A Chance Beginning

A CHANCE BEGINNING

Book I of the Shadow's Fire Trilogy

Christopher Patterson

A Chance Beginning

Rabbit Hole Publishing
Tucson, Arizona 85710 USA

ISBN: 978-0-9984070-0-5 (paperback)
ISBN: 978-0-692-13109-1 (ebook)
LCCN: 2018943790

rev201901

To my wife for always encouraging me,
my grandmother who always believed in me,
and my parents who always supported my dreams.

A Chance Beginning

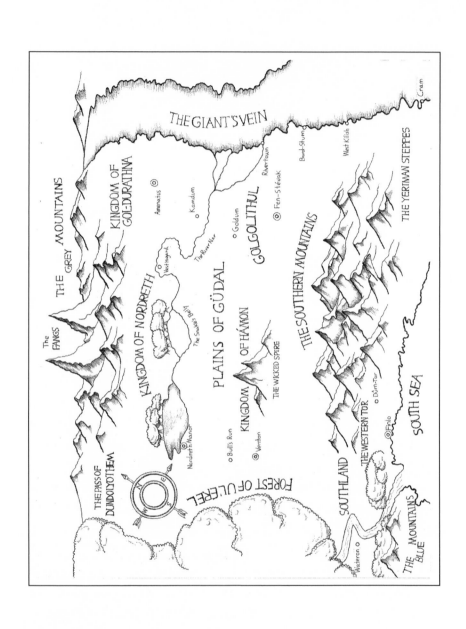

Prologue

I WAS THERE. I FOUGHT at the Battle of Bethuliam so many years ago. I heard the call of the Golden City even in the west, past the cursed forests of Ul'Erel, in the desert wastelands where those exiled fled to so long ago. We took up sword and shield, donned armor, beat drums, and blew horns for the call, for the cause, for righteousness, for the world, and for the Creator. I fought and killed. I felt bone under my steel. I heard the wailing of my victims. I saw brother fight brother, father fight son, whole families—peoples—extinguished from time. I swam in a river of blood, tasted flesh, inhaled burning skin, vomited curses, and, in the end, bled victory; bled freedom. I fought alongside Justus before the world knew him as King Agempi, the Keeper of the Golden Gates. And I watched Justus Guerus sign a treaty with Rimrûk Aztûk, General of Golgolithul and new Lord High Chancellor.

Standing here, staring at nothing but rolling hills and grasslands, I still wonder if the Creator left it all to chance or if he had his hand in it all. Did the Creator will Gol-Durathna and The Alliance to win the battle that ended the age known as The Darkening? Was either side really better than the other? I suppose that is an unanswerable question. In fact, I mean not to answer it, glad I don't have to answer it. I can stand here, in the grasslands and rolling hills of the west, at peace. After a lifetime of battle and bloodshed, loss and taking life, by the grace of the Creator, I can finally settle and rest, build something with these hands rather than destroy.

My brother—the one of four that survived with me—chose to move on, go back to the wilds beyond Ul'Erel, go back to our people and continue to rebuild there. I think this is where I will stay. No more rebuilding for me; just building, creating, loving, growing. I think it has been too long since anyone from my race has lived this side of the Great Forest. It was my people, after all, that turned the tide for The Alliance. I will teach my sons, their sons, and their sons a life of peace, a life in reverence to the Creator, a life of harmony. But, if ever the call came again, the call for a people to save the world once again, my people would be here, close at hand, ready to fight for good in the name of the Creator. Yes, this is where I stake a claim to last generations.

I look back at my people. My heart sinks. A dozen women. A handful of men. All waiting for my move.

"My brothers and sisters," I tell them, "this is where we stay. This is where we will make a new life, a better life, a peaceful life."

They nod in approval. War is hard on them as well. Living in the wilds of the west is even harder.

"How?" one man asks.

"We will use the land," I answer. "We will farm and grow orchards and raise cattle and sheep and pigs as our ancestors did, and we will pray for the Creator's will to favor us."

I look back at this rolling grassland, but what I see, what I see is so much more. I smell the sweet, musky smell of early morning dew. I hear the mourning dove coo just as the sun peeks from the east, a simple line of light along the horizon like candlelight shining underneath a door. I see fields of corn and bean and wheat. I see rows of apple and pear and peach orchards. I hear people singing. I see them dancing at harvest festivals and singing songs of the past, songs they love and yet, know not from where they come. I see a people forgetting about a past filled with violence and war and creating a future of peace.

"Yes, this is where I, Eleodum, will stay." A smile stretches across my face. Then my mood seems to darken, even after my people walk past me, plot where they will build their homes, pick a plot of land where they will plant their first crop. I feel the air thicken. I see a shadow peeking over my shoulder. "But, if there is ever a need again, a need for a fighter, a leader, a champion, I will be here; my blood will be here."

Chapter 1

RIKARD ELEODUM STOOD BEHIND HIS plow, a low moan coming from his oxen as they stamped their feet. He ignored them and the fly that buzzed by his nose. He ignored the heat of the early spring sun and the dusty taste in his mouth. He took no notice of a skinny-tailed rabbit poking its head over a mound of freshly churned dirt. He simply stared, off into the distance to the south, lost in his thoughts.

"Where are you?"

A small tear escaped the corner of his eye, diverted by a week's worth of stubble. He licked the salty tear away when it reached the corner of his mouth and shook his head.

"Erik. Befel. Fool boys. Where are you?"

Rikard Eleodum couldn't ignore the beating of hooves, iron-shod shoes slamming hard against the earth like rolling thunder. The rumbling and billowing dust came closer, and the ground shook beneath his feet as the sound of loud neighs and cracked whips ripped through the air. An army, for all Rikard knew. He cared little for the cultures of feudal lords and knights.

Finally, they appeared, maybe two dozen men, spreading out to line up in front of his barn and house, and those of the four men and families that worked Rikard's farm.

"Less intimidating than I expected."

Rikard let go of his plow and walked toward the entourage, all finely arrayed in polished mail shirts, well-oiled brigandines, and conical helmets that reflected the late morning sun.

Karita Eleodum stormed from the farmhouse's front door, down the stone walkway, and through the fence gate with a speed Rikard had never seen from his wife. Her auburn hair looked aflame, while the ruddiness in her cheeks deepened, and her blue eyes blazed ice cold.

"What is the meaning of this?" she demanded, pointing a finger at a helmetless younger man sitting atop a large horse. "You owe me an explanation!"

The man leisurely pulled off his leather gloves, one finger at a time, and rested them across the horn of his saddle. He wiped a bit of his brown hair away from his forehead and scratched his chin through a close-cropped beard before he yawned.

"Oh, boy, you have no idea what you have just done," Rikard said to himself with a smile on his face. "You have just unleashed a demon that will give you a tongue lashing making you wish she had taken a switch to your behind."

"Now see here!" Karita yelled, closing her fists in white-knuckled rage and stamping her foot like a petulant child denied a favorite treat. But no matter how Karita berated this man, he ignored her, barely offering her a sidelong glance.

"Acwel," the man said lazily.

At his command, another fellow wearing an iron cuirass rode next to him and dismounted. He put his hand up to Karita, and when she pushed it aside and continued her protests, he grabbed her around the torso, pinned both her arms to her body, and walked her toward the gate of her house.

Rikard immediately sprinted to his wife, his smile gone.

"What do you think you're doing?" Rikard shouted. Reaching his wife, he pushed the man away from her, "You maggot infested dung heap!"

Within the flicker of a sheep's tail, ten horses surrounded Rikard and Karita. Lances gleamed in the sun, poised at head level. Instinctively, Rikard moved in front of his wife.

"Burn you to flames and fire, you motherless sons of goats!"

"Rikard," Karita scolded, "your language is so foul."

He couldn't help but smile. Even with steel in her face, she worried herself about her husband's language.

The brown-haired man put a hand up and the lances lifted.

"What is this about?" Rikard spat.

The man leaned forward in his saddle.

"Do you not see the standard on the flags? The symbol on my palfrey's barding?"

He pointed to one of the flags that flickered from the end of a lance. It was blue with a red, four-pointed star in the middle.

"I don't owe you an explanation," he added as he sat back in his saddle and picked at a fingernail.

"I've no idea what that symbol means," Rikard Eleodum said. "And I don't care."

"Well, you should since I, Count Alger, will soon be your lord, and you will farm this land for me. Hence, you have your explanation."

"What?" Karita gasped.

"Don't think so," Rikard argued, shaking his head. "This has been my land—my family's land—for over two hundred years. We've farmed it as free men, just like everyone else that lives in these parts. And, as for lord, I've got but one lord, and you aren't it."

"My dear Farmer Eleodum." The man spoke with a softened, eloquent voice. "Please, do not make this harder than it already is."

"I'm not trying to make it hard," Rikard replied, trying hard to keep his temper and his voice even. "In fact, it's quite easy. This is my land. You leave."

"I leave," Count Alger said with a wry smile, "or what?"

Rikard Eleodum looked around. Him versus all those men with their lances ready.

"Just get off my land," Rikard finally said.

"As I thought," Count Alger snorted and leaned forward in his saddle again. "This is no longer your land. You will work this land for me. You will do as you are told. You will be a good subject. Or I can find another use for you and your wife."

"Fool of a farmer."

Alger gave his seneschal a sidelong glance as he watched Rikard Eleodum's body swing from the wide bough of an oak tree that stood behind the farmhouse. Or what was left of it. Flames shot high into the noon sky, and black smoke stained the clouds overhead, creating a feigned night over the farm. Acwel flinched and jerked back in his saddle when the main beam of the house broke and imploded, red-glaring ash bursting from it before floating calmly to the ground.

"The livestock, my lord?" Acwel asked.

"Slaughter the old ones for the men and dogs," the count replied. "The meat will be too tough to my liking. Give the strong ones to Jovek. Perhaps that might help persuade him to make a choice different than his neighbor."

"As you wish." Acwel bowed. "And the farmer's daughters?"

"Take them to my keep," Alger replied.

"My lord..." Acwel said. It was a question, and Alger knew it was. His seneschal wore that stupid, questioning look on his face.

"Do relax, Acwel," Alger said with a smile. "They are too young for the pleasure houses...for now. Take Eleodum's servants to my keep as well."

"They are free men, my lord," Acwel replied.

Count Alger looked at his servant hard.

"Not any longer." His words were as succinct as they were cold.

Alger rode over to the bodies of Rikard Eleodum and his wife. Despite the distortion of a broken neck, Karita almost looked serene.

"You could have been a pretty woman," Alger said flatly, pushing

9

her body so that it swung back and forth, "with a bit of paint on your face perhaps. Shame."

He pulled on the reins of his palfrey, turned the horse around and slowly trotted toward the train of soldiers walking south toward his encampment.

Chapter 2

ERIK ELEODUM OPENED HIS EYES with a sudden, quick breath. He hated that dream, even though he seemed to have it every night. His nostrils immediately curled as the smell of rotten food, dung, dirt, and stale water hit his nose. He rubbed his face hard and sat up, leaning against the alleyway wall of *The Red Lady*. Befel and Bryon slept, curled up under tattered blankets, bent arms used as pillows. The stars sparkled overhead, at least what he could see of them past the three and four storied buildings. He wanted to poke them as if they were bubbles floating in a gently churning stream. He smiled. What a childish thing to think?

A hacking, phlegm-filled cough from farther down the alley echoed off the walls. He hated the others that slept in this alley. They drank and whored all their money away, and they always stared, looking to take what wasn't theirs. When on his own, Erik had chased away more than a few vagrants, emboldened by the absence of Befel and Bryon. At night, they looked like shadowy ghosts lumbering from wall to wall, stumbling over trash and other bodies.

Erik felt something on his foot. The scratching sound against his boot and the tiny squeak told him it was a western rat—white rats his father called them—and he kicked out. The tiny squeak gave pretense to the rodent's size, as the cat-sized creature flew into a wooden cart across the alleyway. They seemed indestructible, and this one, not as big as they could get, regained its feet quickly and hissed at Erik. He wanted to kick it again, stab it with his knife, but knew better. A bite from a western rat often carried disease—deadly disease. It finally scurried away.

"I prefer the lumberyard to this," Erik said, leaning his head back against the wall. "By heaven, I prefer the pigsties of Venton to this. Pig slop was better eating."

He rubbed his stomach as it grumbled.

"How much longer?" he quietly asked himself.

His brother, Befel, groaned. "Go to sleep, Erik."

Erik lay back down, resting his head against a sack of old rags a cook from *The Red Lady* had thrown away.

"Will they never stop?" Erik muttered as he washed yet another dirty dish in the rear kitchen of *The Wicked Beard* tavern.

"What?" Befel asked.

"The dishes. The glasses. The platters and cutting boards and knives," Erik replied, his irritation clear. "Will they never stop?"

"Not as long as people eat and drink and cook," Bryon, Erik's cousin, replied.

Erik looked at a stack of dishes that seemed shoulder high, a myriad of food caked to each plate. He shook his head.

"This can't be any better than farming,"

"Which would you prefer?" Befel asked. "An endless supply of dirty dishes that we know we won't have to wash one day, or an endless supply of weeds that we would have to pull for the rest of our lives?"

"Weeds," Erik replied.

"Of course you would prefer the weeds," Befel said. "You actually liked farming."

"At least they were our weeds," Erik said, "and not someone else's filth."

A boy, at least three summers younger than Erik, walked in and dumped at least two dozen more dishes into the wash bin next to where the three Eleodums worked.

"Bill says he needs these right away," the boy said with too much joy in his voice.

"Thanks," Erik grumbled as the boy skipped away. "Do you think this was his job?"

"What?" Befel asked.

"Do you think this was that little pipsqueak's job, washing dishes, before we came along?"

"Who cares," Bryon groaned.

"I think it was," Erik said, "and that's why he's always so happy when he drops off more because he doesn't have to do them."

"Will you shut up," Bryon yelled, throwing a scrubbing brush into the water right in front of Erik.

The water splashed up into Erik's face, and he could taste the stale beer and old meat that had mixed with soap. He spat on the floor.

"Damn it, Bryon," Erik said, wiping a dry part of his shirt sleeve across his face before he splashed a bit of water at Bryon. It was enough to sprinkle his cousin's shirt, but not enough to soak it even though it was already fairly wet. He wanted to irritate Bryon, not start a fight.

Bryon shot his cousin a dirty look, but Erik shrugged it off. He had seen so many of those looks, especially in the last two years, that he knew it meant little more than annoyance.

"You said these dishes will eventually end," Erik said. "When?"

"Soon," Befel replied.

"You've said that before," Bryon added.

"This spring will be our second one in Waterton," Erik said. "When are we supposed to make our way east?"

"There's a mining camp," Befel said, "a new one just east of the Southland Gap. I say we go there. As soon as possible."

"What do we know about mining?" Erik asked.

"Nothing. But it's a step in the right direction," Befel replied with a hint of chastisement. "A stepping stone to get east. That's all."

"I'm tired of your damn stepping stones!" Bryon yelled. "Venton was a stepping stone. The lumberyard was a stepping stone. Waterton was a stepping stone. And here we are—washing dishes and cleaning shit from the privies—and penniless!"

"Oi!" Bill was a small man, but he had a big voice, and it echoed through the kitchen when he raised it. "You lot shut your stupid, bloody mouths, and get to washing or you can forget dinner!"

All three dropped their heads as if Bill's voice was a thrown stone and they needed to duck.

"You know, Bryon's right…" Erik began.

"You have no right to speak on the matter," Bryon interrupted, pointing a wet, accusatory finger at Erik. "You're half the reason we're here in this dung heap and not east, living the life."

"What are you talking about?" Erik asked, but he knew what Bryon was going to say. He had said it too many times to count.

"Befel and I wanted to leave," Bryon hissed, "we hated the farm. We hated living among idealistic fools."

"I don't know about hate…" Befel had started to say, but Bryon held up a hand, cutting him off.

"Be quiet," Bryon snarled, and then he stared at Erik. "And I couldn't handle being around my stupid, drunken father for one more moment. And then you come along, with some fool idea about saving your father's farm, and ruin everything."

"I still don't know how I ruined everything," Erik muttered.

When Bryon had first derided him about his coming along, it hurt Erik deeply. He looked up to Bryon, in a way, almost like he did Befel, like any younger cousin might look up to their older cousin. But he had heard this speech so many times it had lost its effect.

"We had saved up enough to get east," Bryon spat, no longer looking at Erik, but aggressively washing dishes while he spoke. "We had enough money. We had a plan. But one more person meant we needed more coin. And then there's your fool brother, trying to cover your ass at every turn, and sticking up for you. Damn it."

Bryon shook his head and continued to mumble and curse under his breath.

"Don't pay him any attention," Befel whispered.

"I never do," Erik replied.

Erik leaned up against the back wall of *The Wicked Beard* and finished off the spiced wine that was now cold and flat. The beef had been tough, and the carrots and peppers a little burnt, but it had been food in his belly, and he was glad for it. His brother snored, a plate of half eaten food resting by his head and a trio of white rats waiting to feast on whatever was leftover. Erik hissed at the rats, and they simply hissed back.

"Damn rats," Erik muttered.

Bryon had left a while ago, eating his food quickly and cursing about it the whole time. Erik shook his head.

"Stale beer and whores," he said quietly. "We're supposed to be saving our money, and that's all you spend your coin on—stale beer and whores. As if that can make you forget home and your father."

Erik looked at the three rats. They had built up enough courage to inch closer.

"Was home really that bad?" Erik asked the rats. They just hissed again. "I liked home ... the farm. So why did I leave? I don't know. To make a fortune and save my family's land? Stupid."

Erik shrugged, and the rats hissed again as he turned his eyes to the sky and his constants—the stars. He remembered a night like this one, cool and crisp and clear as he sat behind his father's barn, watching the moon and the stars. It was the night his father—the ever respected Rikard Eleodum—had returned from Bull's Run, the second largest city in Hámon and the choice marketplace for farmers from Northern Háthgolthane.

His father had returned just before darkness fell, and from the shadows of the barn, Erik had watched him, just sitting in the wagon, turning his straw hat over repeatedly in his hands. His mother had finally walked out the front door of their house and greeted her husband as he stepped down from the wagon. Erik's mother rested her head on her husband's chest and asked that fated question.

"Was the market good to us?"

Erik shook his head. His mother might as well have asked, "Are our lives ever going to be the same again?" or "What day will both my boys be leaving?" or "When should I start uncontrollably crying and screaming as my boys turn their backs on me?"

That was when Erik's father went on a tirade of curses and ridicules of the Hámonian market, much to the chagrin and chastisement of Erik's mother. His father complained about the crops that Hámonian nobles grew, and the prices they received for vegetables and fruits and meat that was half as good. He moaned about the encroachment on the free lands of the north by the feudal lords from Hámon. He spoke in hushed tones of another farmer who had already been removed from his land. He said they would soon be coming for their lands, Eleodum land.

"And if they come?" Karita Eleodum had asked.

"We fight them," Rikard had replied.

"Damn dreams," Erik muttered.

He sighed and shook his head to try and shut out any thought of what increasingly plagued his sleep. Instead, he watched the stars, always constant, always the same. A season might change their position or the time of the night, but they were always there. Now he thought of the last words he'd heard his father say that evening.

"The world is changing, Karita. We can only hope the Creator will have mercy on us."

Chapter 3

BRYON STOOD AGAINST THE WALL of *The Red Lady,* a cup of something strong and pungent in his hand. He looked down at the brown liquid and took another drink. It made him cough, and he looked at it again. It was cheap, nothing like his father's orange brandy. He laughed briefly to himself, thinking that he wouldn't be able to afford his father's orange brandy even if they sold it.

He took another drink.

"Most of the people here wouldn't be able to afford orange brandy," he muttered to himself as he shook his head. "I wonder how that feels, to be able to afford endless cups of brandy?"

Bryon took another drink, draining the cup's contents. He had enough coin for four more cups. He thought of his father again.

"The only good thing you ever made is brandy," Bryon said. He felt lightheaded. This alcohol, whatever it was, was cheap, but strong. "Including me, eh, Father?"

"Who you talking to, sweetie?"

The voice took Bryon by surprise. He looked up to see a young woman, blonde hair pulled into a bun, blue dress hanging suggestively off her shoulders. She was pretty. Prettier than most of the whores.

"Myself," Bryon said.

"Why don't you talk to me?" she asked.

"I need another drink."

Bryon looked to the bar. Whores as pretty as this one were too expensive. Maybe if he had seen her first. But three drinks in…he wouldn't have enough coin. He moved away from the wall, but the woman put a hand on his chest, gently pushing him back against the rough stone. She was slight and slender and shouldn't have been able to push him back, but he was drunk, and she was stronger than she looked.

"Let me get it for you," she said. When she smiled, her red, painted lips revealed teeth that weren't nearly as yellow as most whores'.

"You paying?" Bryon asked warily. "I'm not about to give you a copper penny and then watch you walk out the door with it."

"A copper penny?" she questioned, and then laughed lightly. "My love, I don't want, or need, to steal your copper penny." Then, she shrugged. "I'll buy this one, and I'll get something decent."

She winked at Bryon as she walked away.

"Girls back home are prettier," Bryon muttered as the woman spoke with the bartender, who handed her two cups.

But girls back home were reluctant to open their legs.

"Why?" Bryon had asked one girl.

"Because," she had said, "the Creator saves that for marriage."

"To hell with the Creator," Bryon had replied.

"I don't want to get pregnant," another one had said.

Then, there was his father.

"You sheep-brained idiot!" Brent Eleodum had yelled at Bryon when he caught him lying with a girl behind the barn one day. "You'll end up like me, stuck with your mother, five daughters, and you—a lazy, womanizing, good for nothing."

The girl had run away by that point, embarrassed and crying. Bryon had just stood there, with his pants down around his ankles, and stared at his father as he berated him. His mother could be a nag. His sisters were pains in the ass. But what had he done, apart from work hard for his father? What had he done to deserve this when all he wanted was to be with a girl?

"Here," the woman said.

Bryon shook his head, snapping out of his daze, and took the pewter cup she handed him. The liquid was clear, and when he put it to his nose, it smelled sweet.

"The good stuff," she said, looking up at Bryon over the rim of her cup.

Bryon took a sip and coughed and blinked. His head instantly felt lighter than before.

"That *is* the good stuff," he said through a few more short coughs.

The woman put her hand on Bryon's chest again.

"Hmm," she said, "you're so muscular and strong. Do you work in the lumberyards?"

Bryon shook his head.

"Oh, you must be an adventurer then, heading into the wilds of the west."

When Bryon shook his head again, she raised an eyebrow and pursed her lips, looking irritated.

"Are you going to make me interrogate you all night?"

Bryon smiled.

"Farmer," he said. "I'm a farmer. At least, I was."

"That explains it," she replied. "From where?"

"The north."

"And farming got so droll, so boring," the woman said, stepping closer to Bryon, "that you came to Waterton for more excitement?"

"I'm going to be rich," Bryon said, with a hint of a slur. "I'm going to be famous."

"Aren't we all?" the woman said.

"You can't do that as a farmer."

"I suppose not," she agreed. "So, you plan on making that wealth here, in Waterton, at the edge of Háthgolthane?"

Bryon shook his head. "In the east."

"Ah," the woman said knowingly.

She stepped even closer, now pressing her breasts into his chest as she lifted her head and smelled his neck.

"In the east, the wine flows like a river, and the grass is made of gold," she said quietly.

"Any place away from my father is fine by me," Bryon said, feeling his face grow hot as the woman pressed herself harder into him.

"Interesting," she said, stepping back a little. "I have the same sentiments about my father. Loud, drunk, angry, abusive."

"Sounds like your father and my father could be friends," Bryon said, and she laughed.

He looked down at the woman, and, as she took a sip of her drink, she stared up at him, never taking her eyes off him.

"Look, I appreciate the drink, but I can't afford..."

The woman pressed a finger to Bryon's lips.

"I'm not looking to make money tonight," she said seductively, and she actually sounded like she meant it and not like some bad-acting whore.

"Then, what is this about?"

"I'm just looking to have some fun," she said with a smile, as she stepped in closer again.

Bryon could now feel her other hand playing with the tie to his pants.

"You look like a guy that wants to have some fun."

"I...I like having fun," Bryon stammered as he felt the woman reach into his pants. "Um, w...what's your name?"

"What do you want my name to be?" she asked, a growing smile on her face.

Bryon couldn't think. It might have been the drink. It might have been her hand. But he couldn't think. What did he want to call her?

He let his head fall back, and he closed his eyes for a moment as her fingers worked their magic. Then, the name slipped from his mouth.

"Kukka."

"Very well," she said as she kissed his neck. "My name is Kukka. Kukka will take care of you. Kukka will make you feel good."

"Good. Bad," Bryon muttered, eyes closed and speaking to no one in particular, "I just don't want to feel."

Like piercing arrows, the rays of the early sun shot through the window of a room toward the rear of *The Red Lady*. As Bryon lay next to the woman he called Kukka, he watched her body rise and fall with each sleeping breath. A haze of morning smoke leaked underneath the door and floated along the floor of the room.

She had done as she promised and made him feel good as she took away the memories that pained him. He dared to run his hand along her shoulder, and feel her smooth skin one more time. He worried the callouses would wake her, scratch her, but she didn't move save for her breathing.

"Damned farm," Bryon muttered.

She had said something that made him think, even as they lay together, about her father.

"Are you so different from me?" Bryon now wondered. "You drink. I drink. You whore. I pay whores. Your father was a drunken bastard, and so was mine."

For a moment, Bryon envisioned a life with this woman—a home, children, a place to grow food. Was this how married people felt? How they acted? He shook his head.

"Fool," he muttered. He wanted a life of fame and fortune, a life as drastically different from his father's as possible. What a stupid thing to think.

He turned onto his back and stared at the ceiling, the sunlight picking out the dust that floated in the air, mixing with the rising smoke.

"You're just a whore," Bryon said, "and I'm just an idiot running away from home."

Before leaving the room, he looked back at the sleeping woman— his Kukka.

"Will you remember me?" Bryon asked quietly, then he scoffed. Would he even remember her?

"Why do I care?" he said to himself as he closed the door behind him.

Chapter 4

BEFEL RUBBED HIS FACE, PRESSING the heels of his palms into his eyes, trying to chase the sleep away. Erik lay next to him, breathing slowly and evenly. He looked down at his plate, remembering that he had lost consciousness before he could touch it, but now most of it was gone. He knew it wasn't his brother that had eaten it. The hissing white rats, trying to hide just inside the shadows cast by neighboring buildings, told him that. They fought greedily over the scraps.

Befel spat in their direction, but they only hissed louder.

Erik was here, but where was Bryon?

"Whores and cheap brandy," Befel muttered. "He's more like his father than he will ever know."

The brandy was a certainty. Bryon's father—Befel's uncle—made a sweet, orange brandy that almost tasted like juiced oranges. They had gotten into one of Uncle Brent's casks, once. Not only did Befel and Bryon get so drunk they couldn't even stand, when his uncle found them, he beat them. His uncle had hardly ever disciplined him until then, but on that day, he received a beating like he had never received before, or since. He knew Bryon got it even worse.

As for the whores? Befel didn't know for sure, but he suspected his Uncle Brent of being unfaithful to his wife. He knew his mother, his aunt's sister-in-law, did too. He had unwittingly walked into an argument between his father and mother once concerning his uncle's infidelities.

Befel didn't blame Bryon for wanting to leave. Anyone living in Bryon's house would want to leave. But his fool of a cousin seemed to take with him all his father's worst characteristics and left behind all the good and noble aspects of their culture. Befel shook his head, once again failing to understand his cousin's motivations.

He remembered a hot spring day, staring over the shaft of his hoe while Erik tried desperately to pull a large, bushy weed—witch's brush their father called it—from their planting row. He had stared east as the sun beat down on them, as sweat poured over his face and down the back of his neck, and thought about what Jensen had said.

At the last Peace Day feast, Farmer Jovek's eldest son had been talking about going east. Befel didn't much care for Jovek and even less for Jensen, but nonetheless, he couldn't help but listen to what he'd said.

"Go east, and you'll never farm again. There's riches, gold, and women aplenty. A truly easy life."

At that moment, it had all sounded so good to Befel, and then later, as he had toiled with Erik that day, the last thing he wanted to do for the rest of his life was be on his father's farm. He had watched his father break his back over a farm that seemed to yield less and less every harvest.

As he waited for Erik to free the weed, he had shrugged and shook his head as he stared east. At that moment, he had made his decision and told his brother.

"I'm going."

"Why? Am I doing something wrong?" Erik had asked.

"No," Befel had replied. "I need to leave."

"It's midmorning," Erik had said, still puzzled. "Where are you going? Do we need some supplies?"

"No, Erik," Befel had replied, "I mean I need to leave this place, this farm."

"Why?"

"Because."

"Are you sure? This will all be yours one day," Erik had said.

His comment had stung Befel's ears and did so still to this day, but he didn't reply.

"Why would you want to leave all that?" questioned Erik, a baffled expression on his face.

"Because," Befel had answered, "the only fate I could think of worse than working this farm is death."

"But where will you go?"

"East," Befel had replied.

Now as he stood beside his sleeping brother, his stomach grumbled, and he looked down at the empty plate. He kicked it, and as it flew across the cobbled alleyway, cockroaches scattered, and the white rats hissed again.

"So much for going east," Befel muttered.

He looked down at his brother and thought how peaceful he looked when he slept.

"I'm responsible for you, you know," Befel said. But was he?

He looked up at the sky and once more thought how the night-time looked different here. It wasn't the lack of stars, masked by the torches and street lamps of a border town. It was the different positioning of the constellations. Befel shook his head. No. He couldn't quite figure out what it was, but it was just different.

It was a night similar to this when Erik came to him and woke him to explain that he wanted to go leave with Befel, to travel east with him and Bryon. At first, Befel couldn't understand it. Erik loved the farm, but then he squeezed the truth out of his brother. His younger brother understood the issues their farm faced, understood the problems their father refused to talk about. He wanted to save it. Erik thought the money they would earn in the east might stem the tide of feudal lords from Hámon seizing free farmland.

"Stupid," Befel muttered to the sleeping form at his feet. "I should have never let you come, but you would probably have followed us anyway. Where would I be if I didn't have to keep worrying about you?"

Bryon had not been happy when Befel told his cousin about

Erik coming along too. His younger brother certainly irritated Bryon already, but now the money they had saved up for two people to get east wasn't enough. Now they had another mouth to feed. Now they had another person to worry about and Erik, as far as his cousin was concerned, was just a naïve boy and nothing but a hindrance.

"But you're not so naïve anymore, are you?" Befel said quietly.

Now Erik seemed increasingly annoyed with Befel as he still treated the young man like some clumsy toddler. The thought of his younger brother moving to adulthood almost made Befel smile, but instead, he shook his head and looked to the sky again.

"And now here I am," he whispered, "no further east than I was in the first place, and now with hardly any coin in my pocket. Instead of making more coin, I have to deal with an increasingly distant and troublesome cousin and a younger brother who isn't so young anymore. You're a fool, Befel. Damn you, you idiot. You were the one that was supposed to get everyone east. You were the one with the plan. You were the leader, the eldest, in charge of your kin. And what are you leading now? Damn you."

Chapter 5

Erik Eleodum stood at the eastern edge of Waterton's market, watching the border city's bustling inhabitants. They bartered, sold, bought, and haggled—and sometimes fought. Erik shook his head.

"I hate coming here," Erik said. But needs and hunger often overcome hatred. And he needed to talk to Del Alzon again.

Nearby, the fat merchant stood in front of his cart, rearranging his array of fruits and vegetables, making sure the most appetizing apples, pears, and squash sat to the front. Erik skirted the edge of the market, avoiding most vendors, walking toward Del Alzon.

"Fresh fruit!" he called out, his voice deep and gasping. "The freshest vegetables! Picked just this morning!"

The extra flesh that hung below his chin jiggled from side to side like a turkey's wattle every time he spoke, and his piggy eyes darted back and forth, seeking new targets. However, he didn't see Erik walk up behind him, seeming very unawares for a supposedly savvy, border town merchant.

Erik picked up an apple and turned it over in his hand. The side Del Alzon chose to face the crowd looked polished and clean, a bright yellow and red mixed in long streaks. But on the other side, Erik saw a large brown bruise, soft to the touch. He sniffed, and his nose turned up at the sickeningly sweet smell of rotten fruit.

"Fresh indeed," he muttered.

"What was that?" Del Alzon said, turning and wiping away the sweat that regularly collected on his great, bald head. "Ah, young Erik, it is you."

Erik held up the bruised side of the apple. "You call this fresh?"

Del Alzon shrugged. "If you can find better, you can have it."

Erik dug through the apples, all stacked in neat rows in a wooden crate propped up at an angle by a stick. Erik finally stopped, grasped a smaller fruit, red with a single yellow spot on one side, and showed it to Del Alzon. The merchant presented a large hand with sausages for fingers, palm up: "Be my guest."

Erik took a bite. Juice dribbled down his chin, collecting on his week-old stubble as he showed Del Alzon the crisp, white flesh below the apple's skin.

"Truly, a farmer's son," Del Alzon replied with a sigh, "to find a treasure among the rubbish."

Del Alzon waddled to the back of his cart, his arms swinging out wide to miss his great girth. He grabbed two crates full of more fruit and vegetables and set them in front of the cart, gingerly bending over and, when his stomach finally got in the way with the second one, he dropped it with a crash. A few tomatoes spilled out of one crate, breaking and splitting against the cobbled road. Del Alzon just kicked them below his cart and wiped juice-covered hands on his apron that may have been white at one time.

"So, young Erik, the other day you said you want to go east."

"Yes," Erik replied, "at least, my brother and cousin do."

"And you?" Del asked.

Erik shrugged. "I don't know. I've followed them this far."

"Can you fight?" the fat man questioned, and Erik looked puzzled.

"I think so," he replied, looking at his feet, then back at the merchant. "Yeah, sure. I've been in a few fights."

"But have you ever fought with a sword?"

"Well...no." Erik shook his head. "What's this all about?"

Del Alzon didn't answer Erik for a while, setting about to arranging more fruits and vegetables and shooing away nagging flies and children alike.

"You say you want to go east," Del Alzon said. "But what I've been wondering is why? Why would anyone want to go east? What are they willing to do to get to the east? Those are the questions I have been asking myself."

He stopped and glared at Erik. They were the same height, or perhaps Erik was maybe even a little taller. But just then, Del Alzon seemed to tower over him.

"You have the right build," Del Alzon said. "Your brother and your cousin too. Strong arms. Strong legs. Strong backs. But you've never really fought. You don't know how to use a sword."

"But what about us having the right build? Why would I need to be able to use a sword?" Erik asked.

"I hear Golgolithul is hiring young men from all over Háthgol-lthane to fill its armies. Golgolithul is pushing farther east, you know, past The Giant's Vein, farther into Antolika and the lands of Mek-Ba'Dune."

"Go on," encouraged Erik as the shadowy look across Del Alzon's face dissipated under the high sun.

"For three years of enlistment, the Lord of the East offers regular pay and citizenship."

"So you think we should go off and be soldiers?"

"If you can stomach it," Del Alzon replied. "But with little fighting experience..."

The fat man just shrugged.

"I can use an ax," Erik offered.

"A wood ax?" Del asked.

"Aye," Erik replied. "We all three can. And a knife. And a bow."

"I suppose that would help," Del Alzon muttered as Erik pondered what the man had told him.

"Three years...that doesn't seem so bad, I guess. I've already been gone two."

"Three years of survival can seem like an eternity," Del said quietly, and Erik didn't know if the man meant for him to hear.

"Is the pay good?" Erik asked.

"Better than you're earning now," Del replied with a knowing laugh. Then his round face turned serious again.

"And there is opportunity for booty. The spoils of war. A simple soldier can become a rich man sifting through the pockets of the dead."

Del Alzon's smile sent a shiver up Erik's back.

"But what about our lack of experience?" Erik asked.

"They will teach you," Del Alzon said.

"How do you know?"

Del Alzon pulled the neck of his shirt aside and pointed to the tattoo on his upper chest of a closed fist clenching a black arrow with a red fletching and a red tip.

"The standard of the Lord of Golgolithul," he announced somewhat proudly, and then pointed to a spot on the other side—a blue sun rising.

"This symbolizes that I have served in Golgolithul's campaigns across The Giant's Vein," he explained and then, pushing his filthy shirt further to one side, brushed his hand over a series of scar lines on his shoulder, one on top of the other.

"Each one stands for one year of service."

Erik counted fifteen lines.

"The lands of Antolika are dangerous, the men of Mek-Ba'Dune barbaric," Del Alzon explained. "They are cannibals and necromancers and brutes. The Lord of the East may care little for the common soldiers in his army, but even they can be expensive. He is not known to simply throw away money, so he will ensure you are trained. At least enough to survive."

"Are you trying to test my nerves?" Erik asked, shuddering a little as he pondered the idea of cannibals and worshippers of the dead surrounding him on some distant field.

"No," was Del Alzon's simple answer. "Just trying to be honest."

"What would you do?"

Del Alzon thought for a moment.

"I owe much of who I am today to the army of Golgolithul.

Made a good deal of coin. Met a good deal of women." That made Del Alzon smile.

"Aye, I would go and serve. Service always does a young man good…as long as he survives."

"So how would you recommend that we get east then?" Erik asked.

"Finlo," Del Alzon replied. "Ships leave twice a month from Finlo going east."

"I've heard of Finlo," Erik said. "How do we get there?"

"I hear there is a gypsy train heading that way. You should join that."

"Gypsies?" Erik questioned.

"Aye, gypsies," Del Alzon said, nodding. "Odd as they may be, it'll be a fair bit faster—and safer—traveling in a caravan. What might take you two or three weeks on foot will take you one. Just watch your pockets and your backs."

Erik looked at Del Alzon and then nodded.

"Do you see that man over there?" Del Alzon pointed to a tall, dark-haired man—a giant almost—across the marketplace

"Yes," said Erik nervously.

"That is Marcus, leader of the Ion Gypsies and the caravan traveling to Finlo. There will be other young men like you, travelers going to Southland and miners going east to Aga Kona, a new mining camp just east of the Western Tor. You will want to talk to him."

"Befel told me about that mining camp," Erik said. "He thinks we should go there; try our hands at mining for a while."

"Mining is a dangerous business," Del Alzon said.

"More dangerous than soldiering?" Erik asked.

"Can be," Del Alzon replied. "Takes a lot of skill to do what a miner does. I'd rather go off to some place and fight if you ask me. If it's between dying out in the open with a sword run through my belly, or deep down in the ground, in the darkness, under a pile of rocks, I choose the sword and the open sky."

Erik nodded.

"Will Marcus give me a fair price?"

"He'll give you a gypsy's price," Del Alzon replied. "As I said, just watch your pockets."

"Thank you," Erik said. "You've been a good friend in a strange place."

"Just watch yourself, Erik. The world can be a crazy place."

Chapter 6

"FLAMING GYPSIES!" BRYON YELLED. HIS voiced echoed off the large elm and oak trees of the Blue Forest. "Leave it to Erik to buy our way into a gypsy caravan!"

"I haven't paid them anything yet," Erik replied with more patience than he felt.

He sat on a hollow log, staring at the ground, as Bryon paced back and forth. They were in the little clearing that had become the place where the Eleodums would escape to when they had matters they didn't want to discuss around other people.

"What does it matter?" Bryon spat. "They'll just steal our money while we sleep."

"You want to go east," Erik said, looking up at his cousin. "They are a way east."

"Why can't we just travel on our own?" Befel asked.

"It's dangerous," Erik replied. "Supposedly, there are bandits in the Blue Forest. And wolves and cougars."

"Then how did we make it to Waterton unscathed by forest thieves and wolves?" Bryon asked, throwing his hands up.

Erik shrugged. "Luck, I guess."

Erik looked around the clearing. It was peaceful, save for Bryon's voice, and it reminded him of home.

"Look," Erik added, "it's a safe, quick way to make it to the Southland Gap."

"Safe except for gypsies," Bryon sneered.

"There will be other people," Erik said. "Other younger men going to Finlo. Miners going to Aga Kona."

Bryon huffed.

"And when we get to the Southland Gap," Befel said, "where do we go from there?"

"I don't know," Erik said. "We're not miners, and we're not soldiers."

"We weren't pig farmers or cutters, either," Bryon argued, "but we've shoveled enough pig shit and cut down enough trees!"

"Del Alzon says we'd be better off going to Finlo," Erik said, "and joining the army of Golgolithul."

"What would that fat pig fart know?" Bryon hissed.

"We know how to work," Befel said. "I say we go to Aga Kona."

Bryon shook his head.

"I don't want to go with any damn gypsies, but I say we go to Finlo," Bryon said. "I say we learn to fight. That is where the glory is—the sword."

Yet again, Befel and Bryon started to argue. They accused one another of this and that, cursed one another, and then threatened one another.

We do know how to work, Erik thought, *but we've wasted two years working for other men. Two years away from home, away from Mother and Father. Two years away from Simone.*

The vision of his betrothed popped into his head. When he wasn't dreaming of his parents dying at the hands of Hámonian lords, Simone—her blue eyes, her curves, her soft skin, her pouting lips, her calming smile—filled his unconscious thoughts.

We would have been married by now, Erik thought. *I would have my own plot of land, and her father would have added to it. She might even have my child in her belly.*

"This is your damn fault!" Bryon yelled, shoving Befel. "You think you're the boss, the leader. You think you're your father, but you're anything but."

Erik could see his brother balling up his fists.

"I'm the oldest," Befel replied through gritted teeth, "that makes me the leader."

"But we're not *back* home!" Bryon yelled, his face turning red. "I don't care what you want to do. You and Erik can go mine in some camp and die under tons of rock. I'm going to Finlo to become a soldier."

"You won't last a day," Befel scoffed.

"I'm not going to either place," Erik announced loudly, and his brother and cousin stopped and stared at him, their brows now furled into looks of confusion.

"What are you talking about?" Befel asked.

"You're an idiot," Bryon added.

Erik got to his feet, standing face to face with his cousin. He felt his face grow hot, felt his knuckles pop as he balled his hands into fists. He saw the tension in Bryon's face, that look when he was about to fight. He might have been leaner than Erik, but he was strong— and he never fought fair. Fights with Bryon never ended well. Then his cousin stepped back and shrugged.

"Maybe," Erik said, the tension in his body dropping. "Maybe I am an idiot, but this was a mistake. I never should have come with you two. I don't know how to mine. I don't know how to fight. I'm going back home. I'll travel with you until we reach the edge of the Blue Forest, then I'm heading back north."

"By yourself?" Befel asked.

Erik nodded.

"Why?" Befel asked. "This is more foolishness."

Now Bryon's face was red again, and he started pacing, faster and faster.

"You come all this way. You take the money that was just for us, and now you want to go back! If you had never come, we wouldn't be in this mess to begin with. We are here because of you!" he added, pointing an accusatory finger at Erik. "Damn you, you little shit!"

With that, Bryon began to charge Erik, but Befel stepped in front of him.

"Get out of my way," Bryon hissed, but Befel pushed him back.

"Stop!" he demanded, and then he turned to Erik. "You can't do this."

"Why?" Erik asked.

"We are family," Befel said.

"We don't seem like much of a family," Erik replied.

"I forbid you to go," Befel said, and Erik could now see his brother's face was the one twisting into anger.

"What gives you the right to forbid me to do anything?" Erik asked.

"I'm the oldest," Befel said, "and you're my little brother."

"Like Bryon said, we're not home anymore," Erik argued. "I *am* going back."

Befel shrugged his shoulders in disbelief and shook his head.

"Bryon's right about another thing."

"What's that?" Erik asked.

"We are here because of you."

"Really?" Erik retorted.

"Of course! We had planned on only two of us, and then you up and want to leave the farm too."

"And you think all the mishaps—you think a year in the pigsties of Venton, two years of sleeping on the streets, several seasons in the lumberyards of the Blue Forest, being cursed and beaten and scared for our lives—you think all of that is my fault?"

Erik shook his head and stared at the other two before he continued.

"Let me know if you wish me to send your regards to our mother or father when I go home. Or to Beth and Tia."

With that, Erik turned and walked away toward the Blue River Bridge. He looked up as the wind snapped the two white flags fluttering from poles on the bridge, bearing a crudely painted river—

the emblem of Waterton. He could hear his cousin cursing and his brother trying to command him to stop.

"Fools," Erik muttered, but then he stopped as goose pimples rose along his skin, and a terrifying thought entered his mind. What if Mother and Father aren't there?

Chapter 7

DEL ALZON WATCHED AS ERIK walked through the marketplace of Waterton. The young man looked upset, his eyebrows curled into a scowl, and his lips pursed. He never walked through the marketplace without stopping to speak with Del.

A gnome pulled at Erik's pant leg, but the young farmer pushed the diminutive creature away, causing it to fall backward. Erik didn't give the gnome a second glance—which was also rare—and the tiny man sprang to his feet, spitting and cursing in a high-pitched voice.

"Little bastards. Little, thieving tinkers," Del Alzon muttered. "Worse than gypsies."

They often weaseled their way into homes, purses, and women's dresses, and the creature could have passed for a child if it wasn't for the pointed goatee beard. Del Alzon shook his head as he remembered a story Erik had told him of gnomes back on his farmstead.

"How, by the gods of the east, did they get a wagon on top of your father's barn?" Del Alzon had asked.

"That makes thirty, does it not?" a deep, raspy voice said, dragging him quickly from his reverie.

Not much startled Del Alzon. He had seen terrible things. He had seen terrible people. He had seen terrible creatures. But that voice—that voice startled him every time.

Del Alzon spun to face a pair of dark eyes, half hidden under the cowl of a gray, wool cloak. He looked a slight man, and one would think that amongst the many savvy wolves in a border town like Waterton, a watering hole for adventurers looking to make a fortune from the treasures of the west beyond Gongoreth, he might become prey. But there was something about the way he held himself, however, that removed any suggestion of weakness.

The fat merchant didn't know if it was the well-oiled, pointed black beard that hung from his chin and the way his dark eyes seemed to pierce a man when he spoke to him. Or, perhaps it was the way his thin lips stretched into a fixed smile when he was both angry and pleased. But this was not a man to be treated with anything but the utmost caution.

"Aye," Del Alzon replied, turning back to his fruit stand. "Thirty in total, although I am sure there will be some last minute additions by tomorrow."

The man reached beneath his cloak, and Del Alzon felt his muscles tense. Years of experience, years of practice had taught him to never trust a man, especially one that secretively reaches into his cloak.

"Relax, my friend."

Friend? Del didn't like people who threw around that word either, especially toward him. All of his friends had died many years ago, and he'd never trust this man. Man? Del scoffed at the word. Could one call a Samanian a man?

"It is only money," the cloaked man said.

He retrieved a large cloth bag, heavy with coin, and tossed it to Del Alzon. As the fruit merchant caught it, he realized that his bene-factor's nails were manicured, lacquered with a clear polish. Gold bracelets jingled on his arm.

"Thirty silver crowns, as promised; one for each...person."

"That's a high price for thirty whelps and vagabonds," Del Alzon said.

"Trust me," the man sneered, a wisp of black, thin hair creeping down over one of his eyes, "they will fetch a higher price in Saman, or Tyr even."

Del Alzon felt his lip curl.

"You don't approve?" the Samanian asked.

"Slavery," Del grumbled. "The idea doesn't sit right with me. That's all."

"And what are the fools that fill Golgolithul's armies?" the cloaked man asked. "Can they leave as they wish? Are they masters of their own destiny? What of the men that mine the deep places of the Southern or Gray Mountains? Or the farmers that tend the vast fields of the nations of Háthgolthane? You call them miners, serfs, and peasants, but I call them slaves. They are all the same."

Del Alzon shrugged. He looked at the sack of coin that rested in his hand. It was heavy.

"What do I care?" Del Alzon said as he felt his stomach knot.

Chapter 8

ERIK'S EYES SHOT OPEN, AND he shook his head in frustration. Damn dreams. As the sound of wooden wheels rolling over a well-traveled road rang in his ears, he watched a dark sea of stars twinkle overhead, wisps of clouds and celestial anomalies snaking through the sky like small waves.

Bumps seemed far and few between, but just as he was drifting off again, a wagon wheel hit a hard rock, and he was jolted awake. Giving up on the idea of more sleep—he'd avoid the dreams anyway—he sat up and ran his hands over his face and rubbed his eyes with the heels of his palms. Beside him, Befel and Bryon slept soundly, his cousin snoring loudly.

"Did my driving wake you?"

Erik looked over his shoulder to see Bo, the driver of the gypsy carriage in which they were traveling, looking back at him.

"No, no," Erik replied, shaking his head and returning the smile. "I just had a bad dream."

"Bad dreams often come from worried minds," Bo offered. "What worries your mind this night?"

"Nothing," Erik said.

"That's okay. I know the assumptions people have of my people."

"What assumptions?" Erik asked, shrugging his shoulders.

"You're a bad liar. You don't have to tell me about your nightmares, but if you're going to be awake, come sit with me. I could use the company."

Erik thought for a moment and then nodded, gingerly climbing over the baggage piled in the back of Bo's wagon.

"Do you want any?" Bo asked, handing Erik a hollowed gourd with a cork stuck in the top.

"What is it?" Erik asked, looking at the gourd.

"Grain whiskey," Bo replied. "Mostly rice, flavored with cinnamon and ginger—spices from the Isuta Isles."

"No. Thank you," Erik said, shaking his head.

"I have mead as well."

"Mead," Erik said, almost to himself. "Honey wine?"

"Aye," Bo replied.

Erik smiled. "I'll have…" he began to say but stopped himself.

"Come now," Bo said with a quick laugh. "It's not poisoned. It's not drugged. It's not even that strong. I don't want to steal from you; I'm just trying to make good company."

"Sorry," Erik said, with an embarrassed smile. "That was rude of me. Yes, I would like some honey wine."

"Yes, a little rude," Bo replied with a wide smile, "but I think I'll forgive you!"

Bo reached between his legs and retrieved a clay jar from the floor of the carriage. Just before he handed it to Erik, he jerked the bottle away from the farmer's grasp.

"I'll forgive you if you tell me what worries your mind."

Erik stared at Bo for a moment, trying to read his face. He was never the best at reading people and knew he had a tendency to be too trusting. Finally, he nodded in agreement.

"All right. I agree," Erik said, taking the clay bottle, uncorking it, and pouring some of its contents into his mouth. It was much sweeter than the honey wine from the farmsteads of his people.

"It's good."

"Sweet, yes?" Bo asked.

Erik nodded his head.

"So, what is on your mind, young man?" Bo asked.

Erik waited a moment, suspicion still hanging in the back of his head. Could gypsies be trusted? Bryon had called them cheats and liars. Their grandmother had called them similar names, referring to them as kalifadah—a word given to foreigners not to be trusted in the north—and penges—a word given to whores in the east. But, then again, his grandmother was a superstitious old woman, and his cousin was an idiot.

"Don't milk a cow that has a black tail," Erik muttered.

"What was that?" Bo asked.

"Nothing." Erik shook his head. "Just superstitious nonsense my grandmother used to spout."

"Ah, yes." Bo smiled kindly. "Grandmothers are good at that. And were any of these superstitions in regards to gypsies?"

Erik gave Bo a sidelong glance. Then, he nodded slowly.

Bo shrugged. "I would expect as much. Now, what's on your mind?"

Erik sighed deeply. Above the rumble of wagon wheels, he listened to crickets sing and night birds chirp from the safety of the Blue Forest. He looked up to the sky and his constant, the stars.

"I keep having the same dream, over and over again."

"That could be rather annoying. What is this dream about?"

Erik waited a moment before answering, taking another draught of honey wine and collecting his thoughts.

"I keep having this dream of home—of my parents and my sisters."

"And does home—your parents and sisters—hold so many bad memories that it gives you nightmares?" Bo asked as he flicked the reins of the cart. One of the oxen that pulled the carriage retorted with an irritated moan.

"No." Erik smiled, shaking his head as he gave a brief laugh. "No. In fact, my memories of home—of my family—are quite fond. It was Befel and Bryon—my brother and cousin," Erik jerked his head to the back of the carriage, "that hated home so much."

"Interesting," Bo said. "Then why leave?"

Erik sighed. A chilled breeze escaped the neighboring forest to the south and broke through the thick cropping of elm and oak trees. It rattled branches, whistled through small spaces in the dense foliage of the woods, and crawled up Erik's back. He shivered brief and hard. He shook his head again, a rueful smile still on his face.

"That look says more than any words ever could," Bo said.

"My brother hated working the farm. I don't know why. It's hard work, but he's the oldest boy and would have inherited our father's lands. And my cousin, well, he is my uncle's only boy so he would have inherited his farm as well. But not only does he hate farming, he hates his father."

"So you left because you wouldn't get an inheritance?" Bo never kept his eyes off the road in front of him, but Erik could see a raised eyebrow through a sidelong glance.

"No," Erik replied quickly, "I liked working the farm. Ever since I was little, I found something redeeming in the hard work. And, besides, I would have gotten a bit of land to work. Simone, the woman I intended to marry, would have added to it—a wedding gift from her father. It would have been enough."

"So your brother and cousin left to avoid farming the rest of their lives, but if you enjoyed and saw a future in it, then why did you join them?"

"The feudal lords of Hámon have been encroaching on our lands. They have been farmed by free men for several hundred years…but maybe not for much longer."

"So you left to avoid a fight, but now you fear you have left your family in harm's way?"

"I left because my brother and cousin wanted—want—to go east, where fame is readily available, and fortune is easily gotten," Erik replied, unable to hide his growing doubts.

"And with this new wealth, you thought you could buy off these lords and keep your lands free? You left to save your family?"

Erik nodded, but then frowned.

"I left because I'm an idiot. What a stupid idea."

Bo shrugged, watching the road once again.

"Perhaps," he said.

"We left a little more than two summers ago. I haven't more than a handful of rusted, copper coins to my name, and every night I dream of Hámonian nobles riding through my father's farm, killing him and the men who work for him, raping their wives, and selling my sisters into slavery," Erik explained as a small tear dripped from the corner of his eye.

"And now you are heading east with a bunch of wayward travelers, a company of miners, and a band of gypsies. What does this have in store for you?"

"My brother thinks we can be miners, but my cousin wishes to go to Finlo and become a soldier in the armies of Golgolithul."

"Both can be very lucrative," Bo suggested, "but both are very dangerous."

"Well, I've decided I'm going back home. I'm tired of wasting my time. I'm tired of breaking up fights between Befel and Bryon. I'm tired of having these terrible dreams about my family."

"If you feel that is what is best," Bo said, "then that is what you must do."

"You think that's a bad idea?" Erik asked.

"I don't know, but I will tell you this: fame that's easily won is seldom earned, and fortune easily attained is often ill-gotten. The former doesn't last, and the latter often leads to a man's doom. You are right in wanting to help your family, but people have a veiled understanding of the east. It is not all beautiful women, golden fields, and rivers of flowing wine. Believe me, I would know."

Erik looked to Bo with a tilt of his head.

"Perhaps a tale for a different time," Bo said with a wry smile.

Erik looked forward, still trying to hold back his tears. He could feel them, daring to leave his eyes, but he sought to blink them away. He took another drink of honey wine; alcohol always did seem to stem the tide of tears.

"But I do believe in following your heart," said Bo, breaking the silence.

Erik chuckled. "My grandmother used to always tell me that following your heart can get you into trouble. She told me to follow my head."

Bo nodded and gave a short laugh.

"My grandmother used to tell me the same thing. But she would also tell me that the desires of our heart—the desires of a good man's heart—are put there by the Creator. Therefore, your heart and your head are connected in a way. I don't know you, young Erik, but if you're a good man, then follow your heart. If you don't, then the Creator may have to remind you of what your heart is saying, and sometimes the Creator's nudgings aren't so pleasant."

Am I a good man? Erik thought as he looked down at his chest. *What are you trying to say to me? What are you telling me to do?*

Chapter 9

Patûk Al'Banan, a name that struck fear, commanded awe and reverence, demanded respect—once—sat across his destrier, a giant gray horse, old, hard, and sour like his master. As Al'Banan watched men board a ship in the harbor of Finlo, a long scowl crossed his face. The hard, grumbling snarl that followed it, stretching the wrinkled skin along his jaw, could not be misinterpreted.

"Fools," he muttered under the cowl of his heavy gray cloak.

The tall hillock provided a good vantage point to closely watch the young men of Háthgolthane load onto ships. Sailing east with hope of glory and honor, the salty winds would blast against faces, turning cheeks red and bloody, and blinding eyes for several days. Patûk Al'Banan despised them, and when he spat at the wind, it did not have the will to blow it back into his face.

He clenched his teeth in a grimace and pulled the cowl of his cloak back, revealing close-cropped white hair. He ran a hand through it, wishing once more it would return to the glimmering black shade of his youth. The white hair, the wrinkles, the age spots on the back of his hands, these all belied the fire that burned inside Al'Banan's stomach.

He trained his men hard, but not harder than he trained himself. He often would say to his young recruits, "Any of you. I will take any of you and turn you into a weeping baby . . . if I even let you live. I've bedded more women, killed more men, and seen the passing of three kings." And all who heard knew he spoke the truth.

A sharp gust of ocean air blew up his hill like a swarm of angry bees. His huge steed stamped its feathered hooves impatiently and gave an indignant and fiery snort.

"Easy Warrior," he soothed as he patted the muscled neck of the gray warhorse. His voice turned to a lover's canto when he spoke to his beloved companion. "We will leave soon enough."

"Lieutenant," Patûk Al'Banan barked, his voice back to an iron-hard growl.

A younger man, with high cheekbones, soft skin, and a chin slightly tilted toward the sky that gave away his nobility—once—rode up next to Al'Banan, but when the old warrior gave him a steel-melting sidelong glance, the younger man pulled back on his horse's reins and remained slightly behind his commander.

"Yes, General?" the younger man asked, pushing the cowl of his cloak back, also revealing hair cut short. Although it shone midnight black in the noonday sun, several streaks of gray revealed a middle-aged man. His smooth, pale skin and perfect teeth, his clean and soft looking hands, suggested a man unaccustomed to hard work, a man different from Patûk Al'Banan. However, for all his laziness and self-righteousness, for all his stupidity, this younger soldier proved zealous in his loyalty. It was a quality Al'Banan could not overlook.

"Phurnan, what do we know about this ship?"

Patûk Al'Banan didn't take his eyes away from the men still boarding the ship in the harbor.

"Which ship is that, my lord?" Sorben Phurnan asked, his voice carrying its usual twinge of haughtiness.

"The ship being boarded by all those fool bastards, you imbecile," Al'Banan hissed. Did his subordinate's zealotry really shadow his stupidity?

"Yes, of course, General. My apologies," Sorben Phurnan said quickly, but with the lisping condescendence of Golgolithulian royalty.

"No high ranking officers to speak of, sir. Just seventy or eighty fools that are willing to pile into a boat made to house forty men and

47

risk a voyage around the Dragon's Tooth for the scraps that imposter throws them."

Did his zealotry shadow his stupidity? Yes indeed it did, and Patûk Al'Banan almost smiled. He always enjoyed listening to Phurnan's rants on the Lord of the East, the Ruler of Golgolithul. The curses he invented, the things he said, the claims he made, the lewd jokes and slanderous tales would make a whore's toes curl—and they made Patûk Al'Banan smile. Nothing else ever did.

"How many cross the Plains this month?"

"I am not sure, my lord," Sorben replied, and before Al'Banan could give him another steel-melting stare, he quickly added, "but I will find out, sir. I hear the wagon trains across the Plains of Güdal are slowing, what with summer on the horizon."

"They are easier targets," Patûk grumbled.

"Aye sir, they are," Sorben said. Al'Banan looked back at the Lieutenant over his shoulder. He hadn't meant for his second in command to hear him.

"We sunk one ship last month, sir," Sorben added, a triumphant smile on his face.

"A pittance," snarled the old general, revealing yellowed but healthy looking teeth despite their many years of service to the commander. "A grain of sand on a vast beach. What are seventy fools to a pompous runt who has hundreds flooding through his gates every day, all desiring to die for a cause they don't even understand."

"Even a mountain will fall." Sorben Phurnan, again, had heard what Al'Banan had meant to be his private grumblings. "Even if it needs to be destroyed a stone at a time."

Patûk Al'Banan snapped his head back, a dark shadow looming over his already hooded eyes. He glared at his lieutenant, breathing heavily through his nose, and in the chilled air, the moisture looked like steam spilling from a crack in the earth.

"I grow tired of you listening to my private thoughts, Lieutenant."

Al'Banan's words dripped poison, and Sorben Phurnan made no reply. He dropped his chin to his chest like some wild dog cowering to its alpha, pulled back on the reins of his horse, and practically backed the animal into the horse of another man.

Patûk watched his lieutenant, the anger-filled stare of resentment and hatred fixed on him. A sharp shiver clattered through the younger man's body, and goose pimples broke over his skin. Was it his stare, or the cold breeze coming from the South Sea? Another gust blew across the top of the hillock, throwing dirt into tiny, short-lived tornadoes.

Looking back to the city of Finlo and the South Sea, Al'Banan caught the returning gaze of a man in his middle years, gray creeping along the edges of his temples. The man held a thin hemp line, five plump, brass scaled Perches hanging from brass hooks—a modest catch, and two or three days' worth of food for a half-day's worth of work.

The fisherman, pants cut below the knees and a sleeveless shirt open to bare a leathery, tanned, blond-haired chest, tensed, the muscles in his neck and forearms straining as he scanned the hill of armed soldiers, his blue eyes darting from spear tip to sword handle back to spear tip.

A warm, gentle shiver ran through Patûk Al'Banan, settling in his stomach. It was a welcome feeling he remembered from years past, the one he got when looking at a man he respected, even if he had to kill him. Apprehension dotted the angler's face, with caution in his squinted eyes, and his muscles ready to fight or flee. He slowed his breath, but not in fear.

Another gust blew across the hill, caught Patûk Al'Banan's heavy, wool cloak, and flipped it open for just a split second. It was just enough, and it allowed the midday sun to briefly glare off the steel breastplate. It was embossed with the image of a coiled cobra, hood spread wide, fangs bared, ready to strike.

The fisherman saw that image, and his squinted blue eyes widened. Al'Banan cursed himself and closed his cloak tight. The man couldn't know what it meant. He was too young. But perhaps his looks lied about his age? Perhaps his father or grandfather had told him?

"Fool. Sheep-brained fool," Patûk Al'Banan muttered to himself. "A tiny pebble in our cogwheel, and the whole machine breaks."

He pulled on Warrior's reins, turning him around.

"Lead our men to camp," he muttered to Sorben Phurnan, a look of anger and self-inflicted disappointment still strewn across his furled brow.

The lieutenant nodded, and when he whistled, the company of twenty footmen and four horsemen snapped to attention and fell in behind their lieutenant.

Al'Banan looked down at a man nearly his age, but his white hair was not as neatly kept as the general's. Scars dotted his face, old, faded, and pasty white, but one still glared red and wide. It angled across the bridge of his nose, over the distorted lid of his dead, right eye, and traveled into his hairline, creating a valley through his balding scalp.

Bao Zi had served Patûk Al'Banan faithfully from the time the general stood a fledgling lieutenant with a single silver strand stitched across his purple tabard. And Bao Zi still served his master, answering only to him, and commanding his personal guard. Two other men stood behind Bao Zi, hands resting on long sword hilts, cloaks covering steel breastplates, cowls shielding hard faces.

"Kill him," Patûk Al'Banan muttered matter-of-factly, as he nodded in the direction of the fisherman. Bao Zi glanced over and bowed.

Chapter 10

THE CRUNCHING OF GRASS AND snapping of small twigs under wooden wheels heralded the break in the mid-afternoon silence. As if a switch had been flipped, the hard stamps of wide-flanked draft horses and oxen, the dissonant snorts of hogs, and the sharp bleats of sheep created a dissonant chorus of sound that ripped through the still air.

It was a thunderous explosion of noise that seemed to rattle the ground, and the sudden commotion sent sleeping fowl into the air. The fluttering of their wings caused the green elm buds to swagger gingerly on their long pedicels.

The flapping of wings from thrushes to sparrows to jays sounded a drumming warning to any predators. The screech from a red-tailed hawk from somewhere deep in the Blue Forest of elm and oak and sycamore sliced through the sky and sent each bird flying into a frenzy until they looked like nothing but specks of dust against the sun-scorched blueness overhead.

That cry, that tolling bell of impending doom in the Blue Forest, also sent small mammals scurrying. The sound of their padded feet, pattering through the leaves and underbrush of the forest and up the sides of trees might as well have been a stampede of bison across the Plains of Güdal. With all those helpless creatures stirring from one hiding hole to another, a small red fox darted about, hoping to capitalize on the sudden opportunity for a mid-afternoon snack.

How the presence of humans could send the world into such disarray. Bells jingled, and harnesses rattled. Reins snapped while the creatures of the forest—from predator to prey—watched a train of people as diverse as any large city roll by, unaware that the whole world around it followed its every move.

A pair of piercing dark eyes watched that train slowly roll through that part of the forest. A fox or a wolf? A cougar or a hawk? Those eyes did belong to a cunning hunter, an experienced killer, and a predator without mercy or fear. But when the thin lips below those eyes parted into a devious smile, showing crooked and uneven teeth, they revealed something more than a simple animal trying to survive.

The caravan drove by, several men hanging behind and prodding along errant sheep with sticks just in case some brave wolf decided to make a run at their livelihood. Then, as quickly as it had been broken, silence returned to the Blue Forest, a hushed shadow of fake serenity.

The fox marched back to its hole, the white fur of a rabbit bloodied between its small, sharp teeth. A thrush knocked its beak against the bough of a great oak tree as the fox trotted by, but no one paid any attention to the warning. The cool, thin air of the high atmosphere fluttered under a red-tailed hawk's primaries and ruffled the down-like feathers of its crown. It shook its head, floating gently to earth with its wings outstretched and the limp body of a red-breasted robin clutched between long, yellow toes, and black talons.

Those dark eyes watched the fox sneak underneath the arching, gnarled root of a giant oak, watched it settle into the coolness of its shallow den, hidden by underbrush. They watched the red-tailed hawk float quietly into a canopy of trees, an ocean of green where it nested somewhere off in the heart of the Blue Forest.

"They have their prey," a deep, sweetly nauseous voice hissed from a forked tongue through poisoned teeth, "now it's my turn."

A shadow fell upon those eyes. Thin, knobby-knuckled fingers pulled the cowl of a heavy, gray cloak down over a thin, shallow-cheeked face. A dark form, a black ghost no more than a wisp of dust or a strand of smoke, floated silently through the forest, under low hanging branches and over brush and leaf. It followed the train from a distance, watching its prey, studying them, planning. Two more shadows followed the first, and then others until a dozen or more ghosts slipped through the Blue Forest, under cover of thick oak and elm and sycamore branches. Animals—prey and predator— remained quiet, totally silent, as these specters passed.

Chapter 11

THE JERKING HALT OF THE wagon awoke Befel, and he pulled his blanket tightly around his shoulders as he sat up. As other carriages stopped and sheep bleated, it reminded Befel of home. Then pigs snorted, and it reminded him of Venton. Both made him cringe. He stretched and then slid off the back of the wagon, sidestepping to avoid several children as they ran and played.

"They're probably happier than I am to stretch their legs," Befel mused with a smile.

He looked about the caravan, a small smattering of people from diverse backgrounds and, yet, as segregated as any city, each group of people clumped together in different areas of the camp, including miners traveling to Aga Kona.

"I wonder if I should be over there with them," Befel muttered to himself.

"Finally awake, eh?"

Befel turned to see Bo. The yellow vest the gypsy wore was a stark contrast to his almost black curly hair and thick, dark beard.

"I'm sorry I overslept," Befel said, yawning away sleep.

"What is there to do?" Bo asked. "Go back to sleep if you wish. We are only stopping for a stretch. The little ones can go stir crazy, being cramped for so long."

Befel nodded with a smile. He remembered his two little sisters when they took the day-long trip to Bull's Run as a family, how stir-crazy they would get.

"You know, I didn't see it before, but you could be your brother's twin," Bo said with a smile.

"More like he looks like me," Befel muttered.

"Ah, yes." Bo laughed and slapped Befel on the shoulder. "The plight of an elder brother. Always compared to his little brother. You came first after all, eh?"

Bo bent down and picked up a good-sized piece of a dry and broken branch and inspected it before he drew a small knife from his belt and began whittling at the wood.

"Do you do any woodworking?" Bo asked.

"No, not really," Befel replied, shaking his head.

"I suppose you wouldn't really have time, being a farmer and all," Bo replied.

"How did you know I was a farmer?" Befel asked suspiciously.

"Maybe I read your mind." Bo's face seemed to darken, but then he laughed again. "Or maybe your brother told me."

"Damn Erik, always telling people our business," Befel muttered.

"There's little to do but talk when you're traveling at night," Bo replied. "It's no matter. I care not for where you come from, nor do I care much for where you're going—although, from what Erik said, you haven't quite figured out where you're going."

"Erik has a big mouth," Befel said. "I've figured out where I'm going. It's the others that haven't."

Bo shrugged.

"Stop pestering the boy." The woman's voice cut Bo off.

"Ah, my boy, if you want to meet a gypsy that can read minds and charm people," Bo said with a smile, sweeping an arm out wide toward a short woman with thick, dark ringlets in her hair, "meet my wife, Dika. Why do you think I married her?"

To that, the woman punched Bo in the shoulder.

Now that's a punch any farmwife would be proud of, Befel thought. Bo grabbed his shoulder and rubbed it vigorously where she struck him.

"Dika, that hurts," he pouted. "How many times do I have to tell you that? Now, boy, don't look her in the eyes."

Dika meant to punch her husband again, but Bo sidestepped and ducked. She shook her head with an unconvincing smile.

Befel stepped back.

Can she charm me? he thought.

"Don't listen to him," Dika said, the smallest hint of a chuckle in her voice. "Is there anything you need? Are you hungry?"

Befel ran a hand across his stubbly cheek.

"A razor perhaps?" Befel asked politely. "And some soap and water?"

"Well." Dika wiped her dirty hands on her dress. "You can see that most of our men don't shave. However, I do have soap and water and probably a sharp knife. Will that work?"

"Yes," Befel replied with a short bow. "Thank you."

Dika rifled through several sacks that sat in the back of Bo's wagon. She produced a small jar of white powder.

"Soap," she said, handing it to Befel. "It's the soap we use for our clothes, but it should work."

Then she walked to the front of the wagon and retrieved a long knife. She handed that to Befel as well.

"Here is the water," she said, patting a tall barrel with a spout that sat at the edge of the wagon. "It'll be cold, but I don't think we have enough time to heat it."

The water was indeed cold, but Befel lathered the soap nonetheless. The knife was certainly sharp enough, and it was good to feel smooth skin on his cheeks again.

"Why doesn't it surprise me that you're so trusting of gypsies?"

The deep voice startled Befel, and the knife slipped, nicking his chin. Soon he could feel blood from the cut trickling down his neck. He turned to see Bryon standing behind him, smiling wryly.

"You could go for a good shave," Befel said, pressing a hand against the cut on his chin.

"I think I like the beard," Bryon replied, brushing the whiskers on his chin with his hand. "I think I'll keep it."

"It'll just end up splotchy like your father's," Befel replied.

"I love how you are so wise, cousin." Bryon turned and began to walk away.

"Bryon," Befel called, "I didn't mean...I just meant I think you look better without a beard."

Bryon stopped, looking at Befel over his shoulder with a rueful, condescending glance. "You best get a clean shirt."

Befel looked down. Blood had escaped his fingers, and a red stain grew around the collar of his worn shirt. Befel pulled it over his head, trying to avoid getting any more bloodstains on it.

"I hope that comes out," he muttered, looking at the shirt bundled up in his hands, "I liked that shirt."

He heard several giggles from behind him and turned to see three gypsy girls no older than his eldest sister—perhaps twelve or thirteen summers—cupping their mouths with hands and half-hiding behind a wagon. Suddenly, he was aware of his near nakedness, and his cheeks grew hot.

"Don't be embarrassed," said a low, gruff voice. "They only laugh because you have less hair than the men they are used to seeing."

Befel turned to see a giant of a man standing before him. His open vest made of brown leather showed a chest carved from stone and covered in curly, kinked knots of fur. The man's thick beard crawled up his face, disappearing into his black mane of hair.

"That's certainly the first time I've heard that," Befel replied as he ran a hand through his own chest hair, a somewhat thick carpet of blondish-brown curls. "The noble women of Hámon—Venton—found my hairiness barbaric. They would laugh at me when I worked, shirtless, in the sties."

"That sounds like Hámon," the giant gypsy said. "What do the nobles of Venton know anyway? You must hail from the northwest of Háthgolthane, with a man's chest such that you have and hair that color—and those broad shoulders. Farm country I would guess."

57

"My brother opened his big mouth to you as well," Befel said raising an eyebrow and taking a step back.

"Aye." The large man laughed. "I have spoken with young Erik on several occasions."

Befel stared at the big man for a moment.

"I am Marcus." The giant of a man extended a hand. "We haven't met yet, but I am responsible, the leader if you will, of this pleasant little caravan."

Befel gingerly took Marcus' hand. He looked around the caravan, men and women packing things back onto their wagons and carriages, ready to move on again after their short break.

"Pleasant, yes," Befel agreed. "Little—anything but."

"Well," Marcus said with a smile, "when we are not taking travelers into our company and ensuring them a bit of civility while they travel, we are not so large."

"You certainly are generous with those you allow in your train," Befel said.

"We try to be a generous people," Marcus replied. "People need safety, shelter, just some civil company, so we offer it."

Befel frowned. His brows curling into a thoughtful scowl.

"That look on your face speaks volumes," Marcus said. "It speaks of confusion and irritation."

Befel shrugged. "It's just that the tales people tell and hear about gypsies are so different. They speak of a people who would steal and cheat a person over helping them."

Marcus' smile slowly faded, and his brows cast a brooding shadow.

"I...I'm sorry." Befel took a step back. "I..."

Marcus put up a hand.

"An unfortunate stereotype many of my kin have earned. Our goal is to dispel those myths, so hopefully, your short time with us will help change your mind about who we are."

Befel felt foolish and dropped his eyes to his shirt.

"Do you see that carriage over there?" Marcus said, breaking the silence. He pointed to a carriage made of dark wood and carved swirling, wavy lines. A simple cloth covered the carriage in a high arch. Befel nodded.

"That is one of my carriages. My wife, Nadya, will give you a new shirt in exchange for that one." A small smile appeared under his bushy mustache as Marcus reached out and turned Befel's face, examining his chin. "She'll clean that up for you too. The Creator knows she's had to clean my wounds too many times to remember, and not from shaving either."

Befel tried to smile, but when he thought of what thing could possibly create a wound on this man's body, he swallowed hard.

Marcus turned and walked away, and within only a few steps he raised his arms and roared playfully at a group of little children. The children startled with a combination of fear and jollity as they ran, giggling. Within another few steps, Marcus held at least four of them in one arm, pretending to eat them, gnawing gently at their ribs. Finally, when Marcus set them down with a bellowing chuckle, all the children collapsed with exhaustion, huge smiles on their faces.

Befel chuckled to himself as he walked toward Marcus' carriage. A woman moved about the carriage, folding clothes and packing things away. Her tanned skin seemed to glow in the midmorning sun, just as her dark hair ate up the light. She had a strong face—a farm-wife's face—but where the typical farm wife might look worn and ruddy, this woman looked beautiful, with a rounded chin and pouting lips.

"Nadya." Befel mouthed the name, and it seemed to enchant him.

Marcus seemed serious about dispelling the stereotypes of his people, but if all of his grandmother's superstitions were true, a gypsy woman would have no need for witchcraft or magic. She could simply use her beauty.

"Yes, young man?" she asked.

"Marcus...your husband...said you would have a clean shirt," Befel replied, gingerly holding out the soiled garment.

"Aye, I would. And I'll fix that cut too. Now don't just stand and stare," said Nadya as she waved him over to her carriage. When Befel didn't move, she walked over to him and wrapped her arm around his.

"Will you come over here you silly boy, or do I have to drag you?"

Befel didn't doubt she could have. She stood almost as tall as him, and a sleeveless vest and blouse showed well-toned muscles in her arms.

"Sorry, ma'am," he said, finally reaching her carriage.

"Now sit," she said, pointing to the wooden step.

"Yes, ma'am," he replied as she reached into the carriage for something.

"Hold still," Nadya said, "this might sting a bit."

It might have stung, some sort of rub that washed away old, dried blood, and a creamy salve that stunk sweet like mint and pig urine mixed together, but Befel would have never noticed. All he felt was the soft touch of Nadya.

Chapter 12

BRYON LEANED AGAINST A WAGON, arms crossed over his chest, watching people mill about during the caravan's break in travel.

Despite the sun's warmth, the weather along this road was cooler, full of gentle breezes and shade from tall oaks and elms. Back home, he would have been working his father's fields, planting beans or corn, sweating and burning. Or he might have been in his mother's garden, especially on the days when her back bothered her. Whatever it was, it would have been hot, uncomfortable, and laborious.

He laughed as he watched Befel walk timidly toward a beautiful, exotic woman with long, curled, black hair that shrouded a tanned face and pouting lips.

"Don't stare, cousin." Bryon smiled, putting his face in one hand and shaking his head. "You've never been any good with women."

"What makes you laugh, friend?"

Bryon turned hard on his heels, facing whoever had spoken to him. He expected another annoying, prying gypsy and found himself opposite a slight man, shorter then Bryon, with shaggy, red hair that glared in the almost-noon sun.

That freckled, pale face would surely burn on the farm, thought Bryon as he wondered where the man was from. This was a hobby of his lately, trying to figure out from where people came, to see what he could learn about them for his potential later advantage.

Away from the farm, Bryon realized the world was an ocean

of different people, different languages, and different religions. His cursed father had hidden so much from him, leading Bryon to believe that farming and their people were all there was to the world.

Bryon stared at the red-headed man, thinking that of the ocean of people he had met, this one seemed a smattering of all of them.

"You are a true mutt, aren't you?" Bryon muttered.

"What was that friend?" the red-haired man asked.

"Nothing," Bryon replied sternly, not realizing the man had heard him. He pretended he didn't care. "Why do you call me friend?" asked Bryon, unfolding his arms.

The redheaded man shrugged. "I don't know, friend. It's just something I normally say."

"Well, don't," Bryon spat. "I'm not your friend. I don't know you. I don't even know your name."

"Well, that's easily remedied isn't?" The man smiled. "The name's Ren, my friend, but most people call me Fox. I bet you can't tell why!"

Bryon rolled his eyes when the man pointed to his hair. Wanting to ignore the annoying man, instead, he looked around at some of the other people in the caravan as they threw packs back into their wagons and removed their horses' feed baskets. He turned his head again, and the slight man named Fox still just stood there with a stupid smile on his face, staring at Bryon with those bright, blue eyes.

"What do you want?" hissed Bryon.

"Oh, nothing." Fox shrugged. "Just to make conversation." He paused a moment, tapping a thin finger against his hairless, pointed chin, his other hand resting on his hip. "Where are you from?"

"None of your business."

"Oh, well, I never heard of that place," Fox replied before he burst into laughter that consisted of annoying snorts. "That was a good one, eh? Well, I'm from Southland. Been in Waterton for a couple months visiting family. Grandmother's not doing so well, you know. Figure it's time to get back home."

"I don't care," Bryon said, but something made his eyebrow rise up in a questioning arch.

Waterton had proven to be a city most unwelcoming to families, and the only ones that lived there seemed to be those that thrived on the adventurers and treasure seekers stopping for a while before traveling west. Bryon shook his head slightly but knew that his suspicious nature had gotten him into trouble more than once. He remembered when he suspected the two Wodum brothers of stealing a half dozen of his father's goats. When he accused them openly, they tried to beat him to death. They would've if it hadn't been for Befel. His lip curled at the memory. He hated thinking of Befel helping him. It turned out that his father had already slaughtered them.

"Well, that's nice for you," Bryon conceded as the Fox still stared at him. "What did you say your family did in Waterton?"

"I didn't," Fox said with that stupid smile still on his face.

"Well?" Bryon waited. "What do they do?"

"Merchants," Fox replied quickly. "They sell kitchen wares in the marketplace."

"Kitchen wares," Bryon muttered, "that's an odd thing to sell in Waterton. You must know Del Alzon then."

Fox looked at Bryon with wrinkled brows.

"The fat fruit merchant." Bryon sounded exasperated. How could anyone miss that disgusting blob of a man?

"Oh, yes, yes, of course," Fox cried with an even bigger smile. "Ole Del. What a fellow he is, eh?"

"Aye," Bryon slowly muttered, "what a fellow."

Bryon heard a cracking sound, and he spun around, thinking that a large branch had snapped. Instead, he saw a gypsy holding a long, corded whip, and then he heard the creaking of wooden wheels against a grassy, rocky ground.

"Well, I'd better get back to my wagon. The company I'm traveling with gets mighty upset when I don't help with loading and unloading," Fox said, pointing his thumb to somewhere toward the front of the train. "A bunch of them are going to Finlo—to join up with the eastern army. They're trying to get me to go with them. Almost have me convinced."

"Really?" Bryon asked.

"Sure," Fox said with a smile and shrug. He crossed his arms. "Not sure I really want to be in the family business anymore."

"You're traveling with men sailing east?"

"Yeah."

"I'm going east, too," Bryon said.

"You should come eat supper with us," Fox said. Then he looked over his shoulder. "Well, I'd better go. What did you say your name was?"

"I didn't."

Fox waited for Bryon to give him his name, but the tall farmer never did. Fox finally extended his hand again, and Bryon reluctantly shook it. He watched Fox roam through the train, dodging carriages and wagons already packed and moving. He stopped often, patting some miner on the shoulder or shaking hands with some other fellow. He chatted with one gypsy driver until the gypsy's wife nudged his ribs with her elbow, forcing the man to flip his reins.

"Maybe I will have supper with you," Bryon muttered. If Fox and those other fools were traveling east, he should get to know them. Bryon should show everyone who was boss, so when space was limited on some ship, he knew he'd have a spot.

Bryon stepped up onto his own wagon and saw that Erik and Befel had rolled up several blankets, throwing them over the sides of the wagon to pad the course wooden planks. They had also neatly slid the wagon's water barrel into place so that when they closed the wagon's gate, they had a nice, snug, and relatively comfortable space.

"You're not going to help," Befel huffed, stepping over the gate and into the wagon with a large crate of dried fruits.

"You seem to have a handle on it," Bryon replied as he sat down.

Befel glared at him, but Bryon simply crossed his arms and leaned his head back against the wagon's side. His cousins finished loading the wagon's cargo—more blankets and boxes and a small cask with a thin lid filled with nuts—and then joined him. He closed his eyes, hoping to sleep until they stopped again.

"You boys ready?" Bo said.

Bryon's eyes shot open and looked to the jockey box. His eyes widened when he saw Bo's wife, Dika was going to be driving. Erik told the gypsy they were, and Bo turned back around.

"Figures that a gypsy would let his wife drive," muttered Bryon and shook his head. His father would have never let his mother drive their wagon. "We could have traveled alone."

"I'm not having this conversation with you again," Erik said.

Bryon just continued to shake his head.

"Bo and Dika have been very generous," added Erik.

"Aye," Bryon said, "and when we sleep, they mean to steal what little we have left and leave us with naught but those blankets. Your new gypsy friend jokes about his temptress wife, but there is truth in what he says."

"Oh, please Bryon," Befel jeered, his mouth curled and one eyebrow raised. "That's ridiculous. What could we possibly have that they would want?"

"Our souls," Bryon whispered.

"You don't believe we have souls," Erik said.

"Our wits then," Bryon replied, still whispering with his head ducked low.

"Then they might as well try to steal your money," Befel teased. "They'll get more!"

Erik laughed, and Befel joined him. Bryon squinted his eyes and pursed his lips.

"Piss off," Bryon said.

"Why are you such a stubborn, hoof-brained ass?" Befel snapped. "Are you trying to prove something?"

"Maybe," Bryon retorted. "Is it working?"

"No," Erik replied.

"Oh well, I'll just try harder then."

"You don't have to be like that, you know," Befel said.

"Like what?" Bryon asked, crossing his hands behind his head.

"So standoffish. So mean," Befel replied. "I don't recognize who you are. Don't you remember who you are, where you're from, what we believe in as Eleodums?"

"I don't want to remember who I am, where I'm from, or what I'm supposed to believe," Bryon replied. "I don't want to be a farmer who sticks to silly rules and believes in religious superstitions…and I don't think you want to either."

"Just because I don't want to be a farmer doesn't mean I don't want to hold on to who I am, how I was raised," Befel shot back, hurt in his voice.

"Remember, cousin, you were the one who wanted to leave first, leave our old lives behind. You were the one that kept speaking of the east."

Bryon waved one hand in front of his face as if he were casting some sort of spell or fanning away smoke.

"Go east. We'll be famous. Go east. We'll never have to work hard again. Go east. That's where it rains gold, and the rivers run with silver. Go east and get away from your father. Yes, I'm trying to prove something—prove that I can be a man that won't follow in my father's footsteps, that won't rely on superstition to rule my life. You know, I fear for you two. I fear that you will be on your deathbeds many years from now and realize that all our fathers taught us were superstitious lies—and then what has your life meant?"

"I fear for you cousin," Erik replied. "I fear you will be on your deathbed and realize it wasn't a lie."

Bryon just shook his head and laughed silently to himself.

Chapter 13

Dusk was settling on the Abresi Straits, the stretch of land in which the gypsy caravan traveled.

"Abresi, the man after which this stretch is called, actually built a road," Bo said. "You can still see some of the flagstones if you look closely."

Erik leaned over the side of the wagon to look where Bo pointed, and he could see several flat, square stones overgrown by crawlers and grass. He nodded.

"Odd to build a road so close to the edge of a forest," Erik commented.

"Perhaps," Bo agreed. "Easy access to food and fuel for fires maybe. Maybe it was more to be as far away from Ul'Erel as possible."

"I've heard of the vast forests of Ul'Erel," Erik said. "The land of fairies."

"Aye," Bo said with a smile.

"The land of fantasies," Erik added.

"Perhaps," Bo said with a shrug.

"You believe in elves and fairies?" Erik asked.

"Maybe," Bo replied vaguely. "I've seen stranger things."

"No one has ever seen an elf," Erik replied.

"No one recently," Bo added. "Do you believe in the Creator?"

"Of course," Erik replied without hesitation.

"Have you ever seen him?" Bo asked.

Erik paused at that. Then, slowly, shook his head.

"No, I suppose not."

"See," Bo said. "Your eyes do not always make something real."

Erik could not argue with the gypsy's logic.

"I know farmers steer clear of Ul'Erel," Erik offered. "Is it really so scary?"

"I don't know," Bo said. "Maybe a league north of here is about as close as I've ever been. There are plenty of tales about strange things happening near Ul'Erel. Apparently, it was enough to make Abresi want to build a road as far away as possible."

Darkness finally forced the wagons into circles, and campfires appeared where people congregated. While Dika poured Erik and his kin bowls of stew, he watched a little gypsy girl play with a doll. She had black ringlets in her hair and olive skin, but her deep blue eyes reminded him of Tia, his youngest sister. This was even more so when she chased off three boys threatening to tease her. Like this girl, Tia was a little stubborn, feisty, and certainly devious.

"How much longer?" Bryon asked startling Erik who turned to see his cousin looking pensively at his stew.

"Is it not good?" Erik asked.

"I don't know," Bryon replied, "I haven't tried it yet."

"You're a fool," Erik muttered.

"Even so, but when you die of poisoning, I'll still be alive," Bryon snorted.

Erik shook his head and rolled his eyes. Then he smiled.

"To answer your question, a little while longer. Until you reach Mek-Ba'Dune and die by the hands of some barbarian," Erik added with a chuckle.

Bryon glared at Erik, a look that used to frighten him, but now it only made him smile.

"How much longer?" Bryon asked again.

"Two days, I think," Erik replied. "Two days, and then you can go south to Finlo, Befel can go attempt to be a miner, and I can go home."

Erik looked down at his feet, thinking of springs on the farm, his parents and sisters. And Simone.

"You know, Bryon," Erik said, looking at his cousin again, "the gypsies are traveling south to Finlo as well."

"Aye, but I won't feel so damned confined next to this cursed forest," Bryon replied. "I'll be able to spread out a bit. I won't have to stay so close to these gypsies."

Erik scoffed. "Except for when you have to eat and sleep and travel; unless you want to walk."

Despite the darkness, Erik could see Bryon's furled eyebrows, that all too often seemed locked in a scowl. As usual, Bryon glowered, and Erik and Befel laughed as their cousin stormed off, his stew untouched.

As his brother wolfed down Bryon's meal after his own, Erik crossed his arms over his chest, a multicolored blanket wrapped around his shoulders. He looked up to the mist-covered sky, straining to see his stars, but they weren't there. The moon, barely a thin crescent, peeked through wisps of darkening clouds like a squinting, pale eye.

An uncommon chill hung in the air, crisp with a steady breeze funneling through the Abresi Straights, and the mood of the camp seemed different. The previous night, gypsies had danced and sung, led by Marcus and his sons—Mardirru and Max—in the telling of ancient tales as they drank Sweet Milk, a gypsy concoction of honey, goat's milk, and whiskey. Erik was happy to join in, but his brother and cousin advised against it, both for different reasons. But no one drank or danced, or even talked, this night.

When they finished dinner, the gypsies made final preparations for the night and went to bed straight away. If a family owned a carriage, the women and children slept with the flaps pulled. If just a wagon, then they covered themselves with piles of blankets, huddling close together. The men slept outside on the ground.

Erik knew nights like this. A Thieves' Night, his father would call them. He would sit on their porch with several of his farmhands, watching his barn, his flock of sheep, and his cows and horses as they slept. A Demon's Night, his grandmother would say, a night when the Shadow released his minions on the world to wreak havoc and mischief on goodly people. Erik's mother would scold his grandmother when she told that story, giving her the same look she gave her children when she meant to swat them with a wooden spoon.

Erik hated those nights, and would lie in his bed, blanket pulled up to his eyes, and shiver. Alternatively, he would sit with his mother, curled up with her and his sisters in his parents' room. Befel never huddled with them. He was always too tough for such childishness, and when he grew older, on many of those nights, he would sit with his father on the porch.

Not a thing stirred on those mist-shrouded nights. No owls hooted, no doves cooed, no mockingbird or thrush offered their nighttime songs. No rabbit darted about night-covered fields. No foxes emerged to chase rabbits. It seemed the whole world had been hushed, locked in apprehension of those nights.

Next to them, the Blue Forest with its giant, ghoulish trees loomed over the train of travelers. They swayed in the cold breeze, branches and leaves rattling to a devilish tune of silence save for the creaking of distant boughs and the blowing of air past wide trunks.

"What was that?"

Erik pulled his outlandishly colored blanket tighter around his shoulders. It had been many years since he had huddled in close to his mother on a Thieves' Night, and the last one he experienced back home, he had spent on the porch with his father and brother. But home still offered some semblance of shelter, and now his eyes darted back and forth, inspecting every dark spot of the forest.

"What?" Befel muttered as he pulled a much more somber-colored brown blanket over his shoulders.

"That noise."

"What noise?" Befel asked looking at Erik. "Are you shivering?"

Erik realized he was and sat up but didn't answer Befel's question. As his eyes grew more accustomed to the dark, he watched a small shadow skitter by just beyond the first tree of the Blue Forest. As if that shadow knew some young man watched it from the protection of a circled caravan and firelight, it stopped and stared back. Erik's eyes met tiny yellow ones, and they locked for just moments. Erik felt goose pimples rise along his arms.

"It's just a fox," he muttered hopefully, closing his eyes tight and then opening them again. Those yellow eyes were gone.

"A what?" Befel questioned.

"Nothing."

Befel moved closer to Erik, and even though Erik gave his brother a quick annoyed look, he welcomed the closeness and did nothing to push Befel away.

"A Demon's Night."

Marcus' voice startled the brothers, and they looked up as the giant of a man bent to sit next to them. He had no blanket and an open-chested vest despite the chill of the night.

"That's what my father used to call these nights," Marcus added.

"My grandmother, too," Erik said.

"Perhaps my father and your grandmother hail from the same place," Marcus suggested with a smile.

"Doubtful," Befel muttered, but Erik heard him. The sidelong glance he saw Marcus give them said he had heard as well.

"I suppose not," Marcus agreed, and Erik saw Befel give the big man a worried look.

"While my family is from the Yeryman Steppes, just east of the Southern Mountains, where other gypsies originally hail from is as much of a mystery as any. Some say the Isuta Isles. Others say Wüsten Sahil or the Jagged Coast. I wonder why it matters."

"Isn't it good to know where a man is from?" Erik asked.

"I suppose," Marcus replied with a shrug, "as long as you remember it doesn't define that man."

"What do you mean?" Befel asked, seemingly less truculent.

"Men defined me by my birth," Marcus replied. "I was born to gypsies, in a village of gypsies, and so, even from a young age, men figured me to be like most gypsies they had known—a cheat, a liar, a thief."

"That's not right," Erik said.

"Aye, perhaps," Marcus replied. "But, I am all those things—and worse…"

"Worse?" Erik asked.

Marcus nodded. "I'm a murderer."

"Really?" Erik could feel his face twist in confusion, and he sensed Befel stiffen beside him.

"Aye," Marcus replied. "You could say I embraced the label men gave me. I think most men do that. You were born to farmers, so you're expected to farm. When a boy is born to a miner, so he is expected to mine. When another is born to a rich father, so he is expected to act like other rich men…well, I think you get what I'm saying."

"Yes, I do," Erik replied, and he could see his brother nodding in agreement. "And being labeled a gypsy means you're a liar and a murderer?"

"It means that's the label we gypsies have earned ourselves, and many of us are good at following that label. In fact, I excelled in it. You see, when people throw rotten vegetables at a gypsy, when they spit on a gypsy, that gypsy just leaves. He or she takes what gold they have swindled and goes. Fighting back is bad for business. I was bad at business. Much to the chagrin of my father, I fought back all the time. The problem…I was good at fighting."

"Most people would fight back, I think," Erik said.

"Perhaps," Marcus replied, "but I was so good at it, a nobleman from West Kilish noticed me. He had actually come to run my father off his lands. I beat his men—killed one of them. When he saw me beat a half dozen of his men, Lord Reyloz offered me something I wish to this day I had turned down."

"What did he offer you?" Befel asked.

"Gold," Marcus replied. "He offered me gold and women and a lavish life if I agreed to fight for him."

"I don't understand," Erik said. "He wanted you to fight as one of his personal guards?"

"Oh no," Marcus replied shaking his head. "As a prizefighter, in the fighting pits."

"What are those?" Erik asked.

"Men—rich men—will come from all over to watch two other men fight," Marcus explained. "They will pay money, bet on which one will win, bet on which one will die. Many men bet on me. I made Reyloz a lot of money. I made myself a lot of money."

"And you killed many men?" Befel asked, seemingly not sure if he should be in awe or scared.

Marcus nodded slowly. "Aye. Many men."

"And yet, here you are, leading this caravan that seems all but the typical gypsy caravan," Erik said, clearly puzzled himself. "You simply decided to change?"

"Not so simple," Marcus said and then fell silent.

Chapter 14

EVENTUALLY, MARCUS PRODUCED A LARGE, clay jar and drank from it. He handed it to Erik, and the young man smelled it. It stung his nose and churned his stomach, but out of respect, he took a small sip. That simple swallow seemed to burn away his throat, and Erik coughed hard.

"Brandy," Erik croaked, handing the jar to Befel. "Strong brandy. Stronger than Uncle Brent's."

Befel too took a drink and still grimaced despite managing not to cough.

"Why not simple?" he asked, wiping the back of his hand across his mouth as he passed the jar back to Marcus.

"I made more money and then decided I wanted to leave the employment of Reyloz."

"He just let you leave?" Erik asked, "After making him all that money?"

"No," Marcus replied, "but eventually, he let me go—when he realized his life depended on it. I began lending money to poor farmers, pimping street girls, and selling urchin street boys into slavery. I became a king in Goldum."

As Erik watched, the large man spoke, and he noticed a glimmer at the corner of the gypsy's eye, a tear perhaps. Other men—even himself—speaking of gold and women and being a king, would have smiled and laughed and relished such a thing.

But he only feels remorse, Erik thought. *There is no memory of pleasure.*

"I became even wealthier," Marcus said. "But wealth is no good to a dead man, and many wanted me dead."

"What did you do?" Erik asked.

"I left Goldum," Marcus replied. "I went to Amentus."

"The Golden City?" Befel asked. "Was it there that you stopped your life of crime?"

Marcus shook his head. "No, my friend. It was there that I truly saw the most gold coin fall into my coffers. Even the Golden City has a dark underbelly since, where things are illegal, they are more valuable. I did many of the same things I had done in Goldum, but eventually, I was arrested. In the dungeons of Amentus, I experienced true horror."

Marcus paused to drink, but in his reverie, he never thought to share the jug.

"For two years, I suffered daily beatings, rape, and starvation, but eventually I was released. But now I was poor again, nothing to my name but the rags that barely covered my ass."

"What did you do?" Erik asked.

"At first, I went home," Marcus replied, "and with my father's blessing—once I was strong and healthy again—I took a wife, and I planned to take two of his wagons and do what most gypsies do, go from town to town, entertaining and cheating people out of their money.

"That is when you met Nadya?" Erik asked.

"No," Marcus replied. "My first wife, Silora. We had two children—a boy and a girl."

Marcus stopped. Erik could now undoubtedly see tears falling from the man's eyes. He took a hearty draught of his brandy. The tears collected in the man's black beard, and the wetness shimmered in their campfire's light. Erik thought he could see Marcus' lips moving. He thought he heard him speak names, names he was unfamiliar with, but names nonetheless.

Perhaps they are the names of his wife, his children, Erik thought.

"They killed them," Marcus said softly.

"Who?" Befel asked.

"My wife and my precious boy and girl," Marcus continued. "They killed them. Men not even worth the dirt on their little feet. They took them from me. They burned my wagons. They slaughtered my horses and sheep and pigs."

"Who killed them?" Befel asked again.

Marcus shrugged. "I don't know. The militia of some town I had crossed. The guards of a lord I had cheated. Only the Creator knows. And when I went back to my father, I found he and my mother dead and the small steading I grew up in burned and destroyed. I sat where my father's home had been for three days, cursing fate and the world and anyone in it. I sat there with no food, no sleep, and I meant to sit there until I died. What good was it to live with nothing? But one morning, the dizziness of thirst and hunger filling my head, I heard the call of a donkey in the distance, and beyond the still smoking timber of my father's village, I saw a man on a small horse leading a donkey. He was an older man, plump and short with a gray beard and a head mostly bald. He had a kind face and wore only a gray robe tied with a bit of chord. He didn't even wear sandals."

"He sat with me for three days, never asking my name and never asking why I sat. He just stayed beside me, handing me bits of bread when I would take them, and a bowl of fresh water when I seemed thirsty. Then suddenly, at sunrise on the fourth day, sitting there, he told me he could see pain on my face.

"He told me that he did not know why I sat there so troubled, but he told me this was not the end. He said there were others like me, with pasts that they would rather forget, and that the Creator had a purpose for me. He told me that I was to gather others and, instead of going from town to town lying, stealing, and cheating, we were to spread a message of hope through our song and dance, through our stories. We were to offer a message of greater purpose beyond this life, of greater glory or riches than we thought we could ever achieve.

"I suggested that this would only allow fate to steal from me again, but he argued that fate was a fool's explanation for the unknown. He said that we choose our own paths, and there are consequences for those choices but, if we listen, the Creator does have a plan for us."

Marcus drank again, and now seeming less lost in his memories, he smiled at the boys and passed over the jug.

"So yes, he has a plan for me. I never found out that man's name, and after I finally slept that night, in the morning, he was gone. As soon as I said my final goodbyes, I did what he told me. I found others like me who had grown tired of hurting and cheating. When enough of us had gathered, we formed a caravan, and we do exactly what that man said to do. We go from city to city and town to town. We sing our songs, sell our goods, and put on plays. We make an honest living and try to spread a message of hope, hope beyond this life."

Erik looked down for a moment, and that's when he saw it—sitting across Marcus' lap—a giant, curved sword, sharpened on one side, with a large, golden handle and a guard meant to cover the man's hand as he held the weapon.

"Spreading a message of hope with a sword like that?" Befel accused, having seen it too.

Erik gave his brother a hard look, but Marcus only chuckled.

"Not everyone wants to hear a message of hope," Marcus replied. "Certainly, many do not want to hear a message of hope from gypsies."

"So you fight them?" Befel asked. "You fight them if they won't listen to you?"

"Oh no," replied Marcus and shook his head with a laugh. "My fighting days are done, although this falchion—a gift from a man in Tyr—surely harkens to those lost days. But I must protect my family. Sometimes, people are very insistent on us leaving their lands or cities."

"If we speak of the same Creator," Erik said, "my father always spoke of him as a god of peace. Fighting and war are sin."

Marcus nodded.

"Aye, there is truth to that," he replied. "But do you believe the Creator wishes you to just stand by while other men beat your children, rape your wife, steal your possessions, and kill your friends?"

Erik paused a moment.

"I don't know," he finally replied. "I guess I never thought of that."

"It is wrong to pick a fight, to go out and seek violence," Marcus said and then patted his great sword, one that looked like it could cut down one of the Blue Forest's great oaks or elms better than any woodman's ax. "But when a man comes looking to hurt your family, the lesson they receive may be a very hard one.

"I may be wrong—and if I am, I pray the Creator forgive me—but I believe my past has equipped me with the ability to protect those who are weak and less fortunate. And I will continue to do so, with great fervor until my last breath."

Erik saw Befel sit back, a satisfied grin on his face.

"Well," Marcus said with a clap on Erik's shoulder, "I would encourage you to go to bed, but I will sit here with you as long as you are awake and watch the mysteries of the Blue Forest on a Demon's Night."

Chapter 15

THE CANDLE GLOWED DIMLY, THE only light in the windowless room save for the single torch hanging on a rusted, iron sconce next to the door. The flickering firelight cast shadows along the stone walls like specters coming in and out of sight. The smell of smoke from both fire and pipe permeated the air and thickened it with the same haze one might find on an early winter morning after a heavy rain.

The heavy oak door opened, and the four men sitting around the simple square table rose, wooden chair legs scratching against the stone floor. The light from two more torches flooded into the room, and then disappeared when the door shut. Facing the doorway, each man touched his right fist to his left breast, and steel touching steel signified their guest did the same.

A gauntleted hand rose through the shadows, signaling the four men to retake their seats. Despite an empty chair, the visitor stood, his white tabard and rank—four gold cords and four golden suns sewn across the right shoulder of his outer garment—almost hidden by the room's darkness.

"Perhaps we could spare a bit more light, Amado." A hard voice. Not mean or cruel, just toughened over time.

"Yes sir, of course."

A man with short-cropped hair, so dark it proved barely visible in the shadowy room, stood from his chair and grabbed the lone candle. He put the flame to another torch hanging on the wall opposite the door, and the pitch caught immediately and flared up, chasing some of the shadows away.

Amado, a younger man in his early twenties, blinked rapidly in the new light and looked to his superior.

"Thank you, Amado," the older fellow said, and Amado gave him a quick bow. The visitor, Darius, with neat gray hair and a stern, clean-shaven jaw looked around, the brighter light gleaming faintly off the mail of steel plates on his arms and the helmet tucked neatly under his left arm.

He made eye contact with the four men, nodding slightly to each of them. They returned the favor with a smile. He remained standing but placed his helmet in front of him, the plume of white horse's hair spilling over the pointed visor like a waterfall onto the table.

Darius gave a half smile. His face, the perfect mix of loyalty and humility that comes from the true soldier, told a tale of sacrifice and service. The weight of his stare, his blue-gray eyes the color of cold iron, might have been enough to break a man, but these four knew Darius well enough. They knew he commanded with a just hand and an even mind, and they knew that those eyes were filled with anticipation.

"What news?" Darius asked.

"The messenger will be in Finlo by the end of the month," a taller man replied. With narrow shoulders and a crane's neck, he stood before he spoke and, afterward, bowed. His clothing of dark, woolen robes did not reveal him as a soldier—none of the four men in the room wore more than a dark cloak, trousers, and a simple cotton shirt—but all four were commanders in their own right, even young Amado.

"Is the messenger traveling to Finlo so odd?" Darius asked as he smoothed a wrinkle in his white tabard. He picked at a stray string on one of the gold cords sewn across his right shoulder.

"Several hundred fools a month spill into that city," he went on, "wishing to sail east to Golgolithul and fight for the Lord of the East. Is it so strange that his seneschal would visit and make sure things run smoothly?"

"Yes, Lord Marshal, I think it is odd," the taller, skinny man replied, rubbing his pointy, cleft chin nervously.

"And why is that, Callis?" the General Lord Marshal Darius asked.

"The Lord of the East cares nothing for these young men migrating to his country," Callis replied with a hint of disgust in his voice. "Certainly not enough to send his steward to the other end of Háthgolthane. The minute these young men step off their ships or step foot through the gates of Fen-Stévock, he slaps them in a leather jerkin, gives them a broken shield and a rusty sword, and sends them across The Giant's Vein without a minute of training."

"You disapprove?" Darius asked, his mouth turning into a tiny smirk.

"How could I not," Callis replied with wide eyes. "It is nothing but murder. He would do better to cut their throats the minute they stepped foot on his soil than send them to Antolika with no training!"

Callis slammed his fist against the table. The candle's flame sputtered, and the dim shadows around the room shook like a thousand black butterfly wings fluttering all at once.

"Peace, Callis," Darius said, putting up a gauntleted hand. "You speak the truth, and with care and emotion. I appreciate that. So, why do you think the Messenger of the East travels to Finlo? Please, sit."

Callis wiped an errant black hair from his face, bowed, and took his seat.

"We intercepted a letter meant for a known criminal living within our city's borders," Amado explained. "We believe the Lord of the East is calling for a gathering of mercenaries in Finlo and disguising it as a simple visit to his soon-to-be loyal soldiers. We do not know why he calls for this gathering, but it certainly cannot benefit us, whatever it is."

"No, it cannot."

Darius spoke to himself more than he did to anyone else. He rubbed his strong chin with his right hand, his elbow propped in his other hand. His hand now moved to his eyes, with the heel of his palm knuckling them as if tired.

"What shall we do?" he finally asked, but his voice was neither weary nor weak.

"Before decisions are discussed, that is not all, Lord Marshal."

The bearer of this news was a bald-headed man with no real neck. As he pulled at the collar of his shirt, he inadvertently revealed the black ink of a sprawling tattoo that crept around to the back of his head and ended in the carefully etched tip of a spear that stopped just at the crown of his scalp—the symbol of the Dragon's Teeth.

The crow's feet at the corners of the man's eyes lengthened when he squinted in the dim light. Premature gray peppered the stubble on his face, and dark circles rimmed his hardened eyes.

"Am I so lucky to receive even more good news?" intoned Darius sarcastically.

"I am sorry, Lord Marshal."

Marcel, the Commander of the Dragon Teeth, bowed apologetically and diverted his eyes to the table in front of him. Darius put up a hand, and a small smile crept along his face.

"No fault of yours," he comforted. "Please, speak Marcel, and tell me of this news."

Marcel looked back at the General Lord Marshal.

"News comes to us that the Old Guard is there. We have spotted Patûk, Lord Marshal. We know not how many men are with him, but he is there nonetheless."

"As I suspect he would be," Darius said. "Any place where the Lord of Fen-Stévock might make some gain, Patûk would be there to try and foil his plans."

"Perhaps this is a good thing, Lord Marshal. Perhaps he can help us in this," Marcel stated. "An enemy of our enemy is a friend."

Darius quickly shook his head.

"No, my friend. Make your bed in a den of wolves and, eventually, you will be bitten. We would only postpone the bite. He is to be avoided—for now."

Darius paused for a long while, tapping his gloved fingers on the crown of his helmet. He looked to each man around the table, and then at the flickering flames of the torches in the room and the rolling, inconsistent light of the candle at the center of the table. Inconsistent. The world proved as much.

For once, he would like to live a year, a month, a day even, in relative peace. However, such proved not the life of a man sworn to his country's duty. Such proved not the life of a man who made his living as a warrior and soldier.

He looked back to each of the men at the table—Amado, Marcel, Callis, and Fabian. As would he, each would willingly, gladly, give his life for the Northern Kingdom of Gol-Durathna, for the Golden City, and its king. He chuckled silently. For all the inconsistencies of the world, their sacrifices proved the most consistent. That one constant would make all the difference.

"We must send someone to Finlo, to gather more information."

The other men in the room nodded.

"But who?" Darius muttered.

"The Atrimus, Lord Marshal?" suggested Amado.

"No," General Darius snapped, his voice the crack of a whip.

The Atrimus—the Shadow Men. Darius did not even like admitting that Amentus, the Golden City and capital of Gol-Durathna, employed such men. Agents, spies, assassins—these were the Shadow Men's specialties.

"No," Darius repeated, his voice softer this time, "no, they are not needed yet."

"Ranus and Cliens, sir," said the fourth man, Fabian, speaking for the first time.

A shorter, slightly chubby man, his thin beard of dark brown whiskers stretched from ear to ear, while his upper lip sat devoid of hair. Sweat collected on it and dripped onto his thin lips. Darius nodded, and Fabian sighed with relief and scratched an ear that seemed just a bit too small for his round head.

"A good suggestion, Fabian," the General Lord Marshal replied. "Cliens and Ranus are perfectly suited for this task. You will send for them."

Fabian bowed. The General Lord Marshal touched his right fist to his breast and immediately, chair legs screeched across the stone floor, and all four men stood, saluting Darius in the same way. He smiled and nodded, turned on his heels, and knocked hard on the heavy oak door that served as the only entrance and exit to the room. It opened and, with a final look over his shoulder, he closed the door behind him.

Chapter 16

"Tia!" Erik shouted and jolted awake from his latest dream.

This time, someone had bound and gagged her, and she knelt in a stone cell with nothing but a pile of straw in one corner and a small, barred window to provide a memory of light. Her tattered clothes left her half-naked. Two men laughed at her, cracking lewd jokes as they suggestively jabbed at her. The rag stuffed in her mouth muffled her cries, and the salty tracks along her gentle, rosy cheeks told of an exhaustion of tears.

Erik shuddered and shook his head before he lifted it to see the caravan still asleep. Slowly, he put his head back down and tried closing his eyes, but he saw a movement in the light mist of the dawning morning.

At first, it looked an errant shadow, the undulation of a swirling breeze in the dew-filled fog, but then the shadow took the form of a man. It moved slowly, wraith-like, from the corner of the camp where most of the young men slept, to another carriage, disappearing behind the dwelling of a gypsy and then reappearing on the other side only moments later. Then it crept to another, and another—a hunter stalking its prey, a stalking fox…

"Fox," Erik mouthed as a single strand of sunlight caught the blazing hair of the man who called himself by that name. He stopped at the last wagon before the edge of the Blue Forest and, looking behind him, seemingly checking to see that no one saw him, disappeared into the trees.

Erik blinked and rubbed his eyes with the heels of his hands. He wondered at first if he was seeing things but decided he wasn't. *What was Fox doing? What do I do?*

Erik stood, looking down at Befel who was snoring softly. He wondered about waking his brother but shook his head. If it was nothing, he'd never hear the end of it. He'd just accuse Erik of seeing ghosts.

He walked quietly over to Marcus' carriage, tentatively knocked on the ornately carved door, and stepped back. The door opened and, despite Erik expecting a fuming giant, a bare-chested Marcus emerged with that typical smile on his face.

"Erik, my friend." Sleep muffled Marcus' words, and he yawned. "I would expect a young, hard worker such as you to relish the opportunity to sleep a while longer. What wakes you?"

"I'm sorry for disturbing you," Erik apologized, but the gypsy put up his hand.

"It must be important."

"A bad dream woke me, but that is not why I came to see you. When I awoke, I saw the man called Fox behaving very sneakily before he disappeared into the forest. It may be nothing, but he was skulking around like he was trying to hide something. He went from wagon to wagon, looking over his shoulder each time, trying to avoid watching eyes."

A pensive look crossed Marcus' face. His brows furled, his lips pursed under his bushy beard, his arms crossed his chest.

"You did well to come get me. The Blue Forest bodes no ill will for us, or a group this large, but for a lone fellow in the mistiness of the early morning, nothing but trouble lies in those woods. If not from wild animals, then from bandits or slavers."

Marcus hastily walked past Erik and to another carriage. He rapped on the door hard, and it quickly opened, revealing a tall, thin gypsy with his hair tied into two tails. The man rubbed his eyes and looked rather perturbed, but when Marcus whispered something into his ear, his eyes shot open, and he retreated into his carriage momentarily, only to reemerge with a medium-sized, slightly curved blade.

As he stepped down to the ground, he tightened a red scarf around his neck, buffering out a bit of the cold, and followed Marcus to another carriage. The same chain of events happened; this time, a broad fellow with a bull's neck appearing in the doorway, leaving and then returning with a long boar spear.

All in all, Marcus gathered up five men. Bull Neck and Red Scarf were the first, then he grabbed a younger fellow who carried a bow, and a gray-haired man with wrinkled, slightly sagging skin and a gnarled oak branch for a cudgel. Finally, a fat gypsy without the clemency to wear a shirt who carried a long staff of smoothed wood joined the small group. The gypsy leader sent the five men to the edge of the forest while he returned to Erik.

"Wake your brother and cousin and also Bo. Tell him what you saw. I will rouse the other men."

"What if it's nothing?" Erik almost stammered. "What if I'm just being superstitious?"

"Then we get an early start on the day," replied Marcus with a smile before he walked to another wagon.

Erik obeyed Marcus, waking Bo first. He nudged his brother, who grudgingly sat up, eyes half closed. He smacked his lips, yawned, and looked up at Erik through one eye. "What?"

"Wake up," Erik whispered, "Marcus' orders."

Erik walked to the small cluster of young men sleeping in the corner of the caravan. Bryon slept there often, spending time with other men hoping to find fame and fortune in the ranks of Golgolithul's army. As he approached his cousin, Erik watched Red Scarf sniff the air with his thin nose. He stepped gingerly past the first of the great elms that made up the majority of the Blue Forest, peering cautiously through the mist of the dawning morning.

The slowly rising sun cast weird shadows across the man's path, and at every step he stopped, stooped to touch the ground, and then smelled the air again. Bull Neck stood just behind him, the long blade of his boar spear hovering just above Red Scarf's shoulder. The young bowman stood just behind Bull Neck, arrow nocked, and bowstring half drawn.

Erik kicked Bryon's boot. His cousin grumbled, head rolling to one side. He kicked the boot again.

"Get up."

"Go away," Bryon hissed.

"Get up," Erik repeated. "Marcus' orders."

"I don't give a rat turd what orders that gypsy has given. Now piss off."

"Marcus told me to tell you to get up." Erik backed away, just a few steps. Bryon was volatile, especially in the morning.

"Then he can come over here himself. Damn it, all I want is to sleep in peace and..."

Bryon's voice trailed off as Erik's eyes focused on Red Scarf and Bull Neck again. Through the dawning shadows and the golden glow of a half-risen sun peeking through the crevices allowed by the tall trees, sending threadlike rays to the ground and highlighting the many colors of fallen leaves, Bull Neck saw a gentle movement, a sudden gust of wind or tremble in the earth.

He moved quickly, especially for such a broad man, his spear trained on a spot just beyond a tree. Something moved again and then, with blinding speed, a little red fox danced from behind a thick-trunked oak and raced through the woods, away from the gypsies. Bull Neck's shoulders dropped with a hearty sigh, and he looked to Red Scarf, a relieved smile on his face.

The target must have been irresistible. The space between Bull Neck's collarbone, just above his chest, sat like a fat bull's-eye. The arrow easily slid into his neck, and Bull Neck's eyes widened with surprise. He gurgled and dropped to his knees, spear falling to his side. He grasped at the shadows in front of him. Another arrow thudded into his chest, and he fell sideways, dead.

A howl erupted from Gray Hair, and a corresponding scream

came from somewhere in the gypsy camp. He turned to run, Marcus already heading to meet him, when two arrows thudded into Gray Hair's back with such force that he lurched forward, arms out wide, and hit the ground, face first.

Erik stood, frozen. Bryon now beside him, jolted to his feet by the curdling cry of a dying Gray Hair. Erik saw movement, silhouettes of men just inside the forest who appeared from nothing, rising like specters from hidden graves.

The younger gypsy with a bow loosed an arrow. It harmlessly struck a tree, the sound of iron against wood rattling through the forest. He nocked another and again fired. He still hit nothing. His next arrow seemed to pass through the shadow of a man like rain through mist. Before he could let fly another, two arrows struck him in the chest, and he fell backward, eyes wide, blank and staring.

"To arms!" screamed Red Scarf. "To arms!"

Marcus was there, dragging both the fat gypsy—a mean-looking arrow with a black shaft sticking from his leg—and a dazed Red Scarf back to the wagons. Dropping them none too gently on the ground, he cupped his hands around his mouth and yelled in a thundering voice.

"Awake! To arms! We're under attack!"

Chapter 17

BELLS RANG FROM EVERYWHERE IN the camp and, in expertly rehearsed fashion, the gypsies circled their wagons, women and children crowding the back while the men stood outside the circle, or just inside it, spears and swords, hatchets and clubs at the ready.

The element of surprise gone, the shadowy, ghostly attackers rushed from the forest—a gaggle of men armored in nothing more than leather jerkins.

"Bandits!" a young man standing behind Bryon and Erik cried, but these men didn't have the look of forest bandits—or at least what Erik imagined them to look like. Lightly armored, the men looked well kept. Those who wore beards kept them clipped, and they looked well-fed, strong, and organized.

Erik imagined men confined to a forest living a life of crime as disheveled and hungry, emaciated even. He also noticed their weapons. Some carried swords and spears, but most held thick cudgels neatly carved with faces of animals or angry-looking men. Others held nets, and some carried long poles with what looked to be a claw at the end.

While he and his cousin looked on, frozen in disbelief, bewildered at how a large group of men could sneak up on the group of travelers and attack them, Erik heard a cry rise up behind him. He turned to see one of the attackers, a tall, brawny man with long shaggy hair and thick arms, bludgeoning other travelers—men still thick with sleep and brandy—with a vicious looking club.

Before Erik could react, the man grabbed for his arm, his vice-grip clamping down on Erik's wrist. Bryon already stood three strides away, making for the circle of wagons, but seeing his cousin in distress, he ran back. Just as the attacker raised his club in the air, ready to strike Erik over the head, Bryon brought a fist down on the arm holding Erik. The sound of bone breaking echoed like a thick branch cracking in a heavy wind, and the man cried out in pain, releasing Erik and dropping his cudgel to tend to his broken arm. Bryon grabbed Erik's shirt collar, and half led, half dragged him away.

The two young farmers reached the protective circle as more and more cries of "bandits" and "brigands" rose around the camp.

"They're no bandits," Bo hissed, crouching low with a curved blade in his hand. Erik looked at him blankly, still dazed from the attack on him. "They're slavers. They've come to steal away the young men and women and children and kill the rest."

"How'd they sneak up on us?" Erik shook the daze from his head.

"Look, there," Bo replied curtly, pointing to Fox struggling with a woman traveling with the miners, throwing her back to another man waiting to drag her back into the forest. "I'd say that they've been with us since Waterton. They've been following us, waiting for the right moment to strike when we wouldn't expect them. Damned slavers!"

Bo spat.

Erik watched helplessly as slavers dragged most of the young men, now incapacitated, away, some bound in nets, others trapped in those clawed contraptions, others simply pulled by their limbs.

"Do we do nothing?" Erik cried.

"Slavers are opportunists," Bo replied, eyes trained on the chaotic commotion happening around them. "They prey on the weak. But they misjudged the Ion Gypsies, for we are anything but weak."

With that, he glanced over at Marcus who chose that moment to let out a resounding cry, his falchion raised high in the air. Now, all the gypsy men, including Bo, charged from their hiding places. They crashed into the oncoming slavers, who had advanced on the circled carriages. Erik watched the slavers stop, not expecting such a furious defense from the gypsies.

From what Erik had heard and experienced, it seemed to him that most gypsies proved peaceful, if conniving and deceitful, and he figured that's what the slavers expected. Most of them held non-lethal weapons, their cudgels, and nets. Marcus met them first with a mighty swipe of his sword, removing one man's head from his neck. His sons, Mardirru and Max followed their father, Mardirru with a sword of his own and Max with a woodman's ax.

What first seemed a one-sided routing by the slavers turned to a fight for life and liberty. Both sides clashed violently, while the slavers still sought to extricate their quarry. Erik saw Fox carry away another woman while another man, heavy robe and cowl covering his features, bound another one of the young men and dragged him into the forest.

Erik, still stooping behind a wagon with his brother and cousin while the fighting raged on, saw a thin man, an oily, black beard hanging from his chin and with black hair slicked back and pulled into a tight tail, directing the attackers. He ordered some of them into the fight with the gypsies, while he commanded others back into the forest, newly found slaves in tow.

He, himself, stayed away from the fight, but expertly conducted his force of slave traders to collect contraband while holding off the gypsies. Yet the gypsies pressed harder, and the slavers' leader found it impossible to ignore them. With a shrill, voice, he cried, "Kill them!"

The slavers stopped trying to collect more victims and threw themselves into the defending travelers. With over half the slave traders worrying about smuggling people back to the forest, it seemed the gypsies had the upper hand, outnumbering the attackers two to one, but once the remainder of the outlaws gathered with their fellows, the gypsies were truly outnumbered.

A group of half a dozen slavers turned their attention to the wagons and the women and children huddled in the back of the circle, protected by only a few men. With Marcus and his followers to the front, fighting off the main force, they figured these folks easy pickings.

One man, a tall, gray-haired Goldumarian, leapt over the wagons first, right next to Erik, long-bladed knife in one hand and club in the other. The women screamed, and the children cried, the man standing there with devilish, dark eyes and yellowed teeth bared. Erik slid underneath the wagon with his brother, but before the man could act, Bryon brought a fist hard across the man's face.

The Goldumarian slaver stumbled back, and before he could regain his footing, Bryon struck him again until he fell. Another man jumped the defenses, and Bryon spun, club in hand. He instinctively brought the cudgel up, blocking a quick slash from the slaver's short sword, and returned the favor with the piece of thick wood across the man's face.

As the man collapsed, Bryon dropped the club and bent down to pick up the attacker's sword. He caught Erik's blank stare from under that wagon.

"I'll not sit here and become someone's slave," he hissed. "I've already had my fill of that."

"What are you going to do?" Erik asked.

Bryon picked up the Goldumarian's knife, holding the sword in one hand and the dagger in the other. "Fight."

Chapter 18

Marcus led more than a dozen gypsies, including his sons and Bo, into the fight, at least two slavers for every one of them. Bryon saw some gypsies die, but it looked like the slavers took the brunt of the beating, limping away bloodied and bruised, or trampled underneath feet, mortal wounds stealing away their final moments. But the sheer number of attackers—at least two score—slowly pushed the gypsies back to their wagons, and at every opportunity, they dragged some hapless victim back to the forest.

Trying to decide where best to help, Bryon watched some of the miners and their families run about in chaos, many fleeing north. Those that didn't run found themselves killed or captured. Decision made, he lowered his shoulder and rammed a man with a thin wooden rod raised and trained on another's head. Bryon heard the satisfying sound of cracking ribs as they both fell to the ground.

The man—looking not much older than Bryon—wheezed, lying flat on his back. He struggled to get up, but Bryon kicked him in the head, and his body went limp. Bryon looked at the prostrate man briefly and then at his own weapon, the short sword he stole from the other slaver.

"You would do it to me, wouldn't you, you bloody sheep tick?"

The blade hovered above the unconscious man's neck, but Bryon shook his head.

"I may no longer be a farmer, but I'm no murderer either."

Just then, he felt a slight tug on his ankle and instinctively pulled his foot up hard. A net slid under his boot and along the ground, kicking up a cloud of dust. The netter, a tan-skinned slaver with an oily beard growing on his chin, growled at the near miss. His dark eyes settled on Byron as he twirled his net over his head, ready for another attack. As the man licked his lips and sneered in anticipation of his catch, Bryon rushed him, swinging wildly with his sword and dagger.

He had no training in the use of blades, no training in any weapon for that matter save a boar spear, but he figured well enough what to do with them. His long-bladed knife scratched across the netter's ribs, and the man howled in pain. Dropping his net, he threw a punch, and Bryon dodged it, but then the slaver brought his elbow down hard on Bryon's head as he ducked.

Bryon didn't have time to notice the pain and brought his head back up and hard into the slave trader's face. The man's nose erupted in blood, and as his hand automatically went to his face, Bryon kicked his feet out from underneath him.

The netter tried scooting away, holding his nose with one hand and pushing against the ground with the other, but Bryon stepped smartly forward, meaning to stab the man in the chest with his short-bladed sword. But then, from the corner of his eye, he caught a glimpse of a fiery-haired man running with a little girl under his arms. The red-headed slaver yelled at the crying, squirming girl. Her kicking and fighting only made him squeeze harder.

"Fox."

With his teeth clenched into a grimace, he kicked the tan-skinned slave trader onto his back, still at his shattered nose. Bryon ran hard, splitting the air, pumping his arms until he thought he was close enough. He had never thrown a knife, but nonetheless, he gripped the long-bladed knife's handle hard and heaved it toward Fox's left side; he carried the girl on his right.

The weapon wobbled haphazardly through the air, but luckily the blade turned just slightly enough to graze Fox's arm. It left no more blood than a skinned knee, but it was enough to make Fox flinch, and his hold on the girl loosened.

She fell from his arms and ran, and the fire-haired man looked as if he would chase after her until he saw the lean-muscled farmer, towering head and shoulders taller than him, barreling toward him, red-faced and seething. Fox grinned maliciously.

"That's right, you pompous dung scooper. Come and get some."

When only a hand's reach from Fox, Bryon felt a sharp pain in his ribs and then jerked sideways when another slaver's shoulder crashed into him. His head hit the ground hard and, for a moment, everything around him went black.

"Don't kill him," he heard a voice say. "He'll fetch a fair price in Saman."

Bryon's eyes shot open. "The hell I will."

He kicked out hard, catching the second man—a tall, emaciated man with stringy gray hair and sunken, piggy eyes—in the shin. He screamed, and Bryon rolled away just as Fox's spiked club sunk into the earth where, just moments before, Bryon's head had been lying.

Bryon, on his feet now, jabbed at the gray-haired man with his short sword. The slaver easily swatted the blade away with his own and returned the favor. Bryon sidestepped, but the iron sword scraped along his ribs. Bryon grunted and looked down at his side, a growing stain of red wetting his shirt.

Now Fox attacked, but Bryon caught his arm with his off hand and shoved him away only in enough time to dodge the gray-haired attacker again. Gray Hair swung up hard, the wind from his sword brushing Bryon's cheek. His swing, however, left his side open, and Bryon jabbed again. His sword hit home.

The attacker's eyes went wide, and blood spurted from his mouth as he gurgled an incoherent curse. Bryon retracted the sword, and his victim jerked forward. Hands now shaking, Bryon brought his sword down on the man's shoulder. Shaken, it proved a weak blow, but it was enough to break skin and snap the man's clavicle. The slaver fell to his knees, clutching at his stomach and shoulder, face hitting the ground, gasping for the final breath that was leaving his lungs.

Bryon turned back to Fox, but he was already twenty paces away and running hard. Bryon looked down at the dead man, and then at his blood-covered sword. His hand still shook, and he gripped the handle of his weapon hard, knuckles turning white until it fell still.

Chapter 19

BEFEL WATCHED IN HORROR, HIS cousin on the ground, seemingly unconscious, and two slavers—one he knew as Fox and another, gray-haired man—standing over Bryon, weapons at the ready. He saw a crudely fashioned club lying on the ground and picked it up.

"What are you doing?" Erik asked, still huddled behind a wagon. He had a look of fear on his face that Befel hadn't seen since his brother was a little boy.

"I can't just sit here while our cousin is out there." Befel gave his brother a quick smile and leapt past the protective circle of carriages, rushing to his cousin's aid. He stopped, however, when he saw Bryon leap to his feet, ran again when the gray-haired man raked his sword along Bryon's ribs, and then stopped again, mouth agape when Bryon plunged his own weapon into the attacker's stomach.

Then he heard a mighty cry coming from the head of the fighting and turned to see Marcus, surrounded by a half dozen slavers. The giant of a man looked fine, directing his gypsies, but then the early morning sun glimmered against his beard, normally black, but now it glistened crimson in the bright, dawning light. His vest looked all but tatters, merely hanging on his body by the sticky wetness of blood.

"Marcus," Befel muttered in shock and rushed to the gypsy's aid.

The din of battle almost deafened Befel as the young man closed in on the fighting. From the corner of his eye, he saw the flashing of metal and instinctively ducked when a sword hissed just above his head. Again, instinctively, he swung out with his club, catching his attacker in the arm. The force with which Befel swung his weapon, his well-worked shoulders and arms lending to untapped power, snapped the man's bone, and he went down. As Bryon had done, Befel's boot sent the man's eyes rolling to the back of his head.

Had his mind been right, he might have stopped, but adrenaline propelled him on toward Marcus. He felt blood coursing through his neck, thumping so hard drums rang through his head in a synchronized beat to his breathing. His strong, farm-worked legs carried him faster and faster until he collided with a fat slaver, his face all pock-marks and scars.

The ugly man had already hit Marcus once in the ribs with his long-handled hammer and was preparing to do it again when he turned into a head-over-heels ball of fighting flesh as Befel crashed into him.

Befel felt breathless for a moment, and then a barrage of fists began thudding against his face as his assailant straddled him. He felt blood flow from his mouth, cheeks, and chin, and dropped his club. He covered his face with his left hand and punched hard with his right.

He caught the fat man in the jaw, heard the snapping of his teeth and the mumbling curses as his assailant wobbled backward. Befel retrieved his weapon and slammed the thick piece of wood down hard against the face of the slaver, who slumped to the ground, dead.

As Befel tried to roll to his knees and stand, a brown-haired, blue-eyed slaver tackled, swatting the club away. The two wrestled while the boots of the other fighting men trampled all about them. Befel could tell that this man, surprisingly strong for his spindly arms and thin frame, meant to subdue him rather than kill him. The thought of being taken made Befel fight harder.

His fists thudded into the man's ribs as the slaver's elbow slammed into Befel's cheek. Still, Befel proved relentless in his defense. Befel covered up, withstanding a barrage of fists and elbows, and then returned the favor. Then Befel remembered the homemade knife in his boot, with a deer bone handle and an iron blade honed and sharpened enough to skin even the thick hide of a bull.

His fingertips tickled the end of the handle, all the while fists colliding with his face. Befel felt pain race through his body, felt his head throb, felt consciousness threatening to leave, but finally, he caught the handle and gripped it hard. In one movement, he yanked it from his boot and sliced its edge along the slaver's leg. The attacker instantly let up, squeezing his thigh as blood seeped through his fingers.

"The Shadow take you," he hissed, drawing his own knife.

He lunged at Befel and brought his knife down hard in an arching motion. The blade dug into Befel's left shoulder, and he cried out, his screams at first silent, and then deafening. Now anger pushed away the pain, and he brought his own homemade blade up and into the slaver's gut. The man heaved, vomiting blood all over Befel, but still Befel pressed his knife up, rending flesh and cutting innards until the man fell limp across him.

Panting, Befel lay on the ground, the lifeless body of his attacker pressing against his. The man's face—eyes still open, and mouth wide in a silent scream—rested only a finger-length away from Befel's own. The slaver's bloody and yellowed teeth seemed to sneer at him as Befel closed his eyes, feeling the tingle of sleep.

With pain throbbing at the back of his head, the blood rushed from his face until he looked a ghost of who he had been moments before. Then, just before he fully passed out, he felt a hand on the collar of his shirt, felt the ground move under him. Trying to steel himself for another fight, he looked up to see Bo, nose broken, and lower lip split and bleeding.

The gypsy had a broken arrow shaft protruding from the right side of his chest, but still he managed to drag Befel toward the wagon circle, somehow with a smile still on his face. As Bo let him rest on the ground, Befel closed his eyes, and all was darkness.

Chapter 20

As Erik had watched Befel heading toward Marcus, he saw a little girl running toward the wagons. It was the one that reminded him of Tia, and a slaver was eyeing her, a wolf tracking an unsuspecting hare. Erik scrambled from underneath the wagon and sprinted in her direction.

"Run girl!"

She keyed in on his voice and ran hard toward him, arms stretched out, but she was just too slow, her legs too short. The slaver, a malicious smile spreading across his face, was almost upon her, and now Erik had to move, fast. He ran for the terrified girl and reached her just in time, pushing her behind him. The slaver skidded on his heels.

"Move," the dark-haired man hissed.

Erik shook his head. He stood a little taller than the slaver, shoulders certainly broader, chest and thighs thicker, but this man didn't care. It seemed he knew Erik was an inexperienced fighter, and the slaver licked his lips.

"Move or die."

As the slaver moved in closer, part of Erik wanted to obey, to move, give the man his quarry, and be done with the matter. He knew this man was an experienced fighter and that, despite his smaller stature, he would be more than a fair match for Erik. The dark-haired man breathed hard, his rancid breath beating against Erik's face even from three paces away.

Then he heard the girl whimper behind him and now stood resolute, pulling his shoulders back and pushing his chest out. Would he let someone just take little Tia without a fight? He remembered the dream of his sister crying, chained up and gagged in a stone cell. He shook his head.

"Die then," the slaver announced with an unconcerned shrug.

He drew a curved blade from a baldric on his belt and slashed it front of him, trying to intimidate the young farmer. Erik backed up, nearly stepping on the girl.

"Go to the wagons!" Erik yelled at her.

"She's mine." The slaver's yellowed teeth showed through a ghoulish smile.

"No," Erik muttered. "I don't think so. You'll not have her today."

He balled his hands into fists, eyeing the flashing blade swiping back and forth in front of him.

"Oh," the man chided, "I'll have her, and I'll sell her eventually. But first, I think I might have a little fun."

The slaver cackled, and the visions of Tia from his dream again flashed through Erik's mind. His jaw firmed, his teeth clenched, and he let out a curdling scream. The yell seemed to take the slaver by surprise. He stopped for a second, and that was Erik's chance.

The young man rushed in, underneath the curved sword, wrapped his arms around the slaver's legs, and lifted. Before the slaver could bring his blade down on Erik's back, the younger man drove him hard into the ground. The slave trader immediately went limp.

Erik looked down at the unconscious man, picking up the curved sword. He rested the tip just at the base of the man's neck before he shuddered and shook his head. Instead of finishing the man off, he lifted the sword and looked back at the little girl. She was now huddled with several other children and a woman in the protection of the wagon circle. Then he saw his brother.

Bo was dragging an unconscious Befel from the fight, blood streaming from a wound on his left shoulder. His face was pale and his breathing shallow. Erik meant to follow them and care for his brother, but then he heard a loud cry and turned to see Marcus, riddled with wounds, fighting off three slavers by himself, keeping them at bay with his mighty falchion.

"Marcus!" Erik screamed, rushing to the giant man's side.

Marcus gave a brief nod and muttered something which Erik thought was, "Fight well, my friend," as the gypsy sidestepped, dodging an enemy's sword only to catch another one in the chest. He met the attack with his own blade to the assailant's neck, separating yet another head from its shoulders. Then he lumbered again, his knees buckled, and with a heavy, thundering sigh, Marcus fell forward, face planting into the dirt before him.

Before Mardirru or Max, or any of the other gypsies could move, Erik stood over the body of Marcus, sword extended, and ready to fend off any slavers who might take the opportunity to finish off the gypsy leader. One slaver came in with an arcing swipe of his club. Erik knocked the wood away and swatted the man's shoulder with the broad side of his curved sword.

Another jabbed with a short spear, but Erik knocked that away too. The clubber came in again, a loud yell preceding his attack. Erik lifted his sword over his head, the steel consuming the brunt of the club's blow. Pain rippled down Erik's arm, and he took to holding his sword with both hands, even though the handle seemed too small for such a grip.

Erik saw the spearman from the corner of his eye, turned to swat away the iron tip once again, and retaliated with a hard swipe. The blade scraped along the spearman's chest, drawing a line of blood, and the slaver spat curses.

"A sheep ready for the slaughter," the clubber chided, a man as wide as he was tall with haphazard splotches of black hair pulled into tails.

"Aye. Ripe and plump for a skinning. Just the type of revenge our fallen lads would want," replied the spearman, who had wide shoulders and head shaved bald.

Erik's stomach churned, and he felt his hands shake. For Marcus.

For his brother. For Bryon even. As the clubber swung again, Erik sidestepped, and the fashioned wood thudded to the ground. Now Erik mustered all his strength and, his sword still gripped with both hands, lifted his blade high over his head and brought it down hard. The steel thunked into the man's skull. Bone and blood sprayed, the clubber letting out a mumbled groan before hitting the ground.

The spearman looked on, wide-eyed momentarily, but then he rushed at Erik, frenzied. The young man instinctively swatted the spear to the side and kicked his foot out, catching the bald man on the shin. He tripped and fell to both knees. Straightening his back and trying to turn, Erik was already on him, bringing his steel down on the man's neck. The blade sunk until it hit bone. Arterial blood splashed across Erik's face, and he flinched, letting go of his sword. The spearman's body slumped to the ground, lying awkwardly with the weapon still stuck in his neck.

Erik heard a piercing note blast through the air and turned to see the slavers' leader blowing hard into a curved horn. His face red, his dark eyes tiny fires burning in his tanned face, he blew and blew and screamed as his men passed him. They had crept from the forest under cover of dawn, but now they ran back into the forest as fast as their wounds would allow them.

Erik looked around him. Bodies littered the ground. Slavers, gypsies, miners, women, and children. Death did not discriminate. Just as his cousin reached him, he bent over and retched. Bryon took a step back, Erik vomiting and then dry heaving.

"Do you want some water?" Bryon asked, handing Erik a water skin.

Erik just shook his head, standing straight, closing his eyes, and breathing deeply.

"Do you need anything?" Bryon asked.

Erik opened his eyes and gave Bryon an odd look. It wasn't often that his cousin paid him any concern.

"No," was all Erik could muster.

"I saw Befel," Bryon said.

Erik nodded.

"He is hurt," Bryon added.

"I know," Erik said.

"The gypsies are tending to him," Bryon said. "I think he will be all right."

"He looked pale," Erik said looking around. The smell of blood and urine and feces hit his nose, and he felt his stomach churn again.

"We did it," Bryon said.

"Did what?" Erik asked.

"Won our first battle," Bryon replied.

"Won our first…" Erik began to reply, but then stopped. He looked at his cousin with furled brows. Despite his stomach turning and twisting, he could feel his face grow hot. "You call this a victory?"

Bryon shrugged. "What else would I call it?"

"Tragedy," Erik replied. "What else could it be? Look at the dead. Look at Befel."

Erik saw Dika tending to Befel, soaking his face with a wet rag. He felt his chin quiver, felt tears coming to his eyes.

"Poor Befel," he muttered.

"We're alive, cousin," Bryon said through gritted teeth. "That, in itself, is a victory."

"At what cost?" Erik asked.

"Don't be such a fool," Bryon hissed. "You want to go back home and stick your head in a hole, but this is the mire of shit that real men have to wade through every day. Don't kid yourself, Erik. Every day a man can wake up and breathe breath and say he is alive is a victory."

"And knowing this makes you somehow manlier?" Erik asked. "Knowing this makes you some sort of hero?"

"No," Bryon replied, turning his back to Erik and then looking at him over his shoulder. "No. But I don't want to hide away on a farm trying to escape that truth. I don't want to go work in some rat turd's mine to forget it. I want to embrace it. Use it. Turn survival into my way of making something of myself."

Bryon walked away, and Erik watched as Dika and a few other

women tended to Befel. He wanted to go to his brother, but his feet felt like they were pure iron. He listened as the cries of the dying and those who loved them filled the air. That smell. It made him retch again, and as he lifted his head, he saw Marcus, lying still, motionless where he had fallen.

Erik felt every emotion in his body, from pure hatred to petrifying fear to the deepest sadness, overwhelm him all at once, and he fell to his knees and wept.

Chapter 21

ERIK STOOD OVER MARDIRRU AS he cradled his father's head in his lap. Marcus breathed slowly. He could hear son talking to father in whispers but couldn't make out what he was saying. No matter. They were private words for a dying man.

Erik knelt next to Mardirru. Marcus' seemingly disengaged eyes caught Erik's, and the gypsy smiled despite the blood matting his beard and caking his teeth.

"Erik, you live, and uncaptured," he mumbled.

Erik smiled and nodded. He couldn't speak. He could barely breathe. He felt tears well up in his eyes.

Marcus closed his eyes for a moment and rolled his head to one side, one hand clutching at the sleeve of Mardirru's shirt.

"A king," he mumbled. "They once called me a king—and now look at me. It is what I deserve. My sins have finally caught up with me."

"Don't say that," Erik said.

"My wife?" Marcus asked. He looked to Erik, then to his son, and then back to Erik.

"I don't know, Father," Mardirru replied.

"Nor I," Erik agreed. "But I can find her for you."

Erik meant to stand, but Marcus' large hand reached out and caught his wrist. Even dying, there was strength in that grip, and it pulled Erik back to his knees.

"No, don't leave me," Marcus whispered through labored breaths. "Stay with me until the end."

"I will stay with you," Erik said, nodding, "but this isn't the end. You just need some rest."

"Rest." Marcus spoke the word with an inebriated quality. "Yes, rest. Rest is what I need. Hopefully, the Creator will look kindly on my last years and forgive all the wrong I've done."

Erik wanted to say something but felt more tears coming and thought that if he opened his mouth, he would just sound like a blithering fool through his weeping. So he just stayed there, a comforting hand on Mardirru's shoulder as the young gypsy cried over his dying father.

Erik saw a large shadow spread over them and looked up to see Max carrying the limp body of Nadya. Tears streamed down the young man's face. His expression—pursed lips, crinkled brows, frowning eyes—was one of torture.

"No!" Mardirru screamed when he saw his younger brother holding his mother. He reached for his mother's hand as her arm hung loosely and pressed his face to her skin, weeping uncontrollably.

"Father," Max choked.

"Son." Marcus tried to lift his head to see his boy but couldn't muster the strength.

"Father," Max repeated, "it's Mother. She's dead."

"By the heavens!" Marcus cried. He closed his eyes hard, and his ruined body wracked with heaving sobs. He cried for a long time, and his sons cried and Erik with him.

"Put her next to me, son," said Marcus eventually, and Max obeyed, gently laying his dead mother next to her husband.

"Mardirru, you are the leader of these people now," Marcus said. "Lead these people as the Creator would have you lead."

"I will lead your people to the best of my ability."

"No," Marcus replied between heavy breaths, "they are not my people. They are the Creator's people."

"Yes, Father," Mardirru said.

"Max," Marcus said, turning his head to see his younger son, "support your brother. He will need you in these coming years."

"Yes, Father," Max said with tears in his eyes and a slight bow of the head.

Marcus looked over at Erik.

"Follow your heart, young Erik. If the Creator truly resides there, he will not lead you astray. He has great things in store for you my friend. I know it."

He reached down and gripped his wife's hand. The smile on his face said he took comfort in the touch of her skin to his. Then he looked up again, but it wasn't at Erik. The young man could tell that much, but it wasn't at the gypsy's sons either. It was at the morning sky. One of his big smiles crossed his face. "Look at it—the sky. Beautiful. A beautiful miracle. I am ready."

Marcus continued to mouth the word "beautiful" until he drew his final breath and died, there in Mardirru's arms. Now both sons collapsed on top of their parents' bodies, wailing and clutching at their father's blood-soaked vest. Erik cried with them, for their loss, and for the world's loss of a great man like Marcus. He put his hand on Mardirru's shoulder, gave it a gentle squeeze.

"I'm sorry," Erik whispered. "He was truly a great man."

"None better." Mardirru sat up and wiped tears away from his cheeks. He stood and offered his hand to Erik, helping the young man stand. Mardirru didn't cry anymore. He just stood there, at the feet of his dead parents, his brother by his side, and Erik stood with them.

Eventually, the new leader of the Ion Gypsies bowed—just a slight bow—and blew a kiss to his mother. He looked up at the sky for a moment and then turned to Erik again.

"Come, let us bury them, say our prayers over them, and honor the life the Creator had given them."

Chapter 22

THOSE WHO HAD SURVIVED THE attack and had not fled set about seeking to bring back some sense of order to the embattled encampment, caring for the wounded and laying out the dead so they might bury them.

"The young men your age took the worst of it," Bo said to Bryon as his wife pressed a rag against the wound in her husband's chest.

"What do you mean?" Bryon asked, waiting for Dika to tend to the cut along his ribs, but it had stopped bleeding.

"The slavers targeted them, I think," Bo explained. "If I counted right, they captured all but two of the younger men. That's probably who they came for. Them and the children."

"Why would they want the men my age?" Bryon asked.

"They can sell them for a high price as laborers and such," Bo explained.

"I didn't think slavery really existed," Bryon said. "I mean, I was little better than a slave working in Wittick's pigsties in Venton, but I was still free to come and go. I earned a pittance, but it was still a weekly wage."

"Much of the world still engages in slavery," Dika added, "unfortunately. Even in the places where it isn't legal, you'll find slaves."

"And the children?" Bryon asked.

He noticed the sour look on Dika's face, as a tear collected at the corner of her eye.

"The young ones," Bo replied, "they will sell as house servants... and prostitutes."

"The children?" Bryon questioned. "Brothels?"

"Aye," Bo replied. "Disgusting, I know. The men who steal them away and the men who buy them. It is a terrible tragedy."

"Better they die," Dika said, tears now escaping her.

"Better the men who buy them die," Bryon muttered.

"I have known a few children to escape," Bo said. "We have several in our caravan. Their lives are a true testimony to willpower and the grace of the Creator."

Bryon scoffed. "How could any god let a child be sold into slavery, let alone to a brothel?"

"That's a hard question you ask," Bo said, wincing a little as Dika began stitching his wound. "One many others have asked as well."

Bryon felt his stomach twist. He never had any love for children. He cared for his sisters, cared about what happened to them, but couldn't really stand being around them for too long. He didn't want to be a father, but he recognized the innocence of children.

He had spent a fair bit of time in brothels, and no child deserved that life. The women whose services he had purchased were adults, capable of making their own decisions. He thought of Kukka. A child in such circumstances against her will? He shook his head, trying to push the thought to the back of his mind.

"How is Befel?" Bryon asked, nodding toward his cousin who lay close by, breathing slowly in unconsciousness.

"I will tend to him as soon as I am done with Bo," Dika said.

"His shoulder?" Bryon asked.

"It's bad," Bo replied. "He's lost a lot of blood. The knife struck him just right, it seems."

"Will he live?" Bryon asked.

"Oh yes," Bo said with a flinch. He grunted at his wife, and she returned a stern look as she cut the thread she used to stitch his wound with her teeth. "He will live. The question is, will he ever use his arm again?"

"Seriously?" Bryon asked.

"Aye," Bo replied. "I fear we don't have the ability to help him as much as I would like here. Especially with our caravan in such disarray. We will probably end up cauterizing the wound; it's so deep. He will have to get real help in Finlo."

"He isn't going to Finlo," Bryon said. "He's going to some mining camp in the western part of the Southern Mountains."

"Aga Kona," Dika said, spreading a clean cloth over Bo's chest.

Bo shook his head.

"That won't do," he said. "No. He will not heal properly at best and get an infection at worst if he doesn't go with us to Finlo."

Bryon shrugged.

"He will have to change his plans," Bo said matter-of-factly.

"See to him first," said Bryon, and Dika nodded her understanding.

Leaving them, Dika walked to Befel and patted him gently on the cheek to wake him. Befel groaned as Dika helped him sit up and, even though Bryon knew Befel was pale and groggy from pain and blood loss, something about his look infuriated him. He turned and walked away.

Bryon walked to Erik, who stood and watched as gypsy women gently laid the dead in a neat row.

"They fought well," Bryon said.

"They lived well," Erik added.

They watched women clean wounds and men dig graves. It wasn't just the gypsies who lay there, but miners and other travelers as well.

"They give the others the same burial rites as their own?" Bryon questioned, and Erik nodded.

"What if they don't want to be buried and prayed over?"

"Why wouldn't they?" Erik replied.

"I don't know…" Bryon waited a moment, thinking. "I don't think I would want them to pray over me and then bury me in the ground, only to become worm food. Fire—that's what you'll do if I die. Burn my body and leave my ashes so those bloody worms can choke on them."

Bryon gave a wry, cynical smile.

"Poor Marcus." Erik broke another short silence. "The pain on his face when his son told him Nadya had passed."

Bryon crinkled his eyebrows and scowled. "Why would he tell a dying man such a thing?"

"Why not?"

"Let him pass in peace," Bryon said. "Poor fool is dying. Give him at least a little solace."

"You would've lied to him, even if he asked you directly?"

Bryon shrugged. "Yeah."

"Then he would've known you lied," Erik said, "when he saw his wife in the afterlife."

Bryon chuckled and shook his head. "I suppose that is where we differ. I say let him pass to dust in peace. Give him, in his last moments of existence, as much comfort as possible. Afterlife is just a fool's dream."

"How can you have so little hope?"

"Oh no, cousin; you misunderstand," Bryon replied. "I have hope. I have hope in me, in what I can do, in what I can do with my own hands. I know my purpose. I control my destiny. No greater spirit or almighty god tells me what to do or what my purpose is in this life. My purpose is me, and that's exactly who I will look out for. I won't work my hands to the bone to end up like Marcus."

Bryon turned to walk away but stopped when Erik called his name. "Aren't you going to help dig?"

Bryon shook his head.

"Where are you going then?"

"To search the bodies," he replied, pointing to the bodies of the dead slavers their brethren weren't able to pull back to the forest.

"For what?"

"Whatever they have to offer." Bryon shrugged.

"But they're dead."

"Exactly."

Chapter 23

"WHAT HAPPENS NOW?" BEFEL ASKED, trying not to look at the bloody mass of soiled cloths lying next to him.

He flinched again as Dika probed the wound on his shoulder, making sure it was clean of clothing or other bits of dirt. Bo blew gently on a small fire he had built, waving his hand over it and poking it with a stick. Befel didn't know whether he really cared, at the moment, about what the caravan's next course of action would be. He simply tried to take his mind off the iron clincher—an implement used by the caravan's farrier—sitting in the fire and glowing red from the heat.

"We continue on," Bo replied. "We keep going as we always have, telling stories, singing songs, and spreading the good news."

A quiet sniffle came from Dika. Bo rubbed his wife's shoulder.

"It will be all right, my love," he comforted. She nodded, the back of her hand held to her mouth, holding back sobs and tears.

"I remember when one of my father's mules cut its leg on the barbed fence that divided our land from Farmer Jovek's," offered Befel. "The animal bled so profusely, Father feared it would die right then and there, so we built a quick fire, heated his scythe until it burned red, and pressed it against the horse's leg."

"The best way," agreed Bo.

"It looked so painful," Befel added with a heavy sigh, "and I wanted to cry for the poor animal, but the wound closed up, stopped

114

bleeding, and never became infected. Father still uses that stupid animal. Sure as the sun rises, it's gotten into more trouble since then, trampling through thistle bushes, eating Jovek's apples, gnawing at Mother's roses."

Befel chuckled, and Bo and Dika laughed with him, trying to ease his apprehension.

Bo looked at his wife, and she gave him a slight nod. They tried to do it without Befel noticing, but he saw the affirmation that the clincher was ready, and he began to sweat. His breathing quickened, and he felt his hands shake, just a little.

"Here, dear." Dika wiped sweat from Befel's forehead with a damp cloth. "Bite down on this." She placed a round piece of wood in his mouth. "Bo will be quick, and the pain will be fleeting."

Befel whimpered and nodded, the way he did when his mother would try to comfort him on a stormy night when he was a little boy.

Bo pulled the iron tool from the fire, the metal steaming in the cool morning air.

"All right, son," Bo comforted, bringing the clincher closer. Befel looked away. He could feel the heat from the iron radiating against his cheek. Bo gave Befel no more time to think. He pressed the hot iron tool against Befel's shoulder. The skin and flesh melted, giving off the smell of cooking meat. Befel groaned loudly and then succumbed to screaming as Bo held the clincher in place.

After a few moments, the smell reached his nose, and he retched. The piece of wood fell from his mouth, and the young man slumped to one side, unconscious.

Chapter 24

"THEY'RE BLOODY GYPSIES!" YELLED THE leader of the slavers.

Fox cowered behind a giant elm tree. He knew all too well what Kehl's anger could lead to.

"They're worthless cheats! Gutless con artists! What happened?"

"I don't know, Kehl." Fox crawled from behind the tree, groveled on both knees. Kehl spat on him and kicked the fiery-haired youth hard in the stomach.

"Your job was to know. Your job was to set them up. Gypsies are not supposed to mount a defense that would claim the lives of my men."

He kicked Fox again and turned around, scratching the pointed, oiled beard that grew on his chin. Fox rolled on the ground, groaning and clutching his stomach. Dozens of men and women and children, bound together by lengths of hemp rope, cried and moaned as Kehl raged.

"We still captured most of the younger, able-bodied men that traveled with them, Kehl," a taller, tan-skinned man said. "And we took a fair number of children as well. They will all fetch a good price."

Kehl turned quickly on his heels, eyes bearing down hard on the man that spoke. "And we will have to use all of what we earn from these swine to replenish our losses, you fool."

The man cowered just as Fox had. "What shall you have us do then?" he asked, head bowed so that he wouldn't meet Kehl's gaze.

Kehl paused, leaving a long several minutes of silence, his troop of battered slavers awaiting his next orders.

"Revenge," he hissed, venom rich on his tongue. "We will seek revenge and steal back what we've lost."

"And what of him," the taller man asked. He nodded toward Fox as he withdrew a dagger from his belt.

Kehl eyed the redheaded man then shook his head. He had lost too many men already.

"Kill only the wounded. Load the rest into the wagons," Kehl commanded Fox who skittered away, almost on all fours. Kehl turned to the tall slaver, his brother.

"Ready the men and wagons. We move at dusk."

His brother bowed, and Kehl turned and walked away, hands clasped behind his back. When he knew he was just a shadow in the forest, he turned back around to watch his camp. He watched as Fox pulled an older woman to her feet. She limped forward when he commanded her to walk. The redheaded man shook his head and slit her throat. The children screamed. Kehl smiled.

"Power," he muttered.

Chapter 25

Bryon rode next to Bo's wagon. His horse was a little wide for riding. It had, after all, pulled a gypsy carriage only a day before. However, with fewer people, and the need for so many carriages gone, Mardirru ordered horses unbridled and used for riding.

"I can't believe they buried that scum," Bryon muttered to himself. "They want to bury their own—sure. They want to bury the miners—fine. But the slavers? As if stealing children to sell as prostitutes isn't enough..."

The vision of three people—a woman and two men—hung in his mind. Bryon had found them as they broke camp. The woman and men's throats had been cut, and their bodies left to rot.

Bo had explained that slavers discarded those whom they couldn't sell—the elderly, the crippled, the wounded.

"The leg would've healed up," Bryon muttered to himself, thinking of the first man's broken limb. "Set it, splint it, and in some time, he would be fine. And the cut in the miner's stomach could've healed as well. I thought they could find a buyer for anything."

Bryon gripped the reins hard as he thought of the woman, no doubt too old. That made him think of his mother, who had more gray in her hair than this woman had.

"Leave them to the crows and worms," Bryon had told Max as the gypsy oversaw the burials. "So what if it isn't your way."

Now, he looked to his left. Max, Mardirru's brother, rode many paces away from him. Why did he care? Bryon shook his head; he certainly didn't. He continued to watch Max, thinking he should have punched the man in the face to knock some sense into him.

Even though Bryon had not raised his fist, Max had been needled by what Bryon said, and Mardirru had stopped any fight from happening, stepping between the two. Bryon rubbed his chest where the new gypsy leader had pushed him away.

"I should've punched you in the face as well," he now muttered, looking in Mardirru's direction where he was riding somewhere in the front of the caravan. "I should have socked you right in the jaw— and then kneed you in your balls."

He turned to watch Erik and Dika tend to Befel in the back of the wagon. His cousin hadn't woken since Bo cauterized his wounded shoulder, and fits of shaking overcame him while he slept. Bryon shook his head again.

"You disapprove of my wife's treatment of your cousin?" Bo questioned.

"No." Bryon hadn't realized Bo was watching him. He didn't mean for that to happen.

"Then what causes that disgusted look? Are you still brooding over the burial of the slavers?"

"No," but Bryon thought for a moment and corrected himself. "Well, yes, but that's not it."

"Then what?"

"My cousin," Bryon muttered. "He's a fool."

"I can see that you two don't get along so well," Bo said.

"Like I said, he's a fool."

"I've seen grudges destroy a family, my friend. I'll never understand a family that doesn't love one another," Bo intoned cautiously.

Bryon shook his head again, a quick scoff at what Bo had said. "It's true, I guess. I hold no great love for my cousin."

"I can see that," Bo added. "You can't even say his name. What happened between you two?"

"It wasn't always like this, between Befel and me." Bryon gave Bo a condescending smirk as he spoke his cousin's name. "We acted like brothers, once. Even more so than Erik and him."

"Go on," Bo encouraged.

"We planned on leaving our home together. We planned on going east and making a name for ourselves. We decided that together," Bryon explained.

"As we grew older, our fathers began to prepare us, get us ready for taking over their farms when the time came. They gave us plots of land to farm and animals to tend, but that was not our plan. We pooled the money we made from selling our own crops, our own livestock, and we raised enough, together, to make it east. At the last minute, Befel told me Erik was coming, too. Now we needed more money. Where there were two, now there were three. But we still left."

Bryon paused a moment to take a hearty draught of water from a skin that hung from his saddle.

"We stopped in Venton and sold our labor to this pig farmer named Wittick in order to raise the extra money we needed to buy our way into a caravan and buy the supplies we would need to travel east. That fool Befel…"

Bryon stopped again, fuming silently. His face reddened despite the coolness of the day, and he clenched his reins so hard that the leather creaked under his white-knuckled grip, and his horse slowed practically to a stop. He kicked the horse's side, and it trotted back to the front of the wagon.

"That fool Befel bought our way onto a caravan without telling Erik or me. He used all our money to buy our spots on a train, entirely too much, and he believed them when they told him to meet in Venton's main square the next morning. He gave them our money up front, and when we went in the morning to meet…"

"They weren't there," Bo interrupted. Bryon nodded. "They saw a naïve young man and conned him."

"Because of him, we spent over a year knee deep in pig shit."

"And that is why you harbor a grudge against your cousin."

"Wouldn't you?" Bryon defended. Bo didn't so much ask a question as he made a simple, realizing statement, but for some reason, Bryon felt accosted, attacked.

"Oh, I suppose I would be upset," Bo added.

"Just upset?"

"Aye," Bo replied. "It could be worse."

"Worse?"

"Sure," Bo reassured. "He could've gotten your sister pregnant. Or killed your brother and blamed it on a pack of wolves. Or burned down your barn while it was full of harvest and livestock—even run your family off their land so he might steal it. I've seen all those things happen between families. Yes, it could be worse."

Bryon trotted along silently for a little while longer.

"I won't think about it anymore," he said, half to himself and half to his horse. Then, he looked over to see Befel. He lay in the back of the wagon, Erik stroking his hair and Dika pressing a damp towel to his forehead. Bryon's blood began to boil, and all he could think about was sneering Ventonian nobles throwing scraps of food and taunting him while he worked with his arms sunk elbow-deep in pig shit.

He kicked the horse's ribs hard, and the poor animal jerked, its back legs practically giving out under the sudden shock. It broke into a quick canter, carrying Bryon to the front of the caravan and beyond.

Chapter 26

THE NEXT DAY—BREAKING A COLD, dark night of sorrowful dirges, weeping wives, and wailing mothers—would finally bring the embattled caravan to the edge of the Blue Forest. Erik had never expected it to come.

With its ancient elms and ghostly oaks, the forest had held a certain mystic quality, and yet, despite those barbaric times, it still offered a bucolic sense of peace. Now, through its archaic visage, hailing back to an age when man knew little more than to plant simple crops and pick berries, its simplicity seemed to calm Erik's mind and heart.

Most men sought simplicity in a world filled with decisions of life or death. Erik knew his father did, recanting all the worries he had heard his father mutter.

How do I feed my children? Will my wife's fever ever break? Will my crops make enough at market?

With all of those questions in his mind, Erik's father would sit on their porch and watch his mother's flowers. Simplicity. At the edge of the Blue Forest, Erik too watched life play out in its natural perfection, but his mind was a turmoil as he once again considered his next steps.

"This is still a game of life or death, of kill or be killed," Erik muttered, watching a fox chase after a squirrel as the ancient story of life unfolded in front of him.

But it is simple. Nature holds no jealousy. Nature doesn't enslave. When nature has had its fill, it leaves well enough alone.

Nevertheless, the breaking of dawn did not bring with it any sort of primordial realization. It brought the hard truth of what had happened to the ragtag band of travelers, the harsh reality of the world in which these men and women lived. Morning brought death.

A shrill cry broke Erik's trance. He ran with several other men, rusted sword ready for a fight, to find a gypsy woman kneeling beside the wide trunk of an ancient oak. Her hands covered her face, her back heaving with heavy sobs, as the lifeless body of an older woman dangled above her.

Erik blinked, and the vision, the dream, flashed before him—his mother hanging from a tree just outside their home, drifting back and forth with each gentle breeze. His throat went dry.

"One of ours," a man next to Erik said.

"Y-you recognize...recognize her?" Erik asked.

He could barely speak and never even looked at the other man. He kept his eyes on the woman, watching her twisting.

That was Mother. In my dream, that was Mother.

"Aye," the man replied. "Worked with her husband for a while. Heading to Aga Kona, he was."

"The new mining camp in the west?" Erik asked, noting but not commenting on the past tense—was.

"Aye," the man said with a nod.

Erik looked over his shoulder, wondering if he could see his brother from where he stood. That's where he was going. At least, that's where Befel had planned on going. Erik wasn't sure how useful a one-armed miner would be.

"Slavers did this," Erik suggested, partially to the man and partially to himself. "She was captured, and they discarded her like trash."

"No." The man shook his head. "Did it to herself. Even for her, the tree had been too easy to climb, but then she must have been desperate."

"Why would she do such a thing?" Erik asked, somewhat startled.

"Slavers killed her eldest boy," the man replied. "Took one of her little ones too. Poor Matty. Her husband'll probably end up killing himself as well. Matty's got two other children. What'll happen to them? We'll find Matty's body tomorrow. Sure as the sun will rise."

Erik had presumed the husband had died too, but now he understood the man's words.

As he watched two other men cut her down, Erik heard a scream—a deep, man's scream—from the camp and didn't need to turn to know word had reached her husband. The man he presumed to be Matty came running, dropped to his knees next to her lifeless body, and wailed louder than Erik had ever heard a man cry. Matty cradled the woman in his arms, his tears washing over her face, smoothing out her gray hair as he rocked back and forth.

"That is so sad," Erik muttered. "My heart breaks for that man."

"Feel sad for the world, m'boy," the man said. "This is the way it is. Far worse happens out there, in the east, in the vast cities of the world."

Erik hadn't meant for him to hear his whispers.

This is the way of the world.

He continued to watch the man cradle his dead wife, and then a little boy and an adolescent girl joined him and cried with him.

Is this what will happen to my parents? My sisters? Even if I come home? Is this what will happen to Bryon in the east?

Erik's stomach knotted, and he turned away as some men began to dig yet another shallow grave.

Later, as the caravan finally departed, Erik sat beside Bo at the front of the wagon again, watching the end of the Blue Forest and the last part of the Abresi Straits creep closer and closer.

"Interesting," Erik said as he watched the last elm tree of the Blue Forest pass behind them.

"What is that, young Erik?" Bo asked.

"How much warmer it is," Erik replied, "just a dozen paces past the Blue Forest. I wonder why?"

"The trees hold in the cold, it seems," Bo explained. "And the winds that get funneled through the Abresi Straits make it colder as well. Have you ever been in the Plains of Güdal during this time of year?"

Erik shook his head. "No. Venton. That's as far east as I've been."

"The Plains are hot," Bo explained, "and I think that heat gets pushed into the Southland Gap by winds coming off the Gray Mountains."

"That makes sense," Erik replied. "Winds coming off the Gray Mountains always made springs very cool back on the farm. One year, though, there were no winds. It was much warmer than usual. Almost ruined our crops."

"And that same year," Bo said, "the Southland Gap and the Plains of Güdal were probably unusually cool."

"Are we stopping before nightfall?" Erik asked.

"Aye," Bo said. "We will take a short break before heading south to Finlo."

"The miners are leaving," Bryon said, riding beside them on his horse.

"Are you going with them?" Erik asked his brother, who lay in the back of Bo's wagon with Dika sitting next to him.

Befel's color still hadn't fully returned, and Erik could tell he was in a lot of pain.

"I would advise against it," Bo said. "There's a barber in Finlo you should see—goes by the name of Kevon—but he's also a surgeon of sorts. He's the best in Western Háthgolthane. He'll tend to your shoulder better than anyone."

"You can advise against it all you want," Bryon said. "He won't listen. He's the oldest, after all."

"Shut up, cousin," Erik hissed and then looked back at his brother. "Befel, are you going?"

Befel tried to sit up, but his face contorted in pain as he tried to push to his bottom.

"Stop that," Dika scolded. "You'll reopen your wound."

Without a word, Befel lay back and closed his eyes again.

As Bo had predicted, the caravan stopped, and the miners—what was left of them—gathered up around Mardirru. Erik watched as all the men shook the new gypsy leader's hand.

"Are you sure you still wish to travel west to the Southern Mountains?" Erik heard Mardirru ask one of the miners.

"Aye," the man, hardened by years underground, replied. "'Tis all we know. We can't do nothin' else. I only hope that time— time and gold," he added with a forced smile, "—will help heal some of our wounds. Aga Kona is a big one, it is—one of Golgolithul's biggest mines yet, for sure. And being so far away from the east, it'll practically be like mining a free mine. So I've heard."

Mardirru produced a small sack and dropped it in the miner's hand. It clinked when it hit the man's palm and sounded heavy. The miner squeezed the sack and bounced it in his hand. It continued to jingle like bits of metal. The miner gave Mardirru a curious look.

"Your payment into our caravan," he explained. "Consider it a start to your rebuilding. It is the least we can do after what has happened to all of us. I think it is what my father would've wanted."

"Thank you," the miner said. Erik thought he heard the man's voice crack, and then he shrugged. Erik supposed he might cry too if a man gave him back that much coin.

With that, the miners broke from the caravan and headed east, toward the Southern Mountains.

"Is he going to give us our money back?" Bryon asked quietly.

Erik hadn't realized Bryon was standing next to him. He looked at his cousin with a measure of disbelief.

"You're truly heartless."

"Just a legitimate question."

The caravan turned south, hugging a small wagon trail that ran along the eastern edge of the Blue Forest.

"The Sea Born Road is a little better traveled," Bo explained to Erik, "but it is another day's travel east."

"What is the Sea Born Road?" Erik asked.

"An actual road lined by flagstone and paved with large, flat rock," Bo replied. "It's been there over a thousand years, built by Gol-Durathna when their rule extended this far west. I hear it now stops somewhere in Nordeth, but once it wound its way from Finlo all the way to Amentus—one long road maintained and guarded by the Northern Kingdom. It certainly proves a little safer, so many people using it on a daily basis. And with our numbers so low now, it is perhaps the course I would have chosen, but I am sure Mardirru is figuring on reaching Finlo as quickly as possible."

Chapter 27

A FEW FIRES DOTTED THE hushed camp that first night away from the forest. Erik sat in Bo's wagon and watched his brother for a while, stroked his sweaty hair while the injured man shook and convulsed through nightmares and fitful sleep. He woke once, for just enough time to drink a skin full of water and stuff some bread down his throat. Then he returned to his coma-like state. When it seemed Befel would sleep—rather, half-sleep—through the night, Erik turned his attention to eating some supper and then trying to sleep as well.

The Southland Gap air was warm save for occasional gusts of ocean wind carrying the chill of salty breezes, and Erik decided he'd sleep on the ground. With his back to a wagon wheel, he sat by himself with a bowl of vegetable-laden soup and two hearty slices of bread. The broth tasted good.

Everything Dika makes tastes good, she reminds me of Mother.

He shook his head to rid himself of such thoughts and looked to his right to see Mardirru sitting by himself, Marcus' falchion laid across his lap, and his father's flute resting gently in his hands. He looked so much like the mighty Marcus, sitting there, contemplating.

Erik wondered if he should join him but dismissed the idea.

He wants to be alone, and I would too.

The gypsy stared at the wooden flute for just a while longer and then put it to his lips. He closed his eyes, breathed deep, and blew, making a screeching sound which made Mardirru flinch. Erik knew

128

this man could find his way around an instrument—he'd seen him play the drums, a lyre, and a flute. The same thing happened. The screeching sound of a quieted howling wind wafted through the air. Mardirru wiped a tear from the corner of his eye and placed the flute next to the giant sword in his lap.

"Is there another bowl?" Bryon asked, plopping down next to Erik.

"I didn't expect you to be having dinner with me," Erik said.

"Why not?" Bryon asked, and then again said, "Is there a bowl?"

Erik stood, retrieved a bowl from Bo's carriage, and spooned Bryon several ladles' worths of soup from the large blackened pot that rested next to the fire.

"Thank you," Bryon said.

"Why are you over here?" Erik asked.

"That's a nice welcome!" Bryon replied, a small smile on his face. "Truth be told, I tried sleeping, but with all Befel's tossing about, I don't think I'll ever get to sleep."

Erik stared at him coldly, his blue eyes icy gems.

"I don't mean to blame him," Bryon said. "It is obviously not Befel's fault—all the turning and tossing. But the truth is, I won't be able to sleep with him in such a fit."

"Very well," Erik replied.

He sat next to his cousin, eating and watching the firelight dance off the now distant trees. Then, placing his empty bowl between his legs, he asked, "Did you find anything on the dead slavers?"

Bryon smirked as he gave a wry, sidelong glance. "Not all innocence and naïveté, are we cousin?"

"Just curious. I want nothing to do with anything you found."

Bryon retrieved a leather sack from his belt, opened his palm, and poured the sack's contents into his hand. Coins spilled out, some cut in half, but most full coins of copper and silver. Erik's eyes widened.

"I think I have only seen that much coin two other times in my life," Erik said.

"Oh," Bryon replied. "When?"

"I watched as Marcus put payments to join the caravan into a large chest in the back of his main carriage," Erik explained. "That chest must've had two score of bags like this one."

"Doing what they do for the greater good are they? What do they need with all that money?" Bryon chided.

Erik rolled his eyes and went back to watching the fire.

"Very well," Bryon said. "I am truly sorry for accusing your beloved Marcus of being a thief. He was probably, truly, a good man. So when was the second time you had seen so much coin?"

Erik paused and waited a moment as Bryon put his bowl down.

"It was in Venton," Erik said. "Wittick took me into his house once when he paid us too little. Do you remember?"

Bryon nodded.

"He took me into a room that had two men—men with spears and swords—standing guard," Erik continued. "It was in that room that he kept a chest. He paid me out of that chest. I think it was two pence each. But in that chest...in that chest I saw more coin than I think I will ever see again."

"Hopefully not," Bryon said. "When we get east, you'll see more."

The vision of a woman hanging from an ancient oak tree popped into Erik's head.

What did that miner say? Far worse happens out there, in the world, in the east.

"Wittick is a wealthy man," Bryon said.

"Wittick is a rat turd," Erik replied.

"Aye." Bryon laughed. "He was that. But he is wealthier than our fathers will ever be."

"In terms of coin, I suppose he is richer," Erik agreed.

"How else would you measure wealth?" Bryon asked.

Erik hated that tone—that condescending tone—Bryon spoke with when he felt like Erik was acting childish or stupid.

"Livestock and land," Erik replied.

"All of which you can trade for coin," Bryon said.

"What about respect?" Erik asked. "What about the honor of a name? Men want to work for the Eleodums. They know we will be fair to them, we won't cheat them, and we will honor their labor. My father had that. So did yours."

"Your father, maybe," Bryon said. "Mine? I don't know. The only thing he had in abundance was jugs of orange brandy hidden away from my mother."

Erik laughed. He shouldn't have, and after he did, he quickly looked to his cousin, fearing what might come next. But Bryon laughed as well. Erik looked back at his cousin's hand.

"Is that..." Erik gasped, poking through the coins with his finger.

Bryon nodded. "Yes, it is, cousin. A Ventonian pound. Pure too."

"That right there equals a year of hard work on the farm," Erik said. He felt the smile growing on his face.

"I know," Bryon replied. "And there is more—in the east."

Erik's mouth hung open, but then he saw them again. Scenes from his dreams of his sisters, abused and chained. Dreams of his father and mother...dead. Now came memories of children stolen away and a woman hanging from a tree. He shut his mouth quickly and frowned. A scowl crossed his eyebrows.

"Blood money."

Bryon's mouth dropped open. "Are you being serious, cousin?"

"It's blood money. It's tainted."

"Isn't all money?"

"Men died for that money. Men sold other men for that money."

Bryon shook his head, blinking his eyes cynically as he sighed and laughed in pure, scathing bewilderment.

"Whatever, cousin. When you need food, or shelter, or new clothing, just remember how tainted this money is."

Chapter 28

ERIK AWOKE IN THE DEAD of the night. A cold wind swirled around him, and he shivered. He turned to the forest and stared into the darkness, the shadows of looming elms, oaks, and sycamores taunting him.

A pair of yellow eyes stared back at him, and he thought of the eyes of the first slaver he had killed, the thick clubber with wild, dark, oily hair pulled into a multitude of haphazard tails. In death, his eyes had looked blank, yellowed even, his dark pupils sullen and dirty. However, they still looked piercing, watching and staring from beyond death. They had glared at Erik in disbelief. They accused him and protested at their sudden end. They hated Erik.

Were these the eyes of a ghost? No. A scrawny, spindly wolf darted from behind a tree, ribs poking through its mangy sides. Erik pushed himself up to his elbows, ready to run for the curved sword he had pilfered from a slaver. He was an easy target for the wolf, a week's worth of meat for such a hungry scavenger. Suddenly, it cut to its right hard, jumping and nipping at something. A small hare.

Erik sighed with relief as the two animals, predator and prey, zig-zagged in the black of night. Dashing back and forth, playing a deadly game of chase, they eventually disappeared back into the forest.

Am I the hare? If I am, then who is the wolf?

He continued to stare into the night, sure he'd never get back to sleep. Every time he closed his eyes, he saw dead men. A bald man with a gashing wound, coagulated blood thick like porridge oozing from his neck, taunted him. The clubber, a valley cut into the bone and flesh along the top of his head, eyed him with pure abhorrence. A middle-aged woman, perfect save for a slight, abnormal twist in her neck, watched him with sad, tear-filled eyes, salty lines staining her cheeks. A giant of a man, crimson matting his black beard, flesh about his chest ripped and torn, smiled at him.

Despite the cold, Erik felt their hot, fading breath against his face. He gagged as a pungent, fetid smell hit his nose: Death. He retched again and wiped his mouth with the back of his hand.

He looked over to several of the horses, hearing one snort and another stomp its hooves. He looked at his cousin as he lay sound asleep on the cold ground. He could hear Befel toss and turn in the wagon, still half awake, half asleep, groaning every time he rolled onto his shoulder. But for Erik, there'd be no more rest that night.

The morning still held the cold sting of the fading night. Erik feverishly rubbed his arms, trying to warm up. Bryon had awoken early and had even deigned to help Bo pack the wagon as Erik fed the horses and other animals. Befel finally stirred, shivering in the morning's cold as he tried sitting up. However, any movement sent a chilled, crippling vibration through his body and into his shoulder.

"Erik."

"Yes, brother," Erik replied, running to Befel.

"I need help," he said reluctantly. "I can't sit up."

Erik gently placed his hand behind Befel's back and hoisted him up slowly. Erik saw the look of embarrassment on Befel's face. He patted his brother on the leg.

"Don't fret, brother. Your wound will heal. And when it does, you will not have to ask your little brother for help any longer."

"Is there anything hot to eat?" Befel asked as Erik wrapped two blankets around his brother's shoulders. Erik looked to Dika. The gypsy woman nodded slightly, and within a brief moment, produced a wooden bowl of vegetable soup.

"It's not really hot," she said apologetically, "but it's warm."

Befel nodded his gratitude and dove into the meal.

"That is good. You need to regain some of your strength," Erik said, pleased to see an appetite returning.

"Here." Dika handed the young man a water skin. Befel took it.

"It's milk—fresh milk. It will help you get your strength back."

By the third day of travel along the Southland Gap, an unfamiliar smell filled Erik's nose. It burned his nostrils, and he winced and sneezed at the odor.

"What's the matter, my friend?" Bo asked.

Erik again sat next to Bo on his captain's seat, keeping the gypsy company and listening intently to any stories he had to offer.

"I've never smelled that before."

"What?" Bo asked.

"That odd smell in the air," Erik replied. "What is it?"

"Ah, yes, the sea. The smell of fish, salty water, and sandy beaches. It is peculiar, isn't it? I think at times I welcome that smell, and at times I dread it."

"And today?"

"Hmm," Bo mulled. "I think today I welcome it. It signifies a new chapter in my life and the life of my family. So, yes, today I welcome that smell."

Erik smiled as his eyes followed the line of trees creating the Blue Forest's border and on over a small hillock.

When they reached the top of that hill, that same line of trees stopped suddenly just before a wide expanse of sand, and then, there it was—the ocean. Erik's mouth dropped. A curving horizon of blue, strands of silvery clouds hanging just above it. Black specks weaved through those clouds and dove down to the water.

"Seagulls," Erik muttered.

"Aye," Bo said, hearing the gawking screech of one the birds. "Little better than rats with wings if you ask me."

"Those I've seen before."

"Really," Bo queried. "How so?"

"On especially wet monsoons, they make their way to our farmstead and settle around several of the large lakes. I suppose it might be a little cooler farther north from here, and during rainy seasons, those lakes fill with so many trout and bass there's practically no room."

To the east of the beach, they saw the large coastal city of Finlo, abutting the South Sea. All they could see of the city's port were the tall masts of ships that were anchored in the harbor.

"There it is," Bryon said as he rode up next to Erik and Bo. He pointed to the masts.

"What?" Erik asked.

"That's our ship. That's our future." Bryon said it with such certainty. Erik gave him a questioning look. "It doesn't matter which ship, but one of them will take us east, and that's our future."

Chapter 29

"THERE ARE NO WALLS," ERIK said as they neared Finlo.

"No lad, no walls," Bo replied.

"Even Waterton has wooden barricades," Erik said.

"Southland is a neutral country," Bo explained. "It always has been, never taking sides in any war, just importing and exporting for whoever pays."

"That seems impossible," Erik said.

"Perhaps," Bo replied with a shrug. "I know I wouldn't be able to just sit by and not take sides in a fight. Finlo has survived through the rule of law. That's it."

"I don't understand," Erik said.

"Finlo and its ruling council—the Council of Five—doesn't care who you are, what you believe, what you look like, what food you eat, what you wear, or from where you hail. All Finlo cares about, is that you obey the law."

"Are its laws so different?" Erik asked.

"They are very strict," Bo replied. "Just watch yourself, Erik. You have a good head on your shoulders and a good heart, but it's very easy for a young man to get himself into trouble here."

"A young man like Bryon," Erik muttered.

"Aye," Bo replied and smiled. "So, make sure you watch him as well."

As they neared the entrance to Finlo, three cages were suspended

136

on sturdy poles along the road. Each had an occupant, offering up a sweet meal of rotting flesh for the gulls screeching and hovering overhead.

"Too bad those slavers aren't here," suggested Bryon as he pointed at a wooden placard hanging from one cage that read *Thief, Third Offense.* The body, picked to the bone, clutched the bars of the cage tightly with bony fingers.

"I didn't know you cared that much," Erik said.

Bryon just shrugged.

"They know to stay away," Mardirru said, riding up next to Erik and Bryon. "Their sentence would have been much worse—much more painful—than a simple, poor begging thief."

Erik thought Mardirru's expression was one of sympathy.

"These men got what they deserved," Bryon replied.

"Perhaps," Mardirru replied.

The other two cages held bodies a little fresher. One placard read *Inciting Riots against the Council.* The other read, *Proselytizing and Disturbing the Peace.*

"I hope that's what those rat turds look like right now," Bryon said as he tapped one of the wooden placards. "The slavers. I hope that's what is happening to them. I hope worms are tunneling through their flesh."

"Are you going to keep staring at rotting corpses, or are you going to join us inside the city?" Erik asked over his shoulder as the wagon followed Mardirru and the rest of the gypsy caravan along the main road into the city.

Sand dotted with broken seashells filled the streets of Finlo, and the smell of fish and old seawater filled the air.

"I think I might prefer cobbled streets and the smell of stale beer to this," Erik offered as they slowly rambled down the main street, his nose crinkling at the strange smells.

They stopped in what Erik assumed to be a town square. It had several brick benches and a myriad of carts and vendors where people congregated.

"What will you do now?" Erik asked Bo, who helped the young man pack a few pairs of clean pants and shirts—gifts from Dika—into his pack. Erik looked at the leather haversack, bulging with clothing and food. His throat went dry when he realized that all he owned sat in that pack.

"I don't know," Bo replied, looking over to Mardirru as he bid his farewells to other travelers. "We have a new leader, and therefore, we have a new course."

"Is that a good thing?"

"Aye, I believe it is," Bo replied. "Mardirru is a good man. He takes after his father. His brother, Max, will support him, as will his sister, Melia. And even though he is young, he is wise—wise enough to listen to the counsel of the older gypsies in our caravan when needs be."

"As long as he listens to anyone's advice but yours," Dika chided, walking by.

Bo scowled playfully at her. He turned back to Erik. "Whatever we do, we will stay here, just outside the city's limits, for a few days before we're off again."

"Thank you for all you've done." Erik extended his hand.

Bo laughed, grabbed Erik's wrist, and pulled the young man into a wide embrace.

"We've been through enough together, my friend. I think a friendly embrace is acceptable. While you're in Finlo, I want you to make sure your brother sees that man named Kevon. He will tend to his wound. Tell Befel to say I sent him."

Bo handed Erik his pack, and the two hugged again. With a hearty pat on the shoulder, and a small tear teasing the corner of Bo's eye, they departed. Erik left his brother and cousin saying their goodbyes to Bo and Dika and went over to Mardirru. The younger, slightly smaller version of Marcus stood straight and regal, falchion sheathed at his side, wooden flute tucked into the front of his belt along with a jeweled and golden-hilted dagger.

Erik didn't know what to say and felt relieved when Mardirru finally spoke.

"My father saw something in you. I don't know what. I must admit, I didn't have the opportunity to know you as I should've. I fear, in my youth, I'm still a little cynical of outsiders. That fallacy is something I should've learned from my father sooner."

Before Erik could reply, Mardirru pulled Marcus' wooden flute from his belt. He handed it to Erik, a sad look on his face.

"I am not the dreamer my father was, nor is Max. It pains me to realize that, but I will just have to find where my strengths lie. My father saw you as a dreamer. The way he spoke of you…this flute belongs in the hands of a dreamer."

"I can't," Erik said, trying gently to push the flute away, but Mardirru just held it there, waiting for Erik to take it.

"Thank—" Erik started saying when Mardirru cut him off.

"You do not have a reliable weapon."

He pointed to the curved blade randomly hanging from Erik's belt before he reached for the bejeweled dagger in his belt. It was a long-bladed weapon, with a gold scabbard encrusted with every gem from diamonds to emeralds.

"This belonged to my father also. This is a reliable weapon. I've never seen my father use it, and I've only heard his stories about what it is—what it can do—but just know it will aid you when you are in need of trustworthy steel."

"What it can do?" Erik asked.

Mardirru smiled. "I will leave that to you to discover. And, of course, I am giving you back the money you paid my father for passage into our caravan."

Mardirru dropped a heavy leather sac into Erik's hand, and Erik guessed the young gypsy had returned more than they had originally paid.

"I wish you speed and success on your travels east, Erik Eleodum," Mardirru added. "Go with the Creator, remembering always his steadfast love and unwavering courage."

"Thank you, and may he bless you as well, Mardirru."

The gypsy turned away with a final nod, and as Erik stood by himself in the bustling square of Finlo, he didn't know if he had ever felt that lonely.

He watched the gypsy wagons roll on toward the city's center. He waved at the families he knew, the little girl he had saved, her mother and brother, men he drank with, women who served him hot bread and fresh milk.

"I'll never see them again" he muttered as Bryon appeared by his side.

"Probably not," Bryon said matter-of-factly. He didn't even sound glad or sarcastic.

He handed Erik the reins of a horse the gypsies had given them, and Befel held the reins of his. Erik looked back to see two other horses laden with blankets, food, clothing—anything they might need.

Didn't Bo remember they meant to sail east? Then Erik laughed silently. That seemed just like Bo—leaving them with options.

"We need to find a place to stay. I do not trust this place for sleeping on the streets," Bryon stated.

"Agreed," Befel replied.

Before he could mount his horse, Erik jerked forward as something hard hit him from behind. He looked up to see a thick-shouldered man walking away, looking back at the young man with a sidelong glance and a cruel smile stretching across his wide-chinned face. Erik continued to stare with squinted eyes, disregarding the man's size.

The thick man turned, his bare feet crunching several small, white shells under his heels. The cloth vest he wore opened and displayed a defined chest covered with thick clumps of blond hair obscuring a smattering of blue and black inked tattoos. The tattoos continued down his arms to his wrists, and his clenched hands sent waves of rippling muscle up his arms, the ink undulating under the tension.

At first, Erik felt sure of himself, but as this large, tattooed Fin stared at him, his chest sank a bit. Erik swallowed hard, and he stepped backward. This wouldn't be a fair fight, despite Erik's strength and size and rusted, bent sword. Erik jolted when a hand clamped down on his shoulder. He spun to see his cousin gripping his shoulder firmly.

"Let's go," Bryon hissed in his ear as he looked at Erik, then up at the Fin still standing and staring. The man now began laughing, rolling his eyes and shaking his head.

"Perhaps you should stay closer to your brother and me," suggested Bryon. "The men who walk these streets don't seem the sort we should be messing with."

"I'm surprised to hear you say that," Erik said, looking over his shoulder just to see if the Fin was still there. He wasn't.

"I may like to fight," Bryon said with a dry laugh, "but I'm not stupid."

"Are you sure about that?" Erik muttered so that his cousin couldn't hear him.

Chapter 30

THEY LED THEIR HORSES THROUGH the streets of Finlo, stopping at every tavern and inn they could. They walked what seemed to be the three main streets of Finlo running north to south, and then the three main streets running east to west. Everything was either full or seemed too expensive.

"Said the same thing," Erik said, stepping out into the street to meet with his cousin and brother. "They're full with men sailing east to join Golgolithul's army, traders from Wüsten Sahil, or crews from ships from Crom. The innkeeper said there's nothing in the main city of Finlo."

"Damn it," Bryon muttered.

Erik watched his cousin eye a busty woman walk into the inn, breasts about to burst from a dress cut too low, legs showing through slits cut all the way to her hips.

"Maybe we have to pay more. They'll give us a room then," suggested Bryon.

"This isn't Waterton," Erik said, "Or Venton."

"What's that supposed to mean?" Bryon asked.

"It means the whores here will see your coin," Befel said, "and stick a knife in your belly while you're sleeping. I don't think they'll be as eager for your money here."

"All whores are eager for money," Bryon replied.

"Aye," Erik agreed, "but there are more than enough fools in

142

Finlo to pay. And they're probably paying more. All that coin you found—all the money Mardirru gave us—will be gone in a few days if it was down to you."

"And then we'll be right back where we were," Befel said, "sleeping on the streets."

"No," Bryon said, "we'll be on a ship sailing east, taking us to our destiny."

"The next ship doesn't sail for a week," Erik said. "We need to be careful until then, find a place to stay, and just keep our heads down. We need to find this Kevon fellow to help Befel. I doubt Golgolithul is readily accepting lame men as soldiers."

"Where to then?" Bryon asked. "Where do we stay, oh wise one."

"The innkeeper here said to try the eastern parts of Finlo," Erik replied, ignoring Bryon's sarcasm. "It's older, and not many people stay there because it's out of the way and no one wants to be there. He said there are a few inns, and we should be able to find rooms there."

They headed back through the busy center of Finlo, and the farther east they traveled, the more dilapidated the city looked. Three story buildings towered over them, leaning and swaying in strong ocean breezes. Bits of stone would crumble and fall, and a clay roof tile broke loose and crashed right in front of Erik.

There were more beggars here, too. The center of Finlo seemed to have its fair share of drunks sleeping on the street and sunburnt homeless looking for a generous trader or sailor, but here, in East Finlo, these men looked as destitute as the buildings.

One man lay naked, leaned up against a wall, looking like he'd pissed and shit himself, while another chased after a small rat and then cursed the three Eleodums when it ran under their feet, and they blocked his path to pursue.

The man had no teeth, and his bones almost poked through his skin—and even Befel, with his hurt shoulder—could've bludgeoned him to death with his bare fist, but something in the man's vacant, sunken eyes told them to move on. He didn't even look like a man,

Erik thought, as he stared over his shoulder, watching the man continue to rant and shake.

They found two inns but didn't even bother to see if they had rooms. Erik and Befel had no interest in watching their bags and horses every moment of the day for a week, and Erik suspected Bryon had no interest in the whores, barely more than bones clothed by skin.

After trying one narrow street to another, Erik spotted a solitary, wooden inn with an accompanying stable just beyond a small out-cropping of ramshackle housing and barely-surviving stores.

At what appeared to be almost the edge of the city, the inn sat on a small hill of sand dotted with tufts of fading grass. Without the protection of surrounding buildings, the breeze from the sea con-stantly whipped dirt through the air, building small, sandy mounds around its fence posts.

A shoddy thatched roof held up by several heavy poles made up the vacant stables. Old dried hay lay casually on the ground, and small pieces swirled in a little tornado as the thin planks that formed the back of the stables caught snippets of the ocean's breezes and held them captive.

A waist-high fence made of weather-worn sticks, some too short to fit into the holes of the posts, surrounded the main building, and a short set of broken wooden steps led up to a closed door, several wood slats nailed across what used to be a window.

"I suppose it has the looks of an inn," Erik offered as he shrugged his shoulders.

"Aye," Bryon replied. "An abandoned inn. It doesn't even have a name."

He pointed to a faded sign, now empty of any lettering, thumping against the wall and causing the iron rings that held it just above the door to creak.

"Do you think we should get a closer look?" Erik asked.

"I suppose," Befel replied as they walked past a long-abandoned frame erected to build another group of stores and homes.

144

"How is this shit heap still standing?" Bryon asked incredulously as Erik looked to his right and saw a wretched-looking man sleeping amongst a pile of trash.

"Are you the only tenant here?" Bryon laughed, but the thin, stringy-haired drunk didn't even stir.

"Bryon," Befel said, "I think it best you stay out here with the horses. Just in case our friend wakes up or any of his friends come to visit him."

"Aye," Bryon agreed.

Erik watched Bryon walk the horses to the stables, the animals sniffing and poking at the hay and Bryon smiling childishly. One horse snorted.

"I don't know what to tell you, boy," Erik heard Bryon say as he rubbed sand out of the beast's mane.

"He's nicer to the horses than he is to us," Erik suggested.

"Probably because they are only a little smarter than him!" replied Befel with a grin.

A moldy smell consumed the inside, along with darkness of shuttered windows and a few unlit candles. A mixture of water, spilled drinks, and no doubt blood had rotted the floorboards, and they creaked and moved when Erik and Befel walked across them. Erik looked straight ahead, never down, worried a floorboard would break and reveal what was underneath. He had no desire to know what horrors might lay there.

There were a few round and crooked tables, and the bar was narrow, long enough for two men to stand behind it. Three shelves lined the wall behind the bar, enough room for a myriad of different liquors, but held only four, featureless bottles of, what Erik presumed, to be the same liquid.

Befel coughed self-consciously, and a fat man with a bald head and black beard peppered with gray appeared through a doorway at the end of the bar. He appraised his two prospective customers as he leaned against the wall, his heavy, sausage-like fingers tapping on the loose wood planks of the bar.

"G'day," the bartender finally said with a raspy voice as he looked at the Eleodums with squinted eyes. He scratched his chin through his beard and wiped his hand on a shirt that might once have been white, but was now one of varying shades of brown.

"How can I be of service to you?" he asked with a certain formality, surprising the brothers with his polite manner. His smile showed missing teeth and a black gum line.

Befel spoke. "We wish to purchase a room and some stables for the coming week."

"You don't have the look of a Fin, and you don't have the look of a sailor, and you want to stay on the eastern side of Finlo for a week, do you?" questioned the bartender. "M'boy, these parts of the city are not fond of young outsiders. Even the women in these parts will chew you up and spit out young, good-looking lads such as yourselves. Why don't you let me recommend you to a decent place in the center of the city?"

"This will do just fine," Befel replied. "We've been there."

"Nah," the bartender said, suddenly less welcoming. "I don't think so. Don't really feel like having guests."

"There's no more room anywhere else," Erik said. "I mean, there probably is here in East Finlo, but they seemed to be inhabited by a lot of those people who aren't too fond of young outsiders."

"You two look like you could handle yourselves," the bartender replied.

"Maybe, but we just don't want any trouble," Befel said.

The fat man studied the boys for a moment and then pushed himself off the wall.

"All right. Fine," he said with a shrug. "And what might your business be?"

"Our business is ours to know," Befel replied, perhaps a little too harshly.

"Aye, that may be so lad. And in some city tavern in Goldum or Waterton, or even in the center of town, that might be a good enough reply to my question, but this is my place, and you don't have

146

the look of the men that normally stay at my place. That makes your business my business. You can leave and go somewhere else, or you can tell me why you want to bed down here and have as pleasant a stay as possible."

The bartender now hunched over the bar, crossed his arms, and stared intently at the brothers.

Erik looked at Befel. His brother nodded slightly.

"We are headed east. To Golgolithul," Erik said.

Actually, I should be headed north, to Mother and Father. To Beth and Tia. To Simone.

"Ah." The barkeep laughed. "You're leaving with the rest of those fools to serve Fen-Stévock. Well, if my dingy inn is your last resort, then fine. You can stay here. There will be more men showing up here in four days, but until then you will be alone, and it will be quiet. Just the two of you?"

"There is another," Erik replied. "He's with our horses, in the stable."

"How many horses?" the bartender asked.

"Five," Erik replied.

"Five horses?" the bartender seemed surprised. "That's a fair number of horses for two ... three young lads such as yourself."

Erik just nodded.

"Well, for three young lads and five horses, that'll be twenty-five Finnish nickels."

Erik looked in the purse Mardirru had given back to him. The gypsy had certainly given them back more than they had paid— even some gold and silver—along with two large rubies. Erik smiled inwardly as he rifled through the silver coins, finally producing twenty-five of them, laying them on the bar.

"Will this do?" he asked. "I don't know how much a Finnish nickel is worth."

The bartender looked at the coins Erik had spilled onto the bar, and his hand hovered over them for a moment before he gave an almost imperceptible shake of his head. He pushed back four coins.

147

"That'll do," he said with perhaps a tinge of regret. "And, in the future, don't ask the man you're paying whether or not you have enough money. Most men aren't as honest as me."

The large hands of the bartender scooped up the coins and placed them in the pouch of his apron as Befel and Erik walked out to Bryon.

"Well," Befel said, "we have a room and stables for a week. It was expensive, especially for a place like this. We will be the only ones here for four days."

"Why four days?" Bryon asked.

"More men will be coming, the bartender said," Erik replied.

"Why?" Bryon asked.

"I don't know," Erik said with a shrug, "I didn't ask."

"You should've," Bryon said.

"What does it matter?" Befel asked.

"I don't know. I just want to know how it is a bartender knows a bunch of men will be showing up to his inn—especially a place like this—in exactly four days," Bryon replied. "We should find out."

"Good luck," Erik said.

One look at Bryon and that bartender would probably find himself in a fit of laughter, especially if Bryon tried to get tough. Those meaty hands and thick forearms—they reminded Erik of Del Alzon, and that wasn't a man to be trifled with.

"I think we should take turns staying with the horses," Befel said, pointing to two ragged women hanging a few paces from the inn's fence.

"I'll stay with the horses," Bryon said. "I rather like their company. It'll give you a chance to rest your shoulder, Befel. Erik, maybe you could give me a break every once in a while."

"I think you just relish the idea of scaring off ragged-looking whores and drunken bums," Erik said.

Was he really concerned about Befel's shoulder?

"Perhaps," Bryon replied with a small, malicious smile.

"I'll talk to the bartender," Erik said, "and see if I can't find out why these other men are staying here since you're so eager to know."

"Meanwhile, I need to find Kevon," Befel said.

Chapter 31

BEFEL WALKED BACK TOWARD THE center of town, following what seemed like the main road, so full that he found himself squeezing past people. Much like Venton, the ensuing dusk and waning light seemed to beckon people to come out of their homes and crowd the city. He walked past what looked to be the busiest tavern in Finlo, a place called *The Drunken Fin,* and made sure to give it a wide berth.

With some help from people who looked friendlier, he found his destination, a shop with a pair of scissors painted on its tabard. As Befel opened the door to the shop, he heard the light tinkle of a bell.

"I'll be right with you," someone said.

Befel saw an older man in the back of the shop dragging a razor across another man's face, rinsing the blade off in a wash basin every several strokes. Befel sat in a cushioned chair toward the front of the shop and waited until the man with the razor wiped a towel across his client's face. The now clean-shaven man stood, dropped several coins into a bowl sitting atop a table next to the barber, and walked past Befel.

"So," the barber said in a deep, raspy tone, "what can I do for you?"

"Are you Kevon?" Befel asked.

"Aye," the man responded.

"You double as a surgeon?" Befel asked, getting up from his seat.

"From time to time," Kevon said.

"Can you look at my shoulder?" Befel asked.

"Come have a seat," Kevon commanded, and Befel complied, pulling off his shirt before he did so.

Kevon examined his shoulder, groaning loudly when he saw the cauterized wound.

"Does that hurt?" Kevon asked, prodding and poking at the skin around the wound.

"A bit," Befel replied, biting his lip, "some places more than others."

"I can tell," Kevon said. "It is very red and warm right here. Infection. It probably hurts more there."

When Befel winced and took a quick breath as Kevon pushed on the spot he was talking about, the barber nodded.

"You burned it shut?"

"Yes," Befel replied. "I didn't have needle or thread available. It was the only thing anyone could do. I know it was probably stupid, but..."

"Stupid indeed," Kevon said, "but resourceful if you had no other options."

The barber inspected the wound closer through a smoothly cut, round piece of glass.

"What is that?" Befel asked.

"It's for small things, hard to see with the eye. It makes them larger," the barber replied. "It doesn't look like the infection is bad. I can stop it from spreading. How deep was the wound?"

"The width of a small blade," Befel replied.

Kevon looked away from the wound and stared at Befel.

"I would hate to see how the other man looks," Kevon said. "How well can you move your arm?"

"Some," Befel explained. "I can move it more and more each day."

He raised his arm to shoulder's height and made a circle with it as best he could.

"I think you are lucky. The wound is not too deep, but it could have crippled your arm," Kevon explained. "I will stitch these few places where the heat did not take and patch it with a cream made from Witch's Root and Rain Leaf. The Witch's Root will speed the healing and stop the infection from spreading. The Rain Leaf will reduce the pain and kill the current infection. I'll also give you some Rain Leaf to chew if the pain gets too much. Just be careful. Chew it too much or too often, and you'll wear your teeth away."

Most of the work was painless, but Befel winced as Kevon pulled the thread tight, tied it, and then cut off the excess.

"You will be stiff," Kevon said, "for a few days, and perhaps sore. But the problems will subside. Come see me every day, and I will take another look and apply some fresh ointment. Five nickels today. Two nickels for every other visit."

"A man called Bo said you might give me a friend's price?" questioned Befel.

"Ah, Bo and Dika," Kevon said, a smile growing on his face. "Two nickels today. One every other visit. A friend's price."

Befel nodded his thanks and paid the barber before he asked for a recommendation for buying food and other necessities for the week. He was surprised to be sent to *The Drunken Fin*. Apparently, it doubled as an inn and goods store, and that's why it was so busy.

Dodging the crowds on his way back, Befel avoided several brightly dressed gnomes pinching at the heels of older women, trying to look under the dresses of younger women, and sticking their tongues out at children. He then saw only the third dwarf he had seen in his life.

The man—if one could call him that—wore the customary dwarvish beard and long hair and worked at a blacksmith's anvil, as Befel had heard most dwarves did in the cities of men. The first dwarf he had seen worked in that trade in Waterton, and the second was an adventurer—the other profession many dwarves assumed in the lands of men—stopping in Waterton for supplies before heading into the deserts of Nothgolthane, the continent in which Gongoreth resided.

This third dwarf, as the others, stood at least two heads shorter than Befel, and yet his shoulders were wider than almost any man the farmer had ever seen, his neck invisible amongst muscle. He had heard other men in *The Red Lady*, once, talking about fighting a dwarf, even killing a dwarf and cutting his beard off as a trophy to hang on their spear. After seeing a dwarf such as this one, Befel hardly believed that could've happened.

Finlo certainly did seem to attract many different kinds of people, and just away from the dwarvish blacksmith, standing by a cart that sold silks, velvets, and other fine fabrics, were two men who could only be called giants. They looked like men, only they stood twice as tall as any other on the street. Their arms and legs bulged with muscles, and their hair was long and gray, although their faces showed youth.

Another tall man joined them, this one a full head shorter, with a single eye sitting above his wide nose. A group of three women arrived at the stall, and one giant handed over several yards of fabric to be examined. He moved slowly, every movement deliberate.

"Burn me, what are they?" Befel said to himself.

"Which ones?" asked a man standing next to Befel.

Befel, startled, looked at the man and then back at the cart.

"Both, I guess," he replied.

"The bigger ones," the man explained, "are ogres. Don't know where they come from, and don't know where they go half the time. They're only here a few months at a time, bringing whatever goods they have, but always things of a rich nature. They seem harmless, even though just three or four could tear apart a whole city. I don't trust 'em."

"Why's that?" Befel asked.

"Would you trust something that big?" the man said, pointing. "They're like gypsies. They seem all right on the outside, but every bone in their body is as crooked as a burnt tree. They'll let you slap 'em in the face, only to steal everything you own while you're not looking. That's what I think, at least.

"Once saw one lose its temper. With one step of that ogre's bare foot, he stomped a little pisser of a gnome out of existence. It was just as if he was squashing an ant, you know. Wouldn't mind if they stomped all the gnomes out of Finlo."

"And you don't know where they come from?" Befel asked.

"Up north somewhere," the man replied. "Nothing good comes from up north. They're nomads, you know."

"And the other man," Befel asked, "if that's what he is?"

"Ah," the man said. "That is an antegant. Also, somewhat of a mystery. One moment, they'll be friendly and then the next throw a fit and kill twenty men without even thinking about it. Some are evil to the core, and others you would let watch your little girls while you were out. The wicked ones, well, you won't see 'em in cities, at least not here in the south. You never know what goes on in the east. Nothing good comes from the east, you know. Midius there," he said pointing to the antegant talking to the ogre, "works on the docks. Several of 'em do. Midius will stand there and talk to those ogres all night. I guess big gets along with big."

The man laughed and walked away. Befel watched the man for a moment. He walked to the ogres' cart—the big fellows paying him no attention—and snatched a box of coin. The ogres knew none the better. Thieves indeed.

Chapter 32

As Befel made his way through the crowd and to the bar, trying not to knock into too many people as he went, it felt like half the city had crowded into *The Drunken Fin*. To his right stood another antegant, tall and broad with a shaved head save for a topknot of thick, brown hair. Its one eye glared at Befel as it drained a clear glass pitcher of ale in one gulp. Befel hurriedly looked away and then almost gasped.

To his left stood two men—rather, they had the bodies of men and the heads of wild cats. One had orange fur about its wide head, all streaked with black and white stripes—a cat he had never seen before. Its cat-like ears sat up on its head with black tufts of fur, making them look longer than they really were. The other looked like a Plains cat of some sort, light tan fur about its head except for its mouth and ears, which were a dirty white. Befel could not help but stare at them intently.

Their hands looked human, only covered by orange or tan fur and clawed. They wore clothing like any other adventurer Befel had seen in Waterton, getting ready to travel west. The orange-furred cat-man wore a heavy leather jerkin studded with iron while the Plains cat wore a shirt of mail and a heavy girdle. Travelers' pants made of thick leather covered their legs and hard leather boots their feet.

The orange cat-man carried a long sword sheathed at his side while the other wielded a long, broad-bladed, two-handed sword

155

held across his back. They casually leaned against the bar, speaking a language that seemed to consist of hisses, screeches, and meows.

The one facing Befel, the Plains cat, saw him staring, and his cat-like eyes squinted as he bared his teeth and gave a low growl. Befel now quickly turned away, sweat beading down the side of his face as the cat-man's whiskers quivered.

"You don't seem to be making friends easily," the bartender suggested when he finally made his way to Befel's end of the bar. The handsome, clean-shaven face of the man took Befel by surprise. All the bartenders Befel had met before were fat, bald, and dirty.

"The name's Morgan. Want a drink or did you need something else?"

"Are you still selling goods from your general store?" Befel asked.

"Aye," Morgan replied. "It's open all night, just like the bar."

"Well," Befel said, "then I would like a dozen eggs and a measure of flour. A bit of sugar, enough for a day, and fresh bacon and milk as well."

"The milk will be expensive," Morgan said with a matter-of-fact look on his face. "Not many cows around here, and it's in high demand."

"That's all right," Befel replied.

"Is it?" Morgan asked inquisitively. Befel cursed himself for his quick and ill-advised response.

"I'll have my errand boy go fetch your goods. In the meantime, would you like a drink, my friend?" the bartender asked.

Morgan motioned to a young boy who stood at the end of the bar, and the boy immediately ran off after Morgan had passed on Befel's order.

"I could use a glass of ale," Befel replied.

"You look like you've been traveling hard. A pint then," Morgan said.

"Yes," Befel said.

The antegant that stood next to Befel scoffed and chuckled again.

"A pint!" His voice was deep and reverberated through the bar.

He stared at Befel. "Figures, you men and your pints," he added as he slammed his large pitcher down on the bar, signifying he was ready for another one.

Morgan's errand boy returned with two burlap bags containing Befel's goods. While he sat, bags in front of him, sipping on his ale, he heard music behind him. He turned to see two short men pass by, dancing and playing their instruments.

"What are they?" Befel asked the bartender as he looked down to see that the men's legs were, in fact, the legs of a goat.

"You're not from around here, are you?"

"No." Befel shook his head.

"No matter. Most people in here aren't from around here," the bartender said, nodding toward the antegant and then the cat-men. "Katokiens. That's what we call them."

Befel nodded, still none-the-wiser about the musicians.

"So," Morgan said, "what brings you to Finlo?"

"East," Befel replied. "I'm going east. To fight."

"To join Golgolithul's army?" Morgan asked.

"Yes," Befel replied.

"You're a soldier then?" Morgan asked, serving more ale as he spoke. He seemed able to hold a conversation while hearing orders yelled at him across the bar.

Befel shook his head. "No."

"Interesting," Morgan said as he wiped his bar with a rag. He didn't seem all that concerned with Befel anymore.

"I heard men become rich in the east," Befel said.

"Lots of men going east these days, thinking the same thing," Morgan said. "Not a whole lot coming back."

"Should they be?" Befel asked.

"Don't know," Morgan said with a shrug. "Don't really care."

"Why's that?" Befel asked.

"Don't much care for the east," Morgan said. "Never done anything for me but crowd Finlo's ports with ships full of men that would rather drink on their boat than come to my bar. Don't much care for anything from the east. Don't much care for anything going east."

Morgan gave Befel a hard look before he nodded his head.

"I'll make sure your pint gets a refill, and good luck. Gods know, you're going to need it."

Befel sat for another moment when he heard the antegant next to him grumble loudly.

"East," the antegant said. "What do you want with the east?"

"I'm going to go fight for the east," Befel explained, "for Golgolithul."

"Why? What has Golgolithul done for you?" the antegant asked.

"Nothing. I just..."

"Then why go east? Why even speak of the east?" the antegant asked. "No one likes the east in here, all you men coming through the city, going east. All those eastern ships, crowding our docks. The east—always taking, always imposing, always going where it isn't welcome. The east."

He drank the contents of his new pitcher, slamming it down on the bar again, angrily. Befel felt small as he sat, staring forward, and drinking his second pint.

What am I doing? What are we doing?

Befel looked around the bar, and some of the others looked at him, probably overhearing the antegant's booming voice. Most went about their business.

I should have gone to Aga Kona, Befel thought, but then shook his head. *What do I know about mining? What do I know about life without Erik and Bryon? We can't go east on the ships, though. We won't last a day.*

Befel sat for a while, slowly sipping his ale and thinking.

Chapter 33

ERIK TOOK A DRINK OF what the bartender insisted was ale. It didn't taste like ale. For a moment, he wished he wasn't the only inhabitant of this rundown inn just past the eastern outskirts of Finlo. He had asked Bryon to come in from the stables, but he seemed to enjoy the company of horses over his own kin.

A wooden plate of bread and cheeses was plopped in front of Erik, and he looked up to see the bartender looking down at him with his almost toothless grin.

"Eat, lad," the bartender said, and before Erik could say anything, he added, "my treat."

As the bartender sat down to join Erik, he set a pitcher for himself next to the plate of cheese and bread.

"How's the ale?" the bartender asked, leaning back in his chair.

"It's...different," Erik said, nibbling on some of the cheese.

"Aye," the bartender said, "I thought you would say that. I add a spice to it, from the Feran Islands. They call it cinnamon. Do you like it?"

"I'm not sure yet," Erik replied.

"It takes some getting used to."

When Erik had finished his ale, the bartender poured Erik something from his own pitcher. It didn't look like ale, and when Erik took a drink, he almost coughed.

"Brandy?" he croaked.

"Aye," the bartender replied.

"Also seasoned with…what did you say…cinnamon?"

"Aye. You have a good pallet," the bartender replied. He extended a meaty hand. "The name's Rory."

"Erik," Erik replied, shaking the man's hand.

"You and the fellows you're with—you're all related, yes?" Rory asked.

"Yes." Erik nodded. "My brother, and that's my cousin," he said, pointing outside with a thumb over his shoulder.

"And you wish to go east?" Rory asked. "To fight for Golgolithul?"

Erik nodded again.

"That's good," Rory said. "Serving can turn a boy into a man, make a man a better man, gives a person purpose."

"It seems there are very few people who share your sentiments," Erik said.

Rory shrugged. "I served Golgolithul."

"Its army?" Erik asked.

"Nah," Rory replied. "Navy. Seemed a natural fit. Grew up on a boat, fishing with my father."

"And you enjoyed your time in the navy?" Erik asked. He looked around the bar, the warped wood, and worn furniture and boarded windows. "It made you a rich man?" he added with a smile, and Rory laughed.

"I wouldn't say *enjoy*," Rory said. "It was good for me…to serve. Gave me skills that have saved my life many times. Made me grow up. As for being rich, well, I did, at one time, actually have some coin to my name, my own ship, my own crew. Did that make me rich? Sure, to some maybe. But, as you can see, if I was ever rich then, I am no longer."

"What happened?" Erik asked, finishing his cup of brandy. He noticed Rory finished his own, which prompted the bartender to refill their cups.

"After serving Golgolithul for twenty years," Rory replied, "I had saved up enough money for a business of my own. With my captain's blessing, I left the navy, bought my own ship, hired a crew, and ran goods from Wüsten Sahil all the way to the Isuta Isles. Nothing like being on the open water. Nothing."

Rory drank the whole cup of brandy in one gulp and stared past Erik.

"What was her name?" Erik asked.

Rory didn't answer. He just stared.

"What was her name?" Erik asked again.

"Sorry, lad," Rory finally said, shaking his head. "What was that?"

"What was your ship's name?"

"Ah, Lady Freedom," Rory replied, "and that's what she was—my freedom."

"But now she's gone?" Erik asked.

"That's all that's left of her, lad," Rory said, pointing to a broken, wooden plank with the faded letters 'LADY' painted on it.

"Pirates took her from me. Sailed with the navy for twenty years, fighting pirates and never had a problem. I sail my own ship for four years, and then she's gone. One bolt from a scorpion rips right through Lady Freedom's hull, and down she goes, my crew, and all my dreams. I swallowed sea water for three days before I floated ashore."

"That is all you have left of your ship?" Erik asked.

"Aye. The last piece I have of her," Rory replied sadly. "I didn't have the balls to kill myself, so I figured I'd fight anyone I could—maybe die that way. But no one would kill me. So, I figured I'd just find a quiet bar somewhere and drink myself to death.

"I found this here bar—called *The Green Ghost* then—and sat where you're sitting for a whole year and drank. After I realized I wouldn't die from that either, I bought the bar from the old woman who owned it. She didn't want much for it, which was good because I didn't have much. I built the stables and the rooms in the back and renamed it *The Lady's Inn*. This coming summer will be ten summers running this place. But serving...serving is good for a man."

"I just want to make enough coin to go home and save my father's farm from Hámonian nobles," Erik said, watched as Rory quickly drank two more cups of brandy. His eyelids began to droop, and he leaned hard to one side.

"Bah," Rory replied with a sickened looked. He spat on the floor. "Hámonian nobles. What a disgusting lot. They'll stick their cocks in anything."

Erik didn't want to get into a conversation that reminded him of his dreams and just drank quietly.

"Well, lad," Rory said, slurring and straightening as he realized he was drifting too far to one side. "I hope you don't wind up like me— an old drunk, sitting in his own, rundown bar, whose only way to get by in this world is to be a lackey for the Messenger of the East."

Erik perked up at the name—The Messenger of the East. He'd heard that this was the herald of Golgolithul, the second most powerful man in the most powerful country of Háthgolthane.

"The Messenger of the East?" Erik asked.

"Aye, the Black Mage himself," Rory said, using one of the many names given to the Messenger. "He's coming to my bar. Everyone thinks he's coming to see you lads off. He doesn't give a pig's shit about all the young fools sailing east."

"Why is he coming then?" Erik asked.

Rory's head tilted back for a moment. Then he sat up, eyes wide open, and drank yet another cup of brandy. He poured himself more, and then looked to Erik, who shook his head.

"Mercenaries," Rory said, another disgusted look on his face. "Not even real soldiers. He's meeting a group of mercenaries here, the same day the Golgolithulian ships are sailing east."

"Why?" Erik asked, leaning forward in his chair, his elbows resting on the table.

"I don't quite know," Rory conceded, shrugging lazily. "The Messenger of the East comes by my bar six months ago looking for a discreet place to meet, something off the beaten path. He had heard I once served the east. Well, my bar is well out on the outskirts of the city, and I tell him for the right price, I can be as discreet as he wants me to be.

"He tells me he'll pay me a hundred gold pieces, half then and half when he comes back, but he doesn't know when that'll be. I tell him that's a good price to keep me discreet, and that I trust he'll come back with the other half. By the Shadow, even if he never comes back, fifty gold pieces is more than I make from one summer to the next.

"Now I just got word last week that he is coming. He says he'll be here at four hours past noon. Ships sail out every month taking you lads east, so it's convenient for him. Doesn't look so suspicious. I hear some of the best mercenaries in all of Háthgolthane will be here on his personal invitation."

"Four hours past noon," Erik repeated. "That would be late afternoon, yes?"

"Aye," Rory replied. "An invitation-only meeting."

Erik had heard of this way to keep time—hours—but they didn't use it on the farmstead. Morning, noon, afternoon, evening, midnight—these were the simple ways they used to tell time. Erik sat back in his chair, his eyes staring behind Rory.

"Will any of them have servants? Maybe porters to carry their things?" Erik asked, ignoring Rory's concerns.

"Probably," Rory replied, smiling and shrugging again. "I don't have much experience with mercenaries. They're not welcome most places. Dishonorable lot. I would suppose though that some might hire a few lads to carry their things."

"Will the reward be large?" Erik asked.

"To the mercenaries? Aye, big," Rory replied. "The Lord of the East pays well for this sort of thing. But failure? Well, I don't even want to think of what failure means. A reward for a simple porter, I don't know. Depends on who hires you, I guess."

Rory drank more brandy and smiled at Erik, eyes half-closed.

"Service does a man good," he said once again.

Rory and Erik sat for a while, Rory drinking and Erik thinking.

"Well," Rory said with a final sigh and clapping his hands to his chest, "I am not a smart man, but I have always done one thing, and that is to follow my heart. Follow *your* heart, Erik. It will seldom lead you astray. Follow your heart. Now if you'll excuse me, I think I've once again drunk a little too much."

As Rory staggered off, Erik continued to sit, just staring at the warped and stained wood of the table. He thought of fighting in the armies of Golgolithul. He would be traveling to some place he never heard of, killing someone, or being killed by someone, he never knew. He thought of Rory, fighting for another man for most of his life only to wind up crushed and lost, feeling like he had no purpose.

His thoughts then turned to his farmstead, and of his mother and father and two little sisters, his mother's garden, even his uncle's orange brandy. *Two years goes by so fast*, he thought regretfully. Erik sat at his table, staring at nothing.

With the few candles, his body cast long shadows across the room, and the semi-darkness seemed fitting. His eyebrows curled into a look of disappointment. He looked around the bar, the warped wood, the smell of stale air, the sound of waves crashing on the shore as the tide rose. So different from the chatter of crickets and the songs of night birds, the waning smells of flowers closing with dusk, his mother's clean and well-lit dining room. A small smile crept across Erik's face.

I could be sitting at my mother's table right now, sharing a bowl of warm soup with Simone. She would be my wife by now. Maybe she would have my son in her belly. Father might have given me a plot of land to farm. Her father would have added to it. Brok's a good man. Maybe he would have given me a cow and a bull, some chickens. Maybe some pigs. I would work, just as my father did and his father before him.

Instead, Erik sat alone in a dingy bar, his thoughts lingering on what might have been.

Chapter 34

THE THICK, WOOL COWL OF Patûk Al'Banan's cloak shadowed his eyes well from the harsh reflection of the sun against the South Sea. Then again, the South Sea always seemed much brighter to him for some reason. The Gulf of Shadows—the bit of ocean that flowed inland into Antolika and eventually became the Shadow Marshes—always looked subdued, black even.

The Sea of Knives and the Eastern Ocean seemed to swallow the sun up, their waters so deep they looked purple. And the waters that flowed around the Feran Archipelagos, although technically part of the South Sea, didn't have the same luster. Perhaps it came from the wildness of those waters, the untamed chaos of unclaimed territory that let them blaze a fiery blue like that.

Patûk found it beautiful in a way, and yet here was that imposter, leading his country to ruin and wanting to rule everything. Hadn't he learned anything from history? Some of the world needed to stay unclaimed, uncharted, untouched. He stroked Warrior's nose gently. The destrier, hard, weathered, mean, and loyal like him, snorted and stamped its feathered hoof in approval.

"My lord, we have news."

Lieutenant Sorben Phurnan had rushed to the general's side and knelt, eyes trained on the ground before him. As much as he tried to act servile and subdued, he always carried that noble haughtiness. Even now, kneeling before the general, his back just looked too straight, his head not low enough, his shoulders too square. Patûk couldn't put his finger on it, but he didn't like it.

Patûk decided to let the lieutenant kneel there for a while. He continued to watch the sun, setting beyond the hills of the Western Tor, cast an animated, wrinkled imitation of itself across the crystalline water. He saw, from the corner of his eye, Sorben Phurnan lift his head, a scowl strewn across his face, but when Patûk pretended to turn, the soldier dropped his chin to his chest. The general smiled to himself.

"You do not like waiting, yes?" Patûk Al'Banan finally turned to the lieutenant.

"I will wait as long as you wish me to wait." His subordinate's head stayed low, his eyes trained on the ground.

"That is a good answer." Patûk Al'Banan smiled, although no mirth existed in his voice. "A packaged answer, but a good answer, nonetheless. Your father taught you well. You may stand."

Lieutenant Sorben Phurnan stood, head still slightly bowed.

"You can't wait for the day when men will bow to you, can you?" Patûk sneered as he gathered a length of his cloak up in his right arm so he might walk a little easier without it tugging at his heels. He saw a small smile creep along the lieutenant's face.

"Well," Patûk added, and then he dropped his length of cloak and stepped close, His breath quickened, his hard face tinged with red as his eyes squinted and teeth clenched. "It may never happen, you pompous, blood-sucking worm."

Sorben Phurnan ducked, the general's words a whip, and he backed up so quickly, he fell back on his heels.

"I get tired of hearing about your abuse of my men," Patûk hissed. "This is not Golgolithul, and this is not the courts of Fen-Stévock." He spat when he spoke the name of the Eastern Kingdom's capital city, named after the Stévockians, the family from which the current Lord of the East hailed.

When the Aztûkians controlled much of the Eastern Kingdom's senate, Fen-Aztûk proved the capital city, but the Stévockians quickly moved it when they gained control. Patûk Al'Banan jabbed his index finger into the lieutenant's chest. "These are my men, my soldiers. If I hear of abuse again, I will kill you. Do you understand, Lieutenant?"

"Yes, General," Sorben Phurnan said quietly as he bowed quickly and backed away even farther from his indignant leader.

"Now, what is this news you have?"

Sorben didn't answer at first. He looked over his shoulder and jerked his head sideways. A scout, kneeling just out of the general's sight, rushed forward and knelt just behind the lieutenant. Patûk looked at Sorben, fire in his eyes.

"Speak," Sorben Phurnan said harshly at first and then, remembering the general's words, softened his tone and repeated, "Speak."

"My lord," said the scout, a man no younger than the lieutenant but without the good fortune of noble birth. His close-cropped hair and broad shoulders and lean waist, a scar just above his right eye and a missing half ear, showed a life of service to Patûk Al'Banan. "We have word of the Messenger."

Patûk Al'Banan's posture changed. He stepped back a bit, cleared his throat, and straightened his shoulders. "What word, soldier? Quickly."

"Yes sir," the scout acknowledged. "Our spies have discovered that his presence is expected in Finlo."

"With the imposter?"

"No, my lord," the scout replied and scooted back on his knees, fearful of the repercussions his response might bring.

"What brings the Herald to this place? And without his lord?" Patûk asked calmly.

"I'm not sure, General. But we discovered a call going out to certain men—soldiers, mercenaries," the soldier explained. "Our intelligence says the Lord…"

He stopped quickly. Acknowledging the Lord of the East as such in front of General Al'Banan brought a knife to the tongue at best.

"Our intelligence says the usurper is gathering such men for a mission. Some task of importance—the search for something he holds dear to his family."

Patûk tapped his fingers on his steel breastplate. He turned back to the sun's reflection on the South Sea, slowly fading with the onset of dusk.

"Men from all over have heeded his call," the scout continued. "Men from Háthgolthane and Antolika, my lord."

"Are the Antolikans so starved that they would serve the man who wishes them slaves?" Patûk muttered, more to himself.

"They are barbarians, savages with few desires other than gold and women," Sorben replied.

"What have I told you about listening to my own counsel?" Patûk spat.

"My lord," Sorben Phurnan said quickly, dropping to a knee along with the soldier.

They, the soldier and the lieutenant, waited a long time while Patûk stared at the ocean. Darkness finally overcame the rolling hillocks in which they camped. Warrior stamped and snorted at the chill night the sea brought.

"My Lord," Lieutenant Sorben Phurnan dared to interject, "shall we attempt to intercept the Messenger?"

Patûk turned quickly on his heels. "And come against the Soldiers of the Eye? No, that would prove folly."

"Then infiltrate, my lord? Shall we send men to this meeting disguised as mercenaries?"

"No," Patûk replied. His voice was now even and cool. "No, we will wait and bide our time. We will wait for our opportunity, and when it comes, we will strike. It is the fashion of this imposter to beckon the services of men under a banner of righteousness. No doubt these fools will jump at the chance to serve that bastard. We will wait and follow." Patûk turned to the soldier. "Rise."

The man did as he was told, his head still bowed.

"When is he due in Finlo?"

"Within a week, my lord."

"What is your name?"

The soldier hesitated at the question, but finally answered, "Bu, sir. Sergeant Bu."

"And you are one of our spies?"

Bu nodded.

"You are now Lieutenant Bu," the general said with a smile, "and now in command of our scouts and spies. You have done well. Send Lieutenant Kan to me. Tell him you have been promoted and, as a result, so has he. I have another assignment for him."

Lieutenant Bu bowed low. "Thank you, my lord."

"You will position our spies to watch for the Messenger. Report to me when he reaches Finlo."

"Yes, sir," Lieutenant Bu replied and, with another low bow, turned on his heels and left.

"Lieutenant," said Patûk, with his back to the other.

"Yes, my lord," Sorben Phurnan replied with a visible scowl on his face.

"Bring Captain Kan to my tent when he gets here."

Sorben bowed again, grumbling under his breath as Patûk took up his cloak in his arm again. Without another word, he grabbed Warrior's reins and led the destrier back to his camp.

Chapter 35

"MY LORD, WE HAVE ARRIVED at Aga Kona."

Andragos straightened his robes. He had dozed off, something he rarely did. He had become unaccustomed to long carriage rides as of late, feeling rather uncomfortable despite the relative luxury in which he traveled.

"In Westernese, Raktas," Andragos said.

"As you wish, my lord," his servant replied.

The scowl on Raktas' face, however slight, showed his displeasure in speaking the language of the west. He was uncomfortable with it. Terradyn, Andragos' other manservant, was far more comfortable with the language, and he had long suspected that it was his servant's first language.

Although he found more satisfaction in actually learning a language, he could 'speak' or understand any language he wanted. With the snap of a finger, a man speaking Durathnan sounded as if he spoke Andragos' native Shengu.

"The people of the west are rather suspicious of the east," Andragos explained. "Speaking Shengu around them will make them even more uneasy. They will think we are talking about them."

"Yes, my lord," Raktas replied, "but don't they work for the east?"

"Yes," Andragos nodded.

"They are a backward people, my lord," Raktas suggested.

170

"Perhaps," Andragos agreed. "Simpler I think would be a better word."

Andragos had heard whispers of him being referred to as the Messenger of the East, the Herald of Golgolithul, the Black Mage. Such mutterings used to make him feel powerful, strong, and important. Now, he just found them comical.

"Are you alright, my lord?" Raktas asked.

"Yes," Andragos answered, "just tired."

"Shall I tell Terradyn to send the people away, my lord?" Raktas asked as they heard a commotion outside the carriage.

"No," Andragos replied. "Open the door."

Raktas bowed and knocked on the door of the carriage. It opened and swung outwards, revealing Terradyn standing on the other side, holding back a now growing crowd of miners and their families.

With the open door and the sun barely at noon, light should have flooded the inside of the carriage, but Andragos lifted a hand, and the inside darkened, shadowing his face. He didn't like people seeing him—his face at least—but also didn't feel like lifting the hood of his robes. He relished the spring air. It was clean, here, in the wilderness of the west, next to the Southern Mountains. The air seemed so...so stale in Fen-Stévock.

An older, broad-shouldered man stood next to Terradyn. He looked irritated at being summoned to the carriage. There was a time when Andragos would have bent the man, forced him with an invisible power to kneel and grovel. Defiance would make him rage, but now he found something noble in it, an ant standing up to the spider, a gazelle taunting the lion. He allowed himself a small smile.

"Thank you for letting us stay in your camp," Andragos said from the shadows.

"Don't have much choice, do I?" the master of Aga Kona replied.

Bravery. Stupidity, perhaps. Whatever it was, Andragos liked this man. He heard groans coming from both Terradyn and Raktas. The sound of stomping feet meant his troops—the Soldiers of the Eye—his hundred had snapped to attention. Terradyn must have signaled them to do so, his repost to the man's insubordination. Andragos put up a hand.

"No, you don't," he said. "But, nonetheless, your hospitality, although expected, is welcomed and appreciated. Your service to my lord will not go unnoticed."

The man shifted uneasily at the mention of the Lord of the East, but his stern, defiant visage never changed. He gave a short bow.

"Many thanks, my lord," he said. "Aga Kona is yours while you are here."

"I am sure you will be pleased to know we will only be here for the night," Andragos replied.

"I don't know if we have enough to feed…"

"No need for your people to attend my soldiers," Andragos said, cutting the man off midsentence. "We have all the provisions we need."

The master of Aga Kona bowed and turned to leave, but Terradyn stopped him. A wave from Andragos' hand, and Terradyn let the man go.

Terradyn joined Andragos and Raktas in the carriage, closing the door behind him. As he did, Andragos snapped a finger, and the light brightened as if the whole compartment was luminescent.

"You don't approve of my interaction with the master of this camp," Andragos said to Terradyn.

"He is not even worth the dirt on your boots, my lord," Terradyn replied.

"Not in Shengu," Andragos commanded, his voice deepening a little. "In Westernese."

Terradyn repeated himself, this time in the language of Western Háthgolthane.

Andragos chuckled. "I don't know. I rather liked the man. As for his worth, how can we determine such a thing?"

"Liked him, my lord?" Raktas questioned.

"You think I am getting soft as time passes?" Andragos questioned.

Neither one of his servants replied.

"Come, we can be frank with one another," Andragos said, "after so many years."

"Not soft, my lord," Terradyn said. "But I do think you should be careful with the way you allow Golgolithul's subjects to deal with you, lest you earn a reputation for being soft."

"Noted," Andragos said, sitting back and smiling. "But as the years pass by, I have realized that people are more likely to follow a man who they respect rather than one they fear."

"Why do we have to stay here, my lord?" Raktas asked.

"Why not?" Andragos replied. "What better way to represent the Lord of the East and spread word of his goodwill and charitable nature?"

Both of his servants gave him an unconvinced look.

"I don't even understand why we have to travel to Finlo," Terradyn said. "Couldn't Shinden or some other errand boy have done this for Our Highness?"

Andragos nodded.

"Yes, but there is something I must see in Finlo," Andragos said, furling his eyebrows in thought and steepling his fingers. "Someone I must meet. Discover, perhaps."

"Who?" Terradyn asked.

"I don't know," Andragos replied, shaking his head and fully irritated at his admission.

"You know that fool Patûk Al'Banan is there, my lord," Raktas said.

"I know," Andragos said matter-of-factly. "His spies have been following us, as well. All the way from Fen Stévock."

"Shall we kill them, my lord?" Terradyn asked.

"Much easier said than done," Andragos replied.

The look on Terradyn's face gave away his hurt. Andragos laughed.

"It is not a slight against you," Andragos said. "Patûk Al'Banan is an expert tactician and an amazing leader. It is a shame the Lord of the East and he could not come to some resolution. Losing such a general, along with thirteen thousand men, is a devastating loss to our forces. We would not so easily kill his spies, but if we did, we might find our casualties too much to bear."

"Truly, my lord?" Terradyn asked.

"Truly," Andragos replied. "But, rest assured, our paths will cross. For now, though, let us rest and prepare to receive our audience in Finlo."

Chapter 36

BEFEL FOUND BRYON SITTING AGAINST one of the stable's post. A lantern hung on an iron hook above his head and illuminated his body. Befel could see his cousin's eyes were closed, and as he got closer, he heard Bryon snore softly. Dried hay crunched under Befel's boots, and he thought that might wake Bryon, but it did not. Befel stood over his cousin and nudged him with his foot.

Bryon stirred and moaned. He looked up at Befel, his eyes still halfway closed.

"What?" he asked groggily

"I bought some bacon and milk for breakfast tomorrow," Befel said.

"You couldn't wait to tell me that tomorrow morning," Bryon said, squinting at the lantern's light.

"I guess I could've," Befel said. "Sorry."

"Idiot," Bryon replied, and he leaned his back against the post, closing his eyes. Within moments, he began to snore softly again.

Befel walked through the door of the inn and found Erik sitting silently at one of the tables, arms crossed, chin resting on his arms. He turned his head so he could see Befel, his cheek now lying on his crossed arms.

"I have bacon for the morning," Befel said.

Erik smiled briefly and yawned as he picked his head up and

stretched his arms, accidentally knocking over an empty cup once filled with ale.

"Have you been drinking all night?" Befel asked, a scowl creeping across his face.

"No," Erik replied defensively. "Well, some I guess. I was talking to Rory, and we drank—mostly he drank—while we talked."

"Who's Rory?" Befel asked.

"The man who owns this place," Erik replied, "*The Lady's Inn.*"

Befel walked over to Erik, set his bags on the floor, and sat across from his brother, leaning back in his chair. He rubbed his forehead and scratched his cheek before his shoulders slouched a bit as he yawned.

"Are you all right?" Erik asked.

"I found Kevon," Befel said. "I suppose you could call him a surgeon."

"Good, and how does your shoulder feel? Is it better?"

"It hurts," Befel replied, "but it will improve. Of that, I'm sure. There are all sorts of odd characters here, Erik, ones we would never see at home, and creatures far stranger than gnomes."

"Like what?" Erik asked, intrigued and leaning forward in his chair.

"I went to a tavern to buy some goods and get a pint of ale, and standing right next to me was a giant man with one eye, right in the middle of his forehead," Befel replied, pointing to his forehead. "There were two other men with the heads of large cats. I saw two creatures with the bodies of men and the legs of a goat."

"The world is much bigger than we thought, isn't it?" Erik said.

"That it is," Befel replied with a nod, "the tales we heard are true."

Erik nodded in agreement but said nothing.

"I don't know about sailing east, Erik."

"I don't either. It doesn't seem like a very good idea now."

"So what then?" Befel asked. "Do we continue to live on the streets? What do we do? Do we go home?"

"Not that I mind the idea of going home," Erik replied, "but I think I found another way to earn the riches you want, another way to save Father's farm."

"What other way is there?" Befel asked.

"The Messenger of the East will be here," Erik said.

"I heard," Befel replied, "people on the streets of Finlo were talking about the visit. He's coming to see us off as we sail east."

"Why would he care about a bunch of men, half of whom won't see next year?" Erik asked.

Befel just shrugged.

"Actually, he's here on other business," Erik said, then hushed his voice. "Secret business."

"How do you know about this? What does this have to do with us?"

"Rory told me about the other men coming to his inn," Erik explained. "They are mercenaries, coming at the bidding of the Lord of the East. That is why the Messenger is coming. Some secret mission, and the reward is large."

"We're not mercenaries," Befel replied. "We're not even soldiers."

"No," Erik agreed, "but we're strong and used to working hard. Rory said some of these men might need porters, men to carry their things, make camp, things like that. They might be willing to share their reward. They'll have to feed us. And, if nothing else, a penny or two a day is more than we're making now. It won't be long before our money runs out."

"Can we trust Rory?" Befel asked.

Erik shrugged. "I don't know, but he was drunk. Brandy tends to bring out honesty."

"Can we trust some mercenaries?" Befel asked.

"No," Erik replied, "but the three of us together, I think we will be all right. We can handle our own. We proved that in the Blue Forest."

I don't know about that, Befel thought, rubbing his shoulder.

"Maybe..." Befel said.

177

"What choice do we have?" Erik asked and gave Befel a disappointed look. "Listen, the Messenger will be here, sending these sellswords on their way before he goes to the docks to pretend to see off the men sailing east to join the army. If this doesn't work out, we can still head to the docks and sail east as originally planned."

Befel nodded slowly.

"That might work," he replied. "Now, we just have to convince Bryon."

The next day, the Eleodums sat at one of the tables in *The Lady's Inn*, empty plates in front of them. Rory had been gracious enough to cook up the bacon and eggs and, even though the food the gypsies had fed them was decent, Befel counted the breakfast a welcomed change to meals on the road. It almost felt like back home.

Befel left his brother to the arduous task of explaining this new course to Bryon. His cousin didn't much care to talk to him anymore, so he figured that Bryon might receive enraging news better from Erik. Of course, Erik didn't relish the idea. Over the two years they had been away from home, Erik had grown from a boy to a man, which meant Bryon could bully him less and less. But Befel could tell his brother was still wary around their cousin. Erik finally relented as he normally did. Befel was the eldest brother, after all.

Having listened—surprisingly without interruption—Bryon sat still for a while, and Befel couldn't read his face. His cousin normally laid his emotions bare for everyone to see, either through his body or his face. But not this time.

Bryon finally put his hands on his knees and leaned back in his chair, a small smile creeping across his face.

"All right," he said. "It seems like a good plan—a well thought out plan. I'm a little surprised you came up with it, Erik, but I'll go along. Either way, I'm going east."

Befel let out a silent sigh of relief. The latest step in their destiny had been sealed.

Chapter 37

"THREE DAYS IN THIS SHIT heap," Bryon muttered, once again sitting against one of the posts of *The Lady's Inn's* stables. He threw a piece of straw to the ground with a harrumph and reached up to scratch one of the horse's noses.

"How does this fat fool even stay in business?" he asked the horse. "Just me and my idiot cousins for customers. He must be doing something illegal."

The horse stamped its foot by way of reply.

"All right, Buck," he said, pulling himself to his feet. He'd decided that Buck was a good name for the horse he was growing quite accustomed to.

He grabbed the brush and began running it along Buck's shoulder in long, slow strokes.

"Is that what you wanted?" he asked, but got no further reply.

As Bryon groomed the horse, he heard something behind him and turned to see two men—rather, skin and bones covered in rags—staring at him from just beyond the rickety fence that surrounded the pile of rubbish his cousins called an inn.

"Piss off!" Bryon yelled, throwing a large rock at them.

The rock hit one of the men solid on the shoulder, and the man fell backward with a moaning cry. Bryon laughed as the other man forgot about his friend and scurried away.

"Just like rats," Bryon spat. "Begging, cursed rats."

"Who are you yelling at?" Erik asked.

Bryon jumped at Erik's voice.

"You shouldn't sneak up on people like that."

"Sorry," Erik replied. "I wasn't trying to sneak. Who are you yelling at? It was so loud; I heard you in the inn."

"Just filthy beggars," Bryon explained. "Probably trying to steal our horses."

"You really think they would be able to steal the horses?" Erik asked.

"I don't know." Bryon watched the man who had fallen stumble to his feet. "Maybe not the horses. But something. They're disgusting. Begging. For what?"

"Some coin to buy food, maybe," Erik replied.

"For more ale," Bryon said, shaking his head. "They make me sick. Begging. Scrounging. Slithering like snakes. Why can't they just work like everyone else?"

"What about the times we begged on the streets of Venton?" Erik asked. "Or the alleys of Waterton?"

"That was different," Bryon replied.

"How so?" Erik asked.

"I don't know," Bryon said. "Whose side are you on anyway?"

"I didn't know we were taking sides," Erik replied. "You could come inside the inn. Rory has fresh cheese and bread—and you wouldn't have to bother with these beggars."

"I don't want to step a foot inside that shit heap unless I have to."

"Why?" Erik asked.

"I don't trust Rory," Bryon replied.

"Why?" Erik asked again.

"Because," Bryon replied.

"That's not a very good reason to dislike someone," Erik said.

"Well, it's my reason," Bryon replied, but when Erik gave him an unsatisfied look, he added, "I don't think a man who is a broken old sailor should be that happy. He owns this building he calls an inn, swarmed by whores and beggars, and he's that happy? There's something wrong with that."

"I don't really think he's all that happy," Erik said.

"And you know him so well to say such a thing?"

"Do you know him well enough to say I'm wrong?" Erik asked.

"Whatever." Bryon shrugged. "I don't want to go inside. I can't stand Rory. I can't stand your brother groaning and moaning as he constantly circles his arm."

"Those are the exercises the barber has given him," Erik replied. "He groans because it hurts. You would hold that against him?"

"Maybe I can't stand your constant talking," Bryon said.

"You think you can just end a conversation by being rude?" Erik shook his head with a laugh.

"Was I being rude?" Bryon didn't bother looking at Erik. He went back to brushing Buck.

"All right, Bryon," Erik said and turned to walk back inside the inn.

"He's a fool," Bryon said to Buck. "Sometimes I wonder how we are even blood."

A short while later, a sharp kick to the boot woke Bryon. He looked up and saw a large man standing over him. Bryon shuffled himself up into a seated position and saw three new horses in the stables.

"You the stable boy?" the man asked. His voice was deep.

Bryon shook his head, trying to shake away the sleep that still clung to his mind.

"You just choose to sleep with the horses?" another man asked, and Bryon blinked as he came into view. He glared down at Bryon with gray eyes. Bryon just shrugged.

"That's your thing?" the first man asked, chuckling as Bryon stood. "Animals?"

"No," Bryon replied, rubbing his face.

"You a beggar, boy?" yet a third man asked. "You're not a stable boy, and you claim you ain't buggering the horses, so you must be a little, filthy beggar."

Bryon felt his face grow hot at the accusation.

"I'm a soldier," Bryon shot back.

All three men laughed.

"A soldier!" one of them cried. "Well, I won't say you're the saddest looking soldier I've ever seen, but you're pretty damn close."

"Oh yeah," Bryon retorted, "and what are you three rat turds supposed to be?"

All three men stopped laughing. Bryon swallowed hard. The first man he had seen—he was half a head taller than Bryon, quite a bit wider, and with a dark, bushy beard—stepped forward so that his hooked nose was only a fly's wing away from Bryon's.

"He wants to know what we're supposed to be," the man said. Bryon could smell brandy and black root on his breath.

Bryon looked down and saw the man's hand resting on the top of a wide-bladed ax, rugged and worn.

"Well, then tell him," the second man said.

"We're killers, boy. For money usually, but certainly for pleasure when some little gutter shit calls us names," the first man said, his lips cracking into a narrow smile. Then, he stepped back, and his smile widened. "But I suppose you are too, being a soldier and all."

"A soldier," the third man snickered. "Might as well be a dragon slayer. Or a king. If you're going to pick a fantasy, you should at least pick a good one."

"It's not a fantasy," Bryon retorted and immediately cursed himself for sounding childish in his reply.

All three men bellowed with laughter, and as they walked away, a woman approached them. She was tall and thin with a heavily painted face and hair, which looked to be graying at its edges, haphazardly tied into a bun.

"You look like you could use a good time."

"Piss off wench," the first of the men said. "I stick you, and my cock might fall off."

To that, his companions laughed even harder as the whore hissed her disapproval. She made eye contact with Bryon, and he looked away quickly, but saw her shrug and saunter toward him.

"You look like you could use a friend," she cooed as she neared him.

Bryon scrunched his nose when the smell of sweat and pipe smoke and brandy wafted into his nostrils.

"I'm fine," Bryon replied, turning his head to alleviate the stench.

The woman gripped his chin, turning his face, and even through his beard he could feel the roughness of her fingers.

"Come on," she insisted. "Surely, you would rather the company of a woman to these horses."

Her breath was rancid, and Bryon winced. He slapped her hand away and stepped back, almost knocking over a water bucket.

"I'd sooner stick my horse," Bryon spat.

Bryon expected the whore to back up, run away, but she stood her ground, laughed a little even.

"Looks like that's what you prefer," she chided, looking at Buck, "and the male ones at that."

"Piss off, bitch," Bryon hissed, lifting a hand, "before I beat you bloody."

She waited, a wry, condescending smile on her face. When Bryon dropped his hand, she laughed.

"Don't have the guts," she said, then reached out and grabbed Bryon's crotch, "or the balls, maybe."

He swatted her hand away again, and she turned to leave, needlessly pulling up on her ragged, stained dress even as she stepped on a horse apple. She stopped for a moment, looked at Bryon over her shoulder, and blew him a lecherous kiss.

Chapter 38

ERIK WOKE EARLY, FINDING THAT Rory was the only one in the bar.

"Just us?" Erik asked.

"After the debauchery last night," Rory replied, "I expect it will be just us for a while."

"Good," Erik muttered.

"You don't like my new guests, lad?"

Erik shook his head.

"I don't blame you," Rory laughed. "Neither do I. It's a good thing they're paying me so much."

Rory poured Erik a cup of spiced wine and filled a wooden bowl with porridge.

"What's the matter?" Rory asked after several moments, looking at an untouched bowl and a cup from which Erik had taken only a single sip.

"Nothing."

"You're a bad liar," Rory said.

"Just nervous, I guess," Erik replied.

"I could see how you would be," Rory said.

"Do you think we will be able to sit in on this meeting?" Erik asked.

Rory shrugged.

"I suppose," the old sailor replied. "There'll be quite a few people here. I think it might be impossible for The Messenger to know the face of every single mercenary he's invited. If you sit in the back and make yourselves look small."

Erik nodded in agreement.

"It's a good plan," Rory said. "If no one here wants your services as a porter—you still have time to make it to the docks and sail east like you originally planned."

His breakfast untouched, Erik helped Rory put out chairs and more tables. Apparently, he had never had a need for so many more, at least another half dozen tables and four dozen chairs which he kept in a back room of *The Lady's Inn*. As soon as they had set the last chair, men began arriving.

Some had been staying at Rory's inn, and Erik had seen them before, but most he had never seen. Tall and short, thin and fat, midnight-black skin and snow-pale skin—all combinations of men showed to this special meeting.

"Take that table right there," Rory whispered, pointing to a smaller table in the back of the inn, just a step away from the door. "It'll be away from everything—very unsuspecting."

Erik nodded.

"Where is your brother?"

Bryon's voice startled Erik. He hadn't noticed him walking in.

"In the room," Erik replied, turning. He pointed to the small table in the back. "We'll sit there. It's away from everything."

Bryon nodded. "Let's get your brother."

"Befel," Erik said, walking through the door of their room.

Erik's brother was sitting at the edge of his bed, rubbing his shoulder.

"Men are starting to show up," Erik continued. "We have a table in the..."

"...in the back," Befel said, cutting Erik off. "Aye. It's a good idea."

"Are you all right?" Erik asked.

"What is taking so long?" Bryon asked, standing behind Erik.

Erik looked at his brother. He could see the worry on his face and in his eyes. He knew that look. He had seen it before. His father wore the same worried look when their harvest looked to yield less than hoped for.

"Come on," Bryon huffed, his impatience evident in his voice.

"Why don't you go save us the table," Erik said, "just in case someone else wants it."

"Fine," Bryon said as he stomped off.

"He's like a little child," Erik muttered. What's the matter, Befel?"

"I don't know." Befel shook his head. "Just nerves, I suppose."

"Aye," Erik nodded in agreement. "I thought I was going to throw up this morning, my stomach was knotted so badly."

"Are we doing the right thing?" Befel asked.

"Uh…well," Erik stammered. It wasn't often that Befel asked for his opinion.

"I mean, part of me feels like this is right," Befel continued, "but part of me feels like it's very wrong."

Erik looked at his brother and gave an imperceptible shake of his head.

It's a little late to be second-guessing ourselves, isn't it? Two years away from home, from Mother and Father, Beth and Tia, Simone. It's a little late to wonder whether your conscience has served you well.

"I think," Erik started, and then stopped, collecting his thoughts. "I think it is the best decision—the best option—given our current situation."

Erik waited a moment longer while Befel stared at the floor, taking in deep, thoughtful breaths.

"Come, brother," Erik said, "we don't want to leave Bryon in a room full of men just like him. That might lead to trouble."

Befel looked at him with a smile—almost allowing a laugh to escape—rose from his bed, and followed Erik into the main room of the inn.

The din of talking and laughter, of cups and dice clinking was so loud Erik could barely hear his brother and cousin as they spoke.

"Forty, I reckon," Erik muttered. "Forty men in here. I wonder if *The Lady's Inn* has ever held so many souls."

They ignored him, and Erik couldn't hear what they were saying, but he could see his brother and cousin bickering.

"Stop it," Erik said in a whispering hiss. "You two fighting will do nothing but get us kicked out, and we'll have no choice but to board a ship sailing east. Stop your arguing."

Bryon shook his head. Erik could see him scanning the room.

"They look like the mercenaries," Bryon said.

"What does a mercenary look like?" Befel asked.

"Them," Bryon replied.

"It looks like one giant pissing contest to me," Erik said.

"Aye," Bryon agreed.

Erik saw two men who had the heads of big cats and four dwarves.

"So many different people," Erik muttered. And none of them looked like they had any need for Erik, his brother, or his cousin.

Befel may be right. This may be one huge mistake. Which of these men—mercenaries—would be fool enough to hire us?

"When is he coming?" Bryon asked in a soft voice. "If he's any later—and this doesn't pan out—we'll miss the ship going east."

Just as he spoke, Erik heard the sound of horses and wagons stopping, a deep voice barking inaudible orders, and the shuffling of feet and the jingling of reins. The noise in the bar ceased as if a switch had been thrown, and the sound of a single die sliding off a nearby table resembled something much bigger.

Within moments, a man clothed all in black linens, cowl low enough to cover his face, walked into the bar, the bottom of his robes brushing the floor. A tall, muscular, bearded bodyguard followed him, head shaved and showing blue-inked tattoos. His heavy knee-high boots thudded against the floor when he walked, and with each step even the toughest of men in the bar seemed to flinch. As he looked from side to side, inspecting the men in the bar, large, gold earrings thumped against his cheeks.

The cloaked man gave a slight sideways jerk with his cowled head, and the bodyguard stopped, standing in the middle of the bar and resting one forearm on the handle of his long sword. The cloaked man continued to the front of the bar. He retrieved a bag from within his robes and tossed it to Rory. It clanked when it hit the bar, and the old sailor scooped the purse up and escaped to the back of the inn.

The Messenger of the East. What else had Rory called him? The Herald of Golgolithul, the Steward of Fen-Stévock, the Mouth of Eastern Law, General of the Soldiers of the Eye, Right Hand of the Lord of the East. The second most powerful man in Golgolithul. None of those sounded pleasant and seemed to suit.

The Messenger waggled his fingers as he counted the heads of those in the bar, his gaze alighting on each momentarily. As Erik felt the mysterious man include him, his face invisible under his cowl, Erik's stomach knotted, and he felt sick as the air around him grew heavy. He felt his throat turn dry and found it hard to breathe. He stared at the floor, not wanting to meet the gaze.

"Forty of you have come, bidding the call of Fen-Stévock," the Messenger said. "Forty of you have a chance for glory and greatness in the name of justice and righteousness."

As the Messenger began his speech, Erik's stomach calmed. His breathing slowed, and the air around him seemed to lighten.

The Messenger captivated the mercenaries. His voice resounded through the bar, and the apprehension in the room seemed to ease with every word. When the Messenger talked about justice and righteousness, Erik felt confident if not courageous. It was as if he suddenly could do anything, and goose pimples rose along his arms. He felt compelled to stare at the Messenger.

"My Lord has long sought men of good quality for this task. You are of such quality. You need but complete this simple task required of my Lord, and he will not only reward you with riches but with title and favor. Your names will go down in the annals of history as trustworthy servants of the East.

"In a moment, I will explain the task at hand, and when I have done so I expect that some of you will no longer have a desire to serve my Master. It is a pity, but my Lord, in all his mercy, will honor your decision if that is the case, and you may be on your way.

"But..." the Agent of Fen-Stévock said, his voice even more commanding and powerful, "if you choose to serve the Lord of the East, all his blessings and the blessings of the gods of the east are with you. The courage of the ancients will drive you to victory, and the righteous ones who successfully complete my master's bidding will find a welcome like no other when they walk through the streets of Fen-Stévock. Those who fail will be best to return from wherever they came. The Lord of the East does not look kindly upon failure."

With that last sentence, his voice had become low and menacing as a clenched fist escaped the sleeve of his robe. Erik felt the air grow heavy again, and he rubbed his upper lip as if sweat had suddenly gathered there. The candles in the bar seemed to dim, but then the room returned to normal. Now the Messenger started explaining the task his master had for these mercenaries.

He talked for a long while about the history of the Southern Mountains and its dwarvish inhabitants. Finally, he spoke of a city called Orvencrest, one where the early dwarves had stored a mass of wealth in during the ancient days. The ancestors of the dwarves, living in the south of the country they called Drüum Balmdüukr, still stored many family heirlooms in that city, but not everything in Orvencrest had rightly belonged to the dwarves; some had been taken by force. And some of those treasures were not just gold and silver and jewels. The Messenger referred to those times as *barbaric* and explained that a prized and long-lost treasure of the Lord of the East's family rested among those treasures.

"It has come to my Lord's attention," the Messenger went on, "through much research and many resources spent, that a document of lineage, an old scroll encased in bone and held in a small, golden chest sits in the hidden treasure room of Orvencrest. To you, this may seem of little consequence, but it holds a certain sentimental value for my master."

A low murmur rippled through the crowd, but it seemed odd to

Erik that a simple scroll of family heritage would have such senti-mental value for one of the most powerful rulers in all of Háthgo-lthane. Wouldn't the historians and chroniclers of Golgolithul have kept records of his family's history?

"The location of Orvencrest has long been lost," the Messenger continued, "even to the dwarves of Drüum Balmdüukr, but again, through exhaustive research, my master believes he has located the city, buried deep within the Southern Mountains and hidden by dwarvish ingenuity. For those of you who accept this task, I have a map that indicates where the city is within the mountains. How you get to that point is up to you."

"Your reward," the Messenger continued and then paused for a moment. "Your reward is twofold. You may take whatever you can carry from the storerooms of Orvencrest's treasure. Anything crea-tures of your profession could ever want, you will find in the treasure room of Orvencrest—weapons, armor, gold, jewels, anything. Then, upon your successful arrival to Fen-Stévock with that which my master desires, in addition to a chest of gold, you will receive a seal to be worn upon your breast. Wear this seal within the borders of Golgolithul and all its citizens will recognize you as a Champion of Fen-Stévock. No self-respecting tavern owner will ever charge you for boarding and all will applaud you wherever you go."

Another low murmur went through the crowd. Some smiled loudly while others again shook their heads, looks of pure skepticism scrawled across their faces.

"One last thing," the Messenger said. "You are not to look at my master's document. It will be to your demise if you do, for my Lord will know and you, in turn, will feel his wrath…"

In the ensuing silence, there was none in the room who could not understand what that might mean, and none could avoid the sense of dread. His point hammered home, the Messenger spoke his final words.

"Now, as you leave, please retrieve a map from my menservants, Terradyn and Raktas. May the gods of the east smile upon you."

Terradyn, the first of the bodyguards standing in the middle of the bar, made his way back to the entrance of *The Lady's Inn* and a second tall and large man with a single ring piercing the septum of his nose appeared from outside. Raktas, long, braided, red hair falling to the small of his back and red beard sitting on his barrel chest, handed Terradyn a clutch of rolled parchment, and they both stood at the door, offering the maps and instructions to anyone who would take them. Most of the bar's inhabitants left without taking a map.

"Are even mercenaries that afraid of Fen-Stévock?" Bryon asked, watching sell-sword after sell-sword decline the bodyguards' offering.

"Perhaps it's too dangerous," Befel replied, "or too secretive. I would think that mercenaries are about self-preservation above all else, and from what I've seen and heard, they like to know exactly what they're getting into."

"Or maybe it's just too good to be true," Bryon added.

"This is an adventure of folly," Erik heard one man say. From another, he heard, "A lapdog's mission. That's what this is."

"I won't risk my life for some myth," yet another mercenary said. "And don't think the dwarves are going to just welcome any fool wandering around in their mountains. They'll crack his skull with one of their hammers faster than he can blink."

"A fool's mission," Erik muttered, sitting at their table and watching everyone leave. "Sounds fitting."

Chapter 39

ERIK STARED AT THE COMPANY of soldiers standing at attention outside *The Lady's Inn.*

"The Soldiers of the Eye," a man standing next to Erik said. Erik noticed him clutching one of the maps. "The personal guard of the Messenger of the East."

Close to a hundred men stood in that company, just outside the wooden gate, guarding three carriages made of a golden oak, ornamented with silver bells, and each drawn by a train of six jet black horses, purple-feathered plumes atop their heads. All the guardsmen wore a hardened leather breastplate emblazoned with an open hand centered by a single eye.

"What is that on their chest?"

"The All-Watching Eye. The crest of the Messenger of the East," the mercenary replied.

Each soldier held a long spear tipped by a steel blade that gleamed in the sun and a steel shield also bearing the symbol of the Messenger. All wore leather trousers of the same dark brown color, and all wore heavy boots polished to a bright sheen. When Terradyn and Raktas walked from *The Lady's Inn,* the thunderous sound of a hundred boots, stamping as one, rang through the air as the company snapped to attention.

"Unlike any other soldier in Golgolithul's army, these men pledge fealty to the Messenger and the Messenger alone," the mercenary continued. "People of Golgolithul, and elsewhere, hold only the personal guard of the Lord of the East in higher esteem. These men will give their life for the Herald. They swear oaths of celibacy, keep their heads and faces shaved, and on the back of each man's head is the tattoo of the Messenger's insignia—the All-Watching Eye—in black ink."

He looked over to see Erik watching him and then the guard that stood in front of the inn and then back at him. When Erik's blue eyes caught his, he smiled and winked.

"You seem a little young, lad, to be one of our kind." Before Erik could answer the man, he added, "But, who am I to judge. Watch your step around them, lad. In fact, watch your step around all these fellows."

"Including you?" Erik asked timidly.

The seemingly pleasant fellow chuckled. "Well put, my young man." The man tucked his thumbs into his belt and tilted his head in thought. "Perhaps."

"Wrothgard," one of his companions said, and he looked over to his departing friends. He nodded back to the other two men.

"Peace be with you and fortune smile on you," he said to Erik before catching up to his companions.

Those who did accept the Lord of the East's offer gathered near to the stables, waiting to have a few words with the Messenger who, somewhat to Erik's surprise, welcomed questions and small conversations from the mercenaries. The two cat-men spoke with him for longer than most, even though they did not take a map. Erik heard them speak in their language of growls and purrs and heard the Messenger respond in the same language. When finished, they bowed and left.

Erik then saw the four dwarves talking amongst themselves. They seemed to argue until one of them put up a hand up to stop the conversation. He walked away, his face red and his cheeks undulating as he ground his teeth. He even grumbled at the two bodyguards when he passed them, and the other dwarves shrugged their shoulders and shook their heads. Finally, they put up their hands in capitulation and accepted a map from Terradyn.

"I do not remember sending invitations to you three." The voice startled Erik, and he turned to see the Messenger of the East standing next to him. He and his brother and cousin bowed. Erik felt his heart quicken and his hands shake as he bent low, staring at the ground.

How does he know the faces of those he invited? He could not have met all of them.

"We were in Finlo for the ships, my lord," Erik finally said after a few, uneasy moments. "The ships east, that is. We had intended on going east and enlisting in Golgolithul's armies."

"And yet you are here," the Messenger spoke slowly.

"Yes, my lord, we heard…" Erik said but stopped before incriminating Rory and paused a moment to gather his thoughts. "Rather, we saw all the men showing up to the inn and decided to find out why."

"Ah, I see," the Messenger replied, deep cynicism in his voice. "Have you never heard that curiosity skins a gnome, young man?"

"My father said that to me all the time," Erik said with a smile.

"So, you have a sense of duty then," the Messenger said.

"Honestly, sir, I think it is more that we are tired of begging and living on the street and wondering when our next meal is going to come," Erik replied, hands crossed in front of him, head slightly lowered so he would not meet the Messenger's gaze.

"An honest answer if not a hard one," the Messenger replied. Erik felt his hands shake again. "I like honest answers. Honestly suits you, Erik."

"How did you know my…"

The Messenger put up a hand to silence Erik.

"After hearing my lord's task, what are you going to do?" the Messenger asked.

Erik looked to his brother and cousin. Befel just shrugged while Bryon shook his head, a disapproving look on his face.

"We are clearly not mercenaries," Erik said.

"Clearly," the Messenger reiterated.

"But we aren't soldiers either. I think we will try to sell our services as porters. There is more opportunity for..." Erik stopped. He nearly said gold, but where was the notion of service in that? "There is a better opportunity to serve, this way. We would be just three in a thousand men if we went east, but here, maybe we can do more."

"I told you," the Messenger said coldly, "honesty better suits you. The glimmer of gold, the thought of fame attracts you young men. Gold and fame attracting young men have never been a mystery, and I would be a fool to think otherwise. However, you might find it difficult to hire yourselves out to fellows such as these. Many already have menservants."

He pointed to a richly robed man with pale skin who stood beside his pure white stallion which waited obediently. The man barked orders to two other men, both wearing red trousers and red vests. They packed saddlebags onto two smaller horses, but both still fine looking animals.

"He could probably use your swords more than your shoulders," said the Messenger, "but mercenaries are a greedy lot, and he already has two men serving him."

The Messenger then pointed to three well-groomed men.

"Then there are those that do not have servants because they have no need. You might find luck with those fellows," the Messenger said.

Erik recognized one of them as Wrothgard, the man who had told him about the Soldiers of the Eye. They looked to own few possessions aside from their weapons, and what they did have they carried in simple, leather haversacks. One might think they could at least use someone to fetch wood or food if rations ran low, but each man carried a short bow on his back and a small hand ax for cutting wood on their belts.

He then pointed to another man, a blond haired fellow wearing a simple cloth shirt, its sleeves rolled up revealing the tattoos of a sailor. The scruff of a week without shaving on his weathered, tanned face.

He handed a bundle of rations to another, sandy-headed man a hand shorter than him. The second man wore an iron corselet lying over a brown leather jerkin; both seemed worn and in need of some repair.

Behind them, a third, gaunt fellow with stringy, thinning, gray hair and a simple cotton-stitched shirt that hung loosely from his shoulders, packed more supplies onto another horse. His sunken, grayish-brown eyes squinted, and his weather-beaten skin looked tan and wrinkled. His body, albeit thin and malnourished looking, didn't look a day older than Bryon's father, a man in his early middle years, and yet his face looked the part of the Eleodum's grandfather, long since passed from this life.

"They could probably use your backs and horses—and your swords if the need arises," said the Messenger. "Although seasoned fighters, they are perhaps not as experienced as some of the others here. They would probably welcome your services, for the right price."

Chapter 40

"I DON'T KNOW ABOUT THIS," Bryon said.

"They were the ones the Messenger suggested," Erik said.

"But why?" Bryon muttered, more to himself.

He didn't trust the Messenger, and these three men looked little better than themselves. One even looked sickly, ragged, and worn down. And they all looked well past their prime.

These men won't lead us to riches. They won't lead us east. They'll lead us to our doom.

"It's the choice we've made," Befel said. "Stick to the plan."

"The plan has changed so many times," Bryon replied. "Who knows what the plan is anymore?"

"We agreed," Befel said, looking agitated. "We will sell our services as porters."

"Little more than slaves," Bryon spat. "That's all we'll be for a silver crown a day—slaves to fools on a fool's mission for another fool."

"I'd watch your tongue around all these men who serve that fool," Befel replied. "Besides, the alternative is a crowded boat for several months taking us to a land we know nothing about, fighting for a cause we know nothing about, and for that very same fool. And a silver crown is what we made for a week's worth of work in Venton. I think it's a fair wage, considering what we will be doing."

"Agreed," Erik added.

"Fine," Bryon said with a shrug. "Do what you want. What do I care?"

"You sound like a child," Erik said, and Bryon glared at him, clenching his fists.

Oh, how I would beat you right now if we were home.

"Excuse me, sirs," Befel said, clearing his throat to get their attention. The three mercenaries didn't seem to hear him, so he cleared his throat again. "Excuse, good men."

Bryon rolled his eyes again as Befel cleared his throat one more time.

"Just tap him on the shoulder," Bryon said.

"I don't want to be rude," Befel replied.

"Rude?" Bryon questioned. "Are you kidding me?"

Bryon looked at the skinny one with the gray eyes sunken. He imagined that if the man took his shirt off, he would be able to see his ribs. Bryon shook his head.

This is folly, he thought, and then loudly said, "Hey, you. We want to talk."

"Damn it, Bryon," Befel hissed. "They'll never want to hire us if we speak to them like that."

"What the bloody hell do you want," the gaunt man said, his voice rough and crude. "How'd you beggars slip through the guard here?"

"We're not beggars," Bryon retorted curtly.

"Well," the gaunt fellow said, "you could've fooled me. Did I make you mad, boy?"

He smiled maliciously, showing yellowed, browning teeth in need of attention, and Bryon felt his face grow hot.

Small men. Small men with big mouths. Great.

"We came to humbly ask if you could use our services," Befel said calmly, "that is all."

"Services!" the gaunt man cried. "You must be from the streets of Bard'Sturn, along with the other boy lovers. I prefer women, lad."

He laughed at his own joke, but the blond haired mercenary shot him a dirty look and stepped in front of him.

"What services do you offer?" he asked quickly.

The man crossed his arms in front of his chest and pushed his chin forward, tapping a foot and waiting impatiently for a reply.

"Porters, sir," Befel replied. "We have strong shoulders and two packhorses in addition to our own riding horses. We will provide our own food and clothing—and we'll cook, make camp, and clean, as you need. We also have some skill with the sword if the need arises. We only ask a silver crown a day."

"Each!" exclaimed the blond haired man, starting to turn around and continue to pack.

"No, sir," Befel replied quickly, "between the three of us."

"A silver crown, eh?" the blond haired man said, his interest obviously peaked. He scratched his chin through his stubble. "And how do we know you don't intend to knife us while we sleep? A little odd, young men such as yourselves with two packhorses in addition to your own riding horses wanting a job as a meager porter, don't you think?"

"Indeed," Bryon mumbled.

"It would be a fool thing to try," Befel replied, "to try and knife mercenaries like you. We have little skill with the sword—just enough to get by and maybe help when the need arises. And the horses, well, actually a friend gave them to us. They're nothing special, but they have strong backs and good stamina."

"Maybe you stole the horses. Maybe you slit their owner's throat and took them in the middle of the night" the shorter, sandy-headed mercenary suggested.

Bryon felt a small smile creeping across his face.

These men are truly fools. We could slit their throats, no doubt. Wait until they're asleep, slit their throats, and take what little they own.

"Nah, they don't have the look." The blond haired man said with a coy smile.

He turned to the other two and whispered, their backs to Bryon and his cousins. The gaunt man seemed the most animated, lifting his hands up and down indiscriminately. The shorter, sandy-headed man looked concerned, staring back at Bryon with furled eyebrows and a slight frown. The blond man nodded at the comments being made and then finally turned back to the young men.

"All right," he said, "on several conditions. Firstly, we'll pay an eastern crown. You may not know what that is, but it's made with as much silver as a silver crown, carries a little less weight in these parts, but worth more in Golgolithul."

"How do we know that's true?" Bryon asked, cutting the man off.

"You'll just have to take my word for it," the mercenary replied, "and if you don't like it, leave it. It's nothing to me if you don't want it."

"No," Befel said, "I know what an eastern crown is."

Bryon knew he was lying and seethed silently.

"It's a fair deal," Befel added.

"Very well," the blond mercenary said. "You will make and break camp, cook, and clean. You will also provide for yourselves, including clothing and food. You will have a need to use your swords, of this, I am certain. If you back down, if you fail to fight when we need you, we will not simply dismiss you. We will kill you…all three of you."

Befel looked back at Bryon, and then Erik. Bryon thought he'd like to see him try, but both he and Erik nodded to Befel.

"Agreed," Befel said.

The blond haired man shook hands with Befel and Erik. When he shook Bryon's hand, Bryon made sure to grip hard, tight. The man's hand was rough, and his grip much stronger than what Bryon had expected. And when he looked Bryon in the face, when they clasped hands and Bryon squeezed, the mercenary smiled, almost laughing.

Chapter 41

"WHERE?" KEHL ASKED.

Fox groveled in front of the slaver, panting and ducking, expecting a hard fist from his commander. He had good cause to be afraid—the puffy lip, black eye, and bruised cheeks showed evidence of that.

"Finlo," Fox answered quickly.

"Then to Finlo we go." Kehl turned to walk to his horse.

"Kehl," his tall, second in command said, clearing his throat with a quick cough, "what of the slaves?"

Kehl spun, fists clenched. His dark eyes blazed fire. His second in command backed away. He never hit his brother—he never would—but his brother didn't know that.

"How many men do we have?" Kehl asked.

"Subtracting the men we lost and adding the men we kept in reserve," his brother said, counting on his fingers. "Forty, Im'Ka'Da."

Kehl lowered his head, allowing a small smile to creep across his face. He liked it when his brother referred to him as Im'Ka'Da—leader in their native, Samanian tongue. He stared at the ground for a moment, thinking. He looked at Fox, still kneeling and whimpering. The man disgusted him, and he backhanded the weasely creature across the face. The fiery-haired slaver reeled to the side, crying as an older wound burst open, and blood ran down his cheek. That made Kehl feel better, and his smile widened, When the men, women, and children, all tied in a line by a long strand of rope, cried, shuddered, and cowed at his brutality, that was when he was most content.

"I will take half to Finlo," Kehl finally said, "and you, Kellen, will stay with the slaves and wait for our return. Send for Kilben. I will take him with us. And you, worm," he added, pointing to Fox, rolling on the ground, snaking over an elm's root and trying to crawl to his knees again.

For all of Kehl's brutality and Kellen's wits, Kilben—their youngest brother—seemed to have all of that plus the body of a giant. Kehl would have liked to see his little brother fight that huge bastard of a gypsy. But he needed someone reliable to guard his camp, someone other slavers—the untrustworthy bunch that they were—would be afraid of, someone they wouldn't dare cross.

"Yes," Kehl affirmed, "we will go to Finlo, and we will finish those gypsies. I will have my revenge. I will have my revenge, and I will replenish my ranks with their men."

"And if they refuse to serve, Im'Ka'Da?" Kellen asked.

"Then they die."

Chapter 42

BRYON THREW SEVERAL SADDLEBAGS ACROSS the back of a pack-horse. The animal snorted and stomped a hoof at the luggage. He laid four hemp baskets, two on each side, across the beast's neck. It snorted again.

"I know boy," Bryon said, patting the animal's neck. "The load will lessen while we travel. I promise."

He loaded more bags onto the horse's back, full of food mostly, then firewood and extra sets of clothing. He rolled up several tents, meant only for inclement weather if they ran into any, and decided to load them onto the other packhorse, which proved no happier than the first.

While Bryon loaded the packhorses, Befel fed all the animals but, of course, he fed their new masters' horses first. Erik beat the riding blankets, polished the saddles, and fitted the tackle and bit to the mounts. When he finished tightening the saddle belts, he brushed the dirt from their manes and tails.

"Damn it all," Bryon seethed, accidentally dropping a small basket of apples. "This is no better than farming. Piss on this."

"Well, it's a start," Befel said, "and we're getting paid a fair amount more than farm work."

"Damn you," Bryon hissed, his face red with anger. "This is your fault."

"I suppose I should introduce myself," the blond haired mercenary said, interrupting the cousins' argument. He wiped off a bit of dirt from his hand with a worn rag and extended it to Befel. "My name is Vander Bim."

"Befel," he replied, grasping Vander Bim's hand. "Befel Eleodum. And this is my brother Erik, and our cousin—"

"Bryon," Bryon said, cutting Befel off. He extended his hand again, made sure he squeezed extra hard this time when Vander Bim shook it. The mercenary smiled.

"You'll cramp your hand," Vander Bim said, "trying to squeeze so hard."

"Oh," Bryon said, trying to sound indifferent, "was I squeezing hard? I didn't notice. Sorry if I hurt your hand."

Vander Bim laughed, and that caused Bryon's pulse to quicken, his ears to grow hot.

"Don't worry," Vander Bim said. "You didn't hurt my hand. Shake the hand of an antegant. Now, that's a handshake that might break your fingers. No, after years aboard a ship, you develop a strong grip, one that can withstand the firm handshakes of young, vibrant men."

Bryon fought the frown on his face, fought the urge to throttle this middle-aged mercenary mocking him.

"So, are you also an Eleodum, or shall I call you Bryon with the firm grip?" Vander Bim asked.

Bryon decided he'd had enough of the mercenary's jesting, but he didn't do anything. He just stood there and fumed while Befel laughed. Bryon wiped his brow, his forehead hot since the sun seemed more intense, and he felt his skin burning.

"Eleodum," snapped Bryon as if he couldn't close his jaw quickly enough.

"Very well, then," Vander Bim said. "This is Drake Dreorigan of Nordeth Manor."

He pointed to the sandy-headed mercenary, shorter and stockier than he. The man waved and bowed slightly with a smile on his cheerful, rough face.

"You just call me Drake," he said.

"And that fellow over there," Vander Bim said, referring to the gaunt man, "that is Switch. Drake and I have been fighting together for four years, and Switch joined up with us just a year ago. He can come off as crude, but I guess we all can at times. He's a good chap, an excellent scout and hunter, and an even better fighter."

"Oi, I heard my name," Switch cried, stringing his short bow.

He walked over to the group of men, a large, menacing smile on his face and mischief in his squinted, gray eyes. He didn't bother to shake hands as Vander Bim did. Instead, he pointed a thin-bladed knife at the young men.

"That's right. My name's Switch. Been around awhile, even longer than these two blokes. Been on several of these adventures before. Do what you're told, and I'll keep you alive, make you some money, and get you a little quim while we're at it, eh Vander."

Switch nudged Vander Bim with a knobby elbow and laughed. Vander Bim returned the laugh, but Bryon suspected it wasn't sincere.

"Now that we're all friends," Switch continued, "you three better get back to your duties so we can leave soon."

"We're all done," Erik said. "The horses are packed, cleaned, and fed."

"Oh?" Switch said. "If I'm paying a crown a day for you, you better believe I'll find something else for you to do."

Switch walked back to his horse, sliding his bow into its sheath.

"This is just great," Bryon said. "Thank you, cousin. I love little gutter rats who think they're bigger than they are."

"You keep speaking as if this is my fault," Befel said.

"It is," Bryon replied.

"You're the one that wanted me to come to Finlo with you and not go to Aga Kona," Befel said.

"No." Bryon shook his head. "You can thank your little rat turd brother for that."

"Little?" Erik said. His voice almost sounded hurt.

"I can only put up with so much of that hedge-born churl's mouth," Bryon said, "before I punch him in the face."

"Relax," Befel said. "Besides, I think Vander Bim is in charge, and it seems as if he likes us."

"Well," Bryon replied, "while his back is turned, that sly one will try to work us dead."

"I wouldn't worry about that," Befel said, trying to give Bryon a comforting smile, but it didn't seem to work. "We're their porters. Servants, not slaves."

"What's the difference?" Bryon asked and went over to Buck as Erik mounted his own horse.

"We should leave," he heard Vander Bim say, "if we don't wish to travel by moonlight."

"All right then," Switch said, sitting astride his horse next to Erik, "let's bloody go."

Aside from one other group of mercenaries, Erik's new employers were the only ones left at the front of *The Lady's Inn*. This other bunch—also three men—didn't look like mercenaries, they were all scraggly and thin with worn clothing. They looked more like the beggars.

One man with a square jaw was watching his colleagues nervously, his eyes darting between them, the Messenger's entourage, and the Messenger himself. One of the man's companions, a thin man with a deep cleft chin simply watched the Messenger, who stood alone with his back to the two men. Square jaw said something to cleft chin, and the latter nodded, slowly.

In that instant, they had both pulled crudely fashioned longbows off their backs, nocked arrows, and readied them to fire. The third of the ragtag mercenaries, a man with a huge beard, rode up on a decrepit looking horse, pulling two more sad looking animals behind him. He clenched a fist and shouted, "Lo Hûn Vin Mek-Ba'Dune!"

The bowmen let their arrows fly, straight toward the Messenger. Erik meant to yell, but before he could, the Messenger spun and put up his right hand. His hand flashed twice with blinding light and what once were arrows were now a mere pile of splinters lying on the ground. Three arrows thudded into the chest of square jaw. He stumbled back but still remained on his feet. Cleft chin ran toward the horses, jumping atop one of them and grabbing the thin reins, turning the animal with a savage kick in its ribs. Clearly intent on leaving their doomed companion behind, the two men sped off in a cloud of dust.

Square jaw looked as he might now fall, but instead, he pulled a bronze-bladed knife from his belt and threw it at the Messenger who once more, put up his hand. The knife stopped, simply hanging in the air a blade's-width from the Herald of the East. The blade began to glow white and then melted, the liquid hitting the ground and sending up a thin trail of steam. Five more arrows thudded into the would-be assailant's body, and he fell to the ground with a piteous cry. Terradyn called to the Soldiers of the Eye in a language Erik didn't understand, but the company of soldiers snapped to attention and began to march.

"Let them run for now," the Messenger of the East said, putting up a hand to stop his personal guard. "They will receive their punishment in due time. Those who oppose the might of the Lord of the East will all receive his retribution in due time."

After the shock of the attack had subsided, Vander Bim gave a call to move out. Erik waved to Rory, who watched them from the porch of the inn. Then, much to his amazement, the Messenger stood next to him. He hadn't seen the man—if that's what he was— walk to him, but there he was.

"My lord," Erik said, his voice shaking. He moved to dismount.

"Stay on your horse, Erik Eleodum," the Messenger of the East commanded, although his voice sounded soft and calm.

"Yes, my lord," Erik replied. "Is there something you need of me?"

"Yes," the Messenger replied.

Erik's throat went dry.

"I have been thinking about you," the Messenger said.

The Messenger of the East, thinking about me?

The Messenger reached up and touched the golden handle of the dagger Mardirru had given Erik.

"You are an interesting young man, and I did not see our paths crossing. I have a hard time reading you, Erik Eleodum."

"Reading me, my lord?" Erik asked.

"Yes. Reading you," the Messenger confirmed with a nod. "Understanding you. Knowing who you are by just looking at you. There is something special about you, Erik Eleodum."

Why does he keep saying my name over and over?

"I don't know what it is yet," the Messenger continued, "and that frustrates me. So, I have one question for you before you leave."

"Yes, my lord," Erik replied. "Anything."

"Why are you here?" the Messenger asked.

"Why do you want to know that?" Erik asked without thinking about his words first.

"Your honesty, young Erik Eleodum, is a little refreshing I think," the Messenger of the East replied. "I would like to know, that is all."

"I don't know why I am here, my lord," Erik explained. "I don't think I've known what, by the Creator, I have been doing since I left home. I care little for fame or wealth. I was perfectly happy on my family's farm. I followed my brother and cousin, hoping I might be able to return with enough coin to help my father stave off the advances of Hámonian nobles."

"Just as I suspected," the Messenger said. "A follower of the heart. That is what you are. It will get you into trouble, but the world needs more followers of the heart. Very interesting. Blessings on you, Erik Eleodum. Follow your heart, and I just may see you again one day."

Why would he care to see me again?

Erik gave the Messenger a quick bow, and the mysterious man waved him on before walking back to his bodyguards.

"To Dûrn Tor," Vander Bim called, and Erik asked where that was.

"The only other real city in Southland," Switch replied. "It sits at the feet of the westernmost part of the Southern Mountains, called the Western Tor."

"All right then," Erik said, more to himself than anyone else, "to Dûrn Tor."

⌒

As the six men and their packhorses broke into a trot to head out of Finlo, Terradyn turned to his master.

"Who was that, my lord?"

"I don't know," Andragos replied, steepling his fingers underneath the cowl of his robe. "Perhaps the man I had a premonition about."

"Man?" Terradyn asked with a hint of disbelief in his voice. "He's only a boy."

"He's seen twenty years," Andragos said with a shrug. "And in his twenty years, he has seen much. Many of the soldiers who fight for us are four and five years younger. Would you not consider them men?"

"He is no soldier, my lord," Terradyn replied. "I beg your pardon, but could you be mistaken? Many of these men are trash, but I have seen some that might be worthy of serving you."

"He is not supposed to serve me." Andragos shook his head. "And I do fear his and some of these other men's paths will cross."

Andragos looked down at his feet, watching the pool of bronze from the former knife cool and harden.

Fools. What a waste of a life?

"How old were you when you began serving me?" Andragos asked. He knew Terradyn could not see his eyes even though he stood just a breadth away, and he looked straight at his servant.

"You know the answer to that, my lord," Terradyn asked.

"Still," Andragos added, "humor me."

"Six years old, my lord," Terradyn said with a bow. "Same as Raktas."

"And at six years old," Andragos continued, "did you not do things that most seasoned men could not do?"

"That is different, my lord," Terradyn said.

"Perhaps," Andragos agreed, "but there is something to this Erik Eleodum. Yes. I will see him again. He is the one I was to meet. Now, I am almost sure of it. Be well, Erik Eleodum."

Chapter 43

BRISK TRAVEL ALONG THE SEA Born Road brought the group of mercenaries and the Eleodums to their first destination in only a day. What looked like barely a village at first, Dûrn Tor snuggled amongst low, rolling hills, with a simple grain silo and a few standalone homes. However, it quickly turned to a vibrant city almost the size of Finlo, but where the latter found no need of a wall, the majority of this other city hid behind a complex network of wooden palisades. Neatly constructed between taller hillocks, half a dozen men stood in front of what Erik assumed to the main gate.

All were armored in simple leather jerkins and carrying naught but long spears and round, wooden shields. Two more stood in front of a tavern, *The Hill Giant,* four stories high and built right into one of the Western Tor's knolls. Flags flew above both the tavern and the front gate—a white field and a black ship with three sails.

"We'll stay at the inn tonight," Vander Bim said. "It'll be the last bit of civilization we will experience for a while."

"Halt," one of the armed men in front of the tavern said, a blond haired youth with a clean-shaven face and blue eyes. He grabbed the reigns of Vander Bim's horse, and Vander Bim let go, allowing the young guard to take control of his mount.

"What's your business?" said the other man, a much older man who wore a thick mustache above a lip that was puffy and scarred.

211

"We come from Finlo," Vander Bim replied. "We only wish to stay the night, and then we'll be on our way."

"There's been others with the same story," the older guard huffed, his voice gruff. "You can't enter the city, but you can stay in *The Hill Giant*."

"Very well," Vander Bim complied.

A young groom took their horses. Vander Bim threw the lad—no more than fourteen summers old—a Finnish nickel, and the boy grinned wide, bowed low, and bombarded the party with thanks and promises that he would take the best care of their animals.

"That must've been a giant of an animal," Erik said, eyeing the rack of elk antlers, eight points on each side and a beam the width of a man's arm, that sat above the inn's front door.

"A hunter's delight," Vander Bim agreed as they walked into the tavern.

Around the walls hung the heads of various animals—elk, deer, bear, wolf, cougar, and bison from the Plains of Güdal. A large chandelier hanging from the middle of the high ceiling and made of more elk antlers lit the room well along with dozens of copper candle holders interspersed between animal heads. Two barkeeps stood behind the wide bar and kept patrons' drinks filled with a bit of humor and light conversation. A large mirror, a few cracks sprouting from its bottom, took up much of the lower wall behind the bar, and various stands and shelves displayed an array of alcohols and wines.

A fat woman with a gray bun atop her head and wearing a brown dress covered by a dirtied white smock met the men at the door.

"My name is Elena Minx," she said, the fat under her chin jiggling when she spoke, "and I am the proprietor here at *The Hill Giant*. You may sit wherever you like."

The men nodded and began to move into the bar, but Elena Minx stopped them, putting her right hand in the middle of Switch's chest.

"There're a couple of rules," she said coldly like a grandmother scolding her grandchildren. Her blue eyes squinted as she studied them. Despite her short stature, at that moment, Erik felt as tall as one of his sister's dolls as the old fat woman looked the men up and down.

"There're no whores here, so if you offer a woman money, even if she looks it, she'll probably slap you in the face, and you right deserve it if she does. There's no fighting. Tuc and Boz behind the bar both have nice, big, oak cudgels and believe me, they've cracked bigger skulls than you got with 'em. The kitchen closes at midnight, no exceptions and no bellyaching if you try to get your order in five minutes prior. Drinking—obviously everyone comes here to drink, but if you can't lift your head off the table, you've drunk too much, and you'll find yourself waking up in the street. If you need a room, see Tuc. He's the bald one."

The men nodded, and Elena Minx moved out of their way. They picked a large, round, wooden table in the middle of the tavern, brightly lit as it sat underneath the chandelier. A younger, pretty, blonde haired woman with a soft face, large breasts, and round bottom, came only a few moments later carrying a tray of clean glasses. She smiled at the men and sweetly asked them if they wanted any hot, spiced wine or bread wine.

Switch eyed the woman hungrily and then looked at Bryon.

"Slap her ass," Switch said.

"What?" Bryon asked, a hint of confusion in his voice.

"Slap her bloody ass," Switch said with a smile. "I want to see it jiggle."

"You slap her ass," Bryon retorted.

"I'm not getting kicked out," Switch said. "Now, slap it. That's an order."

"Switch," Vander Bim hissed. "Stop it."

"I thought you were the tough one," Switch chided, squinting his eyes at Bryon. "You're nothing but a yellow-bellied gutter shite. Can't even grab a woman's ass. I was going to pay for your room, but I think you'll just sleep in the stables."

"I planned on it anyway," Bryon replied.

"You like animals, yeah?" Switch said, leaning back in his chair and crossing his arms. He shrugged. "I thought you were partial to men, but who am I to judge?"

Erik thought Bryon was going to hit Switch. He had that look on his face. But his cousin just sighed, and when the bread wine came, quietly drank his glassful.

Vander Bim spread the small piece of parchment, their map, on the table for all to have a look.

"We need to have a definite course," Vander Bim said, and Drake and Switch nodded in agreement.

The map looked simple. A sprawling mountain range was marked *Southern Mountains*. Erik was familiar with the range, at least from stories. It had a few markers. Two mining camps—Aga Kona and Aga Min—and two dwarvish cities—Ecfast and Thorakest.

"Thorakest," Erik muttered, looking over the map while the three mercenaries talked amongst themselves.

"The capital of Drüum Balmdüukr," Vander Bim said. "And Ecfast is an outpost, a gateway almost into the lands of the dwarves."

"What's this?" Erik asked, tracing his finger around the red circle that had been drawn toward the bottom of the page.

"Supposedly," Switch explained, "the lost city."

There was a gap in the drawing between the lost city and Thorakest.

"And what is this?" Erik asked, pointing to it.

"Are you going to ask a thousand questions?" sneered Switch.

"It's all right," Vander Bim said, holding up a placatory hand. "This is a ravine that splits the Southern Mountains into two ranges. It begins somewhere just east of the Western Tor and continues almost the whole length of the mountains."

"We need to avoid Thorakest and Ecfast," Drake said.

"Agreed," Switch said. "Bloody tunnel diggers'll ask too many questions. We'll end up in some dark, dingy dungeon for a hundred years."

"We had talked about sailing around the Dragon's Tooth," Drake

214

said, tracing his finger along a peninsula that extended deep into the South Sea.

"Other than having to backtrack and lose a day," Vander Bim said, "we would have to find a ship and sail through quite treacherous waters with only six men, only one of which is a trained sailor."

"That leaves us with our original plan," Switch said. "We enter the mountain here, from Dûrn Tor, thus avoiding having to cross this ravine, and make our way to the lost city."

"That's settled then?" Vander Bim asked.

Switch and Drake nodded.

"Sounds good," Erik said with a smile.

"No one gives a shit what you think. You're the paid help," snapped Switch.

Instead of feeling small like Bryon used to make him feel, Erik almost felt like acting like his cousin and punching the scrawny man.

Perhaps I'm growing up?

The sun's light had not yet completely left the sky when Befel and Erik turned down their beds. Befel stared at the faint glow of reds and yellows through the western facing window as he rubbed his shoulder and made circles to stretch it. It still hurt, but not quite as bad, and every day it seemed to get better. Befel was glad for Vander Bim's compassion, and he doubted that Switch would have offered to pay for their room. As for Drake, he seemed as indifferent as a leaf carried by the wind. They were a strange bunch for so-called mercenaries, and he wondered if they really could fight but guessed they could because it must have been their reputation which led the Messenger to invite them to his meeting.

Through his window, Befel watched as Bryon walked to the stables. His cousin kept to his promise of sleeping with the animals.

"Fool," he muttered. "He likes those horses more than us."

As the last little glimmer of light twinkled behind the horizon like a yellow diamond, he looked out to sea and thought that the young men that had traveled to Finlo to sail east would be on their ships now. They would have heard an encouraging message from the Agent of Fen-Stévock, and Befel was sure he must have instilled in them great courage and then bid them farewell and gave them blessings. Now Befel imagined cramped bodies, barely able to move, and men retching at the movement of the water, some pissing themselves with fear of the unknown.

Instead, Befel stood in the window of a decent tavern with a comfortable bed waiting and the open road at his feet. The cool, spring morning air would blow on his face and through his hair, and the smell of dew-soaked grass would fill his nose. The freedom he had hoped for, and yet, his thoughts always turned to home, to his mother and father, to his two little sisters, to the wheat and corn and soybean fields. He thought of fishing on afternoons when he finished his duties early and squishing the mud of the pigpen through his toes on a rainy day. He shook his head. No. That was not the life he wanted. He hated farming. He wanted riches, fame, and fortune. Did he?

He closed the window's slats as if blocking off the fading sunset would also block the memories of home. As he sat on the edge of his bed, he looked at the floor for a while, eyes fixed on a single beam of light seeping through window slats. Little particles of dust floated in the air, their invisibility unveiled by the light, but then they were gone as the light disappeared like a snuffed candle. He finally laid back, his head hitting the soft pillow.

As Befel stared at the ceiling, unable to sleep, Erik sat cross-legged on his bed, turning Marcus' flute over and over in his hands. Erik put the flute to his lips, remembering the little his uncle had taught him, and tried blowing a single note. The flute screeched, and Erik recoiled at the sound. Disgusted with himself, he too lay back and stared, dejected, at the instrument.

"How did Marcus make this thing sound so beautiful?"

"Practice," Befel replied as he closed his eyes and put his hand to his forehead. "And now is not the time for that."

Erik went to put it back in his pack when he felt a flutter in his stomach and, for only seconds, his heart raced. His palms felt clammy, and his fingers shook a bit, but he put the flute back to his lips.

He did not think, did not contemplate where he would put his fingers, did not wonder what notes he would play. In fact, he did not know what he did. He simply envisioned a small pond, sitting in the green glade of a dense forest. The rays of a late morning sun sparkled on the pond's surface, and a breeze gently blew through the tall grass. Daffodils and lavender grew along the pond's banks, and a jay, perched high in the branches of an oak, sang a sweet morning song, and a cardinal from across the glade answered with even sweeter words.

Erik played that. The notes floated through the air, and his fingers did what they willed. He just thought of that glade and those birds. Seemingly unsurprised by his brother's new found gift, Befel closed his eyes and fell asleep, breathing gently with a smile on his face. Finally, the cardinal fluttered away and the jay, with no one to sing to, slowed its song and flew away itself. Erik put the flute down, his eyelids heavy. He laid back, the flute resting on his chest, and fell asleep.

Chapter 44

AFTER A HEARTY BREAKFAST OF vegetable soup and bread, Befel went to the stables with his brother and cousin to ready their horses.

"It is a dangerous course you men wish to take."

The voice took Befel by surprise. It was hard and guttural. He turned to see a dwarf standing there, one hand tucked into his belt, the other stroking his long, brown beard.

"Come again?" Befel asked.

"It is a hard road you wish to take, heading into the mountains from here—the Western Tor," the dwarf said. He pointed to two other dwarves standing just a few paces back. "We heard you discussing your plans last night."

"I don't remember seeing you three at *The Hill Giant*," Befel said.

"We dwarves have learned to make ourselves less seen in the lands of men," the dwarf replied.

"I see," Befel said. "It's not really our choice. We're just porters, working for the other three men we were with. That's Vander Bim, right there."

Befel pointed to the mercenary as he walked from *The Hill Giant*.

"He would be the man to tell," Befel said.

"Thank you," the dwarf said, extending his hand. "Turk Skull Crusher, of the Eorthfolk Clan."

Befel shook the dwarf's hand, and that simple handshake proved the myths behind the legendary strength of the dwarves. He thought

Turk had broken his hand, he squeezed so hard, and when Befel retrieved his hand, his knuckles were white and bloodless.

"I remember seeing them in Finlo," Erik said, stepping up next to Befel.

Befel nodded. He remembered them as well, but there were four of them in Finlo, at *The Lady's Inn*. One of them had stormed away, seemingly upset. They watched Turk and the other two dwarves greet Vander Bim. The dwarves all bowed so low their beards almost scraped the ground. Turk and Vander Bim spoke for a while until Drake and Switch joined them. The other two dwarves didn't say anything, but Befel could see them eyeing the men closely, one resting a hand on the handle of a broadsword, its scabbard embossed with iron that looked like a thorny vine, the other resting both his hands on the handle of his mace, a large iron ball studded with four, large spikes around its equator.

"What do you think they're talking about?" Erik asked.

Befel just shrugged.

"Who cares?" Bryon said. "Just make sure the horses are ready so I don't have to listen to Switch whine and complain and curse us."

Moments later, the mercenaries and the dwarves walked over to the stables and the other two dwarves—Demik Iron Thorn and Nafer Round Shield—were introduced. Both had long beards like Turk, although Nafer shaved his mustaches and his hair was a bright blond in contrast to the deep, reddish browns of the other two. As they bowed low again, Befel heard Switch groan, and the look on the slight man's face showed irritation.

"They wish to travel with us," Vander Bim explained, "join forces, I guess you could say. They have already been quite invaluable in reevaluating our travel plans."

"Oh?" Befel asked.

"It seems entering the Southern Mountains here," Vander Bim said, turning and looking to the gently rolling hills of the Western Tor, "would have been a fatal mistake."

"Assuming you can trust them," Drake muttered, and Turk's

bulbous nose scrunched and his bushy brows pinched atop dark eyes.

"And so where do we go, then?" Befel asked.

"Who cares?" Bryon whispered, and Befel looked over his shoulder, giving his cousin a hard look. It was ignored.

"We will follow the Southern Mountains to Aga Min," Vander Bim replied. "From there, our new companions say they know of a secret, underground road that leads directly to Thorakest, the capital of Drüum Balmdüukr. It will let us avoid the many dangers of the mountains and afford us some dwarvish comfort part way through our journey."

"Comfort indeed," Switch whispered, his tone sounding very cynical.

"They have agreed to double your pay," Vander Bim added. "You will care for their things the way you are to care for ours. Agreed?"

Befel looked back at Bryon and Erik. His brother nodded slowly, and his cousin shrugged.

"All right," Befel said with a shrug of his own, and the dwarves bowed again before the six left the Eleodums to their work with the horses.

"I wonder why dwarves want to travel with us," Befel asked as he tightened the saddle of Vander Bim's horse.

"Maybe we look like an easy target," Bryon replied. "We certainly aren't employed by the best of the best here. They mean to kill us and take what we have."

"Doesn't sound like something dwarves would do," Erik said, dropping two haversacks at Befel's feet. "And we don't have anything to take."

"And how would you know what dwarves would and wouldn't do?" Bryon asked.

"I don't know," Erik replied. "How would you?"

Bryon shook his head and started cursing under his breath.

"I think I overheard them saying something about strength and safety in numbers," Erik said.

"That makes a little more sense," Befel said, and that was the end to their conversation until Switch and Drake came back.

"Why are we traveling with bloody tunnel diggers?" Switch asked, grabbing the reins of his horse from Befel without even looking at the young man.

"Strength in numbers," Drake replied, taking the reins of his horse and nodding at Befel. "That's what Vander Bim said. That's what the dwarves said."

"Blood and guts and queen's ashes," Switch cursed. "Strength in numbers. Did you see the one's mace? Bloody crack over the head with that thing. That's what'll happen. Sleep with one eye open, Drake."

"Do you think that's true?" Erik asked.

"Any one of those weapons would crack your skull," Bryon said. "That mace. The broadsword. Even—what was his name—Turk's ax. Did you see that thing hanging from his belt? That blade was big enough and sharp enough to sever through an apple tree in two swings."

"I'm sure they could kill us," Befel replied, "and quite easily. I don't know why they would join up with us just to kill us, though. I think maybe Switch is just superstitious. Doesn't seem like most men like dwarves. And perhaps the feeling is mutual."

"Sleep with one eye open," Bryon said. "That seems like good advice."

"Oi!" Switch called. "Let's go. You're wasting time standing there and talking. What am I paying you for?"

Befel turned to see the three men and the three dwarves waiting, ready to go.

"I don't think I like that man," Bryon grumbled as he walked by with his horse's reins in hand.

Chapter 45

A SCORE OF MEN, MOST unkempt looking, rode into Finlo via the Sea Born Road. Several days of hard travel wore on their horses, and they panted and coughed. Once they tied the animals to hitching posts in the center of the city, the men split up into all directions. They hurried down alleyways, into bars, main streets; all asking the same question: "Gypsies. We're looking for a band of gypsies, small by comparison. They came from the west, Waterton. Were they here? Where did they go?"

"Gypsies," a drunken man sitting next to a large tavern called *The Drunken Fin* muttered. "Gypsies are a strange folk, now aren't they?"

"You saw them?" Kehl asked, looking down at the man.

"Now, I see a lot of people, just sitting here. You know, watching people is one of my specialties. I watch them come and go, and I listen. Listening is another one of my favorites. I remember sitting next to a tavern much like this in Goldum listening to a group of gypsies…"

Kehl's hand around the man's throat cut him off. The slaver stood the man up, the drunk's face turning red.

"I don't give a bucket of shit about you or your stories. Answer me, or I will open you up from your balls to your throat."

The drunk nodded. Kehl released his grip. The man slouched a bit but remained standing.

"The gypsies," Kehl repeated.

"They're gone. They left almost as soon as they got here." The drunk gasped for air and rubbed his neck as Kehl opened his wool cloak a little, showing the man a long-bladed knife.

"But I know a man who would know where they went. He sometimes visits with the gypsies when they're here for a longer time. I think he may be friends with them. I don't know."

"His name?" Kehl spat.

"Kevon. His name is Kevon. He's a barber, just down there," he said, pointing a filthy finger. "Look for the tabard with the scissors."

"If you are lying to me," Kehl pushed the man hard against the wall and closed the gap between their faces, "I will be back."

Kehl hurried down the street, three of his men, including Fox, in tow. He found the shop and pushed the door open. The door hit the wall so hard that one of the small, square panels of glass that sat in the middle of the door broke. A man Kehl assumed to be Kevon looked up from his seat, his hand firmly holding someone's chin, his other hand hovering above the client's face with an unfolded straight razor.

"Can I help you?" the man asked curtly. Kehl nodded to his three men. They rushed into the store. Fox grabbed Kevon by the shoulders and pushed him against the wall. The other two slavers roughly grabbed the client and quickly tossed him into the street. The man stared at Fox through a pair of glasses that sat at the end of his nose. Kehl thought he saw a smirk cross the old man's face as Fox held him there.

"Are you Kevon?" Kehl asked.

"Aye." Kevon nodded.

"The gypsies ..." Kehl pushed Fox aside and came nose to nose with the barber.

"What about them?" Kevon replied.

"Don't play stupid with me," Kehl spat.

"Then don't ask stupid questions," Kevon retorted.

To that, Kehl drew his long-bladed knife and gripped Kevon's left wrist. He pressed it up against the wall and promptly removed the pinky finger on that hand. Kevon let out a low grunt and fell to his knees, gathering up a used cloth on the floor and wrapping his hand in it. He looked up at Kehl, face red, mouth contorted with pain.

"Now, before I remove any more appendages, where are the gypsies that came through here recently?"

"Gone," Kevon said. "They're gone, a week now. Left as soon as they came." Kevon rocked back and forth a little, groaning as the pain in his hand grew.

"Where?"

"I don't know," Kevon said. "They seldom make plans. They're gypsies, after all."

"A fingerless barber. What good will that be?" Kehl kicked the barber in the stomach and then punched him hard in the face. Kevon spat out a tooth.

"I helped a young man who had traveled with the gypsies. I know he stayed here after they left. He may know where they are."

"Where did he stay?"

Kevon didn't answer.

"I will burn this pile of rubbish down around you, old man." Kehl nodded to one of his men. The slaver grabbed a lantern off the wall and tapped it suggestively against the wood of the shop. Kehl waited a while longer, and when Kevon still didn't reply, he looked to his man again. The slaver lifted his hand high, lantern in tow, with the intentions of smashing it against the ground.

"Wait!" Kevon shouted. He clenched his teeth, squeezing his four-fingered hand hard. Spittle ran down his chin. "*The Lady's Inn,* on the eastern edge of the city."

Without another world, Kehl spun on his heel and walked back through to where they had left their horses. His three lapdogs following close on his heels, but not until there was the sound of shattering glass, accompanied by the din of a roaring flame. A woman somewhere down the street screamed, and another man called for water.

By way of forcing people to give him directions, Kehl made his way to *The Lady's Inn,* picking up several of his other men along the way. He motioned for them to follow until he pushed open the inn's door hard, the wood banging against the wall. A tall, fat, bald man looked up from his bar.

"You better have a good reason for barging in here like that."

"Three men, around this one's age," Kehl said as he grabbed the back of Fox's neck and pulled him so that the man behind the bar could inspect the red head. "Where are they?"

"A lot of young men his age come through here."

"No, not this inn," Kehl snapped, "but three in particular were here—and I want to know where they are."

"Don't know."

"Perhaps you would like to see your shit heap of an inn in flames like Kevon's shop," Kehl threatened.

The barkeep frowned. His hand moved underneath the bar.

"You think you're going to intimidate me?" the fat, bald man retorted. "I've dealt with worse and in larger numbers."

Kehl drew his long-bladed knife and nodded to two of his men. They moved forward, toward the innkeeper, one with a cudgel and the other with a short sword. The barkeep laughed and retrieved a huge ax from beneath the bar and struck his bar hard. The ax head sunk into the bar with a loud thunk. He pulled the ax loose, wood splintering when he did.

"I hope you're ready for a fight you won't forget," the innkeeper spat. "Those boys are gone."

Kehl put his hand up, and his men stopped. He squinted, studying the innkeeper. "What about the gypsies they were with?"

"Never saw 'em."

The barber had been easy to intimidate, but this man, he wouldn't be so easy to break. Kehl could ill afford to lose any more men and was sure he would before the fat man had had enough.

"You best watch your back, old fool," Kehl hissed.

"Always do," the innkeeper replied.

The slaver backed out of the inn, eyes trained the whole time on the man behind the bar. His men followed. Outside the inn, when they walked past the stables, he ran into a woman, blonde bun sitting atop her head, mascara and rouge smeared along her face in the humidity, clothes well-worn but good enough for a whore in the eastern part of Finlo.

"You looking for someone?" she asked, her voice a pretense of smoothness and sweetness.

"Out of my way, whore." Kehl pushed her aside.

"If you're looking for someone, I might be the person to ask."

Kehl stopped and turned on his heels.

"Go on," he said.

"For a price," she replied.

"I'll pay it," he said with a wry, malicious grin on his face. "I'm looking for three men. They're young, like this one." He pointed to Fox, who flinched when Kehl motioned toward him. "They were traveling with gypsies."

"I don't know about gypsies," the woman replied, "but there were three young ones here just yesterday. Wouldn't normally notice three young lads except for they were here, and the young ones normally stay in the center and west of town."

"Where'd they go?" Kehl softened his voice and closed the distance between him and the woman.

"I saw them leave with three other fellows," she explained. "A whole bunch of men gathered here just yesterday. They all looked like fighters. Adventurers, I guess. You'd think that sort would want to have a little fun, but hardly any of them did." She cursed under her breath and kicked a small mound of dirt in frustration. "Anyways, one of those boys, he was a mule-headed one, pompous and feisty that one."

"That sounds like Bryon," Fox whispered. Kehl gave the young man a sidelong glance over his shoulder.

"So where'd they go?"

"North," she said, "to Dûrn Tor. That's where a lot of them went."

"Good," Kehl smiled. "I thank your generosity."

He moved to leave, but the woman grabbed the edge of his cloak. He turned and glared at her, lips pursed, and eyes squinted. His gaze went from her dirty hands to her face and back to her hands. She let go.

"What about payment?" she pled. Kehl smiled again.

A short while later, Rory stood on the front step of his inn, watching the dust of twenty horses trail away in the distance. He shook his head.

"Boys, I hope you're long gone."

He walked to his stables, rake in hand, and started piling straw under the stable's roof. When he finished that, he took his shovel and began scooping horse apples into a large bucket. The shovel hit something soft underneath one particular pile of straw. He jabbed again and felt it. He bent low and saw a strand of blonde hair.

Rory pulled the woman out, brushing dirt and straw from her naked body. He recoiled at first, muttering about monsters. He scooped the dead prostitute into his arms, caring little for the blood that now soaked his apron.

"No matter what station in life," he said to himself, "no one deserves this."

He dug a hole some way away from his inn and placed the woman's body inside, covering her with what was left of her tattered dress. He thought he recognized her, but blood covered her whole body, and her face swelled so badly, he couldn't tell if she was whom he thought she was.

"Poor girl," he said as he covered her with dirt.

He wished he could have given her something better than this makeshift burial, but this would have to do. Chances were no one else would have cared enough even to give her this. He stuck his shovel in the ground and rested on the handle, huffing a little and thinking. He looked back toward the north.

"I hope you do find those boys, and I hope they give you what you deserve."

Chapter 46

"WATER," SWITCH SAID, HANDING ERIK a cup.

Erik grabbed the cup, looked at it, and then looked at Switch.

"Get me some damn water you fool boy!"

Erik nodded slowly, walked to his horse, retrieved a water skin, and filled the cup. He handed it to Switch. When he turned to walk away, he heard Switch clear his throat.

"More," the man said, handing his cup back to Erik.

"Are you serious?" Erik asked.

"Do I look like I'm bloody joking?" Switch asked, and Erik just stared at him. "Are you dumb, boy? Get me some more water."

Erik looked to his brother and cousin. Befel just looked back and shrugged, but the look on Bryon's face was one of anger, frustration, and irritation. His face grew red. He could tell he was breathing faster, and he saw him squeezing his fists. If Switch kept this up, then they might get very thirsty before they found more.

Erik nodded. He retrieved Switch more water.

"Are you going to want more?" Erik asked, after handing the man his cup.

"Yeah, I just might," Switch said with a smile on his face that made Erik want to punch him. "Am I making you mad?"

"No, not at all," Erik said with a feigned smile.

Switch laughed.

"I like this one," he said, sitting down and looking at Vander Bim.

Then he pointed at Bryon. "That one over there wants to hit me. I can tell. I guess I don't blame him. He likes to fight. I like to fight, too."

Bryon had turned around. Erik recognized the move. That's what Bryon did when he wanted to avoid an argument or fight, just turn his back.

"Can't imagine you winning too many fights," Bryon muttered. Erik didn't think he meant for Switch to hear him, but he did. The man laughed loudly and slapped his knee.

"That was a good one," Switch said, staring at Bryon with a smile that was certainly insincere.

"You'd be surprised. Growing up on the streets of Goldum, you have to learn to fight. Its kill or be killed. And even a little piss ant, gutter shite like me has to learn how to fight."

"You grew up in the east?" Erik asked. "In Goldum?"

"Aye," Switch replied. "The wonderful east. Grew up thieving and pickpocketing in Goldum. Was pretty good at it, too."

"You were nothing but a thief?" Bryon asked, but it also sounded like a derogatory statement.

"Aye, that's right," Switch replied, ignoring Bryon's tone of voice. "Until I decided to become a mercenary."

"Does anyone else need water?" Erik asked.

Everyone shook their heads, and Erik walked to the horse to return the waterskin. Standing there, he looked up to the sky and could see the faint outline of the moon.

"A damn thief," Bryon muttered, walking up alongside Buck and beginning to brush him. "We're employed by a damn thief. What do you think about that?"

Erik shrugged. "I don't know. Was Wittick any less a thief? Twice the work and less than half the pay. He may not have been a pickpocket, but I call that stealing."

"We have three more hours of light I think," Erik heard Vander Bim say, "and if we go another hour after sundown, that'll be a good day's travel."

"Three hours," Erik repeated. He still hadn't completely grasped the concept of an hour. Rory had tried to explain it to him. Count to a certain number, and that is a minute. So many minutes equaled an hour. And, supposedly, there were so many hours in a day. How could someone split the day up into *hours* and *minutes*? In the summer, the days were longer. In the winter, shorter.

The sun began to disappear to the west as they rode, and Erik watched the shadows lengthen along the ground.

"I hated nights like this back home," Erik said to Turk. The dwarf rode next to him.

"Oh," Turk asked, "how so?"

"There's just something about dusk," Erik replied, "that just seems so unnerving. It's not the daytime, and it's not quite night. The shadows look weird, and the animals don't know what to do. My grandmother used to tell me that this was the time of the day spirits chose to walk our world."

"Growing up in a city built inside of a mountain," Turk said, "it was the deep, darkness of night that always scared me."

"Midnight never bothered me," Erik said. "I love watching the stars."

"Ah, yes. Well, under the mountain, there are no stars. Only darkness," Turk said.

Just then, Erik's horse reared up with a scream. Erik almost tumbled off backward and had to grab a fistful of mane to keep himself in the saddle.

"Oi!" Switch cried. "Can't you control your horse?"

When the horse came back down, Erik looked to the ground and promptly vomited.

"What in the bloody nine hells?" Switch yelled but then threw his head back and covered his nose with his arm.

"Is that a man?" Erik asked, also covering his nose now and watching the ground.

A mist crept across the ground in dusky light, clinging to the horse's ankles and snaking through their legs. A warmth rose from that mist, hotter than the sun-filled day, and it carried the smell of carrion with it. The rot brought on a swarm of flies, hovering just above the ground, flittering in and out of the fog. The haze seemed to part just enough to reveal a nose, a forehead, an arm bent upwards as if reaching for the sky.

The mist dissipated as if the wind had kicked it away, and there lay a body, charred black. Both of the arms were bent at strange angles, elbows driven into the ground and hands in the air. Black skin flaked from the chest and arms, but the face—a man's face— remained flesh colored. His eyes stared upward in a fixed gaze, blank and meaningless, and his mouth lay open, stuck in a silent scream. His ribs lay bare, poking through burnt flesh.

"That used to be a man," Switch said, shaking his head.

"Isn't that one of the men that attacked The Messenger?" Drake asked.

"Aye," Vander Bim said, and Erik nodded in agreement, "See the deep cleft chin?"

"I think I found the second man," Demik, one of the dwarves, said in his rough, Westernese accent.

The guy with the beard wasn't burnt. His head was twisted completely around the other way, the skin on his neck stretched and mangled. His tongue hung limply from his mouth and rigor had set in on his body, hands clutching close to his neck, and his knees brought up to his stomach.

"Bandits?" Vander Bim asked.

"Slavers?" Erik asked, to which Bryon shot him a dirty look.

"What would bandits want with them?" Switch asked. "And slavers—why kill two men who might fetch a decent price?"

"These wounds are unnatural," Demik Iron Thorn said.

"What do you bloody mean, unnatural?" Switch asked, but Erik knew what Demik meant.

Demik said something to Nafer, the third dwarf, in their native tongue, a language that Erik couldn't help to think sounded hard, like the squatty, muscular bodies of the dwarves. Nafer replied and nodded. Turk said something as well.

"No weapon made these wounds. No hand of man either," announced Demik.

"Then what?" Erik asked.

"Magic," Turk said. "Dark magic."

Erik saw Drake shutter.

"You think magic did this?" Erik asked.

"I don't know what else could have," Turk replied.

"The Messenger did say they would get their due punishment," Vander Bim said.

"But we left before The Messenger of the East," Befel said, and the dwarves spoke amongst themselves, again in their own language.

"The Black Mage would be capable of this kind of magic," Demik said with a quick nod and spat. "Yes. This would be within his power. From some distance."

A low murmur rippled through the group of mercenaries and their porters.

"We have maybe an hour of light left," Vander Bim said, looking to the sky. "We need to get away from the dead. Away from this...darkness."

No one disagreed, but the sun had set, and the moon was fully in the night sky before they stopped. The stench of burnt flesh and the vision of twisted limbs still hung in Erik's mind, and he continued to feel his stomach twist. They had only stopped for a short while when Switch returned with several plump rabbits. The thief threw them in front of Erik.

"You skin those up, boyo," Switch said with a smile. "I'll make us a stew."

Erik stared at the rabbits for a while, remembering the ones he used to throw rocks at behind his father's barn at night. Tia had snuck out with him one time, and he remembered her giggle as the cotton-tailed creatures would scurry away as the stones bounced around them. The ones dead at his feet reminded him of his sister's toys, and he felt a sudden craving to be with her.

"What's the matter?" Switch asked, giving Erik a sincere look.

"Nothing," Erik replied, shaking his head. "Nothing. Sorry."

Erik skinned the rabbits while Switch boiled water over a fire Bryon had built, throwing in what looked like leaves and grass.

"What are you putting in there?" Erik asked.

"Pepper, mint, and some grass that tastes like lemons—it all grows wild around here," Switch replied. "Oh boy, this is going to be good."

It was good and, for the first time, Erik was glad for Switch. The man proved crass and crude in some ways but seemed quite resourceful. Even after he had eaten all the meat—he was sure he got less than Vander Bim and Drake, but possibly more than the dwarves—he drank the broth, which filled him, and he leaned back for a moment against his saddle and closed his eyes.

"Reminds me of home," he muttered.

"What was that?" Befel asked.

"This reminds me of home," Erik repeated, looking at his brother. "Mother's cooking, our family around the table."

"I suppose," Befel said. His voice sounded unconvincing and irritated.

"Does home really harbor so many terrible memories?" Erik asked.

Befel shook his head and shrugged slowly. "No. No, I guess not."

Erik closed his eyes but then sat up with a quick breath, his eyes shooting open.

"What's wrong now?"

"I don't know," Erik lied. "I close my eyes, and all I can see are burnt bodies. Dead bodies. Twisted bodies. All I can smell is burning hair and flesh. I can hear screaming."

"Really?" Befel asked.

"We've seen so much death, Befel," Erik said. "So much death."

"Don't worry," Switch said, apparently overhearing Erik and Befel's conversation, "you'll see more."

"Thanks," Befel said, "that is very helpful."

"Just trying to be honest," Switch said.

"I've never seen anything like that," Erik said.

"I don't think any of us have ever seen something like that," Turk replied. "I've seen many things but those men..."

The dwarf's voice trailed off as he stared into the campfire.

"The first time is always the hardest," Drake said. "I remember the first time I saw a dead man. It will pass. In the morning, you will feel better."

Erik nodded with a smile, but his thoughts went from two men, burnt and twisted, to a woman hanging from a great oak tree with a broken neck, slit throats and dead children at the hands of slavers.

"I've never seen something like that," Switch said, "but I've seen some pretty terrible things. In Goldum, my two mates—Shifty and Rat—died by the bloody smile."

"What's that?" Erik asked.

"Man slits your throat," Switch replied, "and pulls your tongue out. Looks like just that—a bloody smile."

Erik covered his mouth, and he saw his brother crinkle his nose as if he had smelled something bad.

"Who would do such a thing to another man?" Befel asked, but Erik thought of Fox and the leader of the slavers. They were certainly capable of such a thing.

"Here," Vander Bim said, uncorking a clay bottle and offering it to Erik, "have some apple rum. It'll make you feel better."

Erik took the bottle and poured some of it into his cup. It was strong and tasted of sour apples.

"Better?" Vander Bim asked.

Erik nodded, lying.

"Here," Vander Bim said. "Everyone have some. My own special recipe."

Erik sat back and savored the rum. Nothing would make him feel better. Nothing would rid his mind of the sight, sounds, and smells of death.

"Are you still thinking of home?" Befel asked.

His brother's voice woke Erik from a half-sleep. His eyes were closed, and he was trying, quite unsuccessfully, to erase the two dead men from his mind. Erik nodded.

"I suppose I am too," Befel said, "at least, a little. The good memories."

"There are no good memories from home," Bryon said.

Erik finally opened his eyes and looked at his cousin.

"You speak as if home was awful," Erik said. "You speak as if you never had a happy moment in your home."

"You didn't have to live in my home," Bryon replied quietly, as he sat and stared at the fire.

"Nights like this remind me of home as well," Drake said, and the firelight caught his teeth as the memory brought out a brief smile. "I remember sitting outside with my wife and children, staring at the stars. When you're mining in the Gray Mountains, you learn to appreciate the stars and the moon, a little light in the darkness."

"I know what you mean," Turk said, and Demik replied in their Dwarvish language. Turk nodded. "Aye. A vein of diamonds can certainly look like stars."

"Where were you a miner?" Erik asked.

"In Nordeth," Drake replied. "For many years before I started doing this nasty business."

"You just didn't want to mine anymore?" Erik asked.

"Mining is dangerous business," Drake explained. "More dangerous than this business if you could believe that. Every man in Nordeth has to serve in the militia. That's where I learned to fight, and I was good at it. Figured I could make a living doing this and, if I die, at least it's in the open, not under a mountain or by some dwarf's ax."

Demik Iron Thorn grunted at that, but Turk put his hand on his companion's arm, silencing him.

"You know, these nights don't remind me of home," Vander Bim said, "but they do remind me of nights on the ocean."

"You were a sailor, weren't you?" Erik asked. "Like Rory?"

"I was a sailor," Vander Bim replied, "but not like Rory. I never served in the navy of some nation. Just sailed on my own, working for merchants or sailing my own ship. I miss those times, in a way."

"Were you worried about dwarf axes on your ship also?" Befel asked. Even Demik laughed at that.

"No," Vander Bim said with a brief chuckle. "But sailing is still dangerous, very dangerous, in fact. Pirates, the weather, creatures that live in the deep darkness of the sea. Five years ago, a storm wrecked my ship, killed most of my crew, and I was damn lucky to be washed up on shore. That's the last time I ever sailed a boat. I met Drake in Finlo, protecting some Nordethian noble, and we've been working together ever since."

Drake patted Vander Bim on the shoulder.

"Here's to good memories," Drake said, lifting his cup.

"Good memories," Erik muttered, echoing to the response of everyone else. "Yes, good memories."

Chapter 47

TURK SAT QUIETLY, REVELING IN the warmth of the campfire. Shadows and light intermittently danced off his face, playing games with the many lines along his cheeks and forehead and highlighting or dimming the different shades of brown in his beard.

"What are we doing here?" Demik said in Dwarvish in case the men awoke. Turk shook his head and laughed softly. Demik did always prove a superstitious fellow.

"I don't know. I suppose we are here because of the very reason we told the men."

"We don't need their protection," Demik scoffed.

Nafer nodded in agreement, sipping on dwarvish ale from a hollowed gourd. As he righted the drinking vessel, the contents promptly hissed, and a bit of a foamy froth spilled over onto Nafer's hand from the small opening. The dwarf cursed silently, waiting for the ale to settle before pouring it into cups for his companions.

"Is this part of your fool idea?" Demik asked, hands on his hips in motherly, scolding fashion.

"Fool idea!" Turk exclaimed as quietly as he could. "A fool idea with which you and Nafer went along."

"It made more sense than what Belvengar was preaching," Nafer suggested, smacking his lips and sighing satisfactorily.

"We take the map to King Skella," Turk said, "find the city for him, and return whatever it is the Lord of the East wants, all the while proving that men and dwarves can work together."

"Anything the Lord of the East wants can be of no good to us in his hands," Demik said.

"No," Turk replied, "but with the lost city in our hands, and its treasure, I would say the scales weigh heavily in our favor."

"What about this so-called mission in general?" Demik asked. "How can we be so certain we will find the city first?"

"Do any men know the Southern Mountains as well as we do?" Turk asked, to which both his companions—Demik clearly reluctantly—gave a quick shake of their heads. "And if we don't find this treasure for the Lord of the East first, we still have a map to the city. We will give the map to King Skella, and within a day, he could have a whole regiment of warriors cleaning and setting things straight and making the city ready to repopulate."

"And the men?" Nafer asked.

"An alliance with men is crucial," Turk replied. "We must show our people, and the men, that we can work together, as we did in the past."

"And how do we do that?" Demik asked. "The short one doesn't trust us, and the Goldumarian is a thief—we can't trust him." He pointed to Drake, curled up next to his saddle, and Switch, sprawled out in front of his and snoring loudly. "I think the sailor is a good man, but that's like saying the sour milk isn't too sour."

"No, my friend, it's not them who we must convince," Turk replied. "It's the young ones. They are the future of our people. Especially that one."

Turk nodded to Erik.

"I don't know," Demik muttered. "I agree with Belvengar more and more every day. You've lived with men longer than both Nafer and I. You've seen their treachery."

"Aye, I have," Turk said, a contemplative look on his face, "and I love our brother dwarf Belvengar Long Spear, but I think he is a bit misguided. I have seen great love in the hearts of men as well, room for true compassion, and acts of extreme mercy. We, more and more, retreat to our mountains, secluding ourselves from the rest of the world."

"Aye," Nafer replied, "but what does the rest of the world have to offer us? What does the world expect of us?"

Nafer waited a little while, but neither Turk nor Demik answered. Perhaps Turk thought it a rhetorical question. Perhaps he knew the answer, knew the sadness of the answer and simply chose not to acknowledge it.

"Smiths and Mercenaries," Nafer answered himself. "And we have done both. My question is, will we even be welcome in our own city after selling ourselves as soldiers to the highest bidder?"

"We have worked as mercenaries with a certain level of morality, I think," Turk replied.

The irony of it was that he felt the same way. A dwarf spent twenty years training to be a warrior, training to be the perfect soldier, training to operate in any climate, any situation. To take that knowledge and sell that loyalty to the highest amount of coin did not sit well with most dwarves. What would his father say? What would his grandfather say? Thank An, the Creator, they would not be there to see him shamed by his choices in the lands of men. Was Demik right? Was Belvengar right to distrust men—hate them even, want to kill them? No.

"No, we have worked within those laws An has set before us and the ethics which we know should guide our lives."

Turk thought back on a wealthy landowner from Kamdum, who had employed their services as bodyguards. He seemed an all right fellow and seemed to appreciate the certain skills the dwarves brought to their job. They seldom had to use them. He treated his servants well, and the people who lived around his estates didn't harbor ill will toward the man. Truly, it seemed a seldom occasion that the dwarves, Belvengar Long Spear—their companion who chose not to join them on this mission—included, had the opportunity to work for an employer from the Northern Kingdom of Gol-Durathna.

They delighted that the lands in which they worked should, by all rights, be dwarf friendly, the Northern Kingdom being a longtime ally of Thrak Baldüukr and the dwarves of the Gray Mountains. For an entire year, they worked for and lived with the Baron—that's what he often called himself—Geyus, living in his home and protecting him and that which was his. Truly, most of the wealth Turk and Demik and Nafer now possessed came from their short time employed by that fellow.

However, in the winter of their second year as Geyus' bodyguards, the Baron called Turk to his room. The dwarf complied, even though it proved the middle of the night. When he reached his employer's room, he fell to his knees when he saw a scene that would probably haunt him for the rest of his years. Unbeknownst to the dwarves, Baron Geyus had a special liking for younger men and women. They would come to him in the middle of the night; he would do what he wanted with them, and they would leave before the first morning light. In fact, most of his retinue of servants and bodyguards had no knowledge of this particular obsession. This night, however, something had gone wrong. Turk never stayed to find out. Two bodies— those of a man and a woman perhaps Erik's age—laid before him, bloody and beaten beyond recognition. When the Baron asked Turk to dispose of the bodies, he wrapped his hands around Geyus' neck and tried to squeeze the life from the man before he hurled him across the room in disgust. Turk gathered his things, along with his companions, and before the sun had crested the eastern horizon, they had left Geyus' estates.

That proved only one example of the many times they left or simply turned down, employment as soldiers or bodyguards because of something they deemed as immoral.

"Regardless of what level of morality we've conducted ourselves, our brethren will see us as what we are: mercenaries, nothing more," Demik said.

"Nevertheless, if something doesn't change," Turk said, "we will eventually retreat to our mountains completely, and then what? We will be no better than the elves, secluded in their forest kingdom of Ul'Erel."

"Hold your tongue!" Nafer hissed as loudly as he dared, pointing an accusatory finger at Turk. "How dare you compare us to those oath breakers?"

"Hush." Demik grabbed Nafer's hand and lowered it. "Peace, brother. Peace."

Nafer took another drink of his ale.

"We should get to bed," Demik suggested. "It is late. We have traveled hard, and another long road awaits us. I think fatigue is wearing on our nerves."

Turk nodded and watched his friends slouch down against their saddles and slowly drift to sleep. He sat there, though, watching the flames of the campfire. They fluttered and flickered, and the wood popped from time to time, sending bits of red ember into the air, their glow quickly dying in the coolness of the night. He stared at his hands, worn and callused. He squeezed them, balling them into white-knuckled fists, and then opened them again, watching the blood flow back into his palms.

"Father," he muttered, "I am sorry for the shame I have brought our family. I only wish I had a brother to honor our family where I have not."

He continued to watch the fire, the growing shadows on his face mirroring the shadow growing in his heart.

"An, Creator and Almighty," he prayed, "give me the strength to do that which you would have me do and not what my own heart desires."

He kept his eyes closed, allowing the intermittent warmth of the fire to wash over him, and then the coolness of nighttime breezes to do the same.

Chapter 48

A RUMBLE RIPPLED THROUGH THE hills of the Western Tor. The older guard at the gates of Dûrn Tor looked south and saw a clear sky. An eyebrow painted with gray rose into a pronounced arch. He gave an exaggerated huff.

"Bonn, did you hear that?" the other guard—a much younger man—asked.

Bonn glanced at him over his shoulder. That look and a simple grunt gave his affirmation.

"Thunder?" the other guard, Trimble, asked.

Bonn's head slowly moved side to side. He stared, one eye squinting under his bushy eyebrows, the other watching carefully. The sound rolled along the hillside again.

"Hooves," Bonn grumbled.

"What was that?"

"Hooves," Bonn snapped. He gave Trimble a sidelong glance and then looked forward again.

A dust cloud swirled into the air, and dark silhouettes broke the horizon. Men. Horses. Hooves.

⟡

Kehl rode hard, not concerning himself with his men, toward the gates of Dûrn Tor, men and women rushing out of his way. Two guards—one old and gray, the other young—stood in front of the

242

city's gate. A thin, menacing smile crept across the slaver's tanned face. This would be easy.

Kehl pulled up on his reins.

"Kilben," Kehl said to his younger brother, "stay here with the men."

"Yes, Im'Ka'Da," Kilben replied.

Kehl smiled when he rode to the two guards, both leveling their spears and keeping that much distance between them and the company of slavers.

"You can't come into the city," the older guard said before Kehl could offer a salutation, make a demand, or say anything at all.

Kehl growled and squinted his eyes. He pushed the cowl of his cloak back. Most men recoiled at the sight of his dark eyes, his oiled, pointed beard, and his snarling whitened teeth. Perhaps his look seemed devilish, wolfish, but the guard didn't move, didn't even notice a change in the slaver. Kehl would kill him first.

"We're looking for gypsies," Kehl snarled.

The older guard just stared at the slaver, the blade of his spear level and steady. Kehl noticed the younger guard glancing at the graying man.

"Did you hear me, fool, or has age deafened you?"

The older guard stayed where he was, not moving and not speaking. When Kehl looked back to Kilben and then cleared his throat, the soldier spoke up.

"I hear just fine, and I heard you just fine. No gypsies here. Haven't seen gypsies in months. Wouldn't let 'em into the city if I did see 'em."

"What about three younger men?" Kehl asked. "They would've come with three other men, fighters, soldiers perhaps. They would've come—"

The guard cut Kehl off. "A bunch of soldiers came through here a day or so ago, coming from Finlo along the Sea Born Road. What about 'em?"

"I'm looking for three of them."

"Don't know. Plenty more than three came through here," the old soldier said, his voice quick and curt.

"I understand that," Kehl hissed. "Let us through. Let us search the city. These men owe me something."

"Don't care," the guard spat back. "No one enters the city unless cleared by the Council of Five. That includes the lot of ya, no matter how tough you try to look."

"You don't want to know what happens if you don't let us through," Kehl replied, grinding his teeth. "Let us through."

"You're in no position to bark orders at me, son," the older guard seethed.

Kehl hissed and buried his heels into his horse's ribs. The animal stepped forward, but the younger guard thrust his spear outward, the steel point stopping just the length of a fly's wing from Kehl's throat. Kehl's head never moved, but he pulled on his mount's reins.

"We let none of 'em in." The grizzled, old guard squinted at Kehl with one eye. "Just like we're letting none of you in. They all stayed at *The Hill Giant*. Go check there." The guard then smiled, a wry, old smile that stretched some of the wrinkles around his mouth. "And if there's any trouble, well, you don't wanna know what'll happen."

Kehl looked over his shoulder. Kilben stared back, waiting for his brother's move. The captain of the slavers huffed through his nose and pulled on his reins to turn his horse. He trotted to the tavern and jumped from his mount without even tying the reins to a post. His men followed suit, Kilben close on his heels. One glare from the slaver caused *The Hill Giant's* stable boy to wish he'd never got out of bed.

Kehl burst through the door of *The Hill Giant*, the doors slamming into the wall and the lively conversations stopping. A woman, her fat body, short and round, weighing her down, ran to the front. She breathed hard and sweat trickled down her cheek when she curtly greeted the men.

"Now see here," the old, fat woman yelled, "you won't just come barging into Elena Minx's tavern like that."

Kehl drew a curved sword in response. Elena Minx backed away a bit, but no fear showed on her face.

"Think you're the first idiot to draw a sword on me?" she barked, "If you get past me—and that's a big if—then you'll have to deal with Tuc and Boz."

Two large men, one of them with a reddening, bald head, stood in front of the bar, large cudgels studded with iron in their hands. A young serving woman, soft-faced, large breasted, and round-bottomed, held a thin-bladed belt knife in one hand and a simple kitchen knife in the other. Even the cook left the confines of his kitchen, cleaver fresh with animal blood gripped tightly and ready for more.

Kehl lowered his blade.

"We're looking for gypsies, a band of them."

"No gypsies 'round here," the older, fat woman replied.

She's lying. She had to be lying. They all had to be lying. Kehl would have to deal with that later.

"We're also looking for six men, then," he said, insistence and impatience in his voice. "Three would be young, twenty years at the oldest, and three would be soldiers or fighters, experienced men."

"Don't know," the fat woman replied, "but everyone who stayed here went north, along the Sea Born Road."

"You better not be lying to us," Kehl hissed.

"And what if I was?" the woman replied. Other patrons in *The Hill Giant* stood, some with nothing but forks or their fists, and some with long-bladed knives or swords or clubs.

Kehl's face grew red, and the grip on his sword tightened to white knuckles. In an instant, he could remove her head, but that wasn't his goal right now. He threw a copper penny, more for insult than anything else, on the floor in front of the fat woman, and he and his crew left, mounted their ragged steeds, and rode north along the Sea Born Road.

"After we find them," Kehl said to Kilben, "we'll come back here and burn that tavern down around that old bitch."

❧

If it hadn't been for her weight, Elena Minx would have stormed past her stables, hands clenched in white-knuckled fists, face red and sweat trickling down her fat cheeks. She headed straight for Bonn, and when she called out his name, the old guard slowly turned, one eye still squinted. Before he could say anything, Elena brought her right fist hard against his weathered jaw and the left one into the middle of his chest.

"Damn it, woman!"

"What, by the Creator and the Shadow and everything in between, gave you the bright idea to send those bloody bastards to *my* inn?"

Trimble stepped back. He once saw a man do just what Elena Minx did to Bonn. He was a foreigner, a man from somewhere in Antolika trying to make his way through to Finlo. Trimble couldn't remember what the two argued about, but the argument turned sour, and that foreign fellow, a man half Bonn's age, hit the old guard so squarely in the jaw, the young guard thought his head might fall off. Bonn had just stood there, unflinching. The next thing Trimble remembered was that Antolikan riding away, half hunched over the horn of his saddle, cradling a broken arm, with a piece of cloth stuffed up both nostrils to stem the bleeding.

Bonn just shrugged at Elena Minx.

"You're a fool," she spat.

"My love," he said, his cold, hard voice seasoned over a lifetime of fighting and drinking softened to a cloudy basket of soft down and rose petals, "you're so callous sometimes."

The old guard's wife glared through a squinted eye, but then, as the old man pouted, lost her glower and rubbed his chest where she had punched him.

"I'm sorry," she said quickly, so no one else might hear the apology.

"You didn't tell them, did you?" Bonn's face looked worried.

"Of course not."

Bonn nodded with a smile.

The old guard knocked on Dûrn Tor's gate with the butt of his spear. The slender covering of a small window in the tall, wide, thick door slid open. A pair of blue eyes peered at Bonn, and the window slid shut with a quick snap. Trimble heard the iron latches and locks of the city's gate and wood creak in thunderous form as the doors opened. Two other guards stood on the other side. Behind them was Bo.

"They're gone," Bonn said.

"My thanks, old friend," Bo replied. He always had a smile on his face. Trimble found that interesting. Every time he saw the gypsy, he smiled—and it was a genuine smile, not one of pretense.

"No thanks are needed." Bonn put up his hand while Elena and Dika embraced, tears in the latter woman's eyes. "Your people have been friends to us here in Dûrn Tor for many years, long enough that you deserve the same protection we would give our own citizens."

Chapter 49

THE SUN HAD RISEN A hand's span and then half again into the morning sky when Erik, Befel, and Bryon finally finished packing the camp and gave a nod to Vander Bim to let him know they were ready to go.

"A late start," Drake said.

"Aye." Turk had been up before the sun even broke the eastern horizon. "A late start."

"I'm glad we're getting to a late start this morning," Erik muttered to Befel. "I slept well last night."

"Enough sleep when you're dead, lad." Vander Bim walked past the young man, saddle in hand. He threw the heavy leather onto his mount's back, the horse snorting and twitching as it felt the weight. Vander Bim winked at him with a smile on his face.

"You'll get a tongue lashing from Switch if he sees you letting Vander Bim saddle his own horse," Bryon said, on his knees stuffing a blanket into his pack.

"Where is Switch?" Erik asked.

"I haven't seen him at all this morning." Befel scratched his chin.

"I haven't seen him either," Vander Bim said.

"Nor have I," Turk added, also saddling his horse.

"He's an odd fellow," Erik said.

"I don't like him," Bryon said softly.

"He's a thief," stated Turk as he brushed some dirt from the side of the wicked, half-moon blade of his battle-ax and then slapped the steel hard against the palm of his hand with an approving grunt and a satisfactory smile. "He's unreliable and unpredictable. But, he is also deadly. I would be careful around him."

"He'll have to catch up," Vander Bim said from his saddle. "We can't afford to delay any longer."

Erik could tell they rode slower than they had the day before, and that they took more breaks than usual as well.

He's worried about Switch, Erik thought, watching Vander Bim scan the western horizon during one of their breaks.

He heard the dwarves speaking in their own language. It sounded like they were arguing, but their faces showed otherwise. It must've just been their language.

"Nafer hears hoof steps," Turk said.

"Is it Switch?" Drake asked.

"I see something," Turk said, shielding his eyes from the sun with a hand.

Only a moment later, the shaggy, gray-haired head of Switch creased the horizon.

"Where have you been, damn it?" Vander Bim asked as Switch got closer.

"Scouting," Switch said, waiting a moment to get a little closer. "And it's a good thing, too."

He pulled hard on his horse's reins, the animal jerking its head and neighing loudly.

"What do you mean?" Vander Bim asked.

"We're being followed," Switch replied.

"Followed? By who?" Vander Bim asked.

"A group of men—a score that I counted," Switch replied.

"How do you know they are following us?" Turk asked.

"I just do," Switch replied. "I saw them sifting through the ashes of our camp from a day ago."

"What did they look like?" Vander Bim asked.

"They looked well taken care of—at least most of them. A couple of them looked Samanian—all brown-skinned and oiled beards," Switch grumbled.

"What could they want with us?" Drake asked.

"I don't know," Switch said with a shrug.

Erik stared at his hands. He looked to his brother and cousin, then back at his hands. They shook. Goose pimples crept along his arms, and despite the warmth of the day, he shivered.

"Who are they?" Turk asked.

"Bandits," Drake said.

Switch shook his head.

"Other mercenaries, maybe," Vander Bim offered.

"Twenty of them?" Switch asked with a hint of sarcasm. "I didn't recognize any of them from Finlo."

"Slavers," Erik muttered.

"What was that?" Drake asked.

"Shut up," Bryon hissed.

"Nothing," Erik replied. He had said it too loud. "It was nothing."

"No," Drake snapped. "It wasn't nothing. What did you say?"

Erik looked to Bryon and Befel. Both were shaking their heads. Befel closed his eyes and rubbed his forehead with his finger and thumb. Bryon glared, eyes squinted. Erik dropped his chin to his chest and sighed.

"When we were traveling with the gypsy caravan down to Finlo, we had a fight," Erik said. "Slavers from the Blue Forest attacked us, and we helped fight them off—killed quite a few."

"Killed quite a few slavers, did you?" Switch said with exasperation. "But left quite a few alive, as well!"

"We fought for our freedom," Erik said. "Any man would do the same thing."

"Aye," Switch said, "any man might fight, but slaver—if you don't kill every last one of them you might as bloody well just slit your own damn throat."

"What would they care?" Befel asked.

"What would they care!" exclaimed Switch. Then he scratched his chin as if it seemed to be a legitimate question.

"Listen, these aren't simple thieves or bandits—these are slavers. Most thieves have no loyalties. I bloody well know. Simple, bottom feeder forest thieves even less. But slavers, well, they're an odd bunch. They have weird allegiances to one another. Their leaders break them, make them believe they're nothing, and then, build them up again like a bloody army or something like that. After that, they would die for their leaders and their company. They act like brothers."

"They were a large company, though," Bryon said. "What would they care if a few of them died?"

"If someone killed your brother, what would you do?" Switch asked with a huff.

"Seek revenge," Bryon said dejectedly.

Switch just nodded his head with sarcasm.

"Can we outrun them?" Drake asked.

"We could, but we would have to run fast." Switch took a quick drink from his waterskin and smacked his lips with a satisfied sigh. "What about our mission? If we concentrate on outrunning these fools, we forget about the real goal here. Blood and ashes and pig guts."

"What about negotiating?" Vander Bim said. "Maybe we could hide the porters."

Switch laughed.

"First of all, slavers are savvy trackers. If they've been trailing us, they'd know we were lying about our numbers. Secondly, slavers don't negotiate. They enslave or kill. And I tell you, any slave trader would pay a good amount of coin—a flaming good amount of coin—to get his hands on a dwarf, let alone three." Switch scratched his chin. "Say, I have an idea. Why don't we sell the tunnel diggers to the slavers, let them kill the porters, and be on our way."

Demik grumbled, his hand sliding slowly to the handle of his broadsword. The smile on Switch's face told pretense, but Erik couldn't be sure. Behind that smile sat a deviousness he didn't like, a malicious undertone that said if he really thought he could get away with such a plan, he would do it.

"What do we do then?" Vander Bim asked.

"Besides get rid of these three idiots." Switch glowered at the young men, his smile quickly fading. "I don't know. But they're pissed."

Nafer spoke to Turk in his own language, and Turk nodded.

"We stand and fight." Turk smacked the broad side of his ax with the palm of his hand. "We should stand and fight."

"I think we'll have to," Switch said. "We've got no bloody choice. Damn it. No bloody choice."

"We will ride up to there." Switch pointed to a group of tall hills, not quite as big as most of the jutting cliffs but big enough to hide half a dozen men. "That will be a good place to hide until the right moment."

"Agreed," Turk said.

"And we will hide the horses farther back," Vander Bim suggested.

Turk also nodded.

"Should someone stay with the horses, just in case?" Drake asked.

"The commotion will scare any predators off," Turk said, shaking his head.

Erik stared to the west as if he could see the oncoming slavers. He saw them. Every time he closed his eyes, he saw them. He saw the dead eyes. Even the living ones had dead eyes. Void of intention except inflicting more death and misery. Vacant of any normal, human ambition. Dead. He also saw Marcus when he closed his eyes. Why couldn't he remember Marcus the way he wanted? Instead of playing his flute and laughing, why did he see him bloodied, struggling for breath, and in and out of consciousness.

Erik saw his brother jerk his head sideways. The others began leading their horses into the hills.

"There's a small hill dotted with ash," Switch said, about an hour later, "just another hundred, maybe hundred and fifty paces away. That's where we'll hide the horses."

Turk and the others nodded.

"Come help me with the horses," the thief said to Befel.

While the others prepared for a fight, picking out good hiding places behind tall hillocks and boulders, Switch and Befel led the horses to the southern side of a shallow mound covered in thin, short, sparse white ashes. They tied the horses to the trees. While Befel worked on the last horse, Switch grabbed his shoulder hard and spun him around. Even though the thief stood a good head shorter than Befel, the farmer felt tiny next to him, felt like he looked up to the Goldumarian.

"If it were just you and me, my son, I would tie you up and leave you for those bloody cutthroats. I have half a mind to do it, but the sailor and miner wouldn't be none too pleased with me. Count your blessings it's not my decision because if it was you and me."

He then turned and ran back to their companions. Befel let him get several paces ahead before he let out a loud sigh. He shivered and rubbed his forehead with the back of his hand. How could such a small man intimidate him so? He envisioned himself punching Switch in the face, cracking that already crooked nose. The farmer shook his head and cursed himself silently. It would never happen.

"What's the plan, dwarf?" Vander Bim asked. He knelt next to Turk, broadsword in hand, head ducked low.

"The thief will be with me," Turk replied. "As the enemy closes in, he will strike with his bow. You should be able to take two, maybe three, before they reach us, yes?"

Switch nodded. Turk shivered at the thief's smile. Evil. Demonic. Malicious at best. Did death and killing truly excite him that much?

Turk pointed to a slightly smaller hill several paces away.

"Drake and Demik will hide behind there and then attack the rear when he fires his second shot. This will confuse the slavers. When they have stopped and begin to turn and fight, I will lead the thief and Bryon. On the first swing of my ax, Nafer will lead the rest to strike the middle. An willing, our skill will overcome numbers."

Turk looked to the sky, then to Befel and Erik, the young men that served them as porters. They looked scared—not shivering or shaking, but unnerved.

"Are you ready to earn your pay?" Turk called to them with a smile.

Erik nodded, and Befel sighed.

"I hope so," Turk muttered. "I truly hope so."

Chapter 50

"They are coming," Drake called.

"Are you ready, thief?" Switch gave Turk a half smile and responded with a nocked arrow and a bowstring pulled tight. Turk nodded. "Remember, two to three arrows and then wait for Demik and the others to attack."

Switch gave a yellow-toothed smile. Turk wished he could trust the man, wished he gave him comfort, but all he did was worry him.

Turk slid a mail shirt over his brightly colored tunic. He patted his chest with the sound of clinking steel. He felt a small smile creeping underneath his beard and couldn't help but feel a bit childish.

"Suddenly, I feel naked," Bryon said. Turk saw him eyeing his mail shirt. "Here I am, just in a shirt and a leather jerkin."

Turk watched as Bryon looked down at the jacket of soft leather, its sleeves tied to the jerkin by sun-stiffened laces.

"Perhaps I will make you such a shirt, one day," Turk said.

"Really?" Bryon asked. "You would do such a thing for me?"

"Sure," Turk said with a shrug. "I feel An has brought our paths together. If so, it would be an honor to give you such a gift."

"An?" Bryon asked.

"Aye. The Creator. It means *The One*, in our language."

"Oh no, not you too." Bryon shook his head.

"What do you mean by that?" Turk asked.

"My cousins," Bryon replied. "They always try to talk to me

about a Creator. My uncle tried talking to me about a Creator. My father—even when he was drunk on brandy—tried talking to me about a Creator. I'm not interested in someone or something else running my life."

Turk tried to force out a smile. He hoped his glare didn't look too hard. He had heard Bryon's argument before.

"Ah, many men I have met have said the same thing."

"And that upsets you?" Bryon asked.

"Yes, of course."

"And you dwarves, you are so sure of the existence of this... An?"

Turk felt his head move slowly from side to side. "No. Many of my own kin have the same doubts. My own father struggled with the belief of An. I only hope..."

Bryon stared intently, and Turk hadn't realized his pause had lasted so long.

"You only hope what?" Bryon asked.

"Nothing," Turk said. "Nothing."

I should've been there, father. I should've been there, to say prayers with you. I'm sorry. I should've been there.

Turk heard a familiar whistle. He looked to the third hill, behind which Demik hid. His friend held up a hand. They were near.

"Don't worry," Switch said to Bryon. "I don't believe in any of that bloody nonsense either. All that talk about a creator and good versus evil." Switch stole his eyes from their gaze just over the hill for a moment to look Bryon in the face. "It's a fool's story to comfort little children at night because they can't stomach the notion of not existing if you ask me."

Bryon nodded, not feeling that comfortable agreeing with a man he had despised.

The thief returned his stare to the field that made up the feet of the Southern Mountains but went on talking.

"Eternity and paradise and all that sound good, but I have a feeling that's not where I would be going." Switch chuckled. "It's just tales, and if there really were a god up there that created everything, then why would the world be so bloody terrible? Most people, if they have the unfortunate luck of being born and the good luck to survive birth, live short, meaningless lives. And those lucky enough to be rich just take advantage of everyone else. Then what about slavers? Why would a god let bloody bastards like that exist?"

Bryon just shrugged.

"He wouldn't." Switch's face turned to a quick scowl.

"So what happens if you die today?"

"What do you think happens?" Switch asked.

"I don't know."

"Nothing." Switch looked at Bryon again. His mouth sat straight, his eyes level. "Nothing bloody happens. You become food for the vultures and crows and wild dogs and worms."

"So." Bryon stopped and thought of his question for a moment. "Are you afraid that you might die then?"

"I do like living…most days," Switch replied with a wry smile. "But live or die, it's all the same to me. We all die someday. Today. Tomorrow. A week from now. Forty years from now. We live and die, and after, we don't matter anymore, and we're not around to care about it."

Bryon frowned. He felt a thick knot in his stomach.

"Don't be worried," Switch added. "You'll be fine. Fight well, and you'll live to see tomorrow."

Bryon would have liked to believe him, but then who could be so sure?

❧

To Erik, the wait seemed to be forever as he stared at the hill that sat in front of him. He closed his eyes briefly, and his mind filled with blackness and death and faces twisted in pain. He opened them quickly, but the images lingered. Marcus, Nadya, the slavers—crude outlines of those killed in the battle—both good and evil—hung in the air, right in front of his face.

Then the sound of galloping horses, iron-shod hooves slamming hard into the earth, filled his ears, and it was as if it had always been there. The echo drummed through the cliffs and hills of the Southern Mountains and sounded like a never-ending explosion, a thousand mallets striking skin stretched tight. Sweat dripped down Erik's forehead and off his nose. He gripped his sword hard and that all too familiar knot in his throat grew hard. His breathing quickened, and he felt the arteries in his neck thump hard against his skin.

If he had given in to the burning desire to allay his fears with weeping, this would not have been a quick cry after a mother's scolding. No, this was deep and mournful, a fear-laden sorrow like that he remembered feeling when his grandfather had lain in bed sick for weeks. He knew his grandfather had lived a long life and welcomed whatever might come and bade his family to do the same. Nevertheless, when his father delivered the news, when that pillar of the community, the solid rock of a family, walked into the house, eyes red, and cheeks streaked white with the salty trails of tears, Erik felt it then, as he did now.

Amidst the ensuing sorrow, amidst the shaking hands and quickened breathing, he felt a slight tug on his side, not a pain, but not pleasant. He looked down to see Marcus' jeweled dagger neatly tucked there, sitting in its golden scabbard. He looked up again, and once more felt a tug, like a little boy might pull at an adult's sleeve. He looked down again and saw only the dagger, but suddenly the shaking in his hands calmed. It didn't stop, but certainly lessened, and the knot in his throat subsided. His breathing slowed, and he was sure he felt...better. Not great. Not unafraid. Just better.

Before he could think about what had happened, he heard the now familiar whisper of Turk break through the deafening sound of hooves.

"Stay down," the dwarf mouthed. He then pointed to Nafer. He would tell them when to go.

Behind his hillock, Erik could hear one, two, three horses close in, then more. They seemed to slow. They knew they were here.

His breath quickened again. He watched Switch poke his head over his hill. He saw a thin smile creep along the thief's face. A man on the other side yelled, a voice Erik remembered. Another voice answered. Switch stood atop the knoll, bow in hand, arrow stretched and aimed.

Switch nodded to Turk, and the dwarf nodded back.

Switch's eye trained on one of the first horseman, and seconds later, with the whistle of steel and wood breaking the air, his arrow thudded into the chest of a gray-haired man. He rolled off the back of his horse, and before he hit the ground, another arrow took flight. It struck in the same spot, this time a yellowed-haired youth who squealed like a piglet as he slid off his saddle.

"Kill him!" yelled a tan-skinned, oily, black-bearded slaver. He pointed his curved blade at Switch and dug his heels hard into his horse's ribs.

When those words left his mouth, another arrow flew by his face. He winced. He touched his hand to his cheek. Crimson covered his palm. The thin red line just above his jaw trickled down to his chin. He slowed and looked back, over his shoulder. Another of his men sat, slouched over the horn of his saddle, arrow point poking through just to the middle of his shoulder blade.

Despite the slowing leader, the slavers closed on Switch, and Turk whistled to Vander Bim. The sailor, already moving into position, gave an affirming nod and he, Drake, and Demik rushed from their hill. Vander Bim slashed his sword across the back of an unsuspecting man, who screamed loudly before he fell from his horse. Drake plunged his pickax into another's chest, one who, hearing his companion's pain-filled cry had turned. Drake then wrenched his weapon back, pulling the man from his mount. He squirmed and fought as much as he could, but Demik stilled him with a heavy hack from his broadsword to the shoulder.

"Behind us!" yelled another man. He looked similar to the leader, only taller, broader. He spun his horse to face the three new attackers. "Kehl, it's an ambush!"

"Kill them!" yelled the leader again. "Kill them all!

Switch threw down his bow and drew two knives from his belt, Bryon and Turk running by him, yelling battle cries. Turk, his stout legs taking him faster into the fight than anyone could have imagined, hit one slaver's horse in the foreleg with his ax. The half-moon blade practically severed the limb, and the animal went down with a wrenching scream. The horse and its rider turned into a heap of tumbling flesh, and the sound of snapping bone and the quick cry of a man hushed by paralysis told Turk his attack did the job. Luckily, the mass of man and horse tripped up another rider going too fast to stop. That slaver crashed hard to the ground, and when he pushed himself to his knees, Turk was there to meet him with his ax to the neck.

Bryon nearly found his fight short-lived. A neatly carved club stopped just short of the young man's skull when a knife dug deep into his assailant's chest. When the slaver hit the ground, Bryon finished the job. He looked back, Switch gave him a quick wink, and he was back in the fray.

"There're only six of them, you fools!" screamed the slavers' leader. "Kill them! Kill them! Kill them!"

Just then, Befel, Erik, and Nafer ran from their hill. Bryon looked to his cousins. Befel caught Bryon's gaze and nodded. Bryon didn't know why, but he returned the favor.

Bryon looked over his shoulder. The thief had thrown one of his knives at an attacker, the short blade lodging in the man's chest. It didn't kill, but it was all the slaver could do to stay in his saddle, dropping his reins and grasping at the knife handle. Bryon rushed at the man, his long arms reaching the enemy. He gripped an elbow hard and pulled. Without a fight, the rider tumbled from his mount. He hit the ground hard, and before he could work to his knees, Switch stood behind him, blade poised at his throat, wicked grin on his face. With the quick jerk of his hand, a crimson line appeared across the slaver's throat, and his eyes went wide, his tongue lolling frantically as he gasped for air.

Both Bryon and thief looked to the man's horse.

"You know how to fight from horseback?" Switch asked. Bryon shook his head. "All right, then. I'll mount up, create some havoc, and you watch my back."

Bryon nodded. Within moments, he saw a slaver, bow in hand, eyes trained on the thief. He didn't think. He didn't have time to think. He saw how fast Switch fired three arrows. It must've been within a heartbeat. Bryon ran. He ran fast, as fast as he could. His legs pumped hard. He dodged several horses and slammed his shoulder hard into the ribs of the bowman's horse. It did nothing by way of injury—actually, it bruised Bryon's shoulder quite badly—but the horse jerked just enough so that the slaver lost Switch in his sights and loosed his arrow off target. Bryon took a step back, the man glaring at him with dirty brown eyes. Out of instinct, Bryon swiped his sword across the slaver's leg. He clutched the wound and seethed spittle through missing teeth.

"You little bastard," he hissed. His shaved head inked in red tattoos sweated profusely under the sun's heat. Before he could say another word, though, Bryon reached up, grabbed the man by his belt, and easily pulled him from his horse. The slaver hopped up faster than Bryon thought he would and easily jumped away from Bryon's ill-trained attack. The man drew his own sword and jabbed it at Bryon playfully, that smile of darkened gaps and blackened teeth glaring like a demon from the Shadow. Before Bryon could return the favor, he heard the sound of bone cracking and metal tenderizing meat. When the wide-eyed slaver fell forward, eyes filled with surprise, he saw Turk standing behind him, hands gripped hard on the handle of his half-moon bladed ax. The dwarf winked.

"Not that I thought you couldn't take care of him yourself," Turk said.

Bryon smiled, laughed. "Your help is appreciated."

Bryon swung at another rider making his way toward the horsed thief. That slaver turned quickly and, seeing a dwarf and a young man, laughed while he dismounted, club in one hand and curved sword in the other.

"Come on then, you pip with your furry rat," the slaver chided.

Turk groaned. With a thunderous roar, he rushed the man. He pushed the slaver back with the top of his ax, swung once with a miss, and then caught a glancing blow from the club while preparing to swing his half-moon blade again. The carved wood didn't seem to hurt the dwarf, but the slaver followed it with a foot to Turk's chest. Turk fell back, his ax falling just a hair's length from his reach. Bryon saw the look in the enemy's eyes and rushed in before he could pounce. He shouldered the man aside, knocking him off balance. He brought his short-bladed sword down, its tip scraping the man's wrist. He dropped his club with a yelp and gave Bryon a backhanded swing with his own curved blade. Bryon stepped sideways and then, noticing his weapon was shorter, moved in close. The slaver tried backing up, but Bryon stood not even an arm's length from the man and punched him in his nose. Cartilage cracked, and blood spilled. Bryon followed with a headbutt and a knee to the groin.

When the slaver fell to one knee, he dropped his sword and looked up to the young man, tears streaming down his cheeks, blood covering a thin blond beard on his chin.

"No, please, I surrender."

Bryon lowered his short-bladed sword for a moment. He had trained it over his head, ready to deliver a deathblow to the slaver's neck. But now—he didn't know. He knelt, defenseless, crying, pleading, begging, and groveling. Then Bryon remembered a woman hanging from an oak tree in the Blue Forest. He remembered three people discarded like trash. He remembered children crying for their mothers and mothers crying for their children.

He lifted his sword again.

"Bryon, he surrend—"

Before Turk could finish, Bryon brought his sword down hard. He felt iron hit bone. He swung again. He felt bone crack. He swung again. He felt bone give way to soft tissue. He swung again. His sword dug deeper. He spat on the corpse.

Bryon turned to Turk and helped his companion up. The dwarf looked at the mutilated mess, then at Bryon. His face was flat, emotionless. He didn't say anything. He didn't have to. Bryon knew what he would say. He knew what Turk was thinking.

When Bryon turned to find another slaver to fight, he caught a ways off, the glint of fiery red hair. Fox. He sat atop his horse next to the man Bryon presumed to be the slavers' leader. Next to him sat another man who looked to be his brother, only wider at the shoulders and a head taller.

"Ren!" Bryon shouted. Fox didn't hear him. "Fox!"

Fox saw Bryon, and his eyes grew wide, those icy, evil blue orbs stretching to their extent. He muttered something to the leader. The man looked at Bryon and nodded. Bryon ignored him. He only saw Fox. Fox pulled gently on his reins. Even his leader looked at him queerly. Bryon stepped forward, even though Fox sat a good fifty paces away. The fiery-headed man pulled a little harder. His leader said something to him. Fox ignored him. Bryon smiled.

"You know," he muttered to himself. "You know I'm going to kill you."

He caught the reins of an errant horse and pulled himself into the saddle. At that, Fox turned his mount and dug his heels into its ribs. His leader yelled after him, but he was already twenty paces away and riding hard. Bryon chased. He flicked the reins with deafening cracks and jammed his heels hard into the horse's side. The animal roared, coughed, and pushed its head forward, galloping faster and faster.

"I'm coming for you!"

Fox looked over his shoulder, saw Bryon gaining ground, and pushed his animal harder. Bryon passed the other two men. It seemed that, perhaps, they tried to stop him, but any attempt to swing a sword or club would've been in vain; he was traveling too quickly.

Fox pushed on faster, and Bryon could hear Fox's horse huffing.

He could hear the man breathing heavy, panting, and see his pale, freckled hand shake as he flipped his reins. He could touch the animal's tail, its flank—he was next to him. He gripped the reins hard and pulled himself into a crouching position on the horse's back before he loosed one foot from its stirrup, and then the other. He stuck his arm out to the side to balance and leapt.

When they hit the ground, Bryon's vision went black. He tried to fight it, to fend off the unconsciousness and knew if Fox was still alive, if he were awake, it would be Bryon who did the dying.

His eyes shot open to the blue sky overhead muddled with smoke and the sound of loudly neighing horses. Despite the pain wracking his brain, he turned on his stomach and pushed himself to his knees. He lost his sword for the moment, and then saw it, tip broken, blade bent completely sideways. He looked over his shoulder. There was Fox, lying motionless.

Bryon crawled to him. He grabbed Fox's shoulder hard and turned him onto his back, catching the wrist of the hand holding a long-bladed knife, aimed for his throat. Bryon shook the blade free and straddled the redheaded man, his weight pinning the slaver's hips to the ground. Fox's left hand, the one that had held the knife, gripped at Bryon's shirt. The other arm lay limply on the ground, twisted weirdly.

Bryon's eyebrows lowered, his teeth clenched, his face reddened, and his hands wrapped around Fox's throat. He squeezed.

The slaver fought hard with one arm. He raked at Bryon's wrist and arm, fingernails scratching away bits of skin. He pulled at the farmer's shirt. He tried to swing at him, but Bryon's arms were too long.

"Please, Bryon," Fox gasped. "I have money. I'll give it all to you. You can take all my money. Just let me live. Have mercy."

When he said that last thing, when he pleaded for mercy, Bryon only squeezed harder. "I'll take your money anyway—when you're dead."

Bryon squeezed harder and harder until even little blurting

grunts from Fox couldn't come through. He squeezed until the pasty, freckled face shrouded by red hair turned blue. He squeezed until Fox stopped kicking, until his good arm fell limply to the ground. He squeezed until the sheer strength of his squeeze forced blood from Fox's nose and mouth. Then he stopped. He stopped...and he cried.

Chapter 51

NAFER CRASHED INTO ONE SLAVER, unhorsed from the chaos. The man flew backward, hit the ground with a large grunt and thud, and when he looked up, the dwarf's vicious, spiked mace met his face. Nafer motioned to Erik and Befel, encouraged them to fight next to him. Befel raced in next to the dwarf, his younger brother close on his heels. The older of the Eleodums watched while one horsed slaver rode past Vander Bim, raking the thin blade of a long-handled wood ax along the sailor's ribs. The mercenary gave a sharp yelp and collapsed, the hind leg of his attacker's horse stepping squarely on the man's thigh. Befel left Nafer's side and raced to stand over the wounded mercenary.

Vander Bim rolled about under the young Eleodum, clutching both his side and his leg. The slaver who attacked him turned around, swinging his ax in wide circles and laughing at the young man holding his curved blade in two hands. He charged—Befel's heart missed a beat—and howled when the iron, pointed end of a pickax dug into his knee. Drake pulled his weapon free with a satisfied grunt, but before attacking again, the slaver turned his horse, its flank hitting the miner hard. Drake, under the force of the animal, fell to one knee. When he tried to rise again, the slaver's horse kicked out, striking the man square in the chest. The mercenary crumpled to the ground.

The slaver turned his horse. A grimaced snarl traced his pale face. Blood gushed from his knee and down his leg, forming a little red pool below his stirrup. The splotchy beard of dark hair exacerbated his ghostly look, with drawn cheeks and drooping eyes. Despite the pain, and despite weakness wracking his body, the slave trader heeled his animal with his good leg and charged at Befel. Every step the animal took looked excruciating for its rider, and only a few paces from the farmer—shaking and gritting his teeth as he readied himself for a fight—the man slid from his saddle and hit the ground with a hard thud. But he was not done for yet.

Befel refused to leave Vander Bim, so the slaver gathered himself up, standing awkwardly, one hand over his knee and one clutching his ax. He hobbled toward the young man, but only two steps in, a knife thumped his chest. His head rolled back, his hands released both knee and weapon, and the slaver fell on his back.

Befel saw Switch run by. Blood stained his shirt, and crimson smeared his face.

"Let's get bloody to it!" he yelled. He threw another knife at a horsed man. The thief cheered when the slaver gave a shrill cry, the blade lodging firmly in his shoulder. He ran to yet another victim and called to Befel, "The sailor will be all right. Get to fighting. We have them on their heels!"

Befel noticed one slaver back away from the fight, riding back to another pair, both with tanned skin and dark, oiled beards. He also watched an unhorsed attacker flee that way. They did have them on their heels. He felt excitement well up in him. His stomach seemed to bubble, his skin crawled with goose pimples, and he let out a yell.

Just then, the smaller of the two, tan-skinned men saw Befel and heard his cry of victory over the din of dying battle. Befel saw the man, clearly the leader, say something to the other beside him. He seemed to growl, his teeth bared, and Befel could not miss the words *"Kill him,"* and a wry, wicked smile grew on the second's face, and the broad-shouldered slaver kicked his horse hard in the ribs. Even as two more slavers fell back to their leader, the tan-skinned man raced toward him. Only paces away, the slaver dismounted at a run and stopped short of where Befel stood. He towered over the farmer, a good hand taller, with shoulders broader than most farmers'. When Befel stepped back, the slaver smiled, showing teeth well cared for, gleaming white. His canines looked sharpened, and with a pointed nose, a long chin, and dark, squinted eyes, he looked a wolf.

"You're one of them," he hissed.

"One of who?" Befel fought to answer the man towering over him. He looked like Marcus—only, a predator's eyes replaced those kind, gypsy eyes.

"One of the men." He smiled. "From the Blue Forest. With the gypsies."

Befel just stared. How could they have remembered him? Out of dozens of people—a hundred people—they remembered him?

"If you remember me, then you'll remember I killed a fair number of your kin."

"Oh, I wasn't there." The slaver laughed. "And any grunt you killed was no kin of mine. But my brother—"

Yes, they did look like brothers—this man and the thinner, slighter slaver with the same face, same skin, same beard. That skinnier man—Befel remembered him now. He remembered hearing the long, low note of a horn. He remembered those dark eyes filled with hate and his words as he ordered retreat filled with venom. He remembered.

"My brother has vowed vengeance on you," the slaver continued. "So I won't kill you. No, no. I wouldn't want to deny my brother his justice. I wouldn't want to deny him his fun."

One hand held a long, curved sword that gleamed in the sun, a thin red line running along its razor edge. The other held a thick piece of dark wood, lacquered and wrapped to its head with leather. The end of the club was shaped into a dog's—or wolf's—head with an open mouth and sharp teeth. A direct hit with that could kill a man. That weapon he held out for Befel to see, to inspect. He would use that. Befel knew it. He would bludgeon him over the head and steal him away and . . . Befel shuddered.

The slaver stepped in, club held high. Befel stepped to the side, sword out wide. He had seen Demik do the same thing. Misdirection perhaps. The club came down, and Befel dodged and struck. The wolf head smacked hard into the ground, and Befel's worn blade glanced off its leather-bound neck. Befel knew that this man could've easily followed up with a jab from his own sword, but he also understood he wanted the farmer alive.

Befel kicked dirt up at the slaver. He saw Switch do that. The man proved too tall, rocks and pebbles hitting his chest. He swung the back of the wolf head at Befel. It hit his hip. It might as well have been a horse's hoof. The farmer stumbled forward but turned quickly to meet another overhanded strike. He ducked and stepped, his sword raking across the slaver's high, leather boot, snug to his calf and stopping short of his knee. The boot was thick, and despite the blade cutting deep, it struck no flesh.

The slaver growled. Befel looked up at him and saw the curved sword raised up, pointing face down, toward him. It jabbed, and Befel jumped, hearing a call from fifty or more paces away. The leader yelled to his brother, and the broad-shouldered man snarled. Was Befel really that important, or was it that this man's brother simply felt that slighted?

You can't kill me, can you? Befel thought. A smile crept along his face.

The next club swing was high, over Befel's head, and the young man punched the slaver's ribs, and he may as well have punched a stone wall. The oil-bearded man laughed, dropped his own sword and responded with a meaty fist to the farmer's face. Befel tumbled backward but kept on his feet.

Befel jabbed, and the sword skimmed along the man's ribs. Cloth tore, and blood seeped through. So much for a stone wall. The slaver howled, and his eyes raged as he swung his club twice in arcing, diagonal strikes. Befel dodged, but the giant of a man rushing at him put him on his heels. He swung. This time, his blade nicked the front of the man's leg. Another howl. Another bull rush of arcing club attacks.

Befel fell back again, tumbled over his head but back to his feet, left shoulder facing the slaver. He saw the wolf head descend and knew he had no time. He put his arm up—as if he had a shield—and lifted his shoulder so that it covered part of his face. The sound of a mallet hitting meat echoed through the battlefield. Befel felt skin tear, felt muscle rend and open, felt the wetness of blood pour down his arm and over his chest. Fire stabbed his skin, and then icy needles drove him down onto his knees. They shook, and he collapsed.

His cheek pressed hard against the earth. Warm or cool, he couldn't feel the dirt. He watched as feet ran about and hooves stamped, hoping they would miss his head and his body. He felt a rough, huge hand grip his shoulder—his good shoulder. The world went black.

Erik watched with pride as Befel fended off a man that reminded him much of Marcus, save for his unkind eyes and snarling smile. His stomach knotted, however, when a wolf-shaped club hit Befel's bad shoulder hard. Blood exploded in a thick mist of crimson, and he watched his brother going down in horror, that giant of a man standing over him, laughing, and reaching down to drag him away.

That tingle of fear, the shaking tremble of uncertainty, crawled up Erik's spine. He pushed it back. It was his brother. He gripped his curved sword and ran. He put his shoulder down, closed his eyes, and wobbled sideways when he finally hit the slaver. The man stood a head taller than Erik, and a bit broader. However, the force and the speed and the unknowing sent the large man forward—to his knees. He looked back, over his shoulder with squinted eyes.

"I'm getting tired of you little maggots," he spat.

Erik wasted no time with talk. He kicked a boot-full of dirt in the man's face. He cried out and blinked. He rubbed his eyes frantically. Erik pulled Befel away and stood in front of his brother. The slaver rose to his full height. Tears filled his eyes, now red and raw.

He growled. He sounded like an animal, some hungry, angry animal waiting, wanting, needing a kill. The slaver looked over his shoulder. Erik watched, saw the other man—the slighter man—nod. What did that mean? The giant of a man turned back to Erik, teeth glaring in a wide smile. Erik saw the fingers wrapped around the handle of the wolf-head club tighten, saw the knuckles whiten. Ah, that's what that nod meant.

"You didn't have me the last time we met. You won't have me today, and you'll not have me tomorrow," Erik muttered.

Erik quickly found himself on his heels. The assault felt impossible. He flinched every time he dodged a club strike and its carved head thudded to the ground. He tried pushing back. His foe batted away every jab with his sword, every swing. He put his shoulder down. He ran into a stone wall. The fist to his face sent him back again, hands flailing to catch his balance.

The man looked over his shoulder again. Another nod. Just then, Erik heard a scream, saw the flashing of steel from the corner of his eye, saw a crimson rainbow spray out in a wide arc, and heard the now too familiar, welcoming grunt of a dwarf. Nafer rushed to his side, fresh blood on his mighty mace. The smile on the slaver's face faded a bit.

The giant looked to Erik, then Nafer, and back again. His smile returned. "A dwarf would be a good addition to our inventory."

Nafer growled.

The slaver attacked again, and this time, he proved less successful. Erik and Nafer together, shoulder to shoulder, pushed him back. The man did not seem to want to give up on his quarry, but he was weakening. Then, Erik saw a few other slave traders—one on horseback and two on foot—running from where Turk and Demik were fighting.

We're winning, Erik thought. Then he heard it. A familiar sound. A low whine breaking through the din of battle. The horn. Erik saw that slight man with the oily beard, saw the curled horn pressed to his lips. The man in front of Erik turned and ran.

He can't get away. How many lives had he ruined? How many lives had he taken? He can't get away.

Erik went to follow but felt a strong hand catch his arm. He looked down to see Nafer holding him back. He shook his head.

"He can't get away," Erik yelled, "they can't get away!"

"We won," Nafer mustered in his broken Westernese.

"Punishment," Erik cried. "That is what they deserve."

Nafer let go, and Erik pursued. The giant slaver proved slower than Erik, and the farmer thought he might actually catch up to him, but the enemy reached his horse and pulled himself into the saddle, kicking its sides hard. Erik swung his sword, and a few dark strands of horsetail fell to the ground. The young man threw his sword. The curved blade wobbled through the air a short distance and then flopped to the ground.

"No!" he yelled. He continued to run, his enemy close to joining with the slavers' leader and a group of four others. He could never reach him. And if he did, a group of six men jumping at the chance to kill at least one of the mercenaries would surround him.

When hope for vengeance seemed gone, when the punishment for these men, at least Befel's brutalizer, seemed a dream, Erik felt a slight tug at his waist. It was the nagging bite from a horsefly, the pinch of a small red ant. He looked down, brows curved, frown on his face. He saw it, calling to him. How could that be? But it was. Trying to get his attention, a childlike tug at his sleeve. That golden, jeweled knife. Erik drew it. He had never thrown a knife before. Never had a need to. How hard could it be?

He gripped the handle, felt the gems in the palm of his hand, and watched the steel blade glisten like a diamond in the sun. He picked a spot on the slaver's back, took aim, and threw. The knife wobbled like his sword. The other slavers laughed. They had been watching him in his futility. Erik hung his shoulders in dejection.

Erik didn't see the knife straighten itself. He didn't see one of the rubies on the gold handle glow, just ever so faintly. He didn't see the whole weapon glow in a brighter red. What he did see was a streak of blood-red rain. He saw it race toward the horsed man, race toward the exact spot for which he aimed. He saw an arrowhead made of white steel, shaft made of golden oak, fletching of cardinal feathers, thump into the slaver's back with a clap of thunder.

Perhaps a normal arrow wouldn't be enough to kill such a large man, even stop such a man, but immediately the giant stood up straight in his saddle. His horse stopped. The arrow glowed red again. It seemed to lengthen. Erik, even from fifty or more paces away, heard the breaking of bone, the ripping of skin as the man's horse seemed to draw to an involuntary halt. He saw the slaver turn in his saddle, his eyes wide with disbelief.

The man looked dumb, mouth open. Blood trickled and stained his beard. The gleaming steel of an arrow point protruded from his chest, streaked in crimson. The man tried to clutch at the steel, but it seemed that his shoulders were just not strong enough to lift his arms. They went slack. The slave trader's breath became short and sporadic, his chest heaving in quick thumps. His eyes rolled to the back of his head, and he slid from the saddle, hitting the ground with a loud smack.

The slaver leader let out a shrill, bone-chilling cry. He snapped his horse's reins and dug his heels deep into its side, face red, spit flying from his mouth as he seethed, but one of his men caught his wrist, and another one grabbed the reins. The look he gave his men might have melted their skin clean from their bones, but after a brief struggle to free himself from their grasp, it seemed they had convinced him they had no chance if they resumed their attack.

"This isn't over, you little bastard!" His screaming curse caused Erik to flinch. "I'll gut you! I'll eat your heart! You'll pay for my brother's death!"

That made sense. The two men looked alike, save for their stature. Erik's stomach knotted, and goose pimples prickled his arms as he looked around. Bodies, blood, guts, parts—it all littered the ground. The smell. He vomited, and when he stood again, Nafer grabbed his shoulder and shook him gently. The look he gave Erik begged the question, *Are you all right?* Erik nodded.

The smell. Blood. Urine. Feces. Hair and skin baking in the noonday sun. Erik covered his nose. A brother dead. How many brothers dead? Sons. Fathers even—maybe. He felt a tear tickle his cheek as Nafer handed him his knife, its blade as clean and unsullied as ever.

Chapter 52

THE BRISK BREEZE WAFTING THROUGH the open window of his bedroom should have cooled his sweat-matted face, given him a stark chill even, but it didn't. Del Alzon sat up. A rough palm across his forehead, quickly retrieved, revealed a head of thinning hair soaking wet. He coughed. His whole body shook as if filled with the worst of fevers. He swung his feet over to the side of his bed, and the wood underneath his girth creaked unsteadily. The fruit seller buried his face in his hands, elbows propped firmly against his knees.

He stood and stared east, through his window. The wind finally made him shiver.

"Poor bastards," he muttered.

Why did he feel so sorry? He sold them out but made a good profit for it in the end. At least for a fruit merchant in Waterton.

"Because they didn't deserve it." Del Alzon spat out the window as he spoke to himself. "They were just young brats looking to do the same thing you did not so long ago."

He turned and walked to a solid stone washbasin sitting in a waist-high wooden stand. He brushed his fat fingers along the carved work that patterned the edges of the bowl. One of the few possessions he brought with him from the east. He looked through the window again. The east. So much hope in the east. Del Alzon shook his head.

"Hope," he scoffed and dipped his hands in the water to splash the semi-cool liquid on his face, not caring how much of it hit the floor.

A towel hung from the side of the basin. He looked down to his tremendous gut that rolled like a sack of water at the slightest movement, noticed at least two stains dotting his dull-white, sleeveless shirt. He wiped the water from his face and threw the towel to the floor.

Some young whelp ran through town the day before last, blood covering his face, cradling a broken arm, limping and coughing, crying for help. Del Alzon had prayed it wasn't the farmer lad. The boy ended up being too young, maybe only fifteen. Why did he care about Erik? He shrugged his shoulders. He just hoped that young man didn't come back, hoped he wouldn't have to look the boy in the face and lie to him again. When did he become a liar?

"Who are you fooling?" Del Alzon looked at the distorted reflection of himself in the mirror. It didn't seem such a misrepresentation. "You've been lying your whole life. The minute you stepped foot on the soils of Antolika and convinced yourself you were fighting for righteousness, you were a liar."

He rubbed the scars along his shoulder, and as he closed his eyes, he saw Erik's face. Then, like a nightmare vision come back to haunt him again, the face morphed into that of the bloodied survivor. How he cried about slavers and the brutal attack and dead women and children. Del Alzon's eyes shot open. He gripped the basin hard and threw it to the side. The wooden stand splintered, cracked, and shattered. The water spilled everywhere, but the stone basin held firm. Not a chip. Not a crack. Just like the vision, it could not be destroyed.

Del Alzon looked down at the water pooled around his feet and clenched his fists until the blood left his fingers.

"There are some things I can't change, but no more lies," he vowed to himself, and moving at a pace which belied his size, he got dressed and went out to the stable at the rear of his house.

It had been a good number of years since he had ridden his horse, and the animal grunted and snorted as Del Alzon settled himself into the saddle. He looked affectionately at the heavy draft horse with squinted eyes.

"You're no skinny beauty queen either, now," he murmured as he patted her thick neck. She tossed her head in response, and the fat merchant managed a brief smile as he looked over his shoulder.

He pulled the horse and kicked her on out of the wooden stable. The thunk of iron-shod hooves on the old timbers, the smell of dust kicked up, and the feel of worked muscles moving underneath him, it all brought back a blur of memories. It felt like...like yesterday...

Riding onto the sandy beach of the Eastern Shores of The Giant's Vein, he saw the crows circling in the air, the smoke rising far away, creating false clouds. A woman knelt just to his right. One sleeve of her simple wool dress lay torn, revealing her breast. Her hair sat in clumps of sweat. Dirt stained an otherwise pretty face. She held the head of a dead man in her lap, her legs curled underneath her. She rubbed his face, his bloodied hair, but her distant stare said the movement was simply ritualistic. She looked...numb.

Two soldiers walked by, grabbed her arms, and dragged her away. She didn't fight. She didn't scream. She just stared. Del Alzon saw the blood running down her legs, saw the rest of her tattered dress.

"Poor bitch," one man said.

"She should've fought harder," another replied. Both men laughed.

Del Alzon looked down at them. His scowl shut them up. The footmen both looked away and continued their march from the boat through the ruined town. He spurred his horse on after the men, the column of twenty men he commanded. A recent promotion, a reward for excellent service in these lands. A reward for survival.

As he rode through the town, he remembered gardens, buildings, statues—all gone, burned and broken. He couldn't put his finger on the name. It didn't seem that important and, like that woman, he was just becoming numb to everything. The slightest hint of true happiness was simply so distant—it was a good day or kind word fondly recollected—but it was never important that he remember such things.

The next day pushed the thought of the destroyed town even farther away. Fighting consumed that day. And the next. And the next. More men off a boat replaced those lost, and in the next place he followed fifty men through stone foundations and scattered bones, all charred black. Didn't he ride through this place before?

The next year seemed a blur of smoke and fire and blood. As did the next. Hundreds of soldiers dead and replaced as if life held no value. Never knowing names or remembering faces, Del Alzon the survivor led them down roads grown over by grass. Mounds of rubble sat where walls once did, but he never thought of them as family homes that might have once see joy and happiness.

Five years of war brought him again to the shores of The Giant's Vein. Two hundred and fifty soldiers, fifty horsemen, five sergeants, and a lieutenant saluted Del Alzon as they made their way off boats and through a field the captain vaguely remembered being different the last time he was there. The familiar sights of crows and smoke couldn't jog his memory, and he simply rubbed his eyes with index finger and thumb, slightly wishing he could go home with the boats now slowly pushing off and away from the beach. If only he could…

Chapter 53

HE GATHERED TWENTY MEN. SIX militia that the city could spare and who agreed to go, the rest much like him. Retired soldiers. Old merchants. It would have to do. He lifted his eyes to the east, toward the Blue River Bridge—toward retribution. Now he sat at their head, them awaiting his instructions, but his mind was back in the old days again.

"Fifteen years of service and for what?" he muttered and rubbed his shoulder again. Even through the heavy wool shirt and leather jerkin, he could feel the scars. "What was the name of that damned town?"

He shook his head.

"Del." A man rode up to Del Alzon's right. The fruit merchant looked at the old man, and a smile crossed his fat, stubbled face.

"That's right."

The gray-haired fellow, a worn jerkin too tight for his waist, looked like he was about to ask a question when Del smiled to himself again and nodded.

"Old Manor. That was the name. Old Manor. I haven't thought of that name in thirty years." He saw the man staring at him. "Sorry, my friend. Just remembered something. An old memory."

"I hope it was a fond one." The older man smiled. He had a good number of his teeth for a man of his age.

Del Alzon shrugged. "There is some fondness to it, I suppose."

"Well, my wife tells me bad memories aren't worth remembering."

Del Alzon shook his head. "If we don't remember them, then we are doomed to make the same mistakes. You've been making the same mistakes, over and over again, haven't you, you fool?"

The gray-haired man straightened quickly, his lips thin and bloodless. "Now what mistakes have I made there?"

"Oh, no, no, not you my friend." Del Alzon laughed. "I do apologize. I was talking to myself. What was it you wanted, Quintus? It is Quintus isn't it?"

Quintus was an easterner like Del Alzon. Then again, not so much like Del Alzon. Many said that everyone who comes west comes to escape something. Del Alzon knew what he came west to escape. He knew what many in Waterton kept hidden in their closets. Quintus, however, he came to build an enterprise. He, his wife, three sons, and two daughters thought they could build a trade in expensive silks and velvets and cottons in Waterton. Who would've guessed that a city filled with people trying to disappear, lay low, getting ready to adventure into the unknown wildernesses of the west or simply drink themselves into oblivion wouldn't be interested in a blanket or vest that might cost a man's whole monthly salary?

Now one boy was back in Golgolithul. Yet another was lost in the lands of Gongoreth somewhere. One of their daughters had married a womanizing lush of a tavern master twice her age. Quintus and his wife seemed happy just to be able to put food on their table. Yet, not so happy that it would be more likely that their remaining son would bear them a grandchild than their youngest daughter, whose penchant for chocolates had given her a girth that rivaled Del Alzon's.

"Aye, it is. I wondered, what is our course of action?"

Del Alzon laughed. Not at Quintus. Not even at his question. He laughed more at the fact that he truly had no idea what his course of action might be.

"Well," Del Alzon replied. "I know roughly where these bloody bastards camp in the Blue Forest. There's enough of us that I don't think simple forest bandits will give us any problems. I figure we just roam around the forest until we find them."

"That's your plan?" Quintus looked less than enthused.

"Aye," Del Alzon said with a smile. "You've a better one?"

"No." Quintus rubbed his clean-shaven chin.

Del Alzon thought it odd, surprising really, that Quintus volunteered to go along. Perhaps some adventure, some time away from the misfortunes of his enterprising escapades, was all he needed. Del Alzon couldn't help but think time away from that bear of a woman he called a wife wouldn't hurt either. With an eyebrow that spanned the breadth of her forehead, more hair on her lip than he, a brutish, callous way of speaking, the shoulders of a bull, and a thick mole just under her chin, the old soldier couldn't figure how she produced such a beautiful daughter. He spoke of the married one, of course.

"I suppose I don't have a better plan," Quintus added.

"Well then." Del Alzon smiled a familiar smile, a toothless quirk of the mouth that spoke of victory—intellectual superiority—however small and trivial. "When you do have a better idea, my dear Quintus, let me know. But for the time being, we'll stick to my plan."

"Sounds good then." Quintus stiffened and stared straight forward, a dumb smirk on his face.

"Does it," Del Alzon whispered. He shook his head with that smile still on his face. As if the old fool had any other choice.

Two days' ride brought them to an old campsite littered with broken wagons, pots, pans, and . . . bodies. They saw one other obvious encampment where one of the fires hadn't been so carefully covered. Gypsies seemed always the most careful about covering their tracks. Del Alzon would have thought it odd, but then he remembered those Ion Gypsies traveled with others—miners and simple travelers . . . and the young men.

Del Alzon tried not to laugh when Quintus threw up, the stench of rotting flesh hanging heavily in the warming spring air of a pre-noon day. Del Alzon could smell it from a mile away, but then again, he knew that smell well. A sickening sweetness, like soft, decaying apples. The others—some of them knew. At least, Del Alzon guessed they knew. They had the look of old soldiers and thought nothing of it until they reached the flies. Thick ones, fat on death, buzzing about aggressively.

"Slavers," one old soldier muttered. His name was Danitus.

Of average height and build, his short hair spoke of either Gol-Durathna or Golgolithul, and he seemed fit for a man his age. His gray eyes spoke of no particular origin, but his speech gave him away. Heavy with the Westernese accent, Del Alzon could pick out elements of the Northern language, a rolling, liquid tongue not quite as 'elegant' as the Eastern language of Golgolithul. It didn't possess the lisps and long vowels that Eastern nobles found so pleasing to the ear.

"What was that?" Del asked, and the aged soldier repeated his comment.

That still hard man, one eyelid seemingly drooping and a number of little white scars on his face sat stiff-backed in his saddle. With a firm hold of his reins, he looked straight ahead. All soldiers worth their salt had that same stare.

"Only slavers lay here rotting."

Del Alzon nodded his agreement and then spat heavily on the ground. Gypsies were little better than slavers. Con artists, liars, and cheats. He shook his head. Were those old stories actually true?

"Aye. They buried their dead and left the slavers to rot."

Danitus pointed to a small circle of rocks. They dismounted and walked their horses to the place. The rest of the men remained a good ten paces away. Bits of wood collected from shattered wagons marked headstones, names and prayers written upon them with charcoal in a myriad of different languages.

"No, they did bury the slavers," Del Alzon said. A line of shallow graves, dirt piled around them, lay open to the air. Wild dogs, perhaps. Thieves. Grave robbers maybe. "Something dug them up."

"Something or someone dug up just the bloody slavers and paid no concern for the gypsies?" Danitus questioned. "And why would they bury murderers who attacked them? It doesn't make sense."

Del Alzon shrugged. "But not just gypsies," Del Alzon said, pointing to one piece of old timber, marked with black letters. "This is the grave of a miner. And this one." He pointed to another wooden headstone. "His wife. It says, *Together in Life, Together in Death.*"

"It looks like the gypsies put up a good fight and did more harm than the slavers," Danitus said. "Look at all the dead. Twenty bodies—at least. Maybe that many graves lay here."

Danitus shrugged as he looked around.

"Aye," Del Alzon added, "but what about the ones those bloody leeches took. The boy that made it back to Waterton said they took a good number of them."

"And why should we care so much?" Danitus' back was to Del Alzon, but the northerner looked over his shoulder to give the fruit merchant a sidelong glance. "You've done deeds just as bad. So have I in the name of justice. That's why you're in Waterton, isn't it? So you wouldn't have to get involved—ever again."

Del Alzon looked away as if the stare Danitus gave him could weigh him down like a sack of rocks on his shoulders.

"Aye. But—as a soldier—can you just stand by?" Del asked. "At some point, didn't we believe in something? And at what point did we lose our faith? It's not just that it's slavers. And it's not that these people were innocent. A man trusted me."

"Hundreds of men trusted me." Danitus gave Del Alzon a hard look and tucked his thumbs into the front of his belt. "Most to their deaths."

"Yes, but all those men knew the chance of death loomed just around the corner. This man—that wasn't part of the deal."

"So this is for a single person?"

"Aye." Del Alzon laughed at his own foolishness. "But the children also. Would you leave innocent children to slavers? And all the other young men I sold into this caravan. And the gypsies—the damned gypsies."

Danitus smiled, even laughed a little, and Del Alzon shot him a hard look. This man would laugh as a seasoned soldier, one who had killed and maimed, raped and murdered, burned and destroyed.

"That's what I hoped to hear," Danitus said. His laugh proved not a jest, but a relieved agreement.

Another man, this one only slightly younger, joined them. A tall fellow with a blond beard that looked well-kept but had a tendency to get a little long and scraggly if the man's wife didn't remind him to trim it. His hair sat under a short-brimmed cap, pulled tight into a tail. His clothing spoke of a hunter, a woodsman, with a loose coat of gray-greens, tight-fitting pants of the same color, and soft boots rolled down to just below the calf. That, certainly, was his profession. Yager made his money by hunting, and he was good at it. He made a comfortable living, and the meat he sold was always fresh, never old and turning.

Del Alzon figured him to be a man from Nordeth. He stood tall enough, a hand's-width taller than his long bow, which—unstrung—was two paces long. Del Alzon thought he had heard the huntsman speak of a child but couldn't remember if the boy was dead or simply living elsewhere. If the hunter started his family early, it could be believable that he had a boy old enough to live on his own. Look at young Erik. He proved barely a man and on his own. By the heavens, the fruit merchant counted a year less than Erik when he first donned a coat of mail and picked up a broadsword in service to Golgolithul.

Yager leaned against his longbow, made of a burgundy-colored yew, as if it were a staff.

"So, fruit merchant, what's yer next move?"

Definitely Nordeth. That accent had the—what did Del Alzon's mother say about the northerners—bucolic twang to it. The corner of the soldier's mouth lifted a bit in an amused smirk. Yager knew his name but always chose to refer to him by some other title. Fruit merchant, peddler, even soldier once when he saw the scars on his shoulder—he knew the world well enough—but never Del Alzon.

"Do you think we can take our horses into the woods? I suppose that's my first question."

Yager peered into the Blue Forest and scratched his chin.

"Aye." A simple response from a simple man.

"My next question, then, is can we ride them through the woods?"

Yager stared again. "Aye. It'll be tight, fer sure, but I think it's possible."

"Too thick to track anything?" asked Danitus.

Yager gave the old soldier a tilt of his head and a raised eyebrow.

"Too thick? Show me a grown over field snowed and rained upon fer forty days, in the dead of a moonless night, with a thick mist setting just above the ground, and I will show you which way the deer have traveled and how many."

Del Alzon grinned, and Danitus nodded with a quirky smile as if accepting a challenge. "Very well then. What are we waiting for?"

Del gripped the horn of his saddle and slowly pulled himself onto his poor horse. The beast stamped and snorted, and all Del could do was rub the animal's neck and calm it with as sweet a voice as he could muster. He motioned for the others. Quintus seemed hesitant, but he followed, taking up a place at the rear of the group.

Danitus pulled the huntsman's mount behind his own as Yager led the way into the Blue Forest on foot. With an arrow half nocked in his great bow, the tracker slowly stepped over root and under bough, always watching the ground, sniffing the air, feeling the leaves, tasting his fingers after he touched them. Slow. The trek through the forest felt slow, but when Del Alzon looked behind him, all he could see was green—trees and brush and creepers.

Night came on fast in the overgrown woods, and they camped with no fire. It seemed even the horses knew the need for silence, and not one of them snorted or neighed or stomped through the night. Truly, the only sound proved Quintus' teeth chattering even though he wrapped himself tightly in not one, but two thick blankets.

"Probably should've left him behind," Del whispered. He stared into the darkness of the forest, picking out the soft scampers of fox feet and the drumming sound of nighttime toads croaking. An owl perched overhead and every so often hooted. That sent Quintus' teeth chattering even more.

Yager shrugged. "Every man serves his purpose."

"And what is, or was your purpose?"

Truth be told, Del Alzon couldn't figure if he really cared what Yager's past life was or if he simply wanted to make the time go by with idle chat. He, after all, kept to himself well enough and normally didn't delve into the business of others unless it suited his own needs. Of course, he was trying to change all that.

"My purpose was my purpose." Yager certainly seemed his own man, there was no denying that.

"And that purpose was?"

"A conversation, perhaps, fer another time."

Yager never loosened the half-nocked arrow, nor did he ever take his eyes off the woods beyond them, but something in his voice spoke of a life more complex than a simple hunter.

Morning came on slowly, bits of light poking through holes in the canopy like strands of blond hair until the entire forest stood dimly lit, a low mist hanging just above the ground. Del Alzon and his band of followers were already moving by that time, but it was noon before Yager stopped the company with a raised fist.

"They're close." His voice sounded a hoarse whisper, cautious and expectant.

"They could be so close to the Straits?" Danitus questioned. "Especially after what seems such a big fight and bountiful quarry."

"Stay here," Yager commanded. "I'll have a look."

He was only gone for an hour. "Twenty, maybe twenty-five, not including captives of course."

"And of the captives?" Del Alzon asked.

"Men, women, children. I didn't get the best look. They're all tied together or stuck in wooden cages."

The soldier nodded. He took a big breath, the girth of his belly expanding even wider, his girdle creaking under the strain. His eyes closed, and he tipped his head back. No one could tell if he was thinking or praying. When he opened his eyes again, he turned to his horse and drew a broadsword from behind the saddle. It looked a worn weapon, albeit capable. The steel no longer shone like it once had, but the edge was just as sharp.

"One more time, my old friend." Del Alzon stroked the broad side of the blade and then slapped it against his open palm. "Let's go."

Yager and Danitus nodded. The three took the lead, and two other men—Gregory the Smith and Maktus the Carpenter—brought bows, and they followed their heels. The weaponry of the group of Watertonians was a mixture of implements, but mostly they all looked like the old soldier's sword, worn and weathered, pulled from retirement for one last hoorah.

A group of about ten men, none too concerned about being quiet or careful, sat amongst wagons and wooden cages in a small clearing of grass and clover and lavender bushes. They joked and drank, most of them looking as young as the two dozen men all bound together by hemp rope at the hands in one long chain, fresh blood and bruises on their faces and bodies. Del Alzon stared at the young slavers in disgust.

One man marched back and forth, hands behind his back and a scowl across his face, ignoring the apparent revelry in which the other slave traders took part. He looked a larger version of the slight Samanian that hired the fruit merchant for his task of convincing young blokes to join the gypsy caravan, all the while knowing the slavers would eventually attack them under cover of night and take the men away to sell in far-off markets. So much for that plan. By the number of rotting bodies spread out amongst the abandoned camp, it seemed the slavers got more than they bargained for. Del didn't see the man who hired him, only this fellow, who looked none too happy, who was probably a brother or a cousin.

"I don't think all of them are here," Del Alzon whispered to Danitus and Yager. "I don't see their leader. There's no sentries posted. No guards. Odd."

"Maybe he's dead," Danitus offered. "Perhaps he died in the fight. It seemed many of them died in the fight."

Del Alzon shook his head. "Not that one. He's too smart to die by the hands of gypsies and miners and young men and—"

The soldier stopped. He spotted one wagon, its wooden bars uncommonly close together. Children. That was the children's cage. A dozen, nearly two dozen. Del squeezed the handle of his sword until his knuckles popped.

"Kill them."

Chapter 54

A FIN PROVED THE FIRST to die. Blood exploded from his mouth as he opened it to take another drink from an ancient-looking bottle. The arrow lifted him off the log on which he sat, and he toppled forward, straight into one of the two campfires. His black hair singed, and the stink and smoke could have been what caught a tall Hámonian by surprise. Perhaps he was just that slow and not as drunk, but Yager had enough time to step from the woods, aim, and hit this second man square between his crystal blue eyes. The arrow thudded against the elm behind him, hair stuck to the shaft in a bloody mass, the man's head fixed firmly to the tree. Next, a stout Golgolithulian who once sat in the slavers' cages until he paid his way into their band, clutched at his neck, blood squeezing through his fingers, soft flesh torn by an iron arrowhead.

Another slaver now charged the exposed Yager, and the man may have killed the huntsman with his boar spear, but Del Alzon emerged from the cover of the forest. He brought his blade down on the spear, and the wood splintered and broke. Then, with surprising speed for a man his size, the blade reversed upwards again and cleaved both hands from their wrists. Steel separating head from neck stopped the slave trader's screams. Danitus took two men before they could even get up, and then more arrows left more slavers dead or dying. Only the man Del Alzon recognized as Kehl's brother seemed willing to put up a fight.

He drew his curved, Samanian sword and fended off two of Del's comrades. He cut both down before the old soldier could reach him.

"You fat piece of cow dung," the slaver spat. "What are you doing? You weren't paid enough? It figures; a traitorous eastern soldier would go back on his word. Thirty pieces of silver would be more than enough for any man living in that forsaken city of denizens and runaways."

"That doesn't mean much coming from a slaver," Del Alzon retorted, readying his sword.

"Can you even move enough to fight?" the slaver chided. "You're disgusting. I think when I kill you, I'll feed you to the slaves."

Del smiled. "If you haven't noticed, in a few moments you won't have much of a slave train left."

He could tell the slaver tried not making his glances from side to side obvious, but he had to see his men fall, to die underneath old, worn steel. In fact, the rout happened all too fast. The old soldier had expected a hard fight, and this seemed a training session. How had these slavers survived as long as they did?

The slaver attacked, and Del Alzon again moved with a speed which belied his bulk. With the weight of his sword gripped fast in his hand behind it, he first punched the Samanian in the nose. It broke with a resounding crack and blood soaked his oiled mustache and beard. Knowing the man would now have trouble seeing, Del lurched sideways and, with a strong backhand, brought his blade along the slave trader's hamstring. He followed with an upswing, and the tip of his sword raked the man's back, creating a neat tear in the black Samanian robes that soon began to turn red.

"My brothers will find you. They will kill you for this."

"More Samanian filth—you're worse than gypsies."

"Then you should appreciate what we did!" retorted the slaver, now down on his knees and clutching at the back of his leg. He looked up at the fat old soldier, a pained grimace tattooed on his face.

"So you killed all the gypsies?" Del asked. "Or enslaved them?"

The slaver didn't answer. Del Alzon responded by driving the tip of his sword a finger's-length deep into the man's shoulder.

"No, no. They fought back. We didn't expect it. We nearly lost a third of our number in the fight. We retreated. Most of the gypsies lived."

"And what of the young men?" the soldier asked.

"You see them, don't you?" It seemed a legitimate response. They did, after all, sit, bound together at one edge of the camp.

Del pressed his sword deeper into the man's shoulder. "There was one in particular. He would've been with two others; family members."

Understanding and recognition brightened the slaver's eyes, and a wry, malicious smile crossed his bloodied mouth.

"I know of whom you speak. They escaped our nets. They, along with the gypsies are the reason my brothers left with the best of our men. They will die with the rest of the gypsies when Kehl finds them."

"Pray to your heathen gods, Samanian, for you are about to meet them."

"No, wait, I . . . we have money."

"I'll take it anyway when you are dead," Del Alzon said.

"My brother will have revenge. He will raze Waterton to the ground for this." The slaver's pleading turned to indignation. As he fumed, the soldier's steel met his neck and, with a single spurt of blood, his curses stopped.

Del Alzon wiped his sword on the dead man's robes and stared indifferently at the Samanian lying at his feet.

"William is dead, Del." Del Alzon found Danitus standing behind him, staring at the dead man. He spoke of William, a woodsman who worked in the lumber mill just south of Waterton. He, perhaps, was the one man in their company who hadn't escaped to the border town from some other life. At just over twenty-five years old, he seemed one of the few men who could say they were natives of the western city. Now he lay dead. "And it seems Syd will soon follow."

The leather worker seemed a much less respectable person. Most found him drunk, even in the morning. Any woman of Waterton with an ounce of decency and a day under fifty avoided him like some disease, and fathers and mothers kept their little girls well away from him too. He did, however, agree to help Del Alzon, so a brother in arms he lay nonetheless.

"Did Quintus survive?"

Danitus nodded. Del walked to the cage with most of the children. They looked dirty, unfed, scared. Most huddled in a corner away from the fat soldier. He figured he didn't look the friendly fatherly type. Some, two little boys, looked too numb to care who came to their cage, and one little girl simply lay on the ground, so weak she was unable to move.

"Poor wee ones," Yager said. Del Alzon felt a tear tickle his cheek. With a loud grunt, he hefted his sword over his head and brought it down on the iron lock that imprisoned the children. With a clang and a spark, the iron snapped, and the door opened slowly. The Golgolithulian tried to climb inside to retrieve the unconscious girl, but his mere size prevented it. As he stepped back, his girth rocked the cage back and forth, and one boy let out a loud cry. That spurred a scream from another cage—a woman, perhaps his mother.

"Come now, children. I mean you no harm. We're going to take you home."

The children didn't move despite Del's best efforts to make himself sound as friendly as possible, and so freeing them from the cages was done by several of the women. Even released, the children remained traumatized and just kept staring and not speaking. Even when fed later on a fresh deer, it took some of the children's own mothers to coax them to eat.

In the morning, Quintus and two other men set out through the forest and back toward Waterton with freed slaves and two dead westerners in tow.

"Where to now?" Danitus asked.

"Find Kehl," Del Alzon replied.

"Feels like old times," Danitus added.

Del nodded, and then said, "Only this time, I have a purpose."

Chapter 55

ERIK STOOD OVER THE DEAD man. An arrow, the red fletching the same color as the thickening blood still oozing from the wound, protruded from his back. He wiped his mouth with the back of his hand. He didn't know if he wanted to touch the arrow—or was it a dagger? As he reached for it, the fletching fluttered gently in a sudden breeze. Erik felt a tingle travel along his spine to the back of his head.

Pick me up. The words passed through his mind again. *Pick me up.*

He furled his eyebrows, taking firm hold of the shaft, and pulled. With a sickening squelch of torn flesh and blood, the arrow was slowly extracted, and he held it in his hand as if it might burn him. The fletching and the reddish-steel arrowhead glowed, and when Erik blinked, he held a long-bladed dagger with a golden hilt. The steel of the blade was as clean and pristine as if it had just been forged.

"What a curious thing you are?" he muttered and felt another tingle crawl up his arm and down his spine before sheathing the weapon.

"You were that man's brother," Erik said, looking down at the body. "I saw him cry for you. Any man would cry over his brother's death."

His stomach knotted. What would he do if his brother had died? Erik shook his head. He couldn't even think of that without feeling sick.

When he stood and turned, he found Turk Skull Crusher watching him.

"What are you doing, Erik?" Turk asked.

"Nothing," Erik replied. "Just…nothing."

"You looked as if you were praying for this man," Turk said.

Erik paused a moment before answering. Then, he nodded. "Yes, I prayed."

"And what did you pray?" Turk asked.

Erik looked down at the dead man again. He closed his eyes and saw the man's brother. He saw red-stained eyes. He heard his wailing. He felt…pity.

"I prayed for forgiveness," Erik replied.

"Forgiveness?" Turk questioned. Erik couldn't help but think the dwarf sounded surprised.

"Aye," Erik said. "For the life I've taken. For the lives I've taken. For the lives I will take." He was surprised how that last part came out and how little the idea surprised him as if it was his given destiny.

"I see," Turk said. "That is a good prayer, although, I don't think you need forgiveness for the lives of these men."

"Why?" Erik asked.

"They are evil men," Turk replied, "and you were defending yourself, and your friends. Death in battle is inevitable."

"It still makes me feel sick."

"You cannot redeem another man." Turk shook his head when he spoke. "Their hearts were wicked."

"How do I know what was in their hearts?" Erik asked. "Maybe Fox was forced into this life. Is that his fault?"

"That is a good question." Turk stepped forward, close enough to put a gentle hand on Erik's elbow.

"An—whom you call The Creator—has told us that a man's actions are like a looking glass into his heart. A man can surely fool those around him. A seemingly righteous man who is truly wicked, or a man who seems wicked but who is troubled because he does what is contrary to his heart. But a man who rapes and murders, enslaves, beats, tortures—I think we can see his heart clearly."

"But he was once a child—just a little boy," Erik said. "He was innocent, once."

Turk opened his mouth to say something else but quickly closed it. He moved to leave, but then turned back to Erik once more.

"When you are finished here, come join us. I will tend to any wounds you might have."

Turk turned and walked toward his horse, where he retrieved a heavy ceramic jar from one of his saddlebags. It looked an odd thing, all brown and tan swirls with a wide cork. The dwarf opened it, and a smell that seemed a mixture of musk and mint and basil and sweat hit his nose. He remembered the first time he smelled that smell. He detested it. It made him gag. He welcomed it now. It had saved his life...more than once.

"That shit stinks!" yelled Switch. "What by the Shadow is that?"

"It will help wounds heal faster and help the pain subside quicker." Turk scooped a healthy portion of the stuff onto his fingers and smeared it over a nasty looking cut just above Demik's left eyebrow.

"Magic?" Drake asked.

"No, not magic," Turk replied as he continued to tend to various wounds. "Medicine."

The dwarf turned next to Befel, who sat up against a large rock. His face had turned a sullen pale, and a smattering of dried blood around his shoulder, some of it partially coagulated, still ran down his arm and dripped off his palm and fingers.

"Let us look at this," said Turk.

The skin looked burned, puffy and red.

"This is an old wound?" Turk asked.

Befel nodded.

"Did you try to burn it closed?" Turk didn't want to be too inquisitive, but he needed to know.

"Aye," Befel replied.

"And then you tried stitching it as well?"

Befel nodded. "A barber in Finlo."

"He did not do a very good job," Turk muttered. "Don't worry. Once I have a look at this, we should be on the right path to healing."

Turk took a clean cloth and pressed it hard against Befel's wound. The young man let out a loud scream.

"I know it hurts, my friend, but the pain is nothing compared to slowly bleeding to death or getting an infection and losing your arm." When Befel gave the dwarf a worried look, he added, "Drink some of the sailor's rum. That will help the pain."

The dwarf smeared a heavy helping of the greenish, gelatinous cream on Befel's shoulder. The young man tensed when the rough hands touched the wound, but the cooling nature of Turk's medicine seemed to ease any apprehensions, and Befel soon drifted off to a half-sleep, vaguely aware of someone tending to him, but too tired to care.

Turk then turned to Bryon and cleaned a cut on his cheek.

"Do not worry about your cousin," Turk said. "He will be all right."

"I don't care," Bryon replied with a shrug. "He's a grown man."

"Your concerned look says otherwise," Turk said.

Turk smiled at the scowl Bryon gave him.

Vander Bim already had his shirt off and arm up, baring a dirty cut along his ribs. Nafer cleaned that one, and after more of Turk's medicine covered that wound, the dwarf adorned it with a wide square of cloth and wrapped more cloth tightly around the sailor's stomach to hold the bandage in place.

Drake seemed a special case. Despite the normal bumps and bruises one might expect to get from such a battle, his true injury was his chest, where the horse had kicked him. He sat and wheezed, clutching his ribcage with crossed arms and looking wide-eyed as if he were suffocating. Turk inspected him, fairly certain he didn't have any broken ribs and then proceeded to mix some of his medicine into a bowl of water.

"Here." The dwarf lifted the bowl up to Drake's nose. "You must inhale this. It will help your breathing and reduce the tightness in your chest."

"I don't need no damn tunnel digger's cream to heal up," Switch said, walking by Drake as the man breathed in the pallid mist rising from his bowl of water. "I've been cut worse than this."

"Good," Turk replied, "then I will not waste any on you."

"You had best reconsider," Vander Bim said. "What happens when those little cuts get infected? Who's going to care for you when you get sick?"

"Hot water and a good scrub," Switch replied. "That's all I need."

"A good scrub indeed," Demik whispered to Turk in Dwarvish. "That man stinks."

"Aye," Turk replied with a smile.

Switch squinted his eyes and peered angrily at the dwarves.

"Do not expect me to take care of you when you get sick," Turk said.

"Don't worry, I won't," Switch replied. "I've been worse off, tunnel digger, and survived. And all without dwarvish medicine."

Turk shook his head as Switch walked away. Some men were so stupid, but this was one of the most ignorant he had ever met.

"Perhaps," Turk said to himself as he remembered several men in his past that were quite dimwitted. He walked over to Erik.

"Do I need to look at you?" Turk asked.

Erik looked up at the dwarf and shook his head.

"Are you sure?" Turk asked.

Erik extended his arms and inspected them. He looked at his legs and patted his stomach and chest.

"I think I'm alright," Erik said. "Not really a scratch on me."

"Alright," Turk said. He saw Erik staring at his brother, concern creeping across his face.

"He will be fine," Turk said.

"He doesn't look fine," Erik replied as Befel breathed heavily, almost snoring.

Turk reached up and put his hand on Erik's shoulder.

"Trust me. He will be fine."

"That sounds like something someone would tell the loved one of a dying man," Erik said.

"I would not lie to you," Turk said.

"Will he be able to use his arm?" Erik asked.

Turk breathed deep. He knew his moment of pause gave away his concern, and he knew Erik would know he was lying if he said yes.

"He won't, will he?"

"He might be able to use it again," Turk replied, "but he has a long road ahead of him. It will hurt for quite some time, perhaps for the rest of his life. But with appropriate rehabilitation and care, it might heal. We will eventually need to get him to a real surgeon."

"He saw one in Finlo," Erik said.

"Like I said," Turk replied, "a real surgeon. One of my people."

Chapter 56

"WATCH," BRYON SAID, "ALL THAT coin, and we will not see a single, rusted iron penny."

Erik watched as Switch moved from one dead man to the next, sifting through their purses, their pockets, their boots even.

"Do you expect a portion of the coin?" Erik asked. "We are just porters after all."

"Whose side are you on?" Bryon snapped.

"What point is there in arguing, Bryon?" Erik asked.

"You always choose other people over your family," Bryon hissed.

Erik balled up his fists.

"You stupid pathetic moron!" Erik seethed. Bryon backed up, his face a mixture of surprise and anger. He opened his mouth to retort, but Erik moved forward and stuck his face right into his cousin's. "If any of us has chosen anything over family, it's you."

"Now, wait just a..."

"Piss on that," Erik spat. He poked himself in the chest with his index finger. "If anyone here has thought about our family first, it's me. I left with you two idiots *because* of family!"

Erik felt tears in his eyes but from frustration and not sadness.

"Nothing to cry over," Bryon replied, trying to be sarcastic.

Erik was about to hit his cousin, and all he could see had turned red. He felt his body tremble, and the only thought crossing his mind was the image of Bryon's bloody face.

"Bryon, Erik," Vander Bim said, and Erik turned, his hands still in tightly gripped fists. "Give me your hands," added the sailor.

The tension diffused a little; Erik looked at Bryon, and they both opened a hand, presenting their palm to Vander Bim. The sailor pressed three silver coins into each one of their hands.

"Consider this a bonus," Vander Bim said with a smile, "for a fight well fought. And I have three more for Befel. I'll give them to him when he's awake, on my honor."

When Vander Bim walked away, Bryon shot Erik a dirty look. Erik returned the look with one of disdain, and then Bryon turned his back and walked away.

Erik could hear Bryon mutter, "Should've given us more."

Erik turned to find Drake staring at him. As soon as his eyes met the miner's, Drake turned, whispering something to Vander Bim. The man's voice was so soft, Erik shouldn't have been able to hear him, but he felt a tickle at his hip and, suddenly, the miner's voice was audible.

"Damned magic," Drake said.

"You're being ridiculous," Vander Bim replied. Erik squinted his eyes as if that would help his hearing.

"I don't like it," Drake said. "Unnatural."

"It's saved my life several times," Vander Bim replied. "By the gods, magic saved your life once."

"That doesn't matter," Drake whispered. "He should have told us."

"Drake, I don't think he knew," Vander Bim replied.

Be careful, Erik thought but knew the words were not from his own mind.

His palm brushed the hilt of the golden dagger and felt a vibration in his hand as it touched the hilt.

"Should have damn well told us," Drake hissed.

Friends can become enemies very quickly. Erik looked down at the dagger, eyebrows furled.

"Erik."

The voice seemed barely audible as Erik just stared at his weapon, trance-like.

"Erik."

Vander Bim's voice finally cut through, and Erik looked up.

"Help your brother onto his horse," Vander Bim said.

Erik didn't reply, just nodded.

With Befel still half asleep, Erik lifted his brother gently by the armpits, nervous about moving the shoulder, and then sat him up in the saddle.

"Don't know what good an injured porter will do us," Switch muttered as he walked by.

"He'll be fine," Erik replied as he made sure Befel was steady.

"Cut him loose I say," Switch said to no one in particular. "His fault this happened anyway."

"It could have happened to anyone," Vander Bim said.

"You and I both know that's not true," Switch replied. "Bloody pricks. Little gutter shites bringing trouble down on us, and all we can do is sympathize over a hurt shoulder."

"Don't listen to him," Vander Bim said to Erik.

"I try not to," Erik replied.

"You earned your pay today," Vander Bim said.

"And some," Erik added. He thought that maybe his voice sounded unappreciative but felt he cared less than he might have done before.

"Aye, and some," was Vander Bim's simple reply as if he too was recognizing the change.

As they rode away, Erik looked over his shoulder. Buzzards had already started circling overhead, ravens bouncing about the dead and squawking, their black beaks glimmering and stained with blood. Later that night, the plains dogs would come in and carry away whatever the ravens and buzzards didn't take. These men deserved nothing better.

Erik thought that, knew that, but nonetheless, the smile on his face faded. The image of Fox crept into his head, but not as a ruthless slaver, but a little, fiery-haired, freckled boy, spindly-armed, and knobby-kneed. Even he was an innocent child, once. Even he had a mother and a father.

Erik knew he shouldn't care, but he couldn't push the image out of his mind. Then his thoughts turned to the dreams of his mother and father, hanging from a tree, of Marcus and Nadya, lying dead in front of their caravan, the other slavers he had killed.

"How many people have I killed?" Erik whispered to himself as he watched the ground pass by.

He was not so much considering the slavers who had died by his hand, but of the people that had lost their lives because of him. Miners and gypsies. Dreams of the dead—dreams of those who he had known and died—haunted him every night. Then another thought grabbed his attention as he looked at the mercenaries he rode with, talking and laughing as if nothing had just happened. That thought stayed in his head, there at the front of his thoughts as he watched six men who killed for a living. Was this what he was becoming? Was this who he would one day be?

"How many men will I kill?" he murmured.

Chapter 57

"Is the young one okay?" Nafer asked. Turk had barely heard his friend speak.

"What did you say?" he asked, and Nafer repeated his question. Turk inhaled slowly as he watched the young man before answering.

"Ah, yes. Young Erik will be fine, but he faces a long road to becoming a man, a treacherous one."

Turk watched the boy, like water in the saddle, head hanging low, chin to chest. Still a farmer really who had never even considered that one day he might hold a sword, let alone kill another man.

"Why so melancholy, do you suppose?" Nafer asked. "He should be celebrating. It makes no sense."

"He grieves for the men we killed," Turk replied.

"Vass?" interjected Demik and his Dwarvish exclamation drew the attention of the other travelers, though it was only Turk and Nafer who understood. Tossing a scowl from beneath squinted eyebrows, Turk returned a guttural chastisement to Demik as Switch scowled again.

Demik opened and then closed his mouth at Turk's look.

"Erik can't stop thinking about the slavers as little, helpless children running to their mothers, or playing with their fathers."

"Ah ha. That is sad." Nafer shook his head and looked back at the boy, reins loose in his grip. "Now I am sorry for the young man."

"That is ridiculous," Demik huffed and flicked his reins as if swatting a fly away. His horse picked its hooves up and began trotting, forcing the dwarf to pull back to slow down the animal. "None of those children had a mother or father."

"He is not like us Demik," Turk said, looking at his friend. His glare at first was firm, but then he let out a forgiving sigh. "Do you remember the first time you took a life? I do."

"You know I do," Demik said. "We all do. And we were all right in our actions. Righteous kills, even if yours was a rude awakening to the world of men."

Turk remembered the woman he had saved from a would-be rapist in an alley in Vestingard. He also remembered the disgusted look she gave him and the warmth and smell of her spittle as it hit his face.

"Aye," Turk agreed, "but we were all trained to fight. We understand the difference between a righteous kill and murder. Erik was not and does not."

"But those slavers ..." Demik paused and shook his head. "It has been quite a while since I've seen men so ruled by wickedness. I don't care how little and innocent they once were, their transgressions warranted death. They got what they deserved."

"I know," Turk replied. "And Erik does too. They did fight well, though, didn't they? These farmers turned porters."

"I will admit that I was quite surprised," Nafer said.

"They did well enough," was Demik's reluctant acceptance.

"They could have fought like an army of dwarvish warriors, and you still would not give them their due credit," Turk said.

Nafer laughed, and Demik scowled.

"They survived," Demik replied, "against a group of untrained, hungry slavers that looked more like wild dogs. The only ones out of the whole lot that looked to have any training were the two Samanians. If you think that is fighting well, then, so be it. Let us see what happens when they are truly tested."

"And what test would that be?" Nafer asked.

Demik looked to the Southern Mountains.

"You know what tests lay ahead of us," Demik said.

"You think he'll be okay?" Nafer nodded toward Erik.

Turk glanced over his shoulder at the young man.

"He never thought he would have to take a life. It is hard, and I understand that. And it does not make this any easier when he is surrounded by men such as these, men whose only hope is the glimmer of gold, the warmth of a woman, and to live another day. But he will be okay, I think. He is coming to terms with it."

"Let us hope An is with him in this time of grief and pain," Nafer said.

"An is with all of us," Turk raised eyes heavenward. Demik just shook his head and gave a wry laugh.

Chapter 58

WHEN THEY STOPPED TRAVELING FOR the day, Switch begrudgingly decided that he would finally let Turk take a look at his wounds, the thief squirming as the dwarf tried to inspect his various injuries.

"I wish he wouldn't bother," Bryon said. When Erik shot him a questioning look, he added, "Maybe he would get an infection and just die."

A part of Erik wanted to agree with his cousin.

"We need him," Erik said.

"Need him?" Bryon questioned.

"Yes, need him," Erik repeated. "He's good at it."

"Good at what?" Bryon asked.

"This," Erik said, slowly nodding his head to their surroundings. "He's good at all this. He's good at killing."

"Well, be careful then. You might find yourself on the end of his skill we need so badly."

"Sit still," Turk commanded.

"That shit bloody stinks." Switch wrinkled his nose, jerking his head away from his wounded shoulder as Turk smeared his medicinal cream sparingly. This was one of the thief's many cuts.

"And, by the gods, it burns. Are you trying to torture me, tunnel digger?"

"The burn is your injuries healing." Turk's face held no emotion, but Erik could see Nafer biting back a smile.

"Give me some rum, or tomigus root, or some flaming heart leaf," Switch cried.

"Ah, flaming heart leaf. We don't have enough to feed you after you wake from the deep sleep heart leaf would give you," Turk replied. "This cream will cure your ailments."

"Rum cures my ailments just fine," Switch argued.

"I told you, *thief*." Turk seemed to hang on the word, to draw it out as Switch emphasized tunnel digger so often. "Rum, and anything else will slow the healing process. Leave your wounds be, and they'll be alright. Continue to fuss with them, and watch them fester and spoil and turn black."

"You speak as if I've never been cut before." Switch huffed and then hissed. "And what of the itching?"

"Healing," was Turk's curt reply as Switch walked off without a word of gratitude. The thief plopped himself on the ground, and moments later, loud snores spoke of his sleep.

Drake shook his head, a palm rubbing his breastbone as he walked, mumbling to no one in particular.

"Not a drink of water. Not a nibble of jerky. Not a splash on the face. Not even a 'good day, I'm going to sleep now.' Such an odd fellow."

To Erik's right, Bryon was being unusually caring and helping Befel settle down for the night in a relatively comfortable, shady spot guarded by a few more tall shrubs and a single, malnourished, rough-barked tree that looked twisted and bent. Its tiny oval leaves all arranged in a neat row along a thin, green branch did little for shade. Befel grimaced with every movement and gripped his shoulder as he waited for Turk to bring more of his medicine.

"Here." Vander Bim passed Erik a cup of rum as he looked down at his brother. At the young farmer's hesitation, he continued, "Rum always seems to dim pain. All kinds of pain." Vander Bim smiled at his own medical advice. Befel reached for it for himself.

"Perhaps a cupful," Befel said before he coughed on one sip, his face brightening at the taste.

Drake laughed until a sharp snort and a chastising stare came from Turk.

"No rum for this one," Turk scolded.

"Can't you see he's in pain?" Drake asked. "You offered it the first time you treated him."

Turk seemed none too moved.

"He was in more pain then. No rum for you, as well," Turk added.

Drake almost looked like a child robbed of his favorite toy.

Turk leaned back, a hand in his satchel. Bottles clinking, he drew out a pouch of something and shook it before he passed it to Drake.

"Spend time you'd be drinking inhaling this medicine. Mix it with water."

"Why?" Drake spouted his plea like a little child.

"Have you ever tended to wounds before—or even dabbled in the healing arts?" Turk asked.

Drake shook his head.

"Then you'll do as you're told." Turk gave a gruff nod of finality to the miner, and Erik smiled for the first time in a day.

"Like a mother scolding a child," Erik muttered with a rare smile as he went off to see to his horse.

Moments later, lost in his thoughts, a heavy thump startled him. Fear jerked his shoulders and, gripping the reins of his mount in his left hand, the right one firmly wrapped around the golden hilt of his dagger.

Turk held his hands up in defense, a saddle dropped at his feet.

"I am sorry, my friend. I didn't mean to startle you."

Erik released his breath and relaxed the hand on his weapon.

"I was just cleaning my horse's coat," Erik said.

"Quite thoroughly I see." Turk nodded to the gleaming patch of brown fur the young man had brushed repeatedly until it reflected the sun while the rest of the poor animal sat dingy and dull.

"I take pride in my work, I suppose." Erik shrugged and turned back around. He moved to another spot and, with as much care as he could muster, stroked his brush across the animal's hide.

"Perhaps. Or perhaps you didn't mean to clean at all." Turk chuckled.

"Then what would I be doing with a brush and a dirty horse standing in front of me?" Erik glowered over his shoulder, hoping his tone spoke more than his words. Inside, he regretted being sharp when he knew the dwarf meant well.

"I don't know. You tell me." Turk's lack of reaction surprised Erik.

"You are still upset about those men—the slavers." Turk didn't need the young farmer to answer.

Erik thought about going back to brushing his animal's coat but instead dropped his brush, his chin touching his chest.

"I wasn't—not at first. I don't know. I can't get them out of my head. I can't stop thinking of ..."

"You can't stop thinking of them as little children—innocent, little children," Turk interrupted.

"Yes." Erik met Turk's blue-gray eyes.

"You know," Turk spoke softly, "there comes a time when a boy's innocence passes away, and he begins to make choices on his own— he becomes accountable for the things he does, both good and bad. Those men held no innocence. They made their choices. Even though they were once little children, and their choices may have been difficult—perhaps they did not have loving mothers and caring fathers— they still made their choices. They are not guiltless, little children."

Turk smiled, not a laughing smile, or a mocking smile, but an understanding smile, one that knew exactly what Erik thought and felt.

"You have continued to pray?" Turk asked.

Erik nodded again. "My prayers do nothing. They don't comfort me, and I think the Creator wants nothing with them."

"Sometimes An answers prayers through his silence," Turk explained. "You must know that An, who you call the Creator, forbids murder without reason, but not killing amidst the bloodshed of battle, defending oneself, fighting for a righteous cause."

"But does the Creator know that I rejoiced when they died?" Erik replied, his voice hard, angry almost.

A part of him wanted to be sorry for the men whose lives he had taken, but he wasn't and prayed for them more because he thought he ought to and not because he wanted to. A part of him wanted to grieve for the gypsies and miners who had died, but he didn't. They just haunted his dreams, night after night. And every ounce of him wanted to hold his mother and father, kiss the foreheads of his sisters, caress the face of his beloved Simone, but they were so far away, and he didn't even know if any of them were still alive, let alone waiting for his return.

"Does the Creator know that I smiled as I watched crows pick at their flesh?" Erik hissed, his words bearing the same intensity as water hitting red-hot iron.

"Aye, that he does," Turk said, "and for that, you must continue to ask his forgiveness. But if he never forgave us, never turned a blind eye to our transgressions even after we've repented, I fear there would be no one dining in the halls of Heaven, and the Shadow would be brimming with the souls of even the most righteous warriors who have walked Háthgolthane."

"I don't think he will forgive me," Erik said and felt the muscles in his jaw ache as he ground his teeth.

"If you truly ask it, truly in your heart ask for forgiveness, An...the Creator will grant it," Turk explained. "That is his promise to us."

Erik nodded slightly.

"You will be all right, my young friend." Turk patted Erik on the shoulder. "This time of uncertainty will pass. I think I would be more worried if you didn't lament the death of another."

Turk remained next to Erik for a short time, making what little small talk a dwarf and young, inexperienced farmer could make. Erik spoke of his father and sisters, his brother and cousin, other things about a farm that could not at all interest a battle-hardened mountain dweller. Nonetheless, he spoke, and the dwarf nodded and smiled as if he truly cared about what Erik had to say. All the while, Erik could not help but think his friend looked nervous, apprehensive almost.

Turk finally took in a large breath, seemingly resigning himself to something.

"Quite a blade you have there." He pointed to the jeweled hilt and scabbard stuck snuggly in Erik's belt.

Erik looked down at the weapon and didn't know what to say. He seemed to stare at it with as much curiosity as the dwarf.

"You didn't know what it could do, did you?" Turk asked.

Erik shook his head. A small smile crept across his face. "It belonged to a friend."

"A good friend to give you such a gift," Turk said.

"Aye," Erik replied, "a very good friend."

The dwarf protruded his lower lip, his brows curved downwards in contemplation.

"Magic," Turk said, "but what kind?"

"Magic?" Erik said. Did that exist? He guessed now that it did, that something could possess powers not normally of this earth, but many in his farmstead didn't believe so. Erik laughed silently. Some in his village, many in the world, believed only men inhabited the earth. Obviously not true either. What would his grandmother say?

"The Shadow," he could hear her rasp in the back of his head. "Magic, my boy, is the tool of the Shadow and all his minions."

He looked at his dagger again, removed it—scabbard and all—from his belt and inspected with at least a little bit of caution.

"I think the others are upset with me," Erik said.

"Why?" Turk asked.

"Because of the dagger," Erik replied.

Turk shrugged.

"Irritated, maybe," Turk said. "Mercenaries aren't as wary of magic as simple folk from Western Háthgolthane. But it is a courtesy, typically, to let your adventuring companions know you have something enchanted in your possession."

"But I didn't..."

312

Turk put up a hand, cutting Erik off.

"I know you didn't know," Turk said. "And they know that as well now. That is why they are merely irritated and not actually upset."

"I think the flute I play is magic also," Erik added. "I don't know how to play the flute, and yet, I do. Or rather, it plays—whatever I think, whatever I imagine, it plays itself. This also a gift from my friend."

Turk nodded and reached for the knife. Erik relented and gave the dwarf his weapon.

You would freely give this dwarf your weapon? Erik thought. *I trust him. I don't know why, but I trust him.*

"And this man," Turk said as he turned the dagger in his hands, "this friend just gave these things to you? Even in lands that scorn magic, it will fetch a high price, one too big for someone to simply gift enchanted things to friends. When someone comes across magical things, they normally keep them, hide them, treasure them, but never give them away. Who was this friend?"

"They belonged to Marcus." Erik's voice cracked. "A gypsy. He died in the slaver attack along with his wife. His son gave them to me. Said they'd be better use to me than him. I couldn't believe it at first. The dagger, even without being magic, must be expensive, that I know for sure. I have often thought that I could sell that dagger and make my father a rich man. And the flute. Marcus played it every night. I thought a son would want to keep such a thing. Perhaps he knew where I would be going."

"Perhaps." Turk looked at the unsheathed dagger and then to the dented, single-edged short sword hanging from the young man's belt. The dwarf handed the weapon back to Erik.

"You say that with some uncertainty," Erik said.

Turk shrugged. "These gypsies, goodly people, yes?"

Erik nodded. "Why?"

"Gypsies have a way of getting their hands on things that don't belong to them." Turk quickly looked up at Erik. He must've seen the look of defiance work across his face. "But, if you say these men

313

were good men, then he must've come across them some other way. I would think if someone, especially in the west, found themselves in the possession of a magic dagger and flute, it would be a gypsy."

Erik felt his face soften.

"Why?"

"They travel all over the world, my friend," Turk replied. "Despite the stereotypes, they are expert tradesmen. I'm sure in a land such as Wüsten Sahil, where things of an enchanted nature are more prevalent, a gypsy would readily take it in lieu of gold, knowing what price it could fetch in Háthgolthane or Antolika. This is a precious gift. One that is truly heartfelt. Treasure it."

Erik nodded and felt better. He took in a large breath and let it out slowly, closed his eyes, and thought of home. He smelled the freshly shorn grass of early spring, the honeyed scents of roses and lilies in bloom. He heard the somber cooing of the mourning dove that, for the past few years before he left, sat on a purple-leafed bush growing just under his window. It serenaded him every day as the sun poked its face over the eastern horizon. He often thought that bird sang only for him. The first couple times he heard it, he sat up in bed, and as soon as the bird saw him, it promptly flew away. But after a week or so, it stayed, grew accustomed to the young man listening to its pseudo-sad song. He wondered if the songbird missed him. He smiled.

"A good memory?"

"Home."

"Aye, a very good memory. If we ever reach my home ..." Turk belly-rubbed himself through a self-critical chuckle. "*When* we reach my home, I will take you to Ilken Copper Head. He is the greatest of smiths in all Drüum Balmdüukr. He could look at your blade if you'd like. Tell you what it is, what it does."

Erik's wide grin offered all the confirmation Turk needed.

Chapter 59

"BLOODY SHADOW! WHERE DID THIS heat come from?" Switch said as he yet again wiped sweat from his forehead before draining his waterskin in a single gulp.

"We should camp early tonight," Vander Bim said. Erik had noticed their pace had slowed, and the sailor must've realized it as well. "We've been riding hard for several days."

Switch scowled and groaned loudly.

"You don't agree?" Vander Bim asked.

"What's it matter what I think?" the pouting pickpocket muttered, but when Vander Bim continued to look at him, said, "what if more slavers are following us?"

"Doubtful," Turk said. "But we are a large group. Single men or groups of two or three could probably gain ground on us."

"Strength in numbers, right Vander Bim?" Switch chastised.

"Aye," Vander Bim replied, "and I still stand by my inclination. We can afford a few more hours of rest. While we sleep unafraid of cougars and wolves, those single men will have to rest with one eye open."

After Erik had seen to the horses, he plopped down next to his brother.

"I know this game, Befel," Erik said. "You feign sickness, and I get stuck with your chores."

Befel didn't say anything. He just lay there, his breathing slow and even.

"How are you?" Erik tapped Befel in the ribs.

"Can't you see I'm sleeping?" Befel asked.

"I know your tricks." Erik smiled.

"If you think this is some trick, then you are more foolish than I thought," Befel said.

"I'm sorry," Erik replied. "I know you're hurt."

"You don't know," Befel replied with a hiss. "This ground is hard and hot. I won't be able to sleep tonight. Every move I make sends ripples of pain down my arm and back. My head aches constantly, and I feel as if I'm coming down with a fever."

"It seems that everything in the world that could happen to you has," Erik said.

"Piss off," Befel said, looking over his shoulder at Erik.

"And where should I go?" Erik asked.

"I don't care," Befel replied.

"I don't like arguing with you, Befel," Erik said, "but don't think I will just sit here while you abuse me and curse me and then whine about your shoulder."

"Whatever," Befel said.

"Vander Bim said we will stop for a few days in Aga Kona," Erik said. "Maybe there, you can get some much-needed rest."

"How far?" Befel asked.

"I don't know," Erik replied, "but it can't be too far."

"Maybe I'll just stay in Aga Kona," Befel muttered.

"And do what?" Erik asked. When his brother didn't reply, he said, "You cannot still be serious about wanting to be a miner."

"Maybe I'll do something else," Befel said. "I'll be a bartender. Run a general store. Something other than this, which I am clearly no good at."

Erik didn't reply as he pushed himself to his feet, looking to the south and then to his brother, now pretending to sleep—perhaps wishing he truly slept—and no doubt hoping this was just one, long dream. Erik wandered back to the campfire and stood at the edge of the encirclement, lively conversation passing between Bryon and the dwarves or Vander Bim and Drake.

Only Switch sat quietly, sipping on a cup of something, his lip curling with every sip, arms wrapped around knees pulled loosely to his chest. He wore a scowl, his typical gaunt grimace of pursed lips and crooked brows. Erik noticed Switch watching him from the corner of his grayish, yellowed eyes. His glance moved from Erik to Befel. Switch's glower grew, and the clenching of his thin, yet prominent, jaw told of grinding teeth.

With a quick snort of finality, Switch poured the contents of his cup out and punched the ground with both fists, pushing himself to his feet. The others stopped their conversations and stared at the thief. He spat into the fire and grabbed his cup. He made for Erik, and the young man backed up a few paces, balling his hands into fists, readying himself for a fight.

Erik saw Bryon tense and move from sitting to crouching on one knee, a cat ready to pounce. But, when Switch reached the young farmer, he said nothing. Erik simply heard the man cursing under his breath. Rather, he stopped short of Befel, stooping over him and grumbling incoherencies. His back to the mercenary, Befel couldn't have seen Switch, so the thief threw his empty cup at Befel's feet.

"My cup is bloody empty!" His yell cracked the now silent night. "Get up and get me some more water!"

Bryon moved to his feet, but a rough, strong hand stopped him from fully straightening himself. Instead, Drake rose, face red, hands clenched and white-knuckled.

"We hired them as porters." Drake's hiss sounded stern, accusing, and hateful. "To break camp and tend the horses; not to wait on us."

Switch looked back at the miner, barely paying him any attention, and then back to Befel. He grunted. He gave him a kick, not too hard, more of a nudge, but nonetheless, it was a boot to the back.

Erik hadn't seen him move. He hadn't seen him traverse the span of the camp. He hadn't seen him run up on the thief. But, Bryon's fist flew, catching Switch square in the jaw, and he reeled backward, toppling over the prostrate Befel and landing on his back.

The sudden silence brought on by the attack proved short-lived as a growl rolled from Switch's mouth. Turk and Demik clamped their hands onto Bryon and wrestled him to the ground. It was a good thing.

Switch jumped to a crouched position, long, straight dagger in hand. The poultice along his right shoulder seeped red through his dirty shirt. Drake ran in front of him, putting his hands on the thief's chest to stop him from charging Bryon.

"That's my family!" Bryon spat as he pushed the dwarves off him. "Employer or no employer, touch him again, and I'll kill you."

Erik joined the dwarves as they moved to stop his cousin again, but the sidelong glance Bryon shot them told them to stay back. Befel scooted away, half kneeling, half sitting, behind Erik.

"I'd like to see you try you little shit! You little maggot!" Switch rubbed his jaw with his free hand, spat blood and a bit of chipped tooth, and, despite his red-faced glare, gave the hint of a smile. "You'll not get another cheap shot like that again."

Bryon made for Switch again, and this time the dwarves blocked his path.

"You won't always have them to step in between us." Switch's grip on his dagger tightened, and his other hand retrieved a smaller, curved blade from the back of his belt.

"Good." Bryon lunged forward again, but Turk put an open palm in the middle of his chest.

"Bryon, stop," Erik said as Turk shook his head, silently saying the same thing.

Switch spat on the ground again and walked off into the darkness of the night, cursing Bryon the whole way.

Erik's eyes met Drake's as the miner walked back to the campfire. His eyes spoke of worry.

"The faults of fights and arguments with Switch normally rest on his shoulders," Drake explained. "And often, he deserves a beating for something he's said or done. However, fights with Switch normally result in someone's death."

"A fight with Bryon might result in his death this time," Erik added. His cousin was a dangerous fighter.

"Perhaps," Drake admitted, "or both their deaths. Whoever might die, there seems no sense in letting it happen tonight."

Befel stood, shaky and pale. Every step caused a grimace, and he clutched his shoulder. When he passed Turk, the dwarf commented, "Give me a moment, and we'll have another look at that wound."

Befel nodded. Erik helped him over to a spot next to the fire, and as they passed Bryon, Befel tried to put his hand on their cousin's shoulder. Bryon pushed his hand away.

"Learn to fight your own battles." Bryon stomped off into the shadows, in the opposite direction of Switch.

"Don't forget who stood by your side when Jovek's boys bullied you, and who came to your aid when the Wodum brothers and their three friends had you on your stomach and would've kicked you until you bled to death!" yelled Befel as his cousin walked away. "Damn you!"

"Let it go," Erik said, helping his brother sit down. "He can't hear you. He wouldn't be able to hear you even if he looked you in the eyes."

Switch now seemed to have disappeared into the night, and as Befel fell into an uneasy sleep, the others gathered again, each with their own thoughts, around the fire as darkness sucked the heat out of the day.

"Those two men we found, all twisted and burnt," said Drake, breaking a long silence.

"Must you really bring them up again?" Erik asked.

"Well, as much as I don't like to," Drake said somewhat apologetically, "it's interesting, what they said in Finlo before attacking the Messenger of the East."

"You understood them?" Erik asked.

"Aye," Drake replied. "I spent time in Gol-Nornor, in the North

River Basin across the Giant's Vein. I was a part of the Nordethian militia, and we are allies with Gol-Nornor and Gol-Durathna. Picked up some of the language while I was there."

"Is that considered Mek-Ba'Dune?" Vander Bim asked.

"No," Drake replied with a quick shake of his head, "but the languages are similar, although the people of Mek-Ba'Dune and the nomads of the North River Basin are quite different."

"So, what did they say?" Vander Bim asked.

"You see, Mek-Ba'Dune means 'Sacred Plains,'" Drake explained. "So, what they said was, 'for the people of the Sacred Plains.' Most of the people of Antolika don't much care for the people of Háth-golthane. We have a history of meddling in the affairs of the people east of the Giant's Vein. I'm sure they were sent to assassinate the Messenger, to try to stop Golgolithul's incursions into their lands."

Drake looked down at his feet, picked up a small twig, and, with the flick of his wrist, tossed it into the fire. Erik watched the twig, watched the fire consume it, and then watched the fire's light dance off Drake's stern face.

"There's much bigger things going on in this world than we know, things much bigger than most could imagine."

Chapter 60

Patûk Al'Banan looked up to the darkening sky and squinted as he traced his index finger around a constellation of stars. They seemed to stand out amongst the million others, floating indifferently in the heavens above the Southern Mountains.

How fitting that you're called the Troll's Shadow in this part of the mountains.

He looked up to the slopes of the mountain range as the waning light cast faint apparitions as if a giant of a ghost moved from one night tree to another, like one of the boulders brought to life. The general stooped, crouched low to pick a bit of dirt between his thumb and forefinger. He leaned his forearm against his knee and looked back up to the sky, now darker than it was just seconds before.

"What do the dwarves call you?" Patûk furled his brows. "The Bear. No, The Great Bear. I don't know which I prefer."

He threw the dirt back to its resting place and brushed his hand off on his pants. Standing up, he pulled his shoulders back and rolled his head, his well-muscled neck popping and crackling. He smiled.

"I think I'll take the Troll's Shadow this night. Tomorrow you can be The Great Bear, protecting the heavens. Tonight, I need something terrible."

He gave a sideways jerk of his head, and Bao Zi walked to his commander's side, Warrior—that loyal, battle-hardened, and equally as surly warhorse—in tow. Patûk took the reins, and Bao Zi bowed and shuffled backward, face always to the ground. The general smiled. Loyalty and humility went far with the old commander.

"Is Lieutenant Bu here?"

"Yes, sir." Bao Zi's responses always sounded abrupt.

When he first took the man on as his personal guard, Patûk thought the man insolent. He even had him beat several times. But when it came time for battle, that old, half-blinded soldier proved his worth. He even gave his right eye for Patûk. The general remembered that day reverently. A dwarf's broadsword meant for his own face had thudded into the guardian's scalp. He thought Bao Zi dead, for sure. Not only was he not dead, but with a single, hateful swing of his long sword—the same one that still hung from his belt—he removed that bearded midget's head from his shoulders.

"Bring him," the general commanded, and Bao Zi bowed, moving silently away.

The lieutenant walked quickly to Patûk Al'Banan's side and knelt, face to the ground. Despite his promotion to officer and his command of all Patûk's spies, Lieutenant Bu chose to continue to wear the leather breastplate of an enlisted soldier. When Lieutenant Sorben Phurnan saw that, he scoffed and the general had given him a hand across the face for it—privately, of course. Sorben, that fool. His privileged upbringing had clouded his senses, his reasoning. Bu was a spy, and silence and stealth were his armor. Lieutenant Phurnan would have given up the requirements of his trade for a simple symbol of status. And since Bu became lieutenant and had chosen to continue to wear the armor of his men, they had worked doubly hard for him.

"News." Patûk Al'Banan's statement seemed simple, but Lieutenant Bu knew what he wanted.

"Yes, sir." The lieutenant remained kneeling and bowed. "Men, dozens of mercenaries heading east from Finlo. In search of a dwarvish city called Orvencrest, my lord. My apologies, sir, but I've never heard of it."

The general grunted his disapproval but waited. Bu shifted uneasily.

"Some went directly into the Western Tor but only a few. One man is dead and two others disappeared a week ago. Most are heading along the northern edges of the Southern Mountains, my lord. Heading to a mining camp known as Aga Kona."

"Any interventions?" Patûk Al'Banan asked.

"No, my lord."

When Patûk gave a glare that could melt steel in the dead of winter, Bu scooted back several paces.

"Th-the mercenaries seem to be doing our job for us, sir. Just three days back, we found over a dozen dead, left for the crows."

"They were killed by mercenaries?" Patûk Al'Banan asked.

"My scouts think so, sir," Lieutenant Bu replied. "They found a dwarf's throwing ax among the dead."

"We are in the Southern Mountains, Lieutenant," Patûk Al'Banan replied. A dwarvish tool may not be so uncommon in a place where dwarves live. In fact, most of the dwarves that live in the world of men come from the Southern Mountains."

"Aye, my lord. But the southern dwarves are not active in this area of the mountains," Lieutenant Bu said, "and we know that three dwarves left Finlo with an acceptance to the Messenger's proposal."

"So they are fighting one another," the general said.

"Yes, sir," Lieutenant Bu replied.

Patûk actually chuckled. "And that is why you never use mercenaries to do something well-trained easterners can do."

Patûk looked up at the sky again. "How far to Aga Kona?"

"From where we are," Bu replied, "a day. We would be there tomorrow by dusk."

Patûk nodded and turned to the captain of his guard. "Send Captain Kan ahead. Tell him we will meet him in two days' time."

Bu nodded, bowed, and left, and Patûk turned back to Bao Zi.

"Now, tell that fool, Sorben. .." Patûk stopped, silently cursed himself for saying what he did in front of his bodyguard. "Go get Lieutenant Phurnan. Tell him to come here with as much speed as he can muster.

"Yes, sir," Bao Zi replied and hurried away again.

Chapter 61

Ranus and Cliens decided to camp up in the rising hills of the Southern Mountains. They knew all too well the things that traversed these parts of the mountains, especially as those rolling hills rose to tall peaks dotted with jutting rocks and huge boulders. Trolls, antegants, wolves, cougars, dwarves. The last might prove the most worrisome of encounters. Some southern dwarves seemed at least tolerant of humans—escorting them away from their homes at the very worst. Others, those disgusted with men and their constant excursions into dwarvish lands, may be polite enough to offer a quick death.

Regardless, dwarves would be the least favorable. Trolls and antegants, well, Cliens shuddered at the thought. Perhaps they were all as bad as each other.

"Shall we tempt fate and make a fire tonight?" Cliens asked.

The click followed by a short hiss spoke of Ranus' disapproval. It spoke of an argument these two soldiers had on many occasions in regards to fate and free will and the role of supernatural forces in people's lives.

"Yes, yes, I know you don't believe in fate. I suppose I don't either."

Ranus gave the Gol-Durathnan a look of disbelief.

"Okay, so maybe a little. But you must admit, how can the Creator know everything, know what will happen, and yet still give us free will? And how can he love us and then allow us to make stupid mistakes that hurt ourselves and others?"

Two clicks, a whistle, two hisses, and another click.

"I guess you're right. Perhaps this is a discussion for another time. Sometimes I wish, however, that my parents raised me to know the gods. It would be so much simpler to leave everything up to their fancies and perverse pleasures."

Ranus put his hand—long, slender fingers that were cold and clammy—on Cliens' shoulder. How could such slender fingers be so strong?

"Yes, yes, I know. Then I would spend eternity with the Shadow. Lucky I met you, right my friend?"

Ranus smiled.

"So, we should tempt all the nasties that live in these mountains and make a fire."

Ranus nodded.

The fire proved a small one. It seemed enough, though, in the way of comfort. It gave a bit of warmth and a bit of light. Enough to ward off any incursions from curious creatures, or perhaps just enough to invite them. Cliens threw Ranus his bag, and the soldier rifled through the Durathnan's things and found a pouch of dried fruit, rattled a hollow gourd filled with nuts, and several small sheets of jerked beef, lightly seasoned with pepper and salt. The soldier from the Shadow Marshes tossed the bag back to Cliens and then, setting his dinner before him on a small blanket, fiddled for something in his pocket. He smiled widely when he retrieved that for which he was looking.

Cliens shook his head. Ranus snorted and presented the contents of his pocket to the soldier in a gesture of sharing.

Cliens stuck his tongue out and curled his lip. "You know I don't like that stuff."

A hiss, a click, a quick gurgle, then another hiss.

"I know I've never tried it," Cliens replied.

Cliens didn't need to. A black ball of something that looked like moss and dirt seemed none too appetizing. Ranus' treats for himself—from home. This was his last one. He studied it, seemed to revel in its presence for a moment, and then tossed it into his wide mouth and moaned with delight as he began to chew.

"Savor it, my friend," Cliens said.

Ranus nodded.

The Durathnan looked up to the sky. Their small crackling fire was no match for the stars above. He figured that his children and their mother were looking at them at that very moment. In fact, they had probably been looking at them for some time. The sun rose and set earlier in Kamdum.

Ranus made a complicated string of sounds.

"I know they are safe." Cliens hated being away from home for so long. He almost turned Darius down this time. He had served the General Lord Marshal well and faithfully for a long time. He had no reservations about turning down the commander of Amentus' forces, and he knew the marshall would respect his decision. But when his eldest son and wife reminded him that duty to the Creator and Country came before family, he had no choice.

Ranus clicked and hissed and groaned again.

"Aye," Cliens replied. "We do need to get as much rest as possible. We do have a long trek tomorrow."

Ranus knew Cliens too well. Watching the stars would put Cliens in a lamentable state. They needed every ounce of energy, courage, and heart focused on their task at hand.

"May the Great Bear watch them tonight and keep them safe. May he watch us and give us a hasty return home."

Chapter 62

"WHAT YOU SPEAK OF IS treason." The older man, Arnif, ran a hand across his gray hair.

Patûk Al'Banan scuffed his own gray head, watching the old man lean back in his chair, right hand resting gently on the table that separated the two. Age had not treated him as kindly as Patûk.

Wrinkles creased Arnif's face, and the white lines of ancient scars crisscrossed his cheeks and forehead unevenly. He tapped his fingers, arthritic and swollen, on the table slowly.

"Not treason," Patûk reasoned in a rare calm, cool voice, "but business. The Lord of the East is a businessman, after all. We all are, are we not?"

"Business?" the other man laughed. "Aga Kona would bring a high price if someone proved foolish enough to consider what you are offering."

"I can pay it. In fact, name your price, and I will double it," Patûk Al'Banan said. "Give the money to the Ruler of Golgolithul if you like."

That threw the man into a fit of laughter. "Oh, yes. He would welcome me with open arms after selling his new mine, one that sits on a fortune of gold. A mine that would bring a hundred thousand times what you would pay over its life."

"Then keep the money for yourself," Patûk Al'Banan replied.

"What do I care what you do with the money? Just don't pass up a once in a lifetime offer."

"And look over my shoulder for the rest of my life." The old man, face long and drawn with a hawk-beaked nose and thin mouth laughed.

"I may have only a few years left, but I plan on stretching those out as best I can. Besides, even if we made no money here at Aga Kona, my only welcome for selling it would be the gallows. No, it is not for sale. Now, if you have nothing else to say, I bid you a good night."

Patûk grabbed the man's wrist before he could move. His steel grip held the man's arm firm, even as he tried to pull away.

"Then abandon it," the general said in a low, whispering hiss. "Tell your king brigands ran you off. Tell him whatever you like. Just leave."

Arnif's thin lips grew even thinner. His white, haphazard eyebrows curled over squinting eyes.

"A sword would run me through the minute those words left my mouth. Or worse."

He stopped struggling to pull his wrist free and studied Patûk's face. The general didn't think the man recognized him, but he couldn't be sure.

"Do you think you are the first thug to try and intimidate me?"

Patûk Al'Banan jerked back; Arnif's words were venom, dirty spittle in his face.

"In my line of work," Arnif added, "I encounter the likes of you all the time. You'll not scare me. You'll certainly not drive me from this mine. And if you don't let go of my arm, you'll not soon forget this day."

Patûk released the man. He nodded a slight approval at the man's defiance even if a storm did rage inside the general's head.

"No," Patûk corrected. "You never before encountered the likes of me," he explained, offering that intentional smile he typically gave right before he killed someone. "I am not some ordinary thug. I am the worst kind of thug. But you are right on one thing, my foolish Arnif. I will not soon forget this day."

"Then get out..." Arnif said quietly but with clear meaning.

"Gladly," Patûk Al'Banan said, standing and giving the captain of the Aga Kona mine a curt bow.

Patûk pushed aside the door-flap angrily, leaving behind a cursing Arnif. He stopped just short of a well-groomed man and watched him getting ready to walk inside. Broad-shouldered and tall, his cloak was surprisingly free of dust and wrinkles when he must have been riding to get to this place.

Wavy brown hair spread evenly over his shoulders gave him the look of a successful adventurer. The finely crafted hilts, bound in richly colored leather, of two long swords poked through the man's cloak, and his attention seemed to be on his riding gloves, pulling them off and stuffing them neatly into his belt. But it was the man's clean-shaven face, his rigid jawline, and the way he held his head when meeting Patûk eye to eye, that gave the look of a soldier. So engrossed in his hands, he did not see the general.

"My apologies, sir," the man said, bumping shoulders with Patûk. "I wasn't looking where I was going. My fault entirely."

Patûk just grumbled under his breath and moved on with a sideways glance at the well-groomed adventurer. Certainly, a soldier at one point. Any mercenary or treasure seeker would have punched him for such an insult of standing in a man's way. It would have been to his death, of course, had he sought to attack Patûk.

As the supposed soldier pushed the tent's flap aside, Patûk heard Arnif yell, "What the hell do you want?"

"My apologies," Patûk heard the adventurer say, "but I wish to beg a night's stay in your camp for myself and my two companions. We have money, of course."

That was what Patûk heard before the tent's flap closed and muffled any more coherent sound. From the corner of his eye, he saw two other men standing by three horses. One nickered and stomped as Patûk walked on.

The fading dusk and oncoming night muddled their features, but he could see their build at least in the waning light. They looked much like the other adventurer—tall, broad-shouldered, well-built. Curious.

"Well?" Sorben Phurnan asked when the general returned to his side, holding Warrior's reins.

"You would do well to watch your tone with me, Lieutenant," Patûk commanded.

"Yes, sir. I apologize most…"

"Stuff your apologies," Patûk Al'Banan said with irritation, "I am tired of receiving apologies tonight."

Sorben Phurnan bowed low in submission. Patûk looked up to the Southern Mountains, its low rolling hills of the Western Tor all but gone, finally turned into high mountain peaks. In the night air, he saw the shadow of another boulder move up among the undulations and dips of the rising slopes. But this time, yellow eyes were highlighted by the soft moonlight, and they met Patûk's steady gaze before they quickly blinked into darkness. The shadow moved, seen no more.

"The Troll's Shadow," the general muttered and smiled.

He turned his attention back to the lieutenant. The man stood smugly in front of the old soldier, head bowed and knees bent in half reverence, half disdain. Patûk remembered a thought he had had many nights before. Did Sorben Phurnan's zealotry outweigh his foolishness? The general shook his head. His foolishness was beginning to outweigh his zealotry.

"What did you make of those three men who arrived?" Patûk Al'Banan pointed to the two darkened silhouettes standing by their horses.

"They were at the Lady's Inn, my lord," Sorben replied. "They are mercenaries."

"Truly?" the general asked.

"Yes, sir. That is, at least, what our spies—Bu—tells us." A strong hint of contempt seasoned Sorben Phurnan's words.

"And you distrust his information?" Patûk asked.

Sorben didn't reply.

"They have the look of soldiers to me," the general said.

"Agreed, sir," Lieutenant Sorben Phurnan replied. "In fact, they move and look like Eastern Soldiers. I heard them, as they spoke with one another, speaking Shengu, and in a dialect that sounded refined, educated. Nonetheless, Bu saw them in Finlo. And he saw them accept the Messenger's offer."

Perhaps mercenaries speaking Shengu—the language of most Golgolithul—didn't seem such an oddity. Perhaps even well-trained, soldier-like men speaking Shengu didn't seem so strange. But all officers of Golgolithul received an education where, in addition to many other things, they learned to speak well. An Eastern soldier speaking an educated dialect of Shengu made an obvious conclusion.

Patûk's lip curled. "Eastern officers selling their training as mercenaries. It makes me sick."

"What would you have me do, sir?" Sorben Phurnan asked.

"Follow them when they leave. Kill them when you have the chance." Patûk's tone was as if he was telling someone to pass him a drink.

Sorben Phurnan gave the general's reluctance to kill former eastern officers a decidedly derisive look. "As you wish, my lord."

Patûk saw the disrespect on Sorben's face, heard it in his voice. He would deal with it later. Lieutenant Bu was proving a loyal soldier, one who did what the general asked of him without question, without needless, negative responses and looks. And Captain Kan had mentioned two other men under his control who could readily serve as faithful junior officers in Patûk's ever-growing army of dissidents. The general's need for Sorben grew smaller and smaller. He looked back up to the mountains. Those yellow eyes appeared again.

"And Aga Kona, sir?" the lieutenant asked.

The general looked at his underling, his head still bowed in mock reverence. "They will not sell. They will not abandon. I think you know what to do."

Chapter 63

Switch, as he often did, rode ahead of the company for most of the day, scouting and surveying their course, and Bryon eyed the thief closely.

"It's a wonder he just doesn't leave," Bryon whispered to no one. "It doesn't seem like he needs us, and we'd be better off without him."

"I wouldn't be so sure." Turk always seemed intent on listening to Bryon's self-directed mutterings as if the farmer would have something of worth to offer. "He may be crude and unruly, and at times we all might question whether he's a foe more than a friend, but I have a feeling his *skills* may come in handy. You must admit, our encounter with those slavers might have gone quite differently without his help."

"I still don't like him," Bryon muttered through ground teeth.

"You don't have to like him." Turk smiled. "You need only tolerate him. Do you think you would've liked every soldier you would've stood next to in the ranks of the Eastern Army?"

Bryon shook his head.

"No indeed." Turk's self-righteous smile irritated Bryon like a thorn in the thumb. The dwarf knew he was smart and had no compunctions about letting others know how intelligent he was. Despite all that, he did seem to make sense most of the time ... all the time, but Bryon would have hated to admit that.

"But you would've tolerated them to survive, and that is what you must do here. I hate admitting it as much as you do, but Switch could very well save your life one day."

Every moment without Switch around felt like a breath of fresh air. So, when the gray-brown head of the emaciated thief emerged from the eastern horizon, cursing his galloping horse, Bryon's heart sank a little. Part of him wondered why the Goldumarian spurred his poor horse so vigorously, to the point of coughing fits, and then part of him didn't care—the part that wanted the fool to keep on riding.

The thief stopped just short of Vander Bim, his mount skidding to a stop and kicking up a fountain of dirt. Bryon coughed and spat and wanted to yell and curse, but a look from the sailor quashed that idea before he began frantic questioning. He'd seen something on Switch's face, and now Bryon saw it too.

"What is it?" Vander Bim asked.

"Blood and guts and maggots." Switch's curses had a particular color to them that, ashamedly, made Bryon smile. Reluctance rolled about the edge of his voice. "You'd best come with me."

Switch didn't wait for Vander Bim, or anyone else, to say anything. He pulled hard on his horse's reins. The animal coughed and neighed and turned. The thief dug his heels hard into its side. It reared up and sped forward, leaving a trail of dust and dirt in its wake.

"I suppose we should follow," Vander Bim said, looking back at the rest of the group.

Drake nodded, Bryon shook his head, and all three dwarves shrugged.

"Onward, then," Vander Bim said with his own shrug.

After following for a while, Bryon saw Switch ahead, circling his horse around a spot on the ground, looking down at something. He stopped, threw one leg over to the side, and slid out of his saddle, immediately going into a crouch.

"What in the Shadow ..."

The encroaching scene interrupted Bryon's question slowly as their horses went from galloping to trotting, to a standstill.

At first, all Bryon could see were bodies. He heard Nafer mumble something in his native tongue and heard Erik gasp. How many bodies, he didn't know. Then, closer, he saw two. And then, even closer, he could see why the thief seemed so frantic.

"By the heavens, what is that?" Bryon felt the corners of his mouth dip and curl under his nose.

Red stained the dirt—blood. It didn't rest just around the bodies, though. It lay all around. Too much blood. At least, too much for just two men. It looked dark, mostly dried, but Bryon thought he saw something else, tissue, bits of organ, stuck in the coagulating liquid.

"By the gods and the four hells of the four corners of the world!" Vander Bim cried out when they finally reached Switch.

Bryon turned his head and covered his nose with his arm. He heard either Erik or Befel gag and saw Drake retching, wanting to vomit, before he covered his mouth and nose with his hand. And there was Switch, crouched, unabashedly sifting through the remains of bodies torn apart like trees in a hurricane. Unworried about the stench of blood and shit, Turk joined the thief.

Bryon could make out the face of one of the men. It looked like a rat's face—a thin chin, a pointed nose, short, wild grayish-black hair. He knew that face.

"*The Lady's Inn,*" Bryon thought out loud.

"What's that?" Switch asked.

"That one is from *The Lady's Inn.*" Bryon pointed to the rat-faced man, his voice muffled by his arm.

"You have a habit of stating the obvious," Switch's voice conveyed a sense of irritation, but his face showed the contrary. He smiled wryly, almost approvingly.

"The other one, then," Vander Bim said. "He's from *The Lady's Inn* as well?"

"Aye," Turk interjected.

Bryon could see it now. He remembered these men, walking into that shit heap of a bar talking loudly about some whore they had shared and the sweetness of the brandy afterward. But something was wrong.

"There was a third," Bryon muttered. No one heard him.

Switch and Turk inspected the bodies. A rock had crushed Rat-Face. Bryon could see the boulder, smattered with blood and lying just a few paces from the body. The dwarf picked up what looked like a small silver coin with a hole in the middle. But when Bryon squinted and leaned forward, he saw that a broken link from the man's mail shirt sat in Turk's hand. He looked about and saw dozens of links lying nearby, bloodied and bent.

"What could have torn a mail shirt like that?" Bryon asked, to which Drake just shook his head in disbelief.

The other man looked as if some wild animal had attacked him, the flesh about his face and neck slashed and torn. His iron breastplate looked battered, dented so badly that Bryon figured it dug into the man's flesh. One of his legs barely clung to the rest of his body by a bit of tendon and clothing.

"What weapon could do such a thing?" Bryon asked.

"No steel or iron weapon made these wounds," Demik said.

"No tunnel digger," Switch said, "that's for sure. Stone weapons, maybe. Or worse."

"What could be worse?" Bryon asked.

"Teeth." Turk's tone sounded flat.

Demik dismounted and joined the other two mercenaries. He knelt beside Turk and gently brushed his rough hands over both men's faces, closing their horror-stricken eyes.

"Who did this?" Vander Bim pondered quietly.

"Rather, *what* did this?" Switch replied without looking at the sailor, finally standing. "That is what you should ask. These poor bastards weren't killed by the same thing that killed those other two we found. That's for bloody sure."

"Not men?" Vander Bim queried.

"No, not men," Switch said, "nor wolves or a cat if that's what you're going say next. Something used the bloody rock as a weapon."

"Dwarves?" Drake questioned. Turk gave him a cold stare. Demik groaned angrily, and Nafer grumbled under his breath.

"No." Switch laughed at Drake's presumption, though, and even more at the dwarves' reaction. "Dwarves don't use boulders. And they don't attack without being threatened first. Eh, tunnel digger."

"Aye," Turk replied and crossed his arms.

"There's only two things in these mountains that could do this," Switch muttered, more to himself than anyone else, "and only one of them would leave their kill behind. Blood and guts and…" Switch stopped. A cold, concerned look came over his face. He pursed his lips and squinted his brownish-gray eyes so that they almost disappeared.

"Mountain Trolls," Turk interjected.

"Blood and guts and mountain trolls," Switch agreed faintly. "Shit, this isn't what I signed up for. Poor bastard's been chewed on."

"They haven't been this far north of Strongbur, whose surface entrances are only four leagues from here, in years," Demik said.

"There are two things that could cause a troll to venture into the lands of men. Either they are hungry, starving even," Turk said, "or…"

This time, Switch cut off the dwarf.

"They aren't acting alone," Switch offered.

"Even more frightening," Turk muttered.

"I don't understand," Bryon said.

"Clearly," Switch replied.

"Trolls are stupid creatures," Turk said, ignoring Switch and walking about as he talked, looking at the ground and, presumably, for clues. "In the past, however, some trolls with more than just typical animal instinct and wild cunning have been known to be adventurous, entrepreneurial. They would sell their strength and cruelty to powerful men—warlords, wizards, the types of men that employ such a creature."

"Like us?" Erik asked.

Bryon shot his cousin a hard look to which Erik returned the same.

Turk shook his head. "No, not like us. The only reason someone would want to hire a troll is to leave a path of destruction. That is all they're good for. They are evil to their very bones. They have no sense of mercy, no pity, and they thrive on agony and the taste of fresh flesh, especially man flesh."

"There was a third man," Bryon said, "in Finlo. Where is he?"

"Escaped, maybe," Vander Bim offered.

"Nah," Switch replied, shaking his head. "It looks like he was killed too. He's probably troll shit by now."

Sweat collected along Bryon's brow, spilled down and stung his eyes. He tried not looking to the mountainside but didn't want the others to see him averting his gaze, so he looked. He didn't think he was worried. He didn't feel scared—until he looked to the mountain.

"What was that?" he muttered.

"What?" Erik asked.

He didn't think he had said it loud enough for anyone to hear.

"Nothing."

"What was what?" Erik asked.

"Nothing." Bryon silently cursed himself. "I thought I saw something."

"This is no way to go," Drake said.

Bryon broke his stare on the mountains and gazed, once again, at the dead men.

"No mate," Vander Bim nodded, "no it's not."

"Just bloody great!" Switch exclaimed. He practically leapt into his saddle. "Not only do we have to deal with magic, and slavers," he cast a sidelong glance toward Erik and Bryon, "but now we have to deal with mountain trolls working for the Shadow knows who."

Bryon hung on one of Switch's words, shook his head, brushed it off as nothing, but, nonetheless, the word passed his lips.

"The Shadow."

Chapter 64

THEY RODE WELL INTO THE night. Making up for lost time—that was Vander Bim's justification. Erik knew he lied. Trolls. That was the reason. And when they did stop, they did so without the comfort of a campfire.

Erik watched as heavy clouds crept over the highest peaks of the Southern Mountains. Intermittent lightning lit the otherwise very dark night and brought an uncommon coolness, but for now, they tempted no rain.

"Every age has a name, you know." Turk's mumble caught Erik unaware. He peered through the darkness to see the faint outline of the dwarf, leaning against his saddle.

"Were you talking to me?" Erik asked.

"Yes, I suppose," Turk replied. "Anyone who would listen, I guess. I find that talk helps pass the time. I very much enjoy history, so I like to talk about history."

"Alright," Erik said. "What is this age, that we are in, called?"

"The Long Peace, in Westernese of course," Turk replied. "It's called different things depending on where in the world you go."

"The world seems anything but peaceful," Erik replied.

"So it would seem," Turk replied. "And certainly, in other places such as Wüsten Sahil or the Isuta Islands, it may not be a very peaceful place at all."

"And the age before this one, the age before the supposed Long Peace. What was it called?" Erik asked.

"The Darkening," Turk replied, "in your language."

"I guess I'll take the not so peaceful Long Peace," Erik replied. "Should I even ask why it was called the Darkening?"

"It was called such for a reason you may not expect," Turk replied. "History books speak of chaos and disorder not because of overwhelming evil and violence."

"From what, then?" Erik asked.

"Education," Turk replied. "Knowledge."

"That was not what I was expecting," Erik said.

"Education, knowledge, learning, language, art, music. These were the things lost during The Darkening," Turk continued, "some possibly lost forever."

"Why would a lack of learning and knowledge, as opposed to some great evil, be called The Darkening?" Erik asked.

"Is there any greater evil than the lack of learning, the loss of a man's desire to know and understand the world around him?" Turk asked.

"I don't know."

"Think, young Erik," Turk said. "Without knowledge, two nations war because they do not share language, or art, or music, or even religion. They do not wish to understand one another."

"Why?" Erik leaned forward.

"Men fear what they do not know or understand," Turk replied. "Without knowledge and education, we become suspicious, scared fools. A man is left to the whims of some *noble* lucky enough to be rich or strong enough to exert some sort of power. Or, he is left to the superstitions of some holy man, some hedge witch who has purposed to understand the world because of the smell of the wind or the patterns of the stars. He does not think for himself. He simply fears his lord's sword, all the while forgetting that knowledge is the most powerful weapon the world has ever known."

"So, the Long Peace is a time of renewed learning?" Erik asked.

"Perhaps," Turk replied. "We are still not where we were in the Elder Days, over a thousand years ago. To hear the tales of grand towers and beautiful poems and moving songs and discoveries being made within this world and beyond, and then to realize in a blink of an eye, in the dropping of a single grain of sand through an hourglass, it all ceased, it makes me sad."

"I would like to read those tales," Erik said.

"You read?" Turk asked.

"Aye," Erik replied. "My brother and cousin can as well."

"Then so you shall," Turk said, "once we get to Thorakest."

"I do feel a change in the winds lately," Turk added after a moment of silence. "Sometimes, I do wish I had lived during The Elder Days."

Silence consumed the night for a while longer. Erik could hear Turk breathing, just sitting there in the dark, awake with him.

"Where are you right now?" Turk finally asked.

Erik slid down a little and leaned his head back so that it rested on his saddle. "I'm home."

"Ah, and a good place to be right now."

Chapter 65

"ARE YOU ALL RIGHT?" Bo's wife said, breaking the monotony of wooden wheels rolling over crunching grass.

"Yes, my dear, I am fine," Bo replied.

"You're lying." Dika sat up with a frown. "I can tell."

Bo quietly laughed. "Just tired, my love."

"Where are we going?" Dika asked in between yawns.

"I do not know, my love. I am simply trusting the Creator, that he will guide our leader Mardirru, show him the way."

"Do you think we will find the missing children?" Dika asked.

"I do," Bo answered, and he meant it.

"Those poor babies," Dika said, sadness ripe in her voice.

Bo looked to the east. The sun faded fast this day. It did so many days, despite the oncoming summer. The sky, only for a moment, lit up in purples and oranges and faint yellows, a streak of red here and there, perhaps pink. Bo smiled. Then, in the space of a butterfly fluttering its wings, the moon appeared.

As the moon rose, it appeared red like someone had sacrificed an animal and covered the normally pale orb in the creature's blood.

"A red moon," Bo whispered.

Mardirru rode back toward his wagon. The young leader, who looked more like his father with each passing day, pulled hard on his horse's reins. Bo slowed his cart.

"Be on guard tonight, Bo," Mardirru said.

"What is it?" Bo asked.

Mardirru looked up. "A red moon, my friend. Wicked things are afoot. Have a keen eye this night."

Bo nodded.

Mardirru looked east, to the same spot, only moments earlier, Bo had looked.

"What is it, Mardirru?" Bo asked.

The young gypsy shook his head.

"What is on your mind?" Bo continued.

He shook his head again, but slowly looked to Bo. "They are out there."

"The children?" Bo asked.

"No," Mardirru's replied. "I mean, yes, I do think the children are out there, and alive, but Erik is out there, and his brother and cousin. Wherever that red moon shines, that is where they are."

The faint glow of a distant fire dared to reflect off Patûk Al'Banan's face. Cries echoed through the black night. Howls and the snapping of teeth abruptly ended pleas for mercy.

"It didn't have to come to this, you old fool miner," the general muttered as he gave the night sky a sidelong glance. "You should just have agreed to do business."

Soft boots stepped over dried leaves behind him. They would have fallen silent on most men's ears, but Al'Banan was too seasoned to be fooled by stealth.

"Report, Lieutenant Bu," Patûk Al'Banan commanded.

"We are almost finished," Lieutenant Bu replied.

Patûk nodded with a grunt. He stared down at the fires again. Surreptitiously, his stomach knotted.

"I take no pleasure in death, Lieutenant," General Al'Banan said.

"Sir?" Bu questioned.

"I've seen thousands die, most by my hand or my command,"

Patûk explained without turning to face Bu, "but I take no pleasure in it."

"It is a necessary evil, sir," Bu replied.

Patûk Al'Banan nodded. He smiled a mirthless smile.

"Yes, Lieutenant," Patûk agreed, "a necessary evil. We are soldiers, and war is our tool."

"War cares only for death, sir," Lieutenant Bu said.

"War cares only for death," the general repeated.

The distant rumble of thunder crept through the high peaks of the mountains. He looked to his left—the west—and saw the silhouettes of clouds, thick and heavy. He hoped it would rain, although he knew it would never make it over the tallest parts of the Southern Mountains.

"Perhaps the rain could wash away the stain of death," Patûk muttered, but then shook his head. Then, he asked. "The three men?"

"Yes, General," Bu replied. "They left late a short while ago."

"Follow them," the general commanded. "I have tasked Lieutenant Phurnan with that command, but I don't trust his efficiency."

"Just follow, my lord?" Lieutenant Bu asked.

Patûk Al'Banan chuckled. Bu proved a good choice. Sorben Phurnan's worth quickly waned again.

"Make sure Phurnan follows the orders I gave him," the general replied.

"And the bodies, General?" Bu asked. "Do we leave them as a warning?"

The general shook his head slightly. No warnings. No chances. No mercy.

"As you wish," Lieutenant Bu replied.

As Lieutenant Bu filtered back into the dark, mountain forest, the cries died, and the reflection of fire began to fade as Patûk looked to the east.

"A Blood Moon. How fitting? Did these deaths appease your

need for blood?" Patûk Al'Banan laughed. "A fool's question. Of course not. You are a god of the old ways. Well, do not worry, ancient Princess of Pain, there will be more blood to come—much more blood."

Chapter 66

Erik stood on the Plains of Güdal in his dream. The moonlight was faint and sickly. Tall grass fluttered about his knees in a breeze that brought neither warmth nor coolness. That's when he saw Marcus, ghostly pale. The man bellowed a deafening cry that sounded oddly stale in this place. Nadya wandered about him, circling him and crying—even though no tears fell from her eyes. He recognized other gypsies, meandering about, moaning and crying. Then, other figures rose from the grass, slowly. Slavers. They limped to him and, even though he tried to run, Erik found himself stuck, unable to move.

The dead slavers closed in on him, and he could hear their subtle laughter, cackling chuckles muffled by blood stuck in their throats. He could smell their stink. He could feel the putrid warmth of their dead breath. As he tried to cry out, he felt a cold hand wrap around his throat. The hand squeezed, and Erik couldn't breathe. The hand was so cold it burned, and he could feel his flesh tearing away under the grip. Fingers crawled into his open mouth, jagged fingernails jabbing into the back of his throat. He tasted blood.

Erik awoke just as the faint purples and reds of the morning streaked across the sky. He turned to see his brother, still fast asleep.

"We should be in Aga Kona by tomorrow morning at the latest," Vander Bim said as they finally broke camp and saddled the horses.

While they traveled, the day carrying on with little signs of civilization, Erik saw something on the distant horizon. It looked odd, in the failing sun of the late afternoon, almost like a thin strand of brown hair trailing in front of him. He thought, at first, maybe it was his own hair, fluttering in front of him, but, no, something was there.

"Do you see that?" Erik asked.

"See what?" Befel replied with a hint of irritation.

"There," Erik said, pointing. "There is something on the horizon."

"There's nothing there, Erik," Befel replied.

"No," Erik continued, "I see something."

"I see it too," Demik said, and he spoke to Turk in Dwarvish, pointing.

"Yes, me too," Turk agreed, nodding.

"What is it?" Erik asked.

Turk leaned forward in his saddle, then sat back with a sigh.

"Smoke," Turk muttered.

"Do you fellows see that?" Switch called back, pulling on the reigns of his horse and turning the animal.

"We were just talking about it," Turk replied. "It looks like smoke."

"Aye," Switch agreed, "bloody smoke. But I don't see a flame."

"Perhaps it's too far away," Vander Bim said.

"Perhaps," Switch echoed with an unconvincing tone.

"Could it be a brushfire?" Erik asked.

"Maybe," Turk replied. He seemed unconvinced as well.

"Those were thunderclouds a few days ago," Erik said. "If the grass is dry, the lightning could have caused a fire."

"Aye," was Turk's simple reply. Then he looked to Switch. "Switch."

Switch nodded, turned his horse, and rode away, in the direction of the smoke. When he returned a short while later, the fact that he said nothing and only shook his head before he galloped off again was enough to get the others to follow him at the same pace, and they covered a league in what seemed a quarter of the time.

The thin wisp of smoke quickly turned into thick billowing

columns swirling into the sky, giving the waning day a premature darkness. A breeze that should have been cool was warm, hot almost. As it intermittently picked up into a brisk wind, black smoke covered the party and caused both the men and the horses to cough and snort and sneeze.

Only a few dozen more paces revealed the origins of the smoke. The charred remains of a once thriving town—a large mining camp owned by Golgolithul, perhaps—sat before them. Some of the wood from the buildings still smoldered. Most had turned to black ash. Even at the outskirts of the town, Erik could see bodies, strewn about, broken and burned.

"I think we reached Aga Kona," Bryon said.

"No," Drake sorrowfully whispered.

"I think he's right," Switch said, causing Bryon to jerk his head around.

Bodies lay all about the camp, all men. None of them had weapons, save for a pickax or a small dagger. Those that still had faces stared blankly into the semi-cloudy sky.

"This was definitely Aga Kona," Vander Bim said, pointing to a pile of rubble and boulders framed by large wood planks. "That was the entrance to the mine."

Erik felt his stomach turn as he led his horse through the camp, looking at the devastation around him. The piece of a tent floated by him, the cloth fluttering as if it were a bird, its edges black and red as a subdued flame still ate away at it. The want, the need to vomit didn't just come from the smell of fire or the dead lying about the camp. It came from the body parts—the arms and legs, bones, mutilated flesh. Erik put a hand to his mouth, holding his retching back.

"Mining camps don't have women and children?" Bryon questioned.

"This one should have," Drake said. "It was as much a small town as it was a mining camp."

"I think I found them," Switch said.

He stood just inside the blackened stone foundations of what looked to be a large building, by the amount of burned timber and ash piled around it. Heavy beams made of white ash, too thick to burn quickly, still smoldered within the foundations, jutting haphazardly this way and that.

They all dismounted and timidly entered the building, joining Switch. Looking skyward, Erik could see some of the roof remained, four stories high. The frame shifted in the breeze. It would collapse soon. Clay pots and melted, pewter cups littered the ground. And then he saw them.

A large pile of wood and ash huddled in one corner of the building, only, it wasn't wood and ash.

"Are those..." Befel began to ask, but then Erik heard his gagging cut him off.

"Those are people," Erik said. He felt tears in his eyes. He felt his hands shake. He felt his face go cold.

"Not just people," Turk said, walking closer. "Women and children. This is where they died."

"This is where they burned alive," Switch said.

Erik felt as if all the wind had been knocked out of him, as if some huge fist had just punched him in the stomach. He heard heavy sobs and saw Drake collapse to his knees. He even saw tears in Bryon's eyes, but then remembered how he'd felt about children back in the gypsy train.

"This is where they came," Vander Bim said, an obvious lump sticking in his throat, "for a last moment of hope."

"Or this is where they were driven," Switch added.

Vander Bim looked at the thief, a questioning arch in his eyebrow.

"These people were driven here," Switch explained, "purposely trapped here so the building could be burnt down around them."

"Why couldn't we have just ridden right past this by night?" Erik muttered with his eyes closed. "Why couldn't this just lay here a mystery?"

"It still would be here, whether we found it or not," Befel said.

"Damn whoever did this," seethed Vander Bim.

"You mean what." Switch patted the sailor's shoulder. "Whatever did this."

Erik tried to force images of women and children out of his mind, but he couldn't. He could see them clearly, crying in the corner and clutching one another as the roars of some evil creature burst through the walls and the heat of fire surrounded them. He saw their faces, heard their cries, felt their pain. More death to fill his dreams. He clenched his fists and breathed hard.

"What ... what could've done such a thing?" Drake sobbed as Vander Bim led him out of the building.

"Mountain trolls," Switch said, "bloody mountain trolls." He turned to Turk. "Where is your god now?"

"Here," Turk replied. "He is here more than you might think."

As Erik and Turk passed through the burned entrance of the building, the roof began to collapse behind them, sending up clouds of black smoke and burying the remains of the people who had spent their last moments there.

Erik watched as Nafer turned to face the building. He bowed and touched an open hand to his chest. He dug in a pouch at his belt and retrieved what looked like dirt. He said something in Dwarvish and threw the dirt to the ground. Then he retrieved a piece of bread from his haversack, tore off a smaller portion, touched it to his forehead— still whispering in Dwarvish—and threw that to the ground.

Erik heard Demik mumble something, and Nafer joined him, and they spoke in unison. Only a moment later, Turk left Erik's side and joined his companions. He chimed in with the cant, joining in perfectly so that their whisperings sounded like a poem or song.

Erik bowed his head, saying his own prayer as he assumed the dwarves were doing. He saw Vander Bim walk by, shaking his head.

"What's the matter?" Erik asked

"Nothing," Vander Bim replied.

"You don't approve of their prayers?" Erik asked.

Vander Bim stopped and looked at Erik with a kind smile. His wrinkles and the gray in his blond hair seemed extenuated in the waning light for some reason, and Erik could tell—perhaps it was the deep redness in the sailor's eyes—that he had been crying.

"It's not that I don't approve, lad," Vander Bim replied. "I just sometimes wonder what good it can do. I suppose it does us more good than anything else, makes us feel better. I hate to say it, but in times like this, I agree with Switch. What loving and merciful god would allow this to happen?"

"Have you never prayed?" Erik asked.

"Sure, I've prayed. I suppose at times I still pray," Vander Bim replied. "For what, I'm not sure. A long life? Money? That I won't be eaten by monsters lurking in the mountains and turned into troll shit? Like I said, I pray more for me than anything else."

Erik bowed his head again and closed his eyes. He didn't know what to pray. He wanted to pray for his dreams to go away. He wanted to pray for his mother and father and sisters and Simone. He wanted to pray for the children who had been stolen away by the slavers, for these people in Aga Kona. He even wanted to pray for the slavers. But it all seemed too much to deal with.

"You are praying?" Turk asked, coming back alongside him.

"Maybe," Erik replied. "But I don't know what to pray."

"Whatever is in your heart," Turk replied.

"That's a lot," Erik said.

"I think An has time," Turk replied with a smile.

"I don't speak Dwarvish," Erik said. "Will the Creator understand me?"

"He understands all languages," Turk replied. "Would you like me to pray with you? Silently?"

Erik thought for a moment.

"Yes," he finally said.

Turk held out his hands. Erik, at first, didn't know what to do. Did he really mean for Erik to hold his hands? Finally, Erik grabbed Turk's rough and calloused hands, and they both bowed their heads and stood for a long time, silent.

"What do we do now?" Erik asked as the sun began to disappear in the west.

"I know I would rather camp away from the dead," Vander Bim replied.

"We may not have a choice," Switch replied. "They are close by—the trolls. I don't know if I would chance traveling with such little light."

"Then what?" Vander Bim asked.

"Hike north," Turk offered, "a league perhaps. Camp in the Plains. It will be hot, but better than being surprised by mountain trolls in the dead of night."

"It's a good plan, tunnel digger," Switch said.

"And after that?" Erik asked.

"Stick to the plan," Vander Bim said. "Make for Aga Min and enter the mountain there."

"And hope it still stands when we get there," Switch added.

Erik stared at the burned building, the final resting place of all those women and children. He looked to the mountains and watched shadows that probably weren't there.

Then, his thoughts went to his home, his farmstead, and his parents. Just two years ago, he was farming, planning a marriage with Simone and dreaming of one day becoming a man like Rikard Eleodum. Adventure, dwarves, mountain trolls, magic, gypsies, fighting... killing were the last things on his mind. What things had to have happened in order for him to be where he was? He'd left for a new life, a chance of a better life.

"Truly," Erik muttered to himself, "a chance beginning. A chance beginning to a new life."

Or was it?

Made in the USA
Columbia, SC
28 May 2020